ARTIFACT

WORKS BY JEREMY ROBINSON

The Didymus Contingency
Raising The Past
Beneath
Antarktos Rising
Kronos
Pulse
Instinct
Threshold
Fracture
Torment
The Last Hunter – Collected Edition
Insomnia
SecondWorld
Project Nemesis
Ragnarok
Island 731
Nazi Hunter: Atlantis
Prime
Omega
Project Maigo
Refuge
Guardian
Human After All
Savage
Flood Rising
Project 731
Cannibal
Endgame
MirrorWorld
Herculean
Project Hyperion
Patriot
Apocalypse Machine
Empire
Unity
Project Legion
The Distance
The Last Valkyrie
Centurion
Infinite
Helios
Viking Tomorrow
Forbidden Island
The Divide
The Others
Space Force
Alter
Flux
Tether
Tribe
NPC
Exo-Hunter
Infinite^2
The Dark
Mind Bullet
The Order
Khaos
Singularity
Hunger – The Complete Trilogy
Nemesis
Point Nemo
Good Boys – The Lost Tribe
Good Boys – Unleashed
Kingdom
Good Boys – The Visionary
The Sentinel Trilogy
Artifact

ARTIFACT

JEREMY ROBINSON

Cover design by Jeremy Robinson
Book layout and design by Breakneck Media

ISBN: 979-8-3470-1218-3

Published in 2025 by Podium Publishing
www.podiumentertainment.com

For the late, great Michael Crichton.
I'm not as brilliant as you, but I hope to
capture a little of your magic in this one.

ARTIFACT

1

Nothing wakes a man up faster than sitting down on a toilet bowl, overfilled with thirty-ish degree well water, baptizing his nethers in the name of the Father, Son, and—

"Holy shit!" I leap up off the toilet, boxers around my ankles. A quick dab of toilet paper dries me up, but the electric cold radiates through my body, sharp sonar waves pinging off my skin's inner wall. Goose bumps prick to life on my forearms and thighs. A shiver transforms me into James Brown for a moment.

A song comes to mind, and I can't help but belt it out with altered lyrics. "I feel cold! Na-na-na-na-na-na-na."

It's my own fault. I like it nippy when I sleep. Not hard to accomplish when it's negative fifteen outside. Raven's Rest, Alaska, situated on the coast of Prince William Sound, is separated from the outside world by a single, three-mile-long tunnel through the mountains. During the winter, it's the only way in or out of town. This isn't a place any normal person would want to be this side of September, and today is... Well, I don't know what day it is. But I'm sure it's February.

Pretty sure. Winter passes by in a cold, boring blur. Not quite perpetual darkness. We get six hours of dark-blue sky... but no direct sunlight. Come winter, we have three big sellers in this town: alcohol, anti-depressants, and daylight therapy lamps.

But only one of them can ruin my day. Or make it interesting. Guess that depends on your perspective. Are drunk people amusing? Most of the time. The few that aren't can muck up your day—the whole week, if you don't get in the first punch.

"Okay," I say to myself, shuffling to the light switch and flicking it on. Eyes clenched mostly shut, I return to the toilet and look down. "Huh..." I need to put the heat on. There's a chunk of ice, floating like a turd, in my bowl. No way it's gonna flush.

Which means, I also need to make the 'twinkle tinkle run.' That's what my deputy, Tali Nuluk, calls it. There's only one bathroom at the station, and if someone is taking their pretty time, or there's a plumbing issue, you're headed outside, where your tinkle...will twinkle as it freezes on impact or drifts away as steam, which is rancid any way you try to paint it.

And yeah, I'm at the station. Sleep here most nights, because 'the Tower' makes me claustrophobic, among other things. Most year-rounders live there. A ten-story apartment building filled top to bottom with people, all of whom know I'm the guy to come see when trouble rears its abominable head. I get a lot of knocks on the door, usually for nothing.

Doreen Parker once came to me because she and her husband had an argument over how many tablespoons were in a stick of butter. They were amazed when I showed them the measurements on the wax paper wrapping. Neither of them was right. Neither of them was close.

Tali tells me I'm avoiding my grief. That I need to move back in and deal with what's there. Not the neighbors.

My wife's things.

Her clothes. Her tea sets. Her smell.

Way I see it, the only thing the Tower has over the sheriff's station is shallow toilet water. And thawed toilet water. And yeah,

Tali is right, but winter isn't a good time to have another breakdown. The dead will still be buried when the snow melts.

After hiking up my boxers, I stumble through the dark station, bare feet stinging as they slap on the cold linoleum floor. I open the front door—yeah, the front. No one is awake at this hour and only a madman would be out. I gasp wide awake as the freezing air wraps around me and caresses every pore.

Takes a moment for my nervous system to adjust and my lungs to start working again. The inside of my nose freezes when I breathe in and thaws when I breathe out. Won't be long before all the moisture leaks out and forms a glacier on my mustache. My skin is already starting to burn, so I need to make this quick. Tali's going to be cranky about the yellow snow, but it will be covered soon enough. Not a day passes without a fresh coat.

I scan the area as I piss, confirming that the town's sheriff—me—won't have to write himself up for indecent exposure.

Main Street is dark. I can see the silhouettes of buildings across the road, backlit by the Tower's outdoor flood lights. But most of the town is a spectral dream, present but unseen.

The crunch of snow to my left spins me around, creating a yellow trail at the bottom of the two concrete steps. Another crunch follows. Then another.

Someone is walking down Main Street.

Or some*thing*.

I shuffle through the possibilities.

Bear? No. Hibernating, unless it's desperate for food, or has rabies. In either case, it would be charging me already.

Human? Unlikely. Unless drunk. But the gait is steady and quick.

Moose is the most likely culprit. Had three spend a few hours in town a few days back, just hanging around.

Drained and on guard, I give myself a little shake, tuck my business away, and then reach my hand over to the exterior light switch. I feel naked without my sidearm…but since I'm already just about actually in the buff, I light up the night.

The whole town—across the street, anyway—comes into view.

Along with my visitor.

"What in God's name?" I gasp, once again feeling the spirit of James Brown in my bones. "How the hell did *you* get here?"

My visitor doesn't answer. Doesn't even look at me. It just hurries on past.

Because it can't speak.

Because…

Because it's a *camel*.

2

I stumble back a step, blinking as the air crystallizes the moisture on my eyes. But it's still there. I'm hallucinating. Have to be.

"Hey!" I shout at the camel.

It snorts and stumbles to a stop, as surprised by me as I am by it.

It's seven feet tall—eight at the single hump. Must weigh in around 1,300 pounds, give or take. The out of place animal side-eyes me. Afraid? Suspicious? I can read a dog's body language from a half mile, but I don't speak camel. Also, its eye is bulging, round, and bloodshot. Almost cartoon-like. Looks close to bursting. The creature's tail snaps back and forth, agitated. I would be, too, if I were out for a stroll in this weather.

With the camel standing still, I can hear the gentle ticking of snow landing on the ground. Only other sound is the camel's breathing. Labored. Tired.

"Where did you come from?" I whisper, trying to mentally recreate a puzzle with no pieces.

Doesn't really matter. Don't think this is the cold-weather variety of camel. "You're going to die out there."

Doesn't seem to care. I'd like to help it, but I have nowhere to put something that big. And if I don't close this door or put on some clothes, I'm going to be in a world of hurt. My whole body is burning already. Going to take some time for the pain to fade.

Now that he's standing still, I can see the frozen froth around his mouth. Something's wrong with this creature. Best guess, one of the Ivanoff boys shipped it in before the first snow and kept it hidden in one of the barns over at Glacier View all this time. Not sure what the purpose would be, but the Ivanoff family is known for its eccentric…hobbies.

And while they sound like a bunch of Russians, they're actually pure blood Chugach Sugpiaq, aka Alutiiq, whose ancestors were baptized by the Orthodox Church. Just one of the lingering effects of Russian colonization during the eighteenth and nineteenth centuries—before Uncle Sam got the whole of Alaska for two cents an acre. Seven-point-two million. In today's dollars, that's about one hundred fifty million for a parcel of land larger than France, Germany, and Spain combined.

The camel stomps its foot and the broad fleshy heel bends out to support its weight, another reminder of just how incongruous the beast is. Those feet were made for sand, not snow.

I stand there, frozen, unsure of what to do or say.

The camel makes the first move. It's a simple gesture—turning its head to look me dead in the eyes. Maybe a final connection with something living before it keels over.

But what I expect to see and what I actually see are as far apart as a dream about oil-wrestling Salma Hayek and a nightmare of a singing Teletubby harvesting my organs.

This nightmare is real, breathing, and staring at me through the one eye on its right side, and what looks to be a dozen or more eyeballs bulging out of the opposite side of its face. They look like engorged ticks, moving as one, locking onto me, each one of them functional.

I stumble back. "Oh my God."

My legs hitch, and I fall onto my ass, unable to look away from the thing.

"What the fuck are you?"

The camel bellows, the agonizing sound of it tearing through me, making me feel nothing but compassion for the creature, despite its disfigurement. Then it sprays froth at me and lurches away. I watch until the beast fades from the floodlight's glow.

Takes about ten seconds for the shock to wear off and for my mind to fully feel the effects of the cold.

"Ahh!" I shout, hopping to my feet. I snap the interior lights on and then hop-run back to the cell I've made my home away from home. "Fuck me."

With shaking hands, I pull on my pants and a shirt. I'm trying to move quickly, but it's not just my hands trembling, it's my arms and legs, too. I sit on the cot to make sure I don't fall over. Then I pull on my wool socks, a sweater, and my brown sheriff's jacket. "Fuck me."

I rub my hands together and then on my pants, but the friction isn't nearly enough to cut through the biting cold.

"Fuck me."

The heat. I need to turn the heat up. I pull my boots on and stand without tying them. Wouldn't be possible if I tried. On my way out of the cell, I pull my black beanie over my head and ears. Fully clothed, I walk through the station more confidently than I did before, even hidden by the dark with no one watching. Takes five strides to reach the thermostat, which I, for some godforsaken reason, have twisted all the way to the left, set at the chilly temperature of 'off.'

I twist it to the right, stopping at seventy degrees. Will be a miracle if the office reaches that temperature before spring.

A gust of wind turns me around. Left the door open. I don't blame myself. The memory of that camel is still gnawing away at me, and it's not something I can let go. Not only is it a mystery, and a crime—I think—but it's by far the most interesting thing that's going to happen in this town for the next decade or so. Can't just let it wander off into the night.

I pull out my iPhone, swipe it on, and let my face unlock it. Takes three tries to open the phone app. Typing is impossible. "S-Siri," I say, teeth chattering. Despite sounding like Max Headroom, the swirling ball of light forms at the bottom of the screen. "C-call Tali."

"Calling Tali," the phone says.

I place the device to my ear and listen to it ringing. I've heard that the first few rings of a cellphone are fake; the phone on the other end isn't ringing. The call is still connecting. That's why no one ever picks up on the first or second ring of a cell phone call.

Tali answers just as the third ring starts, meaning her arm snapped out in the dark, she grabbed her phone, and then tapped the answer button before she was fully awake. Reflexes like a cat, that woman. Wouldn't think so by looking at her. She's five-four with thick thighs. Won't be winning any fifty-yard dashes, but her hands are lightning wrapped in human skin.

"Here. I'm here." she says, trying not to sound groggy.

"Station," I say. "Now."

"What's wrong?" Sounds fully awake now. Guessing she's already on her feet.

"Wouldn't believe me if I told you." I turn on the coffee maker, already prepped for my morning cup. "And rustle up Ethan on your way. He won't want to miss this."

"Colton," she says, "What is going on? Tell me right now or I'm going back to bed."

I sigh. "Fine. There is a thirteen-eyed giant animal loose in town."

The other end of the line goes silent for a moment. Probably debating whether I've been drinking or I'm pulling a prank. Takes her ten seconds to realize I don't do either. "On my way."

3

I pour three coffees into to-go cups, one with cream and sugar (mine), one with extra cream and extra sugar (Tali's), and one black. I don't know how Ethan stands the stuff. I do *not* make good coffee. Tali's been begging me to get one of those pod things. Makes good coffee every time, she says. Her sister, Marit, owner of The Roost, a bar just down the street, has one. Tali said she cried the first time she tried it. Some kind of Blueberry Cobbler coffee. Sounds like a crock of moose pellets to me.

The door swings open, letting in a cold burst of air and snow. Looks to be coming down heavier now. Not great. We'll need to get out there before the tracks are covered.

Ethan follows Tali in and closes the door behind him. Both are wearing parkas, snowpants, and boots, ready for the Arctic north.

"I thought we were in a rush," Ethan says, looking at me, and then turning to Tali. "You said we were in a rush."

I'm confused by the response. Deputy Ethan Ishida is a rookie who stands out in Raven's Rest on account of him being the first and only person of Japanese descent to ever live in and/or visit town. He has never once expressed annoyance or questioned me.

Not sure that he is now, either.

Tali confirms that when she asks, "Why aren't you dressed?"

I look down at my jeans and brown sheriff's jacket.

"What?"

"You're going to freeze your ass cheeks solid dressed like that." She takes on a motherly tone and adds, "Go put on your snow pants and parka. We have them for a reason."

"No one takes me seriously when I wear them," I grumble.

"No one will take you seriously if you get frostbite and lose your fingers. Say goodbye to that legendary right hook of yours. Every fight you ever get in will just be a slap fest." She smiles. "Actually, you know what. Never mind. That would be hysterical to watch."

I turn to Ethan, hoping for some backup.

He shakes his head. "I think you're supposed to be the good example for me, sir. Not the other way around."

"Fine," I say, grimacing. I head to the breakroom, which we also use as Ethan's office, storage, and the locker room. There's a refrigerator, four tall lockers, a round table, four chairs, and a filing cabinet. Boxes line the walls. Nothing important. Really just a glorified lost and found for the town.

I open my locker and pause.

I hate opening it, not because I'm really that against being warm, but because of the photo the locker contains. Part of me thinks I should put it away. Just can't bring myself to do it. I feel like she wouldn't forgive me for not wanting to think about her, but I know that isn't true.

Anya, my wife, wasn't petty like that. She'd probably tell me to take it out. Wouldn't want to see me still grieving two years later. Told me to live a big and bold life the day cancer took her from me. But I don't know what that looks like yet. We met in college. I was so smitten, I moved to this frozen Alaskan hellhole because she was Chugach Sugpiaq and wanted to be among her people and her traditions. I grew to love it here, but that was mostly because she was part of the scenery. Without her, everything just feels cold.

"You'd be laughing at me," I tell the photo. She's sitting on a sun-warmed rock by a glacial river, not too far out of town. One of our favorite spots. She's wearing a flowing skirt and a tank top. Nothing fancy, but the smile on her face, bunching up her apple cheeks, transforms this photo into something worthy of a *National Geographic* cover. Her eyes fill me with hope, and then with despair. I look away before I start crying, snatching my cold weather gear from the locker and slamming the radioactive door closed.

Three minutes later, I'm dressed and composed. Three extra minutes that camel could be out there, hobbling away. I need to overcome this pain. Need to sort myself out. But I'm afraid of what that means. Will I leave this place? Will there be no trace of her left?

Camel, I tell myself after realizing I'd spent another thirty seconds staring at the floor. *Camel in Alaska.* "Wish you were here for this," I tell the locker and then leave the room.

Tali and Ethan are waiting by the door, coffees in hands. Tali raises hers. "Thanks for the caffeine swill."

"Don't start," I say, putting on a smile that masks the sadness tethering me to that photo.

She hands me my coffee, which now has a lid. Won't stay warm for long once we're outside, so I take a long drink, let out a long sigh, and ask, "Okay, who's ready to have their mind blown?"

Their wide, impatient eyes are answer enough. I pick up three high-powered flashlights, from the chargers mounted beside the front door, and pass them out.

"Follow me."

The night air wraps around me once more, but this time I barely feel it. Nose still freezes up. Eyelids, too, but you get used to it, and I'm hoping we won't be out here long. I pull my scarf up over my mouth and nose and then step outside.

"Thanks for pissing on the steps again, by the way," Tali says. "Forget where the bathroom was?"

"Toilet clogged," I say. "With ice."

She's about to complain about how cold I keep the office at night. I swear, Anya's last words to her must have been about doubling her protective nagging to make up for the lack of Anya's. They were a fantastic tag team. Great friends, too.

Whatever Tali's going to say catches in her throat when I crouch, and she sees what I'm looking at.

"What is that?" she asks.

"Footprint," I say.

Ethan crouches beside me, tracing his hand around the compressed snow's outline. "No toes. No claws. Definitely not hooves." He shines his light down Main Street, illuminating the tracks leading straight through the small town. "Whatever it is, it's not from around here."

"And it's bleeding," Tali says.

I turn to where her light is focused. There are four dark pink spots in the snow. She's always had a good eye.

"So, what is it?" she asks. "Aside from probably dead?"

"It's a camel," I say, no trace of humor in my voice.

"A camel," she repeats, trying the word on for size. Probably been a very long time since she said the word for any reason.

"Two humps or one?" Ethan asks. He's dumbing down the question, I know. We don't have animal control in Raven's Rest. We have Ethan. Kid knows everything about every animal you can think of. Most people think it's because he went to college. He told me it's because he watched a lot of *Wild Kratts*, whatever that is, as a kid and wanted to be a biologist before deciding on law enforcement.

"One," I say.

He nods. "Definitely going to die."

"Okay, here's how we're doing this. Tali, you're with me. Ethan, get one of the snowmobiles, and pull one of the eight-by-tens from the shed."

"We have plywood in the shed?" he asks.

"Uh-huh. From when the ceiling was patched. Now, let's go find ourselves a one-humped camel."

Ethan stands up with me, takes a photo of the tracks with his camera, and then looks at me. "Dromedary. The camel. Adapted to life in the desert. Amazing creatures."

"Not for long," I say, patting his shoulder.

4

The trail is easy to follow. Runs straight down Main Street and has yet to be covered by the falling snow. The frequency of blood drops is slowing down. Wound is probably freezing solid. Its eyes—all of them—will go next. Not long after that, it will—

"Holy shit." Tali points ahead, shining her light up the street to the edge of town. Barely reaches, but it's just enough to see a snow-dusted mound. "Colton..."

I shine my light on the beast ahead, doubling the lumens striking the creature.

Both of us snap to a stop when it moves. Its large body heaves up and down. Still breathing. Still suffering.

I draw my pistol.

"What are you doing?" Tali asks.

"You know I can't stand to see an animal suffer," I say. This isn't the first creature I've had to put down, but it is the most unique. Its presence in this town feels almost miraculous...if you ignore the mass of eyes bulging from the left side of the beast's head.

"Of course," she says, a fellow empath for the animal kingdom. "But what if it's sick? What if it's carrying a flu or something?"

"A flu that can jump species? Seems unlikely." I spin the cylinder of my Ruger Super Redhawk .454 Casull revolver, confirming that all six hollow-point rounds are present and accounted for. If I ever had to use it on a human being, it would be overkill. If I put a round square in a man's chest, you could have a Toy Poodle jump through the hole it created. But I don't really carry the weapon for people. It's mostly for hungry springtime grizzlies. In all my time here, I've only had to fire it twice in self-defense. Both times against bears, and each encounter required just a single round.

Never dreamed I'd be using it to put down a camel.

Now that I'm thinking about it, I'm not sure it's the right weapon for the job. If we're going to figure out what's wrong with the beast, I reckon we'll need its head in one piece. I holster the weapon, turn to Tali, and hold out my hand. "Got your pea-shooter?"

She rolls her eyes, draws her 9mm PPS and puts it in my hand. I'm called on for bears. Tali for varmints. She tried my hand cannon at the range once. Damn near flew out of her hands. Had me chuckling for days. I'll be surprised if she fires anything bigger than a 9mm again.

"Thank you, ma'am." I chamber the first round.

"Can we just get this over with?" she asks.

"No time like the present."

Aside from the crunch of snow beneath our feet, we walk toward the fallen camel in silence, each of us lost in thought. I'm focusing on the who, what, and where of the situation, and I'm willing to bet she's considering the why. Always has been more intuitive than me, especially when it comes to people's motivations.

I don't really get most folks, messing up their lives like it's why they were put on this Earth. The world is an amazing place if you've got the right eyes and mind to see it. No need for all the torture people inflict on each other, and on themselves.

The camel groans. It's raspy and tired. The creature is dying, plain as day, but its essential organs are buried under a heap of meat. Going to take a while before the fight is over. Even if we did get it someplace warm, we aren't equipped to treat animals. Closest thing we have to a vet in Raven's Rest is a butcher. His gift at carving meat won't help us keep the beast alive, but when it's dead? He'll give us a look at its insides. Might be the town's first official autopsy.

"All right, old boy," I say, standing above the camel's head. From here, it looks like a normal camel, if you ignore the surroundings. "For what it's worth, I'm sorry it's come to this for you, but walking out into this cold? Sealed your own fate. Best I can do is ease your suffering."

The camel doesn't respond. Can't see me through its frozen eye.

"Right." I crouch down onto a knee and take aim at the side of its head. I'm not familiar with camel bone structure, but in my experience most things shot in the side of the head die. Forehead can be a bit more resilient, especially when it comes to 9mm ammunition.

Finger around the trigger, I start to pull.

A pulse of emotion sucker punches me in the gut. I grunt in discomfort and surprise, my fingers squeezing tighter—including my finger on the trigger.

The gun fires. The bullet penetrates.

The camel stops breathing, lying still and peaceful.

I launch back to my feet. "Did you feel that?"

"Sure did," she says, rubbing an ear.

"Not the gun." I clear the chamber, point the muzzle toward the ground, and hand it back to her.

"If not the gun," she says, giving me a curious look. "You pass gas or something?"

I shake my head. "I felt something."

"You feel a lot of things I don't. Can you be more specific?"

"From…from the camel. I think. An emotion."

"Sure it wasn't *your* emotions?" she asks. "You're not exactly known for understanding your own feelings, right?"

"That's the thing. I felt this clearly. It didn't come from me."

"Well, what was it?"

I meet her gaze, feeling confused. "Fear."

5

"What in the name of Frosty the Snowman's carrot dick do you think—" The woman shouting at us is Marit Nuluk, Tali's older sister and owner of The Roost. Her sudden arrival shifts what I think I heard to the back of my mind, not just because she's a captivating presence, but because camels don't talk, and I don't want to consider the idea that I'm hearing things.

Marit storms out into the night wrapped in an otter fur blanket that I recognize. She has the same high cheekbones as Tali. Same dark-brown eyes and straight black hair, too. Tali keeps hers tied back while on duty, but Marit's is always loose and flowing. Can't see her body under the blanket, but she's built like a taller version of Tali. Where the younger sister is short and all hips, the elder appears to have been stretched out at birth, standing five inches taller with a slender figure that's less skinny and more muscular. The fur blanket covering all that up was handed down from their grandmother and sewn together by their grandfather. Neither of the present day Nuluk women would dream of slaughtering otters for their fur, but when it comes to warmth, it's hard to beat.

"Sorry," she says, pointing her flashlight back and forth between my face and Tali's. "Didn't know it was you two. But the question stands, what are you shooting a—"

Tali and I step to either side, revealing the camel corpse like a pair of magicians.

"Oh..." Marit steps closer, brow furrowing. "*Oh.*"

She looks at her sister and then looks at me.

"We're as clueless as you," Tali says.

Marit rubs her forehead. "It's a camel."

"Uh-huh," I say.

"In Alaska."

"Sure is," Tali says.

"It's a dromedary," I say. "The camel. One humped. Adapted for the desert."

Marit gives me a shove. "Stop trying to impress me."

"You're not impressed?" I ask with a smile.

"Ten bucks says you just learned all of that from Ethan," she says.

The shrill buzz of a snowmobile keeps me from having to respond. She knows me, too well. Feels weird, Ethan being the fourth Musketeer. In the past, Anya would have been with us, not just because she was my wife, but because she was the town's only doctor, and would have been performing the autopsy.

The snowmobile emerges from the snowy night like a JJ Abrams lens flare. I hold my arm up in front of my eyes, until Ethan pulls up beside us. It's a good thing this is all happening here in town and not over by the Tower. All the noise we're making, we'd have half the town out here causing a ruckus.

Ethan lifts the visor of his helmet away from his eyes, looks down at the camel, and says, "Well, it's dead." He gives a wave to Marit. "Hey."

"Made sure of it," I say, motioning to the bullet hole in the side of its head. The 9mm punched its way inside but lacked the *oomph* to escape. Nice and clean.

"No blood," he says.

Tali points out what I already thought was clear. "No exit wound."

It's easy to forget Ethan is a rookie. He's smarter than me. Smarter than Tali. Provides insights on the world and on people that we would miss. He's an observant little bastard. That was Tali's assessment after his first week of pointing out our flaws and inefficiencies around the office. But this might be the first time he's seen a bullet wound in person. He's been with us a little less than a year, and he isn't a hunter.

"Of course," he says, annoyed with himself for not noticing. He pulls his ever-present notebook from inside his jacket and jots down some notes in pencil. Then he closes it, puts it away, and then claps his hands together. "All right, where are we bringing this?"

"Jimmy's," I say.

"Jimmy's," Marit says, her tone sharp.

"Unless you know someone else that can carve open something this big," I say.

"Why do you need it carved open?" she asks. "You know what killed it."

"What I don't know," I say, "is why the other side of its head has a blob of eyeballs."

"A blob?" Now she sounds doubtful.

I sigh. "Marit... It's like...like frog eggs, but the size of golf balls...that are eyes. I'm not bullshitting you."

She smiles at me and pats my shoulder. "You make it too easy, Colt."

I sigh again, this time with a grumble. Marit enjoys getting under my skin. It's not malicious, but I don't always notice she's doing it. Not until she smiles.

Thankfully, it's hard to miss when she does.

"Swing around in front of us," I tell Ethan, "then back it in."

The snowmobile whines as it drags the 8x10 sheet of plywood. I smile when I notice that Ethan took the time to secure two chains to the wood and hook it to the back of the snowmobile. I was going to get the truck to drag it, but this might get the job done.

Might.

Don't know exactly how much the camel weighs, but this utility snowmobile isn't built for speed. It can easily haul 1,500 pounds.

Ethan gets in position and waits for the three of us to pick the wood up out of the snow. He reverses slowly, looking back over his shoulder, until I raise my hand. With the plywood positioned at the camel's rump, the hard part begins.

If the beast wasn't lying in smooth, compressed snow, I don't think we'd be able to move it an inch. Even with the reduction in friction, we have to push in pulses, all at once. We pause every now and again to slap some snow down on the plywood, make sure it's nice and slick. Turns an impossible job into an hour-long job—in the freezing Alaskan night.

When the camel is finally positioned on the plywood, we're overheated and sweating beneath our clothes, and our faces sting from the cold. I think my scarf might even be frozen to my face.

"Come on inside," Marit says. "Warm yourselves up by the fire. I'll pour us some coffee. The good stuff. Town won't be waking up for another hour. Might as well get your energy back before dealing with Jimmy."

"Sounds great," I say. "Thanks."

She gives me a smile and heads back to the bar. When I turn around, both Ethan and Tali are giving me looks I don't quite understand. "What?"

Tali squints at me like she's suspicious or trying to read my face.

"What?" I ask again.

"Nothing," she says, and steps around me, following her sister.

When I look back to Ethan, he's already on the snowmobile, ready to drive away. "I'll get this to Jimmy's and then come back." He doesn't wait for me to respond. Just says, "Ok, bye!" And then attempts to speed off.

The chains snap tight, and for a moment it looks like he won't be going anywhere. Then it makes like *The Little Snowmobile That Could* and starts churning forward, slowly building speed.

"Don't go too fast or it'll slide into your backside!" I shout the words, but I don't know if he heard me over the engine.

I decide it's fine. It'll be a learning moment for him. He might have all kinds of science knowledge rattling around in his head, but there's no better way than personal experience to really understand Newton's first law: a camel in motion tends to stay in motion, especially in the snow while sliding on a smooth piece of wood.

I stand there for a moment, watching him drive off. Then I remember I'm freezing cold and that Marit has hot coffee and a fire going. Woman's a life saver.

6

"Okay, okay," Tali says, having a laugh at my expense. "What about the time you found Lina Shugak and Caleb Winters doing the dirty in the dumpster behind the Tower?"

"Oh, God," I say clenching my eyes shut, trying to erase the memory.

"You could have let them finish," Marit says, approaching the couch Tali and I are sitting on. It's old and comfortable, warmed by a roaring fire in the bar's massive stone fireplace. There's a moose head mounted above—Nicholas, after the Saint, as in Santa Claus, because he's always watching. I rub my feet back and forth on the braided rug. And it's not just because the friction is helping warm my icicle toes. It's more of a compulsion, especially if I'm nervous or excited. Honestly, I'm not sure which I'm feeling now. I have a hard time putting words to my emotions.

I know what other people are feeling. Can sense it when I walk in a room. Hits me in the gut. If the emotion is big enough, it's like a tidal wave. Overwhelmed me as a kid, but I've grown accustomed to letting it crash over me. But when it comes to my own feelings, I'm a mystery to myself.

"You know he just walked up to it and started pounding?" Tali asks.

"Stop," Marit says, trying not to laugh. She hands one of the three mugs in her hands to Tali, and looks at me, aghast. "You *didn't*."

"—know there were *people* in the dumpster?" I grumble, accepting a mug. "No, I did not. Someone neglected to tell me that detail."

Marit's shock rotates back to her sister. "Tali!"

"C'mon," Tali says. "How could he not have known? Like anyone would have reported raccoons in a dumpster. Besides, the whole Tower had a view of those two, half-naked, lying on top of everyone's Hefty bags. They had it coming."

"Still," Marit says. "Look at this man." She points to me. "He's scarred for life."

"Barely sleep anymore," I say, joining the fun.

Marit steps over my legs to the right side of the couch. She gives me a kick. "Scooch."

I do as I'm told, moving to the center of the couch, which is barely big enough to hold the three of us. I'm normally not all that comfortable around people, but there are a few folks in this world with whom I am fully at home. Was lucky to find three of them all in the same town where no one in their right mind would want to live. I'd normally last just a few seconds, seated this close between two people. Would find a reason to leave.

Instead, I take a sip of coffee and try not to react. It's close to divine. "What flavor is this supposed to be?"

"I went easy on you. French Vanilla." Marit drinks from her steaming mug.

"Hrm. What's French about it?"

"Probably just the name," she says.

I take another drink, longer this time. It's hot, but unlike my brews, it isn't scalding. I lean forward and place the mug on the coffee table between us and the fireplace. When I come back, I reach my arms out and around both women. "Listen... I've been meaning to thank you. Both of you. For being here for me since...well, you know. Not sure I would have pulled through without you."

Tali looks like she's going to cry, so I turn to Marit. She's smiling up at me in a way that locks me in place for a moment. The discomfort wanes when she leans into me and places her head on my shoulder. My reaction isn't thought through. I just... lower my hand to her arm and give her a gentle squeeze. It feels... I don't know.

"Hey," Tali says. "You don't just get to be all sappy and then look away from me when I get misty-eyed."

"I don't?"

She whacks my shoulder. A very different response than her older sister. "As much as I appreciate what you just said, you should know by now that it's not necessary. You might be an outsider, but you didn't just accept Anya as Sugpiaq, you learned our traditions, attended ceremonies, and have never once treated us any differently—better *or* worse—than you would anyone else, and that is a true sign of not just acceptance, but love."

"There a point to this diatribe?" Marit says from my shoulder.

"Shut up," Tali responds. "The point is, we're family. We got you. And we know you got us."

I flinch when Marit's hand slides over mine, and squeezes.

If there's a guardian angel watching over me, it spares me from having to address the— I don't know what it was.

The bar's door swings open behind us, letting in a burst of wind and cold that makes the fire dance.

I stand quickly, like a kid who's been caught looking at porn, and turn around to find Ethan stomping the snow off his feet.

"Coffee for you on the bar," Marit tells him. "Should still be warm."

"Uh, thank you," he says. "But I'm not sure we have time to settle in."

"What's wrong?" I ask.

"Well, nothing, really."

"Nothing really, or nothing at all?" I ask.

"I got the camel to Jimmy's, like you asked—"

I tilt my head to the side, letting him know I expect a direct answer. "But..."

"Jimmy's there. He's stringing it up now. Said he wants cuts of the meat to sell, as payment for his services. I told him to wait for us, but you know..."

"It's Jimmy. I get it." I pick up my mug and down the liquid bliss that I'll never admit is in another league from my poison. "Looks like getting warm will have to wait." I look down at Tali. "Deputy."

"Yeah, yeah, I'm coming." She downs her coffee, lets out a delighted moan, and then gets to her socked feet. Gonna take us a minute to gear up again. Hopefully Jimmy waits.

I smile at Marit and give her a nod. "Appreciate the help, and the hospitality."

She gets to her feet. Stands toe to toe with me. "One, knock it off with the formal shit, Colt. Two, you're not getting rid of me that easily." Then she heads for the door.

I look to Tali. She just smiles at me and raises her eyebrows, like we're in on something, only I don't know what it is.

Time to figure it out later. Right now, we need to see about cutting open a deformed camel.

7

"Smells like a skunk's ass in here," I say, waving my hand in front of my face. It does nothing to help alleviate the smell of marijuana clinging to every molecule floating around inside the back room of Jimmy's butchery. The others don't seem to mind as much, but it really stands out to me.

It's not as bad as perfume, mind you.

For me, that's an instant migraine. Happily, people in this part of the world prefer to go scentless, or to use something more natural, like essential oils.

Marit uses a citrus oil that I don't mind at all.

Jimmy appears in front of me, hands raised. He's wearing a hair net that only partly covers his long straight hair. He looks like a Wish.com knock-off of a 1980s Axl Rose figurine—like if Guns N' Roses headlined a county fair and he came free with a corn dog. He should be wearing a winter hat. The backroom is unheated, but he seems oblivious to the cold. Probably high right now, which accounts for the paranoia on display. "Okay, okay…okay. I can explain the smell."

"Jimmy," I say, making sure his eyes stay focused on mine. Of course, I'm the first to look away. Not a fan of looking people dead in the eyes. Feels like I'm jackknife-diving into their souls. I get an instant sense of who they are, and it's uncomfortable. Anya used to say it made me a good sheriff—the ability to read people at a glance, coupled with my sense of what people are feeling. All that might be true, but it also makes me awkward at parties. "You know I don't care about people growing or smoking pot. So long as you keep it indoors."

"Well, I did *that,*" he says, calming down.

Alaska law is fairly lax when it comes to marijuana. My enforcement of those laws is even more lax. Self-medicating is a necessity for some when slogging through a dark winter. I don't partake, myself, but Tali and Marit do on occasion.

Tali steps through the open garage door and joins me in the dark. Then she takes a breath and coughs. "Holy. Wow. What strain have you been smoking, Jimmy?"

"Uh..." He sounds embarrassed. "Super Skunk."

"*Super Skunk!*" she asks. "*Why?*"

"I don't know, it's potent. Twenty percent THC, tops. I got it up to twenty-two with a little bit of horticultural tinkering."

"Can we get on with it?" I ask.

"Right, right." He lifts his pleading hands out to me again as he backs up into the darkness. "Hold on."

"You know," Tali whispers to me, "Might be worth trying a hit every now and again. Might help ease all that hypersensitivity you're always complaining about."

"Always?" I ask.

"Occasionally." She leans in closer. "Also, you might want to consider getting rid of that mustache."

"What's wrong with the mustache?"

"Well, it's creeping people out," she says.

"Creeping people—who?"

"Look, I'm just saying... You're a handsome man, boss. That caterpillar on your lip isn't doing you any favors. And...it kind of makes you look like a pedo."

"Excuse me?"

"Nothing personal. Unless they're shaded by a cowboy hat, or gray and on a wrinkly face, or besties with a full beard, mustaches make every man look like a pedo. Have since the sixties. Next time you're in front of a mirror, have a look. You'll see it."

I'm about to argue when the garage's lights snap on, illuminating the camel, now hung from the ceiling by two meat hooks in its thighs attached to winch cables. Its head faces down, just inches above the dirty concrete floor, stained with the blood. Oddly colored blood. It's light. Almost pink.

"Would it hurt you to bleach the floor every now and again?" Tali asks.

"Can't until spring," he says. "You think it smells bad now, just wait until everything thaws."

"Wow," Marit says, stepping inside the garage with Ethan. "Looks bigger in the light."

"Its size isn't the worst of it," Jimmy says, swinging the carcass around, revealing the left side of the creature's face and the volleyball-sized globule of eyeballs.

Having already seen it, I'm the only one that doesn't reel back in shock.

"Worse than I imagined," Tali says.

Marit walks closer, crouching down. "It's a mutation, right? But how? Radiation? Something from the old base?"

I shake my head. "NovaGen would have cleared out anything like that."

"Speaking of," Marit says. "Haven't seen any of those guys the last few days. The nerds usually come down Monday, Wednesday, and Friday. Like clockwork. They've missed the last two."

Ethan plucks out his notepad, jotting it all down.

It's worth noting. I don't police what they do at the lab. They've got government backing, which I'm guessing is how they got access to the old Cold War research facility. Not very clear on what they're researching, but who's to say it's not some kind of gene-altering research that resulted in a camel growing extra eyes. Wouldn't even be that unusual. We've grown mice with human ears. And they do have 'Gen' in the company name.

"We'll check on them when we're done here," I say, and turn to Jimmy. "Now, cut it open. I want to see what it's been eating."

"Not until you agree to my terms," Jimmy says, crossing his arms.

"How many marijuana plants do you own, Jimmy? Because if it's more than six–"

"Okay, okay. Wow, man. Just trying to make a few bucks for my services."

He's not lying. It's hard to make a living here when everything is thawed, never mind the middle of winter. "I can't let you keep the meat, Jimmy. Could be contaminated. It's probably been genetically altered. Wouldn't be safe. But I'll tell you what, we have a spending budget, and this seems like as good a reason to spend some as any. I'll give you a hundred dollars."

"Two hundred," he counters.

"Fifty."

"Okay, okay! Okay. I'm cool with a hundred."

"Great, I say. "Now, get star–"

A shrill cry sends goose bumps up my back and over my head. If I weren't wearing a winter cap, I think my shaggy hair would be standing on end.

"What was that?" Ethan asks.

"Came from the camel," Marit says.

"Maybe…maybe it's gas?" Tali guesses. "You know, escaping from its ass?"

We spread out slowly, surrounding the camel, examining it from every angle.

"Hasn't been dead long enough for it to get gassy," Jimmy says. "And it'll be frozen through before bacteria can—"

A second cry, this one sounding a little desperate.

"There!" Ethan says, pointing to the side of the camel's leg. "There's a hole."

"What in God's—" my voice catches when a little furry hand pokes out of the hole, scratching at the camel's brown fur—

—trying to escape.

8

I snap my fingers toward Tali. "Knife."

She draws her bone knife, flips it around between her fingers, and catches it by the blade, holding it out to me. The handle was carved from a blue whale's vertebrae. The spinous process. That's what Ethan told us. It's the segment of bone that protrudes up from the vertebrae. I was going to let Jimmy cut this thing open, but this isn't an autopsy now. It's a rescue.

Of something. No idea what could be alive inside a camel, aside from a baby camel, but they don't have little furry fingers.

All I really know is that I'm feeling the same fear that I did out on the street, when I shot the camel. I don't know what it is, but I know this thing is terrified, and it's triggering my overactive sense of empathy.

Without me having to ask, Ethan slides a metal chair in front of me. I step on it, but it's not quite high enough for me to reach the hole. I could ask Jimmy to open it, but he's clearly been smoking. Looks like a piece of cooked spaghetti stuck to the wall. His eyes are wide in shock. He won't be any help.

"Hold the chair," I say and both deputies take a side. Stabilized, I step from the seat to the arms, raising my face up to the hole's height.

I nearly topple off the chair when a small brown eye appears in the hole. Arms flailing, I find my equilibrium again. "Shit."

"What did you see?" Ethan asks.

"An eye," I say. "It's looking at me."

The eye snaps to my hand holding the knife. Then it shifts, like the thing trapped inside gave a nod. It slides out of view.

I'll be damned.

I hold the knife tip against the camel's skin and notice a previous incision, stretching six inches from the hole. It's not sewn shut; it's sealed by frozen blood. That's why the thing inside can't escape. It was trapped by the camel's weight when it fell, and now the wound is frozen.

This is why the camel was bleeding.

Good thing Tali keeps this knife's blade sharp enough to cut Superman's hair. I carry a knife, too, but it's better suited for hacking branches from trees. With a little bit of pressure, the blade slips through the previous incision, separating flesh once more. I try not to rush, despite the little thing's desperate shriek. This blade would take its tiny arm off without me feeling it.

I'm relieved when the cut is finished, and nothing has screamed in pain. Then again, I've just set something free. Something living inside a camel's leg.

I hand the knife back to Tali. She takes it in one hand and sheaths it on her hip without taking her second hand off the chair.

"Okay, little guy," I say, speaking as I would to a dog. "You can come out now."

Two little hands emerge, spindle fingers tipped with little, unimposing claws. Look like they're meant for climbing, more than slashing or pinning prey.

The wound is pulled open and a little face slides into view. It's soaked in blood, or—what I thought was blood, but looks more like red Jell-O. Maybe it's already congealed?

Question for later, I decide.

The little creature is shaking from cold. Its orange, black, and white mane smoothed back. I can see it freezing as the thing extracts itself.

I motion for it to come out, like it can understand me.

"C'mon. I got you."

"Careful, Colt," Marit says. "We don't know what that is."

"Here," Ethan says to Marit. "Hold this. Let me get a look."

They trade places and Ethan moves back for a clear view. At the same time, the little creature pulls itself free, its long-fingered arms shaking.

"C'mon," I say, urging it to my hands. I don't think it will survive another thirty seconds in this cold.

"What..." Ethan's seen it, but I mistake his astonishment for confusion.

"You don't know what it is?" I ask.

"What? No. I mean, yes. It's a golden lion tamarin."

"Dangerous?" I ask.

"Harmless."

That's all I needed to hear. I push my gloved hands into the wound, wrap my fingers around its little body and pull the creature out like I've just delivered a baby. As it slides out, I get a glimpse inside the wound and am confused by what I see, but I don't take time for a second glance.

I hop down from the chair arms to the seat and turn around. Ethan is there to greet me. He holds out his hands, reading my mind. "Get it inside," I tell him. "Warm it under water. Lukewarm to start, and then hotter over time.

He nods. "I know how to do it."

He heads for the door leading inside the butchery.

"You've thawed out more than a few idiots," I say to Marit.

She smiles. "Including three tonight." She follows it up with a nod, understanding what I'm about to ask. "I'll go with him. Make sure he doesn't go too fast."

"Thanks," I say, stepping down from the chair.

"Uh," Jimmy says. He's coming back to himself now that it's just the three of us and a carcass. He digs a winter hat out of his pocket, pulls off the hairnet, and puts the hat on. "The hell just happened?"

"There was a golden lion tamarin trapped in the camel's frozen leg," Tali says, like it's an everyday occurrence and Jimmy shouldn't be freaking out.

Truth is, *I'm* freaking out. I look down at my gloves. They're covered in already frozen, red globules. Both hands are shaking, and not from the cold. My body buzzes with adrenaline. It's not uncommon for me. My body kicks into fight or flight for a variety of reasons: including too much fun, too much stress, or even too much noise. Really, too much of anything, including everything that's happened tonight. Gonna need some downtime soon.

"You okay?" Tali asks, taking hold of my shaking hands.

"You know how it is," I say. She is the only one who knows my secret, aside from Anya, who took it to her grave. It's the kind of thing sisters might normally share, but Tali hasn't told Marit. And Tali only knows because Anya filled her in. Knew I'd need support. She was taking care of me even while dying.

All that said, I'm not about to speak openly about it in front of Jimmy.

"I do," she says, letting go of my hands once I'm safely on the ground.

"Need a minute?" she asks.

"Sixty seconds," I say, stepping out of the garage, into the frigid night, where only the stars can see me. And maybe Anya. She believed in an afterlife, following the traditions of her people. The soul, upon death, embarks on a journey to a spirit world that mirrors the deceased's earthly life. I'm not entirely sure what their beliefs are surrounding the possibility of the dead watching over the living. I'd like to believe she can still see me, at least when I'm out in nature, my thoughts tuned in to her.

It's a bit hokey, but who's going to judge me? I've never said any of this out loud.

I focus on the stars above. They're spectacular this time of year, when the moisture in the air is frozen and most of the town's lighting is off. You can see the Milky Way in a way that's unlike any other place I've been. Like you can reach out and take hold of the stars, galaxies, and cotton candy nebulae.

My chest loosens and my hands stop shaking as I get lost in the view. I take a deep breath. It burns my lungs but still helps ease my nervous system.

A surge of green haze flows past overhead.

The aurora borealis, along with the stars, is what makes this place bearable during the long, dark winter. When everything looks depressing and monochrome, you just need to look up. Three more pulses of green whip past. Almost urgent.

I take it as a sign, and smile. "I'm going, I'm going," I say to Anya. "So pushy." I turn around and head back into the garage, a little better prepared to handle the autopsy of what I could have sworn was an emoting camel, but turned out to be...what? An escape vehicle for a golden lion tamarin.

Going to need a lorazepam before this day is over, that's for damn sure.

"Okay," I say, as I enter the garage, clapping my hands together to remove the frozen gore. "Let's get started."

9

"Jimmy," I say. "Hey, Jimmy."

He blinks a few times before his eyes snap toward me. He's a little more relaxed but hasn't left his position against the wall. "Huh? Yeah?"

"You're here for a reason," I remind him.

"That was..."

I nod. "A monkey—"

"Golden lion tamarin," Tali says.

"Right. Whatever that is." Jimmy grasps his woolen beanie and rubs it back and forth over his head. I have no idea how anyone can wear wool, let alone rub it all over their scalp. Makes me cringe. "But that's not really the point. It was inside the camel, and the camel ain't a normal camel. You know that, right?"

I glance over at the hanging beast, its globule of eyes white with frost.

"Yeah, we figured that out *tout suite.* Look, we're just as lost as you. Only way we're going to get answers is to carve this up, and that's your job."

Tali is unimpressed. "If he's not up to it—"

"I can do it," Jimmy says, pushing himself off the wall. "Just needed a minute."

"You sure?" she asks, "because I've dismantled a few rabbits. How different can this be?"

He scoffs, moving to a table covered in his tools of the trade. None of it looks very sanitary, which I'll need to follow up on another time, but for now, I don't care how clean or rusty his tools are.

When he turns around, he's holding a large cleaver and a honing rod. He slides the cleaver back and forth, ensuring it's sharp. "Where do you want me to start?"

I'd planned on having a look at its stomach first, but what I saw inside the tamarin's hideaway has me curious. "Leg. I want to have a look at its musculature up close."

"To be clear, you are asking me to remove its leg, yes?"

"Yes."

"Fun," he says, dragging over a painting ladder that would have been handy about five minutes ago. He dons a pair of gloves and notes my attention. Holds them up for me to see. "Cut resistant. You know, for safety."

He slides the honing rod inside his belt like it's a sword, then ascends the ladder, cleaver in hand. As he nears the top, everything about his demeanor changes. His nervous jitters disappear. His normally lax expression tightens with purpose. Never seen him like this. Focused.

He places the cleaver on the paint tray, and then takes another step up, using the camel's body to stay balanced.

I take hold of the ladder, steadying it.

"Thanks," he says. "Been a while since I worked on anything this big."

He starts pushing on the flank, almost massaging it.

"Uhh," Tali says. "What...what are you doing?"

"Locating the joint," he says. "I mean, if you don't want every bit of the leg, I can bone saw through the femur, but that might actually take longer, and it'd be a lot messier."

I look down at the gore covered floor.

"Doesn't look like you mind a mess."

"Heh. Yeah. Like I said, I can't really rinse it clear until spring. It builds up during the winter. On the plus side, it's frozen so we can't smell it as bad. If you could, I'd be in here alone. Now, whole leg, or hack job?"

"Whole leg," I say.

He nods and draws a boning knife from his right side. Didn't even notice he had it.

"Right," he says. "So, I'm going to make an incision at the top of the hind leg. Normally would have skinned this thing first, but I'm guessing that's not necessary?"

My imagination provides me with a perfect snapshot of what the camel would look like skinless. "Please, no."

He gives the limb a few more pokes with his fingers, then stops and slips the knife through the skin. It slides in deep.

He stops. "Huh."

"Huh, what?" I ask.

"Creature this big. Should have strong muscles, right? It was walking around. But it feels like I'm just cutting through fat here. No resistance at all." He switches to the cleaver and repeats the process. This time he pulls the blade in a curved path, slicing down beneath the limb and back up on the other side. Then he climbs down from the ladder and looks at the floor beneath the body.

"Double huh." He looks back at me, a squirrely expression on his face. "You didn't bleed this thing, right?"

"Wouldn't know how," I say. "Why?"

He motions to the floor like the answer is obvious. "Just a few drops. Should be gushing. Should have cut through an artery, but...well, I didn't feel much of anything."

He places the cleaver on a nearby table, then folds up the ladder and puts it away. Didn't peg Jimmy as organized, but my experiences with him are generally punctuated by drug and/or alcohol use. He's still buzzing a bit, but I think the camel knocked the high right out of him.

"What's next?" I ask.

He waves me over on his way back. As I approach, he lifts his hand and gives the camel's thigh a slap. The limb tilts a little and then swings down, nearly kicking Jimmy with its club-like foot. "Next..." He takes hold of the lower leg. "...you're going to help me dislocate this bitch."

I stand behind him and take hold of the limb, same as Jimmy.

"On three, shove up, hard as you can. One. Two. Three!"

The leg doesn't move far before I feel resistance. The flesh might be easy to cut, but the bones—and sockets—are thick, heavy, and resilient.

"Harder!" he grunts.

I give it everything I've got.

When Tali pulls the chair in front of Jimmy and climbs atop the seat, my arms are shaking. Won't be able to keep it up much longer.

Tali takes hold of the camel's leg, just above its foot. Then she pulls up, adding her muscle to the task, and a good amount of leverage. Smart.

A loud pop coupled with a sudden increase in weight confirms our success. Unfortunately, most of the hundred pounds are behind me, in the thigh. Unprepared, I let out a, "Whoa!" and am pulled backward. Thanks to Tali and Jimmy holding on, I don't topple to the floor. Instead, I manage to twist around and lower the limb to the floor.

Tali and Jimmy flank me on either side. When I stand, all three of us are looking at the leg's interior where it was cleaved from the body.

Tali is the first of us to break her trance, turning to me and saying, "Seriously, Colt, what the fuck?"

10

I drop to one knee, peering down into the open meat—if that's even the right word—of the camel's severed and dislocated limb. There are membranes arranged in a geometric pattern, creating cells, almost like a network of bubbles, but more complex. They fit together perfectly, no gaps between them. Each wall of every cell is shared by its neighbor...on all sides.

Interconnected.

"No idea," I whisper, and then turn to Jimmy. "Skin the leg. Try not to cut the cells beneath it."

"That what we're calling them?" he asks. "Cells?"

"Unless you got a better idea," I say.

"The devil's work is what I'd call it." He crouches down, drawing his blade. "Ain't nothing living on this planet that looks like this on the inside."

"Didn't know you were religious," Tali says.

"Am now," he says, making an incision. He pulls the blade toward himself, slicing the outer layers of skin. It starts to peel open on its own, revealing the layers beneath. Reminds me of those Internet videos where people slowly cut through layers of balloons to reveal frozen water on the inside. With each gentle drag of the knife, the wound opens further. When a final, translucent film is all that remains, he pinches the knife between his index finger and thumb and drags the blade over it. The only pressure comes from the knife's weight and gravity's tug, but it's enough. The flesh splits open from the inner thigh to the ankle.

Jimmy takes hold of the two halves and pulls, peeling the skin away to either side. When he leans back...well, it's like I'm seeing something I'm not supposed to. Like a glitch in the Matrix—a clue that the world isn't exactly what I believed it to be just a few minutes ago.

I take a deep breath to calm myself and continue my assessment. "Each cell connects to the others seamlessly. The outermost cells form a smooth wall covered in a thick layer of pink gelatinous goo."

"You recording this or something?" Jimmy asks.

"Just saying it out loud so it feels more real," I say. "And so we're all on the same page. See something I don't? Make sure you say it."

"See something, say something." He nods. "Got it."

"They're all filled with the same gunk," Tali says, motioning to the bunch of cells that have been cut open. "Looks like raspberry jam. Kinda making me hungry for toast—hold on. You said it has no tendons or veins. No muscles. And I sure as shit don't see any of that here. So how was it walking? How did the camel control its limbs?"

Jimmy and I look at each other and then back to Tali. We're clueless.

"Okay, then," she says, "time to break the glass ceiling, I guess. Show you guys how a true detective thinks."

"Raven's Rest doesn't have a detective," Jimmy points out.

"Might be time," I say, looking at the limb again, which on the inside, looks absolutely space age.

"I need a power source," Tali tells Jimmy. "Cable with exposed wires at the end."

"Like jumper cables?" he asks.

"Sure, but something we can just plug in."

His eyes light up. "Hold on." He hustles to the far end of the garage and pulls open a filing cabinet. Works his way through each drawer, stopping when he reaches the bottom. Pulls out an old desk lamp, then uses the same knife he used on the camel to cut the cord. He quickly splits it down the middle and whittles away the outer insulation. He then pulls it apart further while moving back toward us, snagging an extension cord from the wall on his way back. He plugs in the cord, unravels it, and then returns. "I got you."

He hands the split cord to Tali and she hands one end to me, smiling at my concern. "Partners, right?"

I sigh. "What do you want me to do?"

She turns to Jimmy. "Be ready to plug us in." Back to me, she says, "Don't touch the exposed metal." She demonstrates by holding the cord a foot from its shaven end.

"Thanks for that, Deputy Obvious."

She gives me a look that would make Beelzebub shrink back.

I just grin.

"Poke it in," she says, and manages to reign in her Steve Carell sense of humor. She pushes her end of the cord into one of the sealed cells higher up on the leg. I shove mine through a sealed membrane, completing the circuit at either end of the limb.

I understand what she's trying to do. Something like this would make a normal arm or leg contract the muscles and make it move. If the same holds true here, we might get a better idea of how it works.

But I feel like we're cavemen trying to discern the meaning of a crashed UFO. We're out of our league. Over our heads.

Probably a dozen other clichés. But we're not out of options. Based on what I've seen here, I know this camel wasn't brought in by a local, leaving only one potential source: NovaGen.

"Okay," Tali says, letting out a sigh. "Plug us in, Jimmy."

Jimmy gives a nod and shoves the plug into the extension cord.

Before there is time to register what happens, I'm struck in the chest and knocked onto my ass and back. Wasn't electrical. Would have felt that in my arm before it hit my chest. Looking up at the ceiling and the upside-down camel, I probe where my ribs meet the sternum. Nothing broken. Nothing dislocated.

A sound like a tuna flapping madly on the deck of a fishing boat beckons me to sit up. Leaning on my hands, I watch the severed limb bouncing and bending, doing an amazing impression of Raygun partaking in the Olympic breakdancing competition.

It kicked me. That's what knocked me back.

"Look at 'm go!" Jimmy says, getting more of a kick out of the spastic leg than I did.

Tali's on the job, bending over, looking at the leg's inner workings as it moves.

"What do you see?"

"The cells are expanding and contracting, controlling the leg like muscles." She takes a pencil from her front pocket and taps the eraser end against one of the cells. It's no longer flexible. "I'm not a physiologist, or whatever you call people who specialize in body stuff, but I think the cell network fills the roles of muscles, veins, *and* ligaments."

"That's enough." I take hold of the cord on my end. I try to tug it out, but the cell is holding on tight. I pull harder, with no luck.

"Same on this end." Tali puts a foot against the severed thigh. Gelatinous sludge oozes out around her boot. She pulls on the cord, gritting her teeth. "Jeezum Crow, how strong is this shit?"

The flailing limb bounces around for a moment while we're lost in thought. Then something cracks and the lower leg's flapping turns its foot into a pendulum. Propelled upward, the camel's foot just misses my face. Would have been a solid hit. Might have knocked me unconscious.

"Unplug it!" I shout at Jimmy. "Unplug i–"

The limb falls flat and goes still. Jimmy stands over it, the extension cord in one hand and the plug in the other.

"Thanks," I say, sliding away and climbing back to my feet.

"That was...that was..." Jimmy's at a loss for words.

"Horrifying," Tali says.

He rubs his wool hat over his head. "Was going to say something more positive, but yeah, that too."

"Okay," says Marit, voice cheery. "Who wants to see the most adora–" She freezes upon seeing the leg. "Shit. What did I miss?"

"Well," Jimmy says. "We can tell you one thing for sure: it ain't no camel."

11

After taking a minute to photograph the camel, its limb, and the strange cells within, we head inside the butchery's storefront, which is kept at a refrigerated temperature, but feels balmy compared to outdoors. To keep the room a nice thirty-seven degrees requires no cooling, but it does take heat.

I remove my gloves, and sit down at one of the two tables between the counter and the windowless front wall. I assume the tables are here in case someone is brave enough to have Jimmy actually make them a sandwich. The baseboard heating pumps out warmth, but it's quickly cooled by the freezing wall above. I lower my fingers down, just above the heater, letting my knuckles thaw a bit. My gloves are some of the best you can buy, but fingers are fingers. They're the first thing to get cold, even when dressed properly.

"Well, where is it?" Tali asks, sitting across from me, pulling her hood back. "Could use some adorable after looking at the insides of an alien camel."

"It's not alien," I say.

She raises her brows at me. "Prove me wrong."

I think on it for a moment, come up short, and offer a very generic, "It makes no sense."

"Aliens wouldn't make sense to us," she says. "Because they're aliens, right? Different planet. Different culture. Rules. Laws. Ways of thinking. All different. A camel sent to Earth as a spy makes some kind of sense, right? Maybe it was meant to watch us? Or see what the life of an animal on this world is like, and it just got dropped off, or beamed or whatever, to the wrong place?"

"And the eye?" I ask.

"Hey, just because aliens can travel through space doesn't mean they never make mistakes." She taps the side of her head, indicating that she's outthinking me.

"That kind of mistake looked very...human to me. We tend to make a mess of things. Aliens. Super intelligent beings. Why would they send a physical abomination as a spy?"

"Mm," she says. "That does make sense."

I smile and tap the side of my head.

The bathroom door opens. Ethan steps out. He's got something inside his jacket. I'm assuming it's the tamarin, and that it's alive, because I can see it moving around beneath the parka.

"Wasn't sure it was going to make it," Ethan says, "but the warm water woke it right up. Once I dried it off—Jimmy's got a hair dryer in there for some reason—it started bouncing around. Then..." He looks down at his undulating jacket. "It crawled inside and—" He twitches to the side. "Sorry. It tickles. Anyway, it seems friendly enough."

I don't bother reminding him that we just removed it from inside a camel that's not a camel, and that it got in there via an incision. It was too clean to be made by the creature's little claws, but something put that cut in the camel, and wanted the tamarin to survive the cold.

And it wasn't aliens.

"Well," Marit says. "Let them see it."

He opens the top of his parka and looks inside. "C'mon out, little man." He talks to it like a dog. "C'mon, buddy. They're nice people. No one is going to hurt you. I promise."

A little head pops up out of the parka. Its two little brown eyes are both cute and somehow wise. The slicked-back hair I saw has been replaced by golden locks on either side of the creature's hairless face. Down the middle of its mane, above the eyes, is a streak of white. The golden hair fades to black where the neck meets the torso.

It looks at each of us, but lingers longer on me.

It remembers, I think. That moment of eye contact between us before I pulled it out.

The tamarin climbs fully out of Ethan's coat and onto his shoulder, perfectly balanced. The black fur covering its torso shifts to gold halfway down its arms and legs, and the whole of its tail. The little guy turns toward me, lifts his head, and lets out a high-pitched squeak.

"I think he wants you," Marit says, giving me a shove toward Ethan.

When I step closer, the tamarin crouches down, ready to spring. I stop and hold out an arm like I'm a damn falconer. Then he leaps the distance between us—and misses my arm.

But I think that was the plan. While the little creature's body swishes past my arm and body, his legs grasp my arm, momentum pulling him down, and then back up. I barely feel it. I imagine his weight would be measured in ounces, rather than pounds. Looks heavier, but I think that's just because he's got poofy hair.

With casual grace, he swings back up into a sitting position like it was no big deal.

Then he locks eyes with me again, peering, like he's assessing me. The tamarin turns its eyes to my clothing, looking me up and down before leaning to the side.

After a quick inspection of Tali, he relaxes once more and lets out another squeak.

"Oh, my God," Tali says. "It *is* adorable."

"And not remotely local," I point out. "Like the camel."

"So, where's it from?" Marit asks.

"Brazil," Ethan chimes in. "And technically, it's not exactly a golden lion tamarin. It's a golden-*headed* lion tamarin. They're omnivores. Territorial. Endangered. And...social. They live in groups."

"We know what 'social' means," Marit says.

Tali leans in close, reaching her fingers out to the tamarin. He watches her but doesn't shrink back. When she starts rubbing the tamarin, he leans into it, turning so she covers both of his shoulders. Lets out a happy little chitter.

"He needs a name," Tali says.

"Dufresne," I say, the name just popping out of my mouth.

"What kind of name is that?" Marit asks.

"You're kidding. *Andy* Dufresne. *The Shawshank Redemption*. Story of a man, wrongly convicted, escaping from prison."

"Never heard of it," she says, shocking me almost as much as the camel's insides did.

"We're going to have to do something about that," I say, petting the tamarin's head. "Isn't that right, Dufresne?"

"Anytime," Marit says to me, smiling in a way that makes me glance away.

"Point is," I say, "Dufresne, the tamarin, escaped from wherever he was being held. Might not have been a tunnel—"

"Spoilers," Marit says.

"—but I think hiding inside a camel—"

"That's not a camel," Tali says.

"—is a pretty ingenious method of escape." I feel a scratch as I slide the little guy's soft fur between my fingers. Used to do the same thing with my dog's ear. I've always been good at connecting with animals. It's a lot easier for me than people.

Without making it obvious, I work my hand back to where I felt the scratch. Feels like a small piece of square plastic attached to his ear.

It's a tag.

Working his hair away from the ear like I'm still just giving him a rub, I get a look at the tag, and frown.

"What is it?" Tali asks.

"He's been tagged," I say, turning so she can see the unmistakable logo—a double helix intertwined with a cross. Gives the impression that they're working on medical research but, after what I've seen today, I have serious questions about what NovaGen actually does. I'm thinking it's high time we find out.

"NovaGen," she says. "Okay, so, not aliens."

"Reckon you'll all be coming with me to pay them a visit?" I ask the group.

"Damn straight," Marit answers, probably because she and Jimmy are the only ones not on the payroll.

I give a nod.

"Meet back at the station in ten. Bring a gun."

"You expecting trouble?" Ethan asks, looking nervous.

"I'm expecting... Well, I don't know what I'm expecting. Just want to be ready for anything, much as we can be. And the ability to put down another rogue camel, rhinoceros, or giant sloth seems warranted."

12

The smell of my home brew used to get me salivating for the caffeine boost, but now, after having Marit's French bullshit coffee, I understand why no one likes mine. This second batch of the day isn't about waking up, though; it's about staying warm. Our winter gear does a good job, but NovaGen is on a mountainside. Windy enough to pull the dentures from a grandpa's flaccid face, and cold enough to freeze them before they hit the ground.

So, we'll take my brown swill in thermal cups and keep our cores nice and warm. Shouldn't be up there too long. They're nice people for the most part. Smart. Don't cause problems. Back down from fights even if they have a right to put a roughneck in their place. Granted, the NovaGen folks probably wouldn't get in too many punches and, even if they did, there wouldn't be a lot of power behind them. Some of the brutes in town have stared down polar bears without flinching. Not a one of those nerdy fellas would win a fight unless lightsabers were involved, but they'd have my blessing.

The office is warm now by Raven's Rest standards. I've shed my parka, to keep from getting sweaty, while we wait for Ethan to finish bringing around the snowmobiles. He's scrawny, like the guys at NovaGen, and he might not be a genius, but he does work hard and is loyal. No one's given him a hard time since he arrived a year back, but that's mostly on account of whoever messes with him, messes with me.

And no one wants that.

He likes to think it's because of his fierce gaze. Eye of the tiger. Closer to eye of the fainting goat. But there's no one else in town that could do the job as well, aside from me and Tali, of course.

The high-pitched rev of a second engine grows louder as it rounds the building. That's our cue. I pour two cups, cap them, and carry them to the back room where the Nuluk sisters are having a conversation. Probably trying to process the massive dung pile of weird we've collectively stepped in.

I approach the open door and hear hushed voices.

"He'll come around." It's a whisper. Can't tell who's speaking. "Don't worry about it, you have—"

My boot squeaks on the floor, and the room ahead goes silent. I nearly freeze in place, but I don't want them to think I was eavesdropping.

"Alright," I say, entering the room as casually as possible. "Liquid shit for both of you, and no complaints. I'm man enough to admit that Marit, and her pods, are superior."

I place the cups on the round table and note their expressions. Hands deep in the cookie jar, trying to dig to China, or whatever is on the opposite side of the world from Alaska.

"You guys good?" I ask.

"Fine," they both say far too quickly. But I get it. I walked in on sister-talk. None of my business. "Sounds like Ethan's got the snowmobiles ready to go." I look down at Marit's 9mm handgun resting on the table. "Sure you don't want something with a little more oomph?"

"A little more oomph would probably break my wrist," she says.

I wave her off. "Hogwash. You're a strong woman. Don't underestimate yourself."

She and Tali share a quick glance and a subtle smile that most people would normally miss. But hypersensitivity to other people's emotions has its benefits, and causes a lot of confusion, because I also can't read their minds. Something I said struck them as funny, but I'm not going to ask what. I struggle to understand the female mind and its collective sense of humor.

Anya was like that. The three of them together, would just start saying random things, and the others would burst out laughing. Over and over. Felt like they were delivering punchlines to psychic jokes I couldn't hear. It's nice to hear a semblance of that again.

I back out of the room. "Finish up the chit-chat. Time to go."

Ethan comes in just as I return to the front. He shakes the snow from his jacket and stomps his feet on the mat. He's not trying to keep the floor dry, he's making sure he doesn't fall on his ass. Again. Packed snow on the bottom of a boot and a smooth floor are not a good combination, which he learned the hard way, week one.

"All set," he says. "Gassed them both up, too. Have enough fuel to go up and back a few times. Prepare for everything, right?"

Kid makes me feel a semblance of pride. He pays attention.

I give him a nod and motion to the coffee. "Pour yourself a cup and drink it as we go. It'll help keep the cold at bay."

"Yes, sir," he says, and pours two cups. One for him, one for me. Good fucking man. Tali better watch out or I'll have the kid outranking her soon.

"Hey, you want to be the big man, today?" I ask him.

He stops pouring. "Seriously?"

"Long as you think you can handle it."

He gives me a sidelong smile. "You read my resume before hiring me, right?"

"Maybe you're rusty," I say.

He laughs at that. "Uh-huh."

Kid was apparently some kind of wizard with a shotgun in the academy. A close-range guru. Won't need to shoot anything, but I call it 'being the big man,' even when Tali takes a turn. Means you're a threat. It's probably sexist, but I have yet to meet a woman that wants to be called a large woman.

Before I can head to the armory, the station door bursts open. Snow swirls around the figure that's just stepped inside. Guessing it's Jimmy based on the jacket. He stomps his feet and turns around. Holds up some kind of thick, pale balloon with a tube extending from its top. Looks like there was another tube at the bottom, but he's tied it off.

"Got what you were after!"

"And that is?"

He looks to the balloon, thrusting it forward. "Camel's stomach."

I stretch my neck one way and then the other. "I just needed to know what was inside it, didn't need to— You know what, let's just have a quick look."

"Thought you'd say that," Jimmy says. "Already drained it, but I gotta tell you, the bile in this thing didn't look or smell right. More like coolant. Like for a car. But it wasn't coolant, either. Saved some in a bucket. Probably should have brought that with. Anywho..."

Jimmy crouches down, slaps the organ on the floor and draws his knife.

"Seriously?" Tali says, walking toward us with Marit. "You can't do that on the floor."

I agree with her. It's all kinds of unsanitary, but it's this or the table we eat on.

Jimmy doesn't wait. With one clean slice he cuts a straight line from top to bottom. "Here comes the fun part." He peels the stomach open like a haggis laying its insides bare. Problem is, there's nothing there.

"Huh," he says. "Well. That is... huh."

Sounds like he has something to say.

"Spit it out, Jimmy," Tali says before I can.

"Well, it's just that I've seen something like this before."

"You have?' Ethan says, sounding astonished.

"Not exactly, but close enough," he says. "Was a deer. Newborn. Didn't live longer than ten minutes. And its stomach was like this. Empty."

"Because it hadn't eaten," Marit says, crouching down for a closer look. "Ever." She reaches down to the stomach and plucks a small nugget from the lining. She holds it out in her palm.

"It's a tiny oval," Jimmy says.

Marit looks at him long enough to roll her eyes and then says, "It's a partially digested pill."

He gives a vigorous nod. "I see it. I see it."

"I've seen enough," I say, standing up and taking my parka from the hook. "Let's go have a chat with our friends from the lab."

"Should we call them first?" Ethan asks. "Let them know we're coming?"

He's already on the way to the phone when I say, "Never let them know you're coming, kid. Never. Get the boomstick and let's go."

I head out into the cold. I'm not a fan of mysteries I can't solve on my own. And I'm not keen on animal experimentation, which might be legal on mice, rats, and other small things, but a camel? Can't be legal.

I climb on one of the waiting snowmobiles. Beside me, Tali takes the second.

A pair of arms slide around my waist. I think it's Ethan, until I feel a helmeted head resting on my back for a moment. A kind of nervousness, which I haven't been acquainted with for a very long time, sneaks up on me and pounces. Before I can make sense of anything, Ethan hops on the second snowmobile and wraps his arms around Tali, shotgun slung over his back.

Jimmy stands there, just watching us like a lady seeing her husband off to war. I snap him out of whatever thought he's lost in by saying, "Dufresne is locked inside my office. Has water and a Snickers bar. Should be fine but stay here and keep an eye on things." Before he can respond, I turn over the engine, hit the throttle, and we're off.

Can't help but wonder if I'm running toward something or running away.

13

Cold doesn't begin to describe the situation on the mountain pass. There's nothing to stop the wind. We're carving a path through two feet of snow on what we call 'Laboratory Lane.' And there's a twenty-foot drop on either side of the road. Which is why Nova-Gen keeps it immaculately maintained.

But not today.

And probably not for the past week.

Which is the real concern. If there are animals from the lab on the loose, and they're not maintaining the facility, I don't imagine the reason is a good one. I've been trying to work out what could have gone awry whilst not plunging over the snowy road's edge with Marit. Her grip has gotten stronger. She knows the deal. Up here in the frozen north, one mistake is all it takes to wind up dead.

Haven't come up with much. Maybe they all came down with something? Could be some of them got tired of combing ice out of their beards. Moved back to the lower forty-eight. Happens all the time. But it doesn't feel right. I don't know where Nova-Gen's money comes from, but they've got plenty of it. Should be easy for them to fly in new personnel on a chopper. Seen them do it before.

Brake lights flare in front of me. Tali pulls to the left, giving me space to slide up alongside her. She cuts her engine, flips up her visor, and I do the same. We'll be able to hear each other better.

"You okay?" I ask.

"What?" she says. "Fine. I grew up here, remember? This is just another day."

She's joking. No one goes on the mountain during the winter without a good reason. Some of the lab guys make the trip down, but they've got all kinds of fancy winter vehicles that help them make the journey, safe and warm. Like I said, plenty of money.

"Why are we stopped?" Marit asks her sister, sounding impatient. She's probably been rethinking her decision to come.

Tali waves her off. "You've got this big space heater of a man buffering the wind for you."

"Tali," I say, using my boss voice.

"Right. Sorry." She points up the slope. "No lights."

She's right. We're just a few hundred feet from NovaGen. Can't see it from here, but the place is usually lit up at night like they're trying to ward off the boogeyman. Should be a bright glow. The falling flakes should be radiant in the sky. It's usually a beautiful sight.

I should have noticed. But I'm distracted by…something. As usual, my out-of-date mind is processing my emotions at the pace of a quadriplegic turtle.

"Doesn't change anything," I say, trying to hide how unnerved I feel. "Something ain't right. Unfortunately, it's on us to find out what."

"Yeah," she says, resigned to the task. Same as me. And since we're less than a minute from reaching the top, there's no backing out now. No matter what's going on in the lab, we need to warm up before heading back.

I give her a nod, start my engine, flip my visor down, and flinch when Marit wraps her arms around me again. Then

I gun it, taking the lead. Snow bursts over and around us as we torpedo through the fresh powder. If there was an actual sun in the sky, this might be fun.

We crest the incline and get our first look at the facility—which isn't much. There's no light outside, or in. Power outage is my first thought, but this place must have multiple backup generators. Hard to believe they all failed, but if they did, and there was no way to leave, the people might have headed underground.

I haven't seen it, but the NovaGen facility was built on the remains of a Cold War bunker of some kind. Supposedly multiple levels down there. And if there's no heat on the top floors, the bottom is the safest place to be. The temperature underground is stable and warmer than the surface. Still uncomfortable, but warmer.

I take us down into the parking lot, illuminating their fleet of snow-cats and heavy trucks, their tires wrapped in chains. Hard to believe that the lab rats wouldn't just come to town for help. Or even further. But the lot is full.

Turning so the snowmobile is facing back the way we came, I park in the middle of the lot.

Not expecting the need for a hasty retreat, but the Boy Scout in me demands preparation.

Tali pulls up beside me and kills her engine. Ethan is the first on his feet, leaving his helmet on the snow machine, and flicking on his flashlight and hustling toward the door.

"Hold up there, young'n," I say.

He stops, but I can tell he doesn't want to. Eager to help the people inside, no doubt, but until we know what happened, we're playing it safe.

Marit stretches with a grunt.

"You good?" I ask her.

"Been a while since I rode shotgun on a snowmobile," she says.

"Suspect it won't be your last."

She smiles. "Unless we all freeze to death up here."

Both Nuluk sisters have a dark sense of humor. I enjoy it for the most part, but I'm not sure Marit would find it funny if she remembered how many people froze to death every winter.

I head for the door, flashlight in hand. Ethan walks with me as I pass him. Nervous energy radiates from him.

As we approach the door, I say, "Problem number one..." I take hold of the handle and pull. It moves, but is stopped by the snow drift covering the first three feet. "Give me a hand," I say to Ethan.

He joins me and gives it everything he's got. It's not nearly enough.

"Look out," Marit says, giving Ethan's shoulder a friendly backhand.

She takes the handle in both hands, gives me a nod and then we both pull. The snow puts up a fight, but gives in, sliding back a foot before stopping again. But now we've got leverage. I move to the gap, turn around and place my foot against the door. Tali takes my place, and the sisters are ready to pull. I nod and push. The sisters pull. The snow drift doesn't stand a chance.

The door opens three feet. Plenty of room.

I step inside the vestibule...and gasp.

Heat washes over me. The fans are running. This place has electricity. No reason people should have abandoned the upper lab and gone underground.

"Oh my God," Tali says, stepping in and removing her parka hood. "This is divine."

"We'll see," I say, opening the second door and realizing maybe I shouldn't have. Could have been some kind of airborne contaminant. Gas leak, maybe. But I don't smell gas. I smell—"Wait here," I say, putting some gruff behind the word so everyone takes me seriously.

I step through, making sure the door closes behind me. Then I draw my pistol. Flashlight under the gun, I sweep the lobby. Usually just one person here—a redhead who looks more like a model than a receptionist. She mans the desk despite NovaGen almost never having visitors. We had a few fancy cars come through town during the summer, but nothing since.

The space isn't large. Closer to a doctor's waiting room, than some place people might want to hang out. Stylish, but not exactly welcoming. Doesn't take me long to clear the room. All that's left is the space behind the desk. The redhead's territory.

Pistol leading the way, I creep up on it like I'm stalking prey. I finish with a quick step to the side of the desk and thrust out my pistol, ready to fire—at nothing. Nothing living.

But my suspicion is confirmed.

I flick my flashlight off and on twice. Tali opens the door. "What was with all that John Wick shit?" She sees the look on my face. Her smile disappears and she draws her sidearm. "What is it?"

"Blood," I tell her.

14

"That's a lot of blood," Ethan says, covering his mouth and stepping away. "Do you think whoever that blood came from could still be alive?"

I look down at the puddle of coagulated dark red. The edges have already started to dry. And then there are the drag marks that stretch a few feet before disappearing. I recreate the attack in my head. The attacker came head on, and fast. Red Head reeled back, taking her coffee mug full of pens with her. The attacker came straight over the desk, fast enough that he caught her before she'd reached the wall. Slammed her head into it, resulting in the splotch of red blood that then smeared upward. She was lifted off the floor. And her throat was slashed, left to right, resulting in the spatter streaking to the right.

Then she was dropped, and left to bleed out, after which she was removed from the scene.

A forensics investigator would come to the same conclusion, except that it makes no logical sense.

Red Head, despite her supermodel good looks, was only five foot two. Probably why she ended up behind a desk. But the spatter is nearly seven feet up, meaning she was held high off the floor, with one hand. Happens in movies. Not in real life. An impossible feat of strength. I'm sure some people could manage it, but the same person would be too bulky to manage the speed and agility required to quickly vault the desk.

I can't guess at who killed her.

Perhaps there were two of them. But there's no question about the result. "She's dead."

"Wait, who's dead?" Marit asks from the other side of the room. She has no desire to see the pool of chunky blood.

"Receptionist," Tali says.

"How do you know it was her?" Ethan asks, sounding almost emotional.

"Don't for certain," I admit, "but she's the only one I've ever seen behind this desk."

"Right," he says. "Got it. So, she could still be alive."

"At this point, we don't need to worry about who the victim was," I say. "Our primary concern is who killed her. Might be long gone. Might be in the first room down the hall."

"So, what do we do?"

I look at him, confused. Kid must be rattled. "We clear the NovaGen facility, room by room, floor by floor."

He looks down. "Okay. Right. Should've known that."

"It's okay," Tali says. "First murder jitters. It's normal."

Thing is, this is Tali's first murder, too. She's cool as an Icelandic cucumber.

"Sorry, kid," I say to Ethan. "I'm going to need the shotgun."

"Right," he says, unslinging it from his back. Pretty sure he forgot it was there. "Of course."

I holster my sidearm and accept the shotgun. I give it a pump, chambering the first shell. "Here's how we're doing this. First, this isn't some kind of horror story bullshit. We are not splitting up into teams of two. We are not separating for any reason. I will lead the way through whatever lies ahead. Tali and I will clear each room. Ethan and Marit will stand guard, watching our twelve and six. Everyone got it?"

"Got it," Tali says.

Ethan nods. "Yes, sir."

Marit and I make eye contact. She purses her lips and gives a slight tilt of the head. The eye contact lingers for a moment, until I get nervous and look away. It's hard for me to make eye contact. It's nearly impossible for me to maintain it for long. But it was easy with Marit just now, and when I got nervous it felt... different. But familiar.

Strange.

I head for the lone hallway leading from the reception area to who knows what. I've never been inside. No idea what to expect.

I take a deep breath, flip on the shotgun's mounted flashlight, and lower mine into a pocket. I shoulder the weapon, illuminating the hall. There is only one door on the left side and a set of solid looking double doors straight ahead.

"Why are we doing this in the dark?" Ethan asks. "Won't it be hard to see?"

"Kind of what darkness does," Tali says. "Yeah."

"But why?"

"We turn on the lights, we announce our presence. I'd prefer to sneak up on a murderer. They'll be just as blind as—"

"Well, yeah, but won't they see our flashlights anyway?"

It's not a bad point, but there are a couple benefits to flashlights. "Sure," I say, "until we turn them off. We control the light, we control the fight."

"Got it," he says.

I glance back at Tali. She's got her pistol in hand, finger ready to slide over the trigger.

"Moving," I say, creeping forward.

"Copy," Tali whispers, following me closely.

I glance back to confirm that Marit and Ethan are with us. They are, but I'm not a fan of how we're arranged. "Ethan, watch our backs." He steps to the side, allowing Marit to pass him, then follows us backward.

To my surprise, everyone moves in silence. No one is heavy on their feet. Good thing.

I head for the lone door and grasp the knob. I move in front of the door, allowing Tali the space she needs to follow me through. Then I mouth, "One…two…three," and shove the door open. I swirl in first, finger on the trigger.

I only make it two steps when something hairy engulfs me, coiling around me as I attempt to twist free, rattling as its ambush subdues me.

15

Just as my finger slips around the trigger, Tali shouts, "Whoa, whoa, whoa!"

I nearly fire the shotgun anyway, but her hand finds my arm and squeezes. She's calm. Undisturbed. Safe.

Which means that I'm safe, and have just made a fool of myself. I lower the shotgun and stop struggling. I'm released as whatever wrapped around me—whatever I wrapped around myself—loosens and slips away. I stand in the darkness, hoping no one will shine a light on what I've just mistaken for a bear. Maybe a Sasquatch.

Three lights hit me, illuminating...a coat closet, which includes a fur coat. Not the fancy kind, but the kind Chugach Sugpiaq wore a hundred years ago. Looks authentic, too. Not a replica. It's not unusual in town, but I wouldn't have expected to find one at NovaGen, let alone one assaulting me in a closet.

"Can we all agree to forget this?" I ask.

"Not a chance," Tali says, smiling.

Marit follows with "Nope."

I turn to Ethan. Can tell he's torn between his loyalty to me and solidarity with the sisters. He settles for the middle ground. "I mean, it would be hard to forget."

"You nearly re-killed the bear that gave its life to keep people warm," Tali says. "Also, I think you just blew any chance we had at sneaking up on anyone."

My brows furrow. I'm confused.

She stares at me, squinting. "You screamed."

"I did not."

She turns to her sister, asking the question by raising her eyebrows.

I shift my gaze to Marit. She gives me an apologetic nod.

Damnit.

Wrestling a bear skin jacket is bad enough. But screaming?

I'm beyond ready to move on. "If you all can handle not laughing, we need to push on."

"Oh, lighten up," Tali says. "We needed to break the tension."

"Ethan," I say, and he steps to the back again, predicting my instructions. "Tali, with me. Marit—"

"Already here," she says, pointing out that their positions haven't changed.

I head for the door, shotgun ready once more, a bit more relaxed than before. Tali is right. My mistake did cut through the tension. And I'm sure it will be told a dozen more times before the story stales.

The double doors loom ten feet ahead. The thin gap between them glows with a dull blue light. Computer monitors maybe. Just outside the doors, I pause. One of them is open slightly, hence the gap. I press my boot against the door's edge and nudge it further. The hinges don't make a sound as the space widens enough for me to slide through.

I stop halfway through, shocked by what I'm seeing. The lights are off, but the large octagonal space, thousands of square feet, is surrounded on all sides by massive panes of glass, providing views of the mountains to the west, Raven's Rest to the east, and the sea to the south. It's a view only those brave enough to climb the range to the north get to see.

But it's accentuated by a luminous sky. Well, not quite luminous, but it's what passes for day this time of year. Morning has arrived. Dull light emanates from the sun beyond the horizon and attempts to pierce the cloud cover, casting gray, shadowless light over the town.

Including the insides of what appears to be a summer camp playroom...for adults. This is not what I was expecting. There are hammocks by the windows. Arcade games. A large-screen TV mounted between windows. Couches. Lounge chairs. A pool table that looks like it converts into a ping-pong table, and a foosball table for good measure. A refrigerator. Cabinets. Bookshelves crowded with what looks like novels. There is one door, and what I think is an elevator. And at the center of it all, a wood burning fireplace. Its black metal chimney hovers a few feet above, rising to the ceiling.

A gentle hand on my arm.

Then a whisper. "What is it?"

I look back at Tali. "Not a closet." I place my hand on the door and let the others get a look.

"Umm," Tali says, and I step into the room, still ready to fire. There's no movement, but one of these couches or game tables could be hiding a killer.

Once everyone is inside, I close the door behind us and deadbolt it. No one will be sneaking up on us from behind.

"Tali, Marit, sweep right," I say, "Kid, you're with me."

We split apart, circling the room, all of us shifting our weapons toward every nook and cranny we pass. We stop when we reunite on the far side.

"Clear," I declare.

We lower our weapons and relax a bit.

"Seems abandoned," Marit says. "Didn't see any more blood, either."

"Same," I say. "But we've barely scratched the surface of the old facility."

"You been down there?" Tali asks.

I shake my head. "Just a guess. The Cold War US government wasn't known for building things small. Just secret and big. This room is large, but beneath us? Probably a concrete maze."

"Makes sense," Ethan says, moving toward the center of the room. Crouching by the fire, he holds a hand above the ashes. "Cold."

Already gathered that by the faint scent of smoke lingering in the room, but I'm glad he thought to check. Been a while since someone lit a fire in here.

In fact, most everything looks new.

Or rarely used.

"Everyone feel good about pushing on?"

"Yes, sir," Ethan says.

"Let's do it," Tali adds.

Before Marit can say anything, a muffled scream rips through the single door. Every hair follicle on my legs springs to attention and stabs my skin with little daggers.

"Umm," Tali says, "Can we change our minds?"

The scream... It's not human.

The camel and the monkey should have been warning

enough. The lab is experimenting on living things and one of them is still alive and very unhappy. Given the blood and the lack of people, I'd guess it's also violent and deadly.

I give a nod and whisper. "Fall back, double time. We are leaving."

A second scream, closer now, chases us to the double doors. I unlock them, swing the door open, and we sprint like Pompeiians trying to outrun a volcano.

16

The sudden cold slaps me across the face and sucks the air from my lungs. I whirl around, covering our retreat, shotgun aimed at the facility's lobby doors.

Behind me, a snowmobile roars to life, engine revving.

"Let's go!" It's Marit. She waves me over.

Beside her, Tali mounts the second snowmobile. Ethan tries to hop on behind her but he's moving too fast. Slips in the snow. Ends up on his ass. But it doesn't slow him down much. He bounces back up and throws himself on the seat behind Tali, wrestling with his helmet.

I make it a step before a shifting shadow inside, beyond the two sets of glass doors, catches my attention and locks me in place.

It's not moving quickly...because it's stalking us. If I hadn't heard the screams, I might write the shadow off as a trick of the eyes. But it's there, just beyond the dull gray light of what passes for day.

When the second engine revs to life, I break free of my trance and haul ass to the waiting snowmobile. I grab my helmet and climb on backward, shotgun leveled behind us.

"Hit it!"

The snowmobile lurches forward so quickly that my butt comes off the seat and I nearly sprawl over the backrest and into the snow. Marit must have been expecting it. Her left hand catches my jacket and holds me tight enough that I can shove myself back down. I adjust my stance, feet extended on the running board, leaning back against her.

"You good?" she shouts.

"Peachy," I say, and then immediately need to take it back.

Two sets of metal and glass doors explode outward from the lab. Reflective shards fill the air, commingling with snow, creating a wall of debris through which I can't see much more than a shifting of light. As we crest the mountainside, I catch a look at the outer doors. The left side hangs by a hinge. The door on the right has been torn free. Both are bent like a car plowed through them.

Because something did…and it wasn't a car.

It was a living thing.

That is now outside.

I lean the shotgun against the backrest and watch the snow-covered road behind us. There's a shift in the falling snow, like something large moved through it.

I see nothing.

But I feel it.

Some kind of instinctual primitive sense, lying dormant since the days when humanity was a prey species, has been triggered. I can feel it out there. The thing from the facility. It's hunting us. It's—

I flip up my visor to try to see better.

"Gah!" I shout as a blur bounds onto the road beside us. It's as white as the snow-laden sky and ground, almost impossible to see. I get off a shot, but I turned the weapon at an awkward angle. The shotgun snaps out of my left hand, swivels up in my right, and cracks me in the temple. That's what I get for opening the visor. My aim is shit.

But I see a momentary splotch of pink, which is followed by a different kind of scream.

Sounds like a woman. Suffering.

It's followed by another woman screaming. Marit. "Did you get it!?"

"With a few pellets," I say, gripping the backrest to steady myself. My head is spinning from its collision with the shotgun. I can feel warm blood running down the side of my face. *Problem for later,* I think and turn my thoughts to the wound I inflicted on the...whatever it was.

Hit it with five pellets, I'd guess. Could have been four. Could have been six. Either way, it's not enough to kill much of anything bigger than a human without getting lucky. A pellet to the brain or heart would do in most living things, but it's unlikely. I didn't get a good look at the creature's body, but it was tall. And girthy. Closest thing I can compare it to, that makes any kind of sense, is a Yeti. And that hardly makes any sense at all.

"You get a look at it?" I ask her.

"My eyes are on the very slippery, steep, and winding road covered in snow," Marit says, sounding frazzled.

Don't blame her. Driving on this mountain is a tough job on a good day. Going full speed downhill in deep snow? Not many people who could pull that off. The Nuluk sisters? They've been riding these mountains since they were big enough to reach the throttle.

I scan the area behind us, searching for any signs of movement. It's a futile effort. *Everything* is moving. The air is filled with falling snow. But nothing is chasing us. The nagging feeling of being hunted fades.

We're five hundred feet down when I stop worrying about a second attack. Not because the creature hasn't attacked a second time, but because I hear its angry roar once more, now far away uphill. Whatever it was, it's not chasing us now, but it did *not* want us at the lab.

Territorial maybe.

Would help to know what the hell it was.

Ten frigid minutes later, we reach the mountain's base, where the road meets the outer edge of Main Street. Tali pulls to the side and slows to a stop. Marit and I pull up beside her.

Tali yanks her helmet off so we can see the expression on her face. I know it's not good, but it's hard to tell what kind of not good she's feeling until she speaks. "Colton, what the fuck?"

I stand up, turn around, and sit back down, facing forward now. "Wish I knew."

"Well…what are we going to do?" she asks. "A lot of people work at NovaGen. And at least one of them is dead."

"We can't just run away. We need to go back," Ethan says, showing surprising bravery. "We need to find anyone alive and get them out."

I nod in agreement. "We're not defeated. We're regrouping. Reinforcing."

"Reinforcing?" Tali asks, putting her helmet back on. "With *who?*"

"It'll take State Police days to reach us in this weather," Marit says.

I nod again. "That's why we're going to recruit people from town."

Tali lifts her visor and looks at me. "People from town. You're insane."

"It's the obvious choice," I say, "when it's the only option."

"Where do we start?" Marit asks.

"Where we began," I say.

"Got it," she says, revving the engine.

As we peel away, I catch a grumble from Tali. "Well, we're all gonna die." Then she and Ethan are behind us, speeding toward town in search of anyone skilled and brave enough to face an unknown killer, in the hopes of saving people from a secretive lab that most Raven's Rest residents don't want here.

17

When we pull up to the sheriff's station, I feel like I've returned home after being away for two years. It's an odd sensation, because I'm not really fond of this place, and since Anya passed, I've mostly just felt trapped here. Because I like change even less than I do the cold.

But tonight, something has changed. Not entirely sure what or why, but I'm guessing it has something to do with being hunted by an abominable snowman. Or maybe it's just a concussion.

I'm a little uneasy on my feet when I climb off the snowmobile. Marit notices and catches me by the coat.

"You okay, Colt?" she asks, her voice full of enough concern that I feel a little embarrassed.

"Took a hit to the head," I say. "I'll be fine."

She pulls my helmet off. "You're covered in blood."

"It's nothing," I say, letting machismo guide my addled mind. I lift a hand to the helmet, attempting to tug it from Marit's hand. "I'll be—"

She strikes with the speed and snap of a rolled up wet towel, slapping the top of my hand. "Now is not the time for little dick syndrome."

My face screws up. "Did you just say... You think I have a little—"

"What? No." She averts her gaze, which is typically *my* go-to move when speaking to people. "I meant that you were acting like—you know what, pretend I didn't say it."

Before I can tease her, Tali and Ethan pull to a stop beside us. Tali looks back and forth between Marit and me, and she's about to say something, but then does a double take when she sees my face. She just shakes her head at me. "Get your ass inside."

Despite my position of authority, I do what I'm told. With both Tali and Marit on my case, the fastest way forward will be that of least resistance. Right now, that means letting them patch me up.

Which is what I would insist on doing, if it was one of them hurt. So, I don't complain.

After so long in the cold, the warmed station feels like the thirteenth level of Satan's sauna. Anyone looking in from outside would think we were a bunch of horny swingers, peeling clothing and dropping it to the floor. But for me, shedding the heat-retaining winter gear is a desperate need for regulation. When my body is overheated, from a baseboard heater, from the sun, from exercise, I'm assaulted by pinpricks all over my body. It's not exactly agonizing, but it's hard to focus on anything else until the sensation fades. Nothing to do about it except cool down. As a result, I end up removing more clothing than the others, all the way down to my T-shirt and boxers.

I sigh with relief and turn toward the motion on my right. It's Marit. She's still dressed in black pants and a black long-sleeved thermal shirt. She's stretching, hands linked above her head, back arched, and…

My stomach twists as I find myself overwhelmed by her—

She glances toward me.

Our eyes link.

She's caught me looking.

I'm embarrassed. Marit is one of my closest friends. She was Anya's best friend. It's not appropriate to look at her like that. But...

Marit lowers her hands and motions to one of the three chairs we have for visitors. "Sit."

Once again, I do as I'm told, mostly because I'm grateful that she hasn't acknowledged my *faux pas,* and I'm eager to move past it.

Ethan arrives a moment later, first aid kit in his hands. Didn't even notice him leave.

"Leave it here," Marit says, patting the empty chair to my left.

"What should we do?" Ethan asks.

"Not sure if the bossman is the best person to ask right now," Tali says, looking mischievous.

Shit. She must have noticed what happened with Marit. Which means I'm never going to hear the end of it. My only consolation is that Tali isn't a gossip. She'll keep it between us, but she'll bring it up on occasion, because she knows that little things—errors in judgement—drive me nuts. I like to think things through. To analyze. To understand. When I do or say something, there's intention behind it. But sometimes I just... react. And somehow, she's always there to see it.

Tali raises her eyebrows at me. "He's got other things on his mind."

Marit glances back at her sister, making a face I can't see. But it gets the job done.

"Ugh. Fine. What do you want us to do?"

"Make a list," I say, wincing as Marit starts cleaning my face with the gentleness of my grandmother who would spit on a rag and set herself to the task of scouring dirt—and several layers of skin—away from my skull, when I was a child. "Write down anyone you think might be useful. Anyone who can shoot. Then pare it down to the ones you'd trust with your life."

Tali huffs. "Going to be a short list."

I nod. "We don't need an army."

"What about me?" Ethan asks. He doesn't know the town well enough to help with the list.

I glance to my office. Then to its open door. I grunt. "You can figure out where the hell Jimmy is, and what he's done with Dufresne."

"Huh?" Ethan spins around, spots the open door, and hurries to the office. He leans his head inside. He backs out and then disappears around the hallway's corner. Returns a moment later, shaking his head. "They're not here."

"I know that," I say.

"So, you want me to...go back outside..."

"And find them," I say. "Yes. Jimmy is a creature of habit. You'll probably find him, and hopefully Dufresne, back at the butchery."

He grumbles but doesn't put up a fight. Starts putting his winter gear back on. Think I'll give him a raise when this mess is cleaned up. He's put in the work, especially tonight. Best way to keep a good officer is to pay them well and actually give a shit.

"Hold still," Marit says, grasping my chin with her right hand while using a wad of gauze to apply pressure to my head wound. She turns my face back and forth, looking me over. "Good news is, you only have one gash. Bad news is, you're still funny looking."

I drop my jaw. "Not nice to tease a man while he's injured."

"Yeah, well, you know I don't mean it. But this—" She taps a finger on the gauze, indicating my wound. "This is going to leave a scar. It's a doozy."

"How big is it?"

"About an inch long," she says, "but it's not the size that matters, right?"

I smile. "You're in rare form today."

"Nothing like a brush with death to make you think about what you want in life." She looks at me, expectant, waiting for a response, but I'm confused by the statement. Does she want to make more jokes in her life?

I have no idea, but I know what I want. "Butterflies."

Her face screws up like I've just been possessed by Mephistopheles and growled something in Latin. "You...you want *butterflies* in your life?"

"On my head," I say. "Don't do stitches."

She's squinting at me now. Blinks out of it. "You mean— Right." She digs through the first aid kit with her right hand. Brings it up. She's holding a butterfly stitch. "This kind of butterfly."

I nod.

She gives her head a gentle shake, closing her eyes. Beneath her lids, I see her eyes roll. I've done something to irritate her. I'm good at detecting other people's emotions, but not great at understanding potential causes for them.

While she pulls the two sides of my temple together and tapes them closed, I consider how I might have hurt her feelings.

When did I sense the change?

'Butterflies.'

Wasn't the answer she was looking for. But what answer *could* she be looking for? The question of what I want in life... It wasn't meant to be practical. She didn't ask what I needed. She asked what I wanted. And she was hoping for a different answer.

She wanted me to say—

"You alright?" she asks. "Looks like you're in a trance."

I suck in a breath, stomach churning again. "Sorry. I was just..."

She leans back. There's blood on her hands.

My blood.

"Thank you."

"'I was just thank you?'" she says, smiling at me now. "We need to check you for a concussion. You seem a bit off."

She's right about that. I *am* off, but it's not because of the blow to my head. It's because I know what's happening. I recognize it. I *remember* it. But, it's not right. And this isn't a good time to be distracted.

She wiggles her bloody fingers in my face. "Probably should have worn gloves. Sorry. Be right back."

A moment later, I'm alone with my thoughts, which is an uncomfortable place to be. Doesn't last long. Tali approaches. List in one hand, rolled up magazine in the other. Looks angry.

She stops in front of me. I'm sure she's about to deliver bad news. Instead, she asks, "Where are you in pain?"

"Just my head," I say. "Why—"

She swats my shoulder with the magazine—some kind of mail order catalog. Puts some muscle behind the first swing, then hits me another three times, just a bit lighter. Then she leans down, points a finger in my face, and says, "You–are an idiot."

She stuffs the list into my hand, spins around, and walks away before I can say anything. I look down at the list. It's short. Just three names, none of them what I would call pleasant, but I understand why she picked them. Now we just need to convince the trio to cancel their plans, take a brutal journey, and risk their lives for a bunch of outsiders.

My day is about to go from shitty to social nightmare shitty before I can fully wrap my head around what we're up against—if that's even possible.

All I know is that we can't just leave those people.

Wouldn't be right.

And that is something I cannot abide.

18

I've chosen to go on this mission alone. Need some time to spin down before I reach the Tower. I've never been a fan of the place. Even when living there. Just too many people, all the time, in each other's business. If one person on your floor has salmon, you might as well all be having salmon. The smell of other people's food, cannabis habits, and pets commingle in the hallway. It's like steam-breathing a bowl full of cat piss, decomposing snails, and skunky pot. If I'm alone, I walk through the place with my shirt over my nose and mouth. If there are people around, I hold my breath as much as possible, breathing in through my mouth only when instinct forces it.

But that doesn't mean people don't notice my discomfort. I've been teased about it by at least two dozen people. One of the residents calls me 'crinkle nose.' Oversensitive. A born complainer. Penelope Pussycat–known for fleeing the stench of Pepé Le Pew. These are the kind of things people whisper about me when they think I can't hear them. I wonder if they'd say the same thing if they knew all my senses are as jacked up.

That's not accurate.

My physiology is the same as anyone else's. The difference is in my brain. The easiest way to explain it is that I've got no filter. I get all the information from my senses all the time, while a normal human mind filters out everything it deems unimportant. It's like watching every cable channel at once, rather than one at a time.

My eyes are sensitive to light, making broad daylight painful, but boosting my night vision. Despite that, I still need reading glasses. Aging sucks. My hearing is exceptional. My sense of smell is…annoying. All of them have their benefits, but it's my exaggerated physical senses that really mess with me. Clothing, temperature, external sensory inputs, like a texture or unexpected touch, can be overwhelming. I can mask most of it, but if I don't get enough time on my own, I get overwhelmed, exhausted, and grumpy. Even if I'm just with people I like.

Any stimulation eventually leads to overstimulation.

I've considered telling everyone in town why I'm like this but decided against it. Would likely just result in more teasing. Given society's cliché understanding of my condition, they'd likely stop trusting my ability to do this job, despite the fact that my 'symptoms' make me an exceptional investigator, and my desire for honesty means that I'm trustworthy. Sometimes to a fault.

Fully dressed in my winter gear again, I rev the snowmobile and take the road to the Tower, which also runs past Jimmy's place. From a distance, I can see lights on inside. A moment later, I spot our second snowmobile parked outside Jimmy's. Before I can pass the butchery, Ethan steps outside, waving his arms at me. Heard me coming.

I slow to a stop in the road and wait for Ethan to arrive. I lift my visor to look him in the eye. "What is it?"

"Jimmy's inside," he says. "Has the tamarin with him. They're kind of hitting it off, I think."

"Huh…" Didn't take Jimmy for an animal person, unless he was going to cut them up and sell them.

"But that's not why I stopped you," he says.

Good thing, that.

Would have been annoyed if this was just about Jimmy finally making a friend with the same IQ. I smile on the inside. Tali would have laughed at that, but then we'd both feel bad about it. Jimmy is eccentric in his own special way, but he's only dumb when he's high...which is most of the time.

"It's the camel," Ethan says.

"What about the camel?"

"He took it apart."

"How much of it?" I ask.

"All of it." He looks back at the butchery. "He's got limbs in a pile. Organs in a bowl. And he's managed to cut out a bunch of those...cells. Even tried to cook one."

"He *cooked* one? Please tell me he didn't eat it."

Ethan shakes his head. "Didn't get the chance. Whatever's inside didn't solidify when heated—it boiled. The membrane expanded to the size of a cantaloupe, he says, and then exploded. A few drops hit his hands and burned him, but he's fine."

"And where was the tamarin during all of this?" I ask.

"On his shoulder. It keeps a hand on his ear. Tugs it every now and again. Kind of reminds me of that movie. *Ratatouille*. The rat controlling the chef kid by yanking on his hair."

"Never saw it," I admit, but I understand what he's getting at. "Nothing out of control?"

"Depends on how you define control," he says.

"Has Jimmy endangered himself or anyone else?"

He shakes his head. "He's just being weird."

"Then you can catch me up in detail when I come back."

"Heading to the Tower?" he asks, looking up to the tall building at the top of a hill to the north. Its concrete structure and complete lack of style makes it look like a Soviet-era building, but it was built long after the US bought the state from Russia.

"Recruiting," I say.

"Want company?"

I shake my head. "Not remotely. Just keep an eye on Jimmy. I'll stop by on my way back. ETA...thirty minutes." I think about the list of people I'm about to visit. "Maybe an hour."

"The people at the lab could all be dead in an—"

"I know, kid. But if we don't do this right, *we* might all end up dead."

He doesn't like it. Clenches his mouth shut, stopping himself from complaining. Then he says, "Thirty to sixty minutes. Got it."

I give him an appreciative nod, rev the snowmobile engine, and then zip away and uphill, straight toward a building that contains my worst fears and most painful memories. I'd rather be back at NovaGen. The people I find dead there won't be anyone I love.

19

I open the door to the Tower's lobby and snap to a stop. Been a month since I stepped through the door here. Let Tali and Ethan handle all the domestic issues that have come up. Nothing serious.

I glance to my left, at the mailboxes. Mine is likely packed tight. Might even be holding some in the back for me. Don't really care.

"As I live and breathe, Sheriff Graves."

I turn to find Milton Norval, the lobby's security guard/welcoming committee, who seems to always be at his post, no matter what the time of day. "You ever go home, Milton?"

"Home is six floors straight up," he says, voice gravelly and calm. "But I avoid it as much as I can. Same as you, I suppose."

Milton is the best thing about this building. He's a font of knowledge, friendly, the town's only black man and, as fate would have it, the elderly father of a name on my list. He's also straightforward and honest, two traits that are both exceedingly rare and welcome.

"Not many things harder in this world than losing a wife. When my Lani passed, I was a mess." He huffs. "Going on ten years now and I'm still a wreck."

I ask the first question that comes to mind. "You ever think about dating someone?"

He shakes his head. "I'm eighty years old, Sheriff. Not much I can do to please a woman. Besides, I've already watched the woman I love die. Why would I want to put myself through that again?" He searches my face for a moment and then changes his tone. "If I were young, like you, things might have gone differently for me. You're not short on lady friends, are you, Sheriff?"

I feign a smile, but I'm no longer comfortable with the subject. "Reason I'm here, Milton, is to find your daughter."

"Grizz in trouble again?" he asks.

"Not at all," I say. "In fact, I need her help with a problem."

He looks skeptical. "What kind of problem?"

"The kind that someone like Grizz has a talent for solving," I say.

He grins. "Bear come out of hibernation early?"

"Something like that," I say.

"Well, I'm sorry to tell you, I stopped keeping track of that girl when she was eighteen. A wise man knows when a wild horse can't be tamed. But if it helps, I haven't seen her leave the building, and her apartment is seven twenty-one."

"It does," I say, stepping toward the elevators. "Thanks for your help, Milt."

"Any time, Sheriff. Don't be a stranger."

The elevator door pings and opens the moment I push the button. I step inside, suck in a breath, and hold it as the elevator rises to the seventh floor. The elevator is bad, but the seventh floor is worse. A well-known fact—to me—is that the higher you go, the smellier things get. My place is on the third floor, and even that bothers me. It's like the smells seep through the Tower's layers, rising upward to be trapped on the tenth floor, held in by the thick rooftop.

This building is like Dante's levels of hell, flipped on their head, getting worse as you ascend. When the elevator doors open again, I've got my jacket open and my shirt pulled up over my nose. Don't care if anyone sees me right now. Job takes precedence. But I'm still glad to find an empty hallway. The red carpet is worn down to nothing just outside the elevator, slowly receding away like a bald man's last stand, from the still visible threads the further away you get. By the time I reach seven-twenty-one, the carpet is almost half its original height.

I stand in front of the door, take one last, long drag of air under my shirt, and lift my fist to knock. I give the door three swift raps with my knuckles and am caught off guard when the well-oiled door opens inward.

"Oh, shit!" a man whispers. It's Stephen Burton. He's naked, hands cupped over his junk. Runs back into the living room, through the kitchen, and into the bathroom, glancing over his shoulder with nervous eye contact as he goes.

I don't get into people's business, so I'm not going to repeat what I've just seen, but Burton is a married man. A lack of loyalty is one of the greatest faults a man can have. Women, too. I have no respect for it. Burton slams the bathroom door behind him and doesn't emerge again.

When Grizz steps out of the living room, naked and proud, I almost wish the philandering Burton would come back.

"He's a married man, Grizz," I say, working hard to keep my eyes on hers. Eye contact is hard in general. When there's something else to look at, it's even harder. Not that Grizz is what I want to be looking at. Not at all. But it's like facing down a tidal wave of dead baby hippos. It'd be a horrible thing to see, but you still wouldn't take your eyes off it.

"Hate to break it to you, but there ain't much else to do around here come winter than jump on the merry-go-round of pound town. And I'm the main attraction." She waggles her chubby body as she struts toward me, forcing my eyes to divert to the ceiling.

"It's okay, Colton," she says. "Get it over with and have an eyeful."

When I resist, she waves a hand at me. "Prude. You know, I bet Anya would want you to—"

I snap my fingers and point at her, locking eyes once again. "Don't say her name."

"Whoa, cowboy," she says, raising her hands, exposing her ample bosom. "There he is. Knew there was a lion beneath your timid exterior."

She's trying to get a rise out of me, in more ways than one, but I'm not interested in either and let my face communicate it.

She frowns. "No fun." She picks up her underwear from where it hangs on a dining room chair. "What can I do you for, Colton?" She pulls on the far too small panties, which are, in fact, a thong.

"Need your help."

"With?" She glances up and sees the new message in my expression. Her demeanor changes in an instant. She straps on her resilient bra next. "What's happened?"

I lean in closer as she approaches, conspirators in the communist bloc. "Up at the lab."

She glowers for a moment.

"At least one person dead," I whisper.

Her eyebrows rise. "Murder?"

I shake my head.

She looks almost excited now. "Animal attack?"

"Maybe," I say.

"Well, it's one or the other, Sheriff. When it comes to getting killed out here, it's one or the other." She furrows her brow, searching my face. "Unless there's a third option I don't know about."

"I don't want to get into it here." I glance at the bathroom door.

She gets it.

"Assuming we're meeting at the station?" she asks.

I shake my head. "Jimmy's."

"Jimmy's?" She rolls her eyes. "You know that man hasn't visited me in two years. I think he might be fucking those animals before he—"

I raise my hand, silencing her. "What I need to know, before moving forward— Is it true? Did you kill a grizzly with a knife?"

"Sure as Santa's reindeer drop pellets all over the planet." She turns to the side, lifts her chubby upper arm so I can see it. There are four round scars. "Bit my arm." She turns the other way and unfurls a breast before I can look away. Four more round puncture scars mar her skin. I cringe.

She finishes the display by turning away from me, revealing five scars down her back from left to right, and a second set from right to left, forming a striated X pattern across the center of her back. "He got me from behind. Tore me open. My spine was exposed when I fought back. Fucker wasn't expecting me to have a knife. Sure as shit wasn't expecting two. Got a few bites in while I stabbed his back. It was a blade through his temple, put the man-eating bastard down."

"Good," I say.

She eyes me while pulling on her pants.

"So, it's a bear, then?"

"If it was, it wasn't a grizzly. Chased us in the snow. Couldn't see it. Because it was white."

"Polar bear?" she asks, almost smiling. "They don't come this far south, Colton. And if one did, it's either sick or desperate for food."

"Let's hope that's all it is," I say.

"Ominous."

"You have no idea." I turn to leave. "Be at Jimmy's in thirty."

"Hey, Colton," she says. I pause in the hallway without looking back. I've already lifted my shirt back up over my nose. "Thank you. For seeing me as more than a quick lay."

"Looking forward to the day when you do, too, Grizz."

With that, I head for the elevator, mentally preparing for my next encounter. Grizz was the easy one. I knew she'd want in. It's 'Old Red' that concerns me. Man is unpredictable, strange, and a common visitor to the station–behind bars. I take a deep breath through my nose, step into the elevator, and begin my descent toward clear cold air, and the surliest sonuvabitch I've ever met.

20

"Thought we had an agreement, Sheriff," says Amaq Taqtuq, one of two brothers living in a trailer on the outskirts of town. His tone is one part aggression, one part defensive. He's not happy to see me and is probably racking his mind trying to figure out how I know about whatever illegal activity he's up to now. "We stay out of town; you mind your own business."

His brother, Pamiu, steps out of their trailer cradling a shotgun. He's not holding it in a threatening way, but it's still a threat. And that's why neither of the Taqtuq brothers made the list. They're about as trustworthy as a chimpanzee with a fist full of shit.

Can't turn your back on them.

"Today's your lucky day," I say.

He spits some brown chew to the side. "How's that?"

I note that both brothers are outside in nothing more than jeans and flannel shirts. Don't seem to mind the cold at all. "I'm not here to see you." I point to Pamiu. "Or him. But that's going to change if he doesn't put that shotgun away."

"And if I don't?" Pamiu says.

"I reckon you'll find out how much faster I can draw a pistol than you can swivel that thing around, get off a shot, put your own brother in the dirt, be arrested for murder, and spend the rest of your life in Spring Creek Correctional. Which would be fine by me, because then neither of you would be a pain in my ass for much longer."

Amaq, the elder brother, comes to his senses first. Motions for Pamiu to go back inside. "I got this."

"You sure?" the younger brother asks.

"Go on!" Amaq shouts, quickly losing his patience.

Reminds me of his father before he passed. Except that their father was a respectable man and a member of the community. The sons are twenty-two and twenty-four and have spent the past year without their father to guide them. That and the fact that their brains are still developing, are why I've shown them leniency. That will come to a swift end if either of them points a weapon in my direction.

Amaq faces me, trying to be the tough bigger brother. "What do you want?"

"Old Red," I say.

Amaq laughs. "Out of the frying pan and into the fire, huh?"

"Like a Hot Pocket fresh from the microwave. Know where he is?"

"I don't help pigs," he says. "Especially pigs from the lowers. You have no business in this park. No business in this state, on our ancestors' land, especially now that your wife is—"

My glare silences him. Might have also been my hand lowering toward my pistol. Either way, he got the message just in time to avoid spending the next few days in a cell.

I calm myself.

"You were saying?"

"I don't keep track of Old Red, man. That'd be a dangerous thing. He's not exactly stable. Why do you want him, anyway? He finally kill someone?"

"You'd have known if he left," I say. "His truck is loud enough to wake the dead."

"Well, I haven't heard it the last few days, so I guess he's either dead or holed up like all the rest of you lowers."

"Thank you," I say. "See how easy that was?"

"Fuck off, pig," he says, reverting to his big man act.

I start walking deeper into the trailer park.

"Instead of spending all your time out here being assholes to everyone you come across, it sure would be nice if you boys respected what your father left you and tried to do something to honor his memory."

The comment must sting, because Amaq has no comeback when he'd normally just keep right on mouthing off, which isn't against the law, but it's sure as hell annoying.

Old Red's trailer isn't hard to find.

It's lit up in Christmas lights year round and covered with antennae that let him communicate with the outside world. Not everyone in the world. Just with those *old school* enough to still have functioning ham radios.

Some people think the Christmas lights are an inner reflection of the nice man beneath the gruff exterior. But I know better. They provide lighting for the entire periphery of his trailer, which is surveilled by six cameras mounted to his roof. I'm not sure where he's storing all the data, but I suspect he's keeping everything those cameras capture.

I assume he already knows I'm coming. Probably has motion sensors, too. He's paranoid, but I'm not sure he's as crazy as everyone thinks. He made the list, so Tali must agree. Sometimes people have good reason to be paranoid. And if the rumors about Old Red are true, I don't blame him for all the cloak-and-dagger shit.

I pull my glove off to knock on the door.

My bare knuckles create a thump loud enough to be heard, but not hard enough to be considered pounding. "Hey Edgar, it's Colton."

He doesn't bother playing mouse, and he doesn't mince words, which is fine by me because it is far too cold to be standing out here for long. "Don't you mean *Sheriff Graves,* Sheriff Graves?"

"You're not in any trouble, Edgar, I just—

"Old Red," he grumbles. "Don't go by 'Edgar' anymore. You know that."

"Sorry, Old Red. It's been a day."

"So, this isn't police business?" he asks.

"It is," I say, "but not the kind you're thinking. I need your help."

The door swings open, revealing a yellow-lit interior. Old Red is front and center, a hunting rifle leveled at my chest. It holds my attention.

"Ahh, don't worry, Sheriff. Betsy ain't loaded." He opens the rifle, demonstrating that it is, in fact, harmless. He leans back with a grin that accentuates the wrinkles around his face, and the crow's feet framing his eyes. His grizzled beard keeps the smile from making him look friendly. His long salt-and-pepper hair is a mess. Looks like he cuts it himself, probably with a knife. He's got a real Ted Kaczynski vibe about him, except for his eyes. He wouldn't like me saying it, but there's kindness in him. Hidden way down deep.

"Why not?" I ask, genuinely curious. Doesn't really fit his profile.

"I might shoot someone for trespassing, looking at me sideways, or talking shit about any one of my old gals, but I'm not the kind of person to go shooting a lawman, and I know I haven't broken any laws. 'Sides, you've always been fair to me. Ain't got no beef."

"In that case, mind if I come in?" I ask.

"So long as you don't mind a mess."

I do. A lot. But I'll mask it to get the job done. "Not at all."

He steps aside, allowing me in. Then he cleans off a bench at a small table by using his arm to bulldoze wrappers and cans, along with something wet and green, onto the floor. There's a smear left behind. He gives the bench a pat and sits down on the opposite side, which must be his usual spot, because it's already clear.

If I weren't wearing my thick winter gear, I don't think I'd be able to sit, but the layers protect me. A quick slide in the snow should scour it away before I get back on the snowmobile.

"Listen, Red. Is just 'Red' okay?"

"Ayep."

"Red, we've got a problem in town."

"Sounds like a you-problem, Sheriff Graves."

I choose my words carefully. "That's true...but we could really use your help with something."

"What in the hell do you think I know about camels?" he asks.

"Red...I didn't tell you about the camel." I glance around the space. For the most part it looks like a normal, but messy, trailer home. That said, there are three doors closed. One being the bathroom. One a bedroom. And the third. No idea what he uses it for, but I also don't see any computer equipment out here, so I'm guessing that's where it is.

"No, you did not, Sheriff."

It's clear he's not about to elaborate, but it's also clear he's got cameras in town.

He grins. "I see what you're thinking. And you're wrong. I know about the camel because it came through here heading toward town. Figured it'd die on its way. Creature like that ain't meant for these parts."

I nod. "It's dead."

"Problem solved," he says.

"Not remotely."

He gives me a squinty side-eye. Takes a deep breath. Lets out an exasperated sigh. "Lay it on me."

"We tracked the camel back to where it came from," I say.

"Ambitious."

I ignore the comment. "Red, the camel came from the laboratory. From NovaGen."

His expression shifts from interest to angry dread.

"There's at least one person dead, and the others…they're all missing."

He leans back in his chair, scratches his chin, clucks his tongue. "Sounds like I should'a loaded Betsy after all."

"Do you know what it is?" I ask.

"Come again? *It?*"

"We entered the top floor. The new construction. Found a lot of blood, and something else found us. Chased us. Didn't get a clear look at it, but I think it was white. Mean anything to you?"

"Not a damn thing," he says. "But if you need something shot, I can do that. If you need a tour guide through the seven layers of Hell on Earth, I'm the only one still alive that can provide that particular service. And it's the only reason I'm still in this frozen wasteland of a town. I'm the last one who knows what happened there before the government cleaned everything up and swept it under a very thick rug. The others were caught when they ran. The G-men never found me on account of me not running. Only place they didn't think to look was right here."

"Might need both of those skills," I say, refusing to bite on the morsels he's dangling. I've always wanted to hear his story but now is not the time.

"When is go-time?" he asks.

I look at my watch.

"Fifteen minutes. At Jimmy's. Your snowmobile running?"

"It'll get me where I'm going. Not fast, but she's reliable, sturdy, and has seats for two. Assuming it won't just be the two of us taking this little trip. Who did you con into joining your mob?"

"Tali and Ethan—"

"That's the new kid, yeah?"

"My deputy, yeah. Good kid."

"'Good kid' doesn't mean he's a good officer."

"He's both," I assure him. "We've also got Marit, Jimmy, and Grizz."

"Whew. Grizz? She is one hell of a woman."

"I've heard," I say.

"Not in a sexual sense," he says. "I've heard the rumors. Have no need for it. No, what I'm talking about is that bear. I was here to see it. The aftermath. Hard to imagine anyone surviving an attack from a grizzly that big, but she cut it up good. Severed its head, you know."

"Sounds like she was a brute."

"Brute? Son, she was a killer. Reckon she still is." He stands up. "Now, fifteen minutes isn't long to get ready and get to Jimmy's."

"You're going to help?" I ask, relieved to have another person who can shoot on board, but even happier to have someone along who knows the subterranean laboratory's layout.

I stand up and offer my hand. He shakes it. Not a fan of physical contact, but I understand the importance of it to other people. Creates a bond. In this case, we've come to an agreement: comrades—until we succeed in our endeavor, or die trying.

21

On the long, straight, cold ride back to town, I reflect on everything that's happened. The camel, its strange insides, Dufresne the tamarin, the murder scene at the deserted lab, and the thing that chased us away. None of it makes sense. It's the strangest and most mysterious case I've ever come across during one of the most boring times of year.

And yet, it barely holds my attention.

Marit does.

My recent encounters with her crash into the part of my brain that's good at solving puzzles, flipping every table, scattering pieces, and demanding my attention.

This isn't the time to be thinking about such things.

People are dead. At least one. I shouldn't be entertaining the idea of a relationship.

My stomach sours. I...just can't. Anya would—

"Whoa!" I shout, swerving around a moose standing in the road. It doesn't react to the whine of my engine, my headlight, or my sudden arrival. Narrowly avoiding an accident that would have been an annoyance to the massive bull, but would have ended my life, I slow to a stop and look back.

The immense head swivels toward me.

The moose is not concerned. He's an old bull. Like me, I suppose. He's survived the Alaskan wilderness and, judging by the scars on his haunches, at least one encounter with a grizzly. But now, no one messes with this guy.

"You real?" I ask the moose.

He doesn't flinch.

He's real, I decide. Belongs here. He's got the typical, 'I don't give a shit,' gaze of a confident bull. And those scars speak of a violent past, likely long before NovaGen ever arrived in Raven's Rest. "Never mind. Stay off the mountain."

The massive creature doesn't respond. Just waits for me to leave.

So, I do.

Wind whipping against my helmet, I'm once again lulled into something like a meditative state, driving by muscle memory while my thoughts turn back to Marit. I attempt to redirect myself to the case but fail.

I need to confront these thoughts head-on, or I'll never be able to focus.

Marit is...amazing.

Beautiful. Funny. Patient. And I'm pretty sure she...cares about me a lot. All of that even though I have strange—sometimes obnoxious—needs, and I'm particular about most aspects of my life. She doesn't even know why I'm different from most people. But she's never shown me anything other than kindness. And that's a rare thing.

She was Anya's best friend, though. How would Anya feel if she knew about Marit's feelings? If she knew about mine? It would break her heart. If she's watching us right now, she might be screaming in my ear.

I have no concrete beliefs about the afterlife. I know what all the religions say. I know what the tribal beliefs are. But me... I'm not sure. Maybe we just cease to exist. Maybe there *is* an afterlife. Maybe we care about the people still living. Maybe we're just happy to be free of the mortal coil. But if there's even a chance that Anya is aware of what's transpiring in my thoughts—in my heart—I can't imagine following through on any of the things I've been thinking about. After work. Lying in bed. And now at work, during the most dangerous and intriguing events in Raven's Rest since my arrival.

It's Marit that I think about when my brain has a moment to itself. Sometimes even when I should be thinking about other things. She just...makes me feel at peace, which is something I have not felt in a very long time.

Up until now, they've just been thoughts. A fantasy. But... despite being slow to pick up on people's subtle, and not-so-subtle, cues, I eventually suss things out. And suss them out, I have.

The question is, what do I do about it?

Should I do *anything* about it?

All I really know is that now is not the time.

This distraction could endanger the others. A lot of people would think I was crazy for thinking about these things at a time like this, but they don't know how my brain works. How single-minded it can be.

"Gonna have to wait," I tell myself, not just because it's a dumb time to be pondering affairs of the heart, but because I don't yet fully understand my own feelings about it. And there is no way to predict when it will suddenly make sense to me. Emotional processing is basically out of my hands, controlled by a little demon in my mind who likes to catch me off guard, at inopportune times, with emotions generated by things that happened a week ago. A month ago. Six months ago.

"Heeeeey," the doppler effect voice snaps me out of my

thoughts and back to reality. I'm still on the snowmobile. Still zipping along. But I've just passed Jimmy's and am cruising into town. When my mind catches up with the here and now, I hear Tali's shouting voice. "Where are you—"

She stops when I pull to the right and then turn hard to the left, making a U-turn. She waits for me, hands on her hips. Classic power pose. She uses it a lot. Builds her confidence, she says. Which means I might be in for an earful.

I pull up beside Jimmy's and cut the engine. "What took you so long?"

Hand raised, I extend my index finger. "Caught Grizz with her pants down. Literally. Was propositioned by her." I extend a second finger. "Then I had a run-in with the Taqtuq brothers. Shocker, they still don't like me." A third finger goes up. "All that followed by a sit-down chat with Red inside his trailer."

She's surprised. "He let you inside?"

"That unusual?"

"You're the first person I've ever heard of going inside. Guess it means he likes you. Or trusts you. What was it like?"

"Dirty," I say, extending a fourth finger. "And I ran into a moose. *Nearly* ran into a moose."

"A real moose?" she asks.

I nod. "Had old grizzly scars. Saw the wisdom in his eyes."

"*His* eyes? It was a bull?"

"Biggest I've seen, I reckon."

"Wow," she says. "And why did you speed past? Looked like you were in a trance."

I climb off the snowmobile. "Was thinking."

"About?"

"I'm sure you can guess."

She smiles at that. "And?"

"And nothing," I say. "This isn't the time."

"Can't really argue with that," she says, "but I also know you. You need to focus on one thing. Might be a good idea to speak your mind and get it out of your head now."

I grunt. "I'm not there yet."

"And only God knows when you'll get there," she sighs. "I know. Just...please remember that I'm not just your deputy. I'm your friend. Probably your best friend. And I'm *her* sister. You know I keep my mouth shut about these things, so if you need to talk it through..."

"Maybe later," I say.

She rests a hand on my shoulder. "Moment we walk back into Jimmy's, later is going to become *much* later."

"Downside of the job, I'm afraid." I look toward the open garage door. "Death before I... You know what I'm trying to say."

She's all smiles now. "Yes. Yes, I do."

I sigh and give my head a slight shake. "All right, just...show me what's going on."

She motions her head for me to follow her to the garage. "Most of what I know Ethan told me, so don't ask a lot of questions. I don't have answers. Mostly try not to puke. It'll freeze and be there all winter."

"Got it," I say, stepping into the garage behind her.

She moves to the side, giving me a clear look at what's become of the camel.

I'm not one to lose my lunch. I've cleaned up more than a couple moose crushed beneath an eighteen-wheeler. I'm accustomed to blood, guts, brains, you name it. But what I find hanging from the ceiling and collected in a series of metal bowls lining the floor is not just disgusting, but downright otherworldly. And that, more than the gore, twists my stomach into knots.

Tali extends her hands toward the mess. "You see?" She turns to me. "You have any clue about any of this?"

"Only one thing I'm certain of—we're about to host a nudist yoga class at a porcupine sanctuary."

Her face scrunches up. "What?"

"About to juggle babies in a minefield during a lightning storm?"

She stares up at me.

"Trying to baptize a cat in hot sauce?"

"Are you trying to say, we're in over our heads?" she asks.

"Yeah. Just in a more interesting way. I've been working on them."

"I can tell," she says, feigning being impressed. "We're about to put out a dumpster fire with a flamethrower."

"Ahh, shit," Grizz says, making us both jump and spin around.

She's dressed for the weather, including her bearskin, and carrying an array of weapons. Revolvers. Shotgun. Rifle. "If I knew this was a flamethrower kind of party, I'd have—" Her eyes widen, focused between Tali and me, locked onto the mess behind us. "What in the goat-milking disaster porn…"

22

“Sheriff, someone got some splainin’ to do,” Grizz says, doing her best impression of Ricky Ricardo from *I Love Lucy*. And by ‘best,’ I mean horrible. The accent sounds more Russian than Cuban. I’ve heard that the line was never actually in the show, which might account for her bad impression. People say it’s some kind of collective memory fart like, ‘Luke, *I* am your father.’ The Mandela Effect, I think it’s called. Merging universes affecting memories or some kind of nonsense like that.

“Hey!” Grizz says to me with a shove that would get her locked up in a city with an uppity police force. “Seriously, what the hell is this, Colt?”

I’ve never seen Grizz freaked out before. Don’t like it. “Used to be a camel. Found it walking down Main. It was freezing to death. Had to put it down.”

“Well, shit,” she says. “Here I thought it disassembled itself.”

Her sarcasm stings, but I get it. Being confronted with something like the camel’s remains, without warning, would make a mousy preschool teacher demand answers.

“It’s a lot,” I say, “and it’s already a long story. Let’s wait for Red to arrive and then I’ll fill you in. Every detail. Nothing held back.”

She grumbles, but nods. “Old Red, huh? Surprised he’s coming. Surprised you asked him.”

“It was easy after asking you,” I say.

She laughs.

"Oh, Sheriff. Now, now. You've seen what I have to offer. You'll be back."

"Oookay," Tali says. "I'd rather focus on the dismembered camel—not a camel—situation."

"Mm," Grizz says, shedding her shotgun and rifle. She squats down beside the large bowls full of pale, clean, organs. "So...it's got no muscles that I can see. No tendons. Skeleton looks normal, if you ignore how clean they look. And...huh. No veins." She removes her gloves and moves from bowl to bowl, lifting and moving body parts that have begun to freeze.

"I'm not sure that's a good—"

She cuts me short with, "No heart." Looks to me. "You say this thing was alive and walking?"

"Yes, ma'am," I say.

"Don't you 'yes, ma'am' me, Sheriff. I'm not that old, and I'm sure as hell not respectful enough." She drops some kind of organ back into a bowl. Lands with a metallic clang. "Also, I'm calling bullshit. No way this thing was walking around. Sure the cold didn't get to you? Lots of people see things during the winter. Spirits. Pale mermaids. Fuckin' yeti."

Tali and I share a quick glance.

Grizz is sharp. Doesn't miss it. Whispers, "Fuck's sake," as she stands. Levels her gaze at me. "Sheriff. Shoot straight with me now, or I'm walking back up to my warm bed. We're not risking our lives looking for sasquatch turds, are we?"

"Wasn't a yeti," I say. "Or a sasquatch. So, no. But *something* came at us, and I didn't get a good look. Best guess..."

I motion toward the camel. "It was something like this, but not friendly."

"And by something like this, you mean..."

"Created," I say. "At the lab. But like I said. Long story and Red isn't—"

"Right behind you, Sheriff." I flinch and turn around, jump-scared twice in five minutes by two people who look like they'd stomp around like frost giants. "Easy, hoss." He grins. Missing a tooth. "Gonna shit yourself before too long if you react to a voice like you've just been impaled by a Tsuchi."

"A what?" I ask.

He shakes his head. "Before your time. Government program that was scrapped after a bunch of people died."

"You were there?" I ask.

"Nuh-ah. Before my time, too." He steps around me, into the garage, sizing up the camel's remains. "The Tsuchi were a remnant of a World War II project that we inherited from Japan's Unit 731. Nasty business. The kind you deny all knowledge of, if word gets out. The project I was involved in up on that mountain was born out of the Cold War. When that fiasco of a 'war' ended, funding dried up and everyone working up on that mountain that wasn't useful for another project... Well, they went to work for the Devil or Jesus, if you catch my meaning. One of the two, though I suspect most of them are a might warmer than they'd like to be right now."

"Hey, Red," Grizz says, greeting him.

He turns around and gives her a smile. "Grizz. Been a while."

"Too long," she says, a gleam in her eye.

"Don't get any ideas, woman," he says. "Plumbing ain't what it used to be."

"Ugh," she says. "It's a shame." She turns to me and Tali. "This man's cock—"

"No!" Tali says. "Uh-uh. Don't need to know. Don't want to think about it. God, no."

"Missing out," Grizz says, getting a kick out of Tali's reaction. "Say, Tali, why is it you don't have a man? You and your sister are the two most prized bachelorettes in town. Spend too much time waiting for mister perfect, you're going to miss mister good enough. And that's all a woman can really hope for."

"Thanks for the unsolicited advice," Tali says, doing her best to reign in her feelings on the subject. There's a reason she hasn't found a man yet, but similar to my situation, only a few people know why—myself included. Not an easy thing, keeping a big part of yourself hidden because of what people might think.

"Any time," Grizz says, and then turns to Red, "Now you. Mind telling me why you're not surprised to see a camel made of fleshy cubes hanging from Jimmy's ceiling and contained in bowls that I'm guessing he also uses to make meatloaf and his horrible chicken salad?"

"Sheriff explained it all before I agreed to come," he says.

Grizz swivels, full body, around to me, eyebrows raised. A look of mayhem in her eyes.

I raise my hand. "Sorry, Grizz. I forgot."

She's not convinced. "Forgot..."

"It's been a day already, Grizz." Don't want to piss her off, but I'm not about to relinquish my authority.

"Uh-huh. You just remember which of us was willing to show up for a fight, not knowing a damn thing about what's going on."

"Ahh, don't be sour with him," Red says. "He's in over his head. Trying to make sense of something that might not make any sense at all."

"Which is why you're both here," I say. "If there's something killing people up at the lab and we can stop it before they're all dead, then that's what we're going to do."

"Ain't gonna be killin' much in that concrete maze with the shit you all are carrying," Red says.

"You got a problem with my guns, Red?"

"I got a problem with getting killed and going deaf. In case you missed what I just said, every tunnel and room in that subterranean hellhole is made of concrete. You fire any one of these weapons in that situation, you're not going to be hearing anything except for a high-pitched squeal for the rest of your life."

"Suppos'n you have a solution?" Grizz asks him.

"God damn right, I do." He heads to the garage's open door. "Any of you know how easy it is to get a firearm in Alaska? Legal and otherwise? Not to mention ancillary equipment that would come in handy during tunnel warfare? Doesn't matter. Point is, I've been preparing for shit to go down in that facility since my project was shut down."

I follow him out into the cold with Tali and Grizz. He steps to the side and spreads both hands out toward his snowmobile like a magician revealing his fully reformed assistant. There's nothing directly impressive about the snowmobile. Like the rest in town, it's a dependable old workhorse. It's the sledge he's pulling that's the magical part.

There's a heap of black weapon cases, big and small, bungee corded to the sledge. Dozens. Along with old, metal, olive drab bullet cases. How he's not on a terrorist watch list is beyond me. Probably because the government doesn't know he's alive.

"Now," he says, "we gonna circle-jerk all day, wondering who's going to solve the camel mystery, or are we going to arm up and go storm the castle to save a bunch of peasants?"

23

"It's like Christmas," Red says. "Right?"

He looks over his weapon cases spread out across Jimmy's tables in the front of the shop where we've all gathered.

Marit leans into me. Whispers.

"How many guns are in there?"

"No idea," I tell her.

"Can't be legal," she says.

"Depends on what they are." I look down at her and smile. "But I'm thinking you're right."

"Going to do something about it?"

I've been considering that possibility since he revealed his portable armory five minutes ago. It's my job to uphold the laws of Alaska, but I'm pretty sure everyone in Raven's Rest is breaking one law or another, dang near every day. I focus on what keeps people safe and alive. You take a snowmobile to the top of a mountain and barrel down for kicks, whatever happens, that's on you. Try that shit in the center of town and your snowmobile becomes my snowmobile.

"Not sure I will," I admit. "Just...keep your eyes open for explosives."

She nods.

"All right," Red says, weapon cases behind him. "Some ground rules. First, you point one of these things at anyone else, armed or empty, you lose it."

"Sounds like your snowmobile rule," Marit whispers.

Feel like I'm in the back of the classroom again, goofing off while–

Two finger snaps draw my attention back to Red. "I'm sure you know weapon safety guidelines, Sheriff, but I'm gonna need you to pay attention regardless. You're not used to handling these darlings."

Sufficiently scolded, I refocus on his presentation.

"Now, rule two, fingers off the triggers until you aim to kill something. You're liable to misfire when the shit goes down and your fingers get all twitchy from adrenaline." He looks us over, one at a time, making sure he has our attention. "Rule three. Keep a round chambered at all times. If a sonuvabitch tries jumping you, won't be time to chamber and fire. That said, if things are calm and clear, keep your safety engaged. Once you get used to it, switching the safety off will only add a fraction of a second to your fire time, and will likely save a life in case you happen to break rules one and two. Am I understood?"

I'm genuinely surprised that Red's speech to the group is about safety. Didn't see it coming. I was expecting a conspiracy theory and a kind of a yippee-ki-yay Bruce Willis vibe. Instead, he sounds downright responsible. "Yeah," I say.

Red doesn't budge until every one of us has confirmed our understanding of his safety rules. I can tell Grizz wants no part of a safety plan. Not her style. But she says the words anyway, "I hear you."

"Good," Red says, unlocking the cases. "Each one of these cases contains the same set of weapons so it doesn't matter which one you claim. Wasn't sure how many of us there would be, so we've got some extras…which is fine. Fewer people means fewer dumb mistakes."

He opens a single case revealing two different submachine guns that I'm not familiar with. There are four loaded magazines for each, encased in foam. Both weapons are sound suppressed and have collapsible stocks. The last item in the case is a knife with a handle that looks too thick.

"Any one of you know what you're looking at?" Red asks.

"All I know," Grizz says, "is that I'm not using that thick-ass knife over these gals." She raises her hands, spinning two curved karambit knives from their finger rings. The rotating blades snap to a stop in her strong grip, ready to slice or stab. "They were good enough to take down a grizzly, they'll be good enough for whatever's wait'n for us at NovaGen."

"You killed that bear with *those*?" Ethan asks, looking like he's just seen his first nude woman.

"And it's why I'm happy she brought 'em," Red says, and turns to Grizz. "But you are taking a firearm, yes?"

"Hell, yes," Grizz says. "Both of them."

He grins and continues, "Now, listen up, because I'm only going to explain all this once." He motions to the two weapons in the case. "These here are what adults call submachine guns." He shifts his hand toward the larger of the two. "This is a PP-19-01 Vityaz-SN, which is a mouthful, so let's just call it a Vityaz."

He pauses, waiting for someone to say something.

No one does.

"Any dumb questions? No? Great. The Vityaz is compact, light, and allows for greater maneuverability in tight quarters. Hallways, tunnels, rooms full of shelves. You get the idea. What they are not good at is distance. Don't bother trying to hit something long-range. You'll miss."

"What are we calling long-range?" Tali asks.

"Hundred meters," he says. "Hundred fifty in the hands of a pro."

He sees that only half of us have understood the distance. Closes his eyes. Rubs his forehead. "Dear, Lord... Look, let's just call it a football field. You all get that?"

"Yessir," Jimmy says, nodding with enthusiasm. Perched on his shoulder, Dufresne mimics the nod. "Ready to rock 'n' roll."

"You most certainly are not." Red takes the weapon from the foam and demonstrates how to deploy the stock. "Release button near the stock hinge. Press it and unfold. When you hear a click, it is engaged."

He turns the weapon so we can see the safety switch. "This is the safety. There are three settings. It's currently set to safe, meaning it cannot fire." He flicks the switch down to the middle position. "This is semi-auto, meaning you will have to pull the trigger every time you want to fire a single bullet." He flicks it to the lowest setting. "And this is full auto, which I recommend, again, because you're all new to the weapon, and because it fires 9mm rounds, which I suspect you all know don't pack a lot of punch. If you want the target dead, the more bullets the better."

Full-auto was my biggest concern. Because they are very illegal in the United States, and since I'm not familiar with either of these models, I take a guess. "These are Russian. Black market imports."

"Yes, indeedy. And you have every right to be uncomfortable using them, being full-auto and all, but if you don't tell, I won't tell." He gives me a wink and carries on like the matter has been settled. Since I don't bother arguing the point, I suppose it is.

Red turns the weapon around and points to the charging handle. "You all know what this is. Give it a yank to chamber your first round. Each magazine carries thirty rounds. Sounds like a lot, but I promise it will feel like a lot less. This little bastard can drain the entire mag in three seconds, so unless you have a bona fide Kodiak bearing down on you—and Grizz ain't around—don't hold the trigger down long." He flicks the safety back on, ejects the magazine so we can see how. Then he ejects the chambered round, pushes it back into the magazine, slides it back into the SMG, and gives it a slap. "You all get all that?"

Nods all around.

"Good," he says, folding the stock and putting it back. He takes out the second weapon. "This little bitch is a SR-2 Veresk but is more commonly called 'The Beast.' Everything I said and demonstrated on the Vityaz is the same here, except that this carries 9x21mm Gyurza rounds. Greater stopping power and penetration. If you're capable enough to switch weapons based on targets, this is for bigger ones. Any questions."

Tali's hand goes up. "What's with the knife?"

"Last resort," he says, sounding almost grim. He pulls the knife from the foam and holds it for everyone to see. "This is a Weaponized Amphibious Stabilized Platform, or WASP."

"Amphibious?" Marit asks.

Tali follows her sister with, "Stabilized?"

Both are questions I was going to ask.

"Amphibious because it was originally designed for defense against big swimmy things in the ocean. Like sharks." He scrunches his nose, not thrilled about what he says next. "Stabilized because when something is dead, it's not moving, hence being stable. Kind of a sloppy way of forcing an acronym."

"So," Jimmy says. "What do you call it?"

Red cranes his head around with his eyes closed and stops when he's facing Jimmy. "Say again?"

"What...do you call it?"

Red sighs and whispers, "We're all gonna die" under his breath so lightly that only the person with hypersensitive hearing (me) catches it. Then he speaks very slowly, like Jimmy is hard of hearing. "A. Wasp."

"And. What. Does. It. Do?" Jimmy replies, using the same slow cadence.

"You have any thawed meat?" Red asks.

"In the fridge, but it's from the–" he motions his head toward the garage.

"Works for me," Red says.

A moment later, Jimmy slaps down a chilled camel thigh on the counter between the 'kitchen' and the front of the shop. "Doesn't make for good eating, but it's thawed and it's...kinda meat."

Dufresne lets out a high-pitch squeak before using Jimmy's long hair to swing around his head to the other shoulder. The limb makes him nervous.

"Good enough, Jimbo." Red holds the knife up again. "There is a button, here." He taps a button positioned between the handle and the blade using his thumb. "You want to stab your target deep enough for this hole to be inside the body."

He taps a hole I hadn't noticed on the top of the blade. It's only about an inch from the tip and is followed by a serrated edge. "If you can manage that, and you are absolutely sure you want the target to be...stabilized..."

He grins. "Just push the button."

He smiles at Jimmy. "You have a change of clothes?"

"Well, I live upstairs, so–"

Red stabs the leg, plunging the blade deep. There's a big smile on his face when he pushes the button. The leg explodes from the inside out, the force directed straight ahead, toward Jimmy.

Chunks of the camel's geometric insides, along with a red slurry from burst cells, slap against Jimmy's face and body.

Jimmy sputters, looking down at the gore covering him. He spits twice and then, to my surprise, smiles wide. "Sick."

A very pleased Red spins around to the rest of us. "And that is how you kill any motherfucker you might encounter on land, in the ocean, or on another damn planet. Any questions?"

24

"Can I talk to you for a minute?" Marit asks me.

We've distributed the weapons among us and are waiting for Jimmy to finish changing. He's taking longer than I expected, but maybe he's taking the time to wash the chunky gore off his face and out of his hair. I would, too. So, I've got no reason to say 'no' to Marit, even though saying 'yes' terrifies me.

"Sure," I say.

She heads for the garage and motions for me to follow her. She's got the Vityaz slung over her back. The Beast is hidden beneath her jacket, as is mine, along with my revolver and the explosive WASP blade that I hope we have no reason to use.

Honestly, this feels like overkill. But I appreciate the thought Red put into his weapon selection, even if they are illegal. Sound suppressed weapons will save our ears, which in turn will allow us to continue communicating. Had we rushed down there with a bunch of folks carrying big guns and shotguns, we'd have all come out deaf.

I'm going to withhold my judgement about overkill until we're done.

Might turn out to be just the right amount of kill.

I close the door behind me as the cold burns my face.

"Look..." I scratch my chin stubble. "I know what you want to talk about."

"You do?"

"It's obvious at this point, right? And, yes, I agree that we just need to speak about it openly and honestly. I'm just not sure that now is the right time."

"To speak about..."

"Us," I say, uncomfortable with the word.

"Us..."

"You have feelings for me," I declare. "And...I have feelings for you."

Her eyes widen.

"You do?"

"But I don't know how I feel about any of that yet, on account of me being me, and feeling guilty for, well, all of it. Anya... I just... And there are things about me you don't know."

She places her hand on my cheek. "Take a breath, Sheriff."

I look up to find her smiling at me. Our eyes lock and linger. I'm charged with nervous energy, but I don't look away. Can't look away. I've fallen into a trap, unable to escape until—

"I was going to ask you to go over the weapons with me again. Felt embarrassed about asking in front of everyone else."

An ejection seat launches me straight up and out of the trap. I topple through the air, wondering how I got to this point, hoping I'll hit my head upon landing and knock myself unconscious. Waking up in a hospital with no memory of the past few minutes would be merciful enough that I might reconsider my thoughts on God.

"Colton," she says, both hands on my cheeks now. "It's okay. Really. Everything you said...it's true. And you have no reason to worry. I'm still me. You're still you. When this is all done, we'll have an entire winter with nothing else to do but talk this through."

"Right," I say, still pin-wheeling through the air, waiting for impact. "All winter."

"Nothing will happen until we're both comfortable with it," she says, her voice soothing. She brings me back down to the ground, placing me gently on my feet. "Okay?"

"Okay."

"Good." She smiles and pulls the Vityaz around into her hands. "Now can you please tell me if I'm using this thing right?"

She runs through the steps that Red showed us. Loading and unloading. Opening the stock and snapping it in place.

Chambering a round and switching the safety through its three settings. Keeps the SMG pointed at the ground and her finger off the trigger.

"You're good," I tell her. "Sure you weren't just trying to get me alone?"

She gets a mischievous look in her eyes. "If I ever try to get you alone for a different reason, you'll know right away."

A fist of energy punches me in the gut. Hard to describe the way it feels. Easiest just to say it doesn't feel good. Just another sign that my nervous system is on high alert, picking up stimuli like a shark does blood in the water. Most of the world views reality through foggy glasses—protection from harsh truths. But me, and people like me, we see and feel reality without a buffer. As cool as that sounds, I'd prefer to be ignorant with filtered senses.

"Where does your mind go?" she asks, pulling my attention back. "It's like you suddenly can see into another world."

"Same world. Different lenses." I say. "Sorry. Wandering mind syndrome."

"Interesting," she says.

"Interesting?" That's a new one. "Polite way to say 'weird?'"

"My favorite people are weird," she says.

"If that's true, why don't you come see me, eh?" We turn toward the voice. Grizz is outside the garage, securing her new gear to her snowmobile. "I'm an equal opportunity weirdo, if you catch my meaning."

"Oh, I caught it," Marit says, chuckling. "What I'd rather not catch is a handful of STDs."

"Oh, honey," Grizz says with a smile. "You can't get herpes or crabs on your hand."

My discomfort with the conversation grows like a supercharged beanstalk I wish I could climb away on. That said, I'm also realizing something I've missed in all my years living in Raven's Rest. Marit and Grizz are friends.

Huh. Sometimes feeling more than other people also means I miss a lot. Divided attention is not my strong suit, which is why I need to turn my attention away from affairs of the heart and start thinking about saving those who are hurt, and maybe gunning down whatever killed at least one person up at the lab.

"Later?" I say to Marit.

"Later," she agrees.

"Jimmy back?" I ask Grizz.

"Right behind you," she says, as Jimmy, face and hair clean, clothing changed, enters the garage. He's got an orange-and-white truckers cap on backward, is strapped with weapons, and has a goofy grin. "All right, mother-cluckers, let's go pluck this chicken before it lays another egg."

I'm not sure if there was a metaphor in there or if it was just nonsense, but the meaning is clear. And I agree. "Everyone load up. We're leaving."

25

The ride back is just as cold, windy, and bleak as it was the first time. The gloomy blue sky providing us with shadowless light makes seeing a helluva lot easier, though. There's also a trail to follow from our last visit, allowing us to go faster without fear of driving off the road.

What's missing are footprints. And blood.

There's no sign of anything on this road aside from the deep snowmobile tracks.

Could the animal have leapt over the road without touching down, taking a swipe at me as it crossed our path? Seems an impossible feat, but I'm guessing a camel made of flesh LEGO bricks is, too.

When we reach the parking lot at the top, NovaGen comes into view, its doors still wrenched open and shattered. The pieces of debris have all been covered by fresh snow, but the damage supports our tall tale. Once again, we turn around in the lot, parking side by side, facing back the way we came.

"Well, I'll be damned," Red says, climbing off his snowmobile, looking at the broken doors. "You all weren't exaggerating."

He's the only one of us that traveled alone. Said he didn't want another man wrapping his arms around him. So, Jimmy clung to Grizz and neither of them seemed to mind much at all.

"Not in the habit of exaggerating, Red," I say, standing on his left side, already armed and ready to go. "It's a lot like lying."

"That's right. Heard you weren't a fan of untruths." He pulls off his helmet and looks back at me. "Man after my own heart. How you feel about secrets?"

"Secrets?" I ask.

"Guessing you're going to learn a few before the end of the day," he says.

"If I'm told something in confidence," I say, "it stays that way. If I learn something someone would rather I hadn't—in the line of work—and it's related to a crime, well, that's fair game. If it's personal, it ain't none of my business."

"And secrets that might get you—and those you love—murdered just for knowing 'em? What do you do with those?"

"Keep them locked away, and a gun in reach."

He has a good chuckle. "You're a rare man, Sheriff."

"Anyone comes to Raven's Rest looking for trouble is going to get a lot more than they bargained for," Marit says, standing on the other side of Red.

"Guys," Jimmy says, stepping around us. He's got a goofy grin on his face, and a matchstick between his teeth, which is usually present if he's not working or smoking. "Honestly, thank you for letting me come. I would have been a lot more excited if I knew it was going to be a bonding experience. Seriously. I don't have a lot of friends, on account of the way I smell, but—what I'm saying is: I'm glad to be here."

"Well," Red says, "you really shouldn't be." Red chambers a round in his Vityaz, flicks the safety off and heads for the broken doors.

"Hey," Ethan says to Jimmy. "I get it, man. Friends can be hard to come by when—" He gives Jimmy a hearty pat on the arm. It squeaks in response.

Even Red freezes in place. "Would someone check on that, and please tell me he did not do what I think he did."

Tali approaches Jimmy head on. "Arms out to your sides."

He obeys. Has had multiple run-ins with the police, in Raven's Rest and elsewhere. Nothing major, but he's learned how to keep officers happy: do what they tell you.

Tali unzips the coat and peels it open. Dufresne is inside, looking back with wide eyes, like he knows that he and Jimmy have been busted.

"He did," Tali says.

Once again, I hear Red's whispered curses. Then he says, "Jimbo, I'm only going to warn you one time. If that creature gives our position away or otherwise puts any one of us in danger, I'm putting it down. You get me?"

"Y-yeah. I'm sorry. I just—never mind. Can I ask a question?"

"Oh, by all means," Red says, controlling his building annoyance, which helps me reign in mine.

"Is *this* that one time? Or do I get—"

"*This* is the one time," Red grumbles. "Now fall in line, shut the fuck up, and if that little thing starts squeaking, feel free to muffle the sound until it's dead. If you don't, a single nine mil will erase its head. Painless, if that's a concern."

"Okay, okay," Jimmy says.

Red storms toward the open doors.

Jimmy glances at me.

"Geez. That guy is hardcore."

I force a smile because I feel like it's what other people might do. It's a practiced grin, in that I actually stand in front of a mirror trying to judge if my forced smile appears genuine. It doesn't do much to soften the blow of what I say next. "Hardcore, sure. But he's also right. Bringing Dufresne was a bad idea. I'm not going to lose people over a monkey."

"You won't," he says, zipping his coat up over Dufresne again. "Word is my bond, Sheriff. Just like you."

"Uh-huh," I say.

"If it gets out of hand," Grizz says. "I'll take care of it."

I give her a nod of thanks and then follow Red, who has just entered the lab's top floor lobby. Taking my time, I watch Red move. He might be familiar with what's under the ground, but he seems off balance in the lobby.

He stands still, like he's heard something. I do the same and the others follow suit. If he hears something, charging in there isn't going to help. He raises his head to the side.

"Is he…sniffin'?" Jimmy asks.

Red's nose twitches like a dog's. No doubt about it, he's sniffing. But I don't bother answering. To some people, their sense of smell is just as sensitive as their hearing or eyesight. Maybe Red's like that, too. I used to think everyone's sensory experience of the world was like mine. Couldn't be further from the truth. I feel, hear, see, taste, and smell things that most people don't notice. Pain in the ass most of the time, but when you really need to be in touch with your surroundings, it comes in handy. Maybe Red and I have that in common.

And I already know what he's smelling.

The blood.

But Red doesn't head for the lobby's reception desk. He stands still, Vityaz in hand, looking at a row of chairs where people might wait for a meeting. They look as unused now as they did the first time I visited. But he's only interested in the chair directly ahead of him.

"Hang back," I say, and step through the broken doors. The lobby is a little warmer than outside, thanks to the heat still pumping out, but the Arctic winter will claim this open top floor when night falls.

Red's head cocks to the side when he hears my feet crunch over broken glass and snow. "You said there was one dead in the lobby?"

I step closer. "Someone died, yes. Based on the amount of blood behind the reception desk. There wasn't a body."

"Well, there is now," he says, stepping to the side, revealing what might be the most revolting sight I've had to look at in my entire life. "I think it's a man. But...it's kind of hard to tell."

26

"You don't need to see this," I tell the others as the cold compels them to ignore my request that they wait. When all five sets of feet keep moving, I turn to Tali, make eye contact, and she understands that, while I'm being polite, it's an order.

"Everyone hold up." When Tali is the only one that stops, she reaches out and takes hold of Marit and Ethan's arms and pulls them to a stop. "Not a request."

Both of them stop but still attempt to see around Red and me.

Grizz hears the exchange, but chooses her own path. "Ain't nothing I ain't seen before, I'm sure." She steps around me and looks down at what vaguely resembles a human body. "Well, I was wrong. That's...ahh...that's new."

Might be new to her, but she seems undisturbed by the gore. Makes me wonder what other kinds of violence she's seen during her lifetime. After all, it's not a normal person that can go toe-to-toe with a bear and come out on top.

Jimmy hasn't voiced dissent but, given his line of work, I suspect he might be the most prepared for what he's about to see. So, I don't bother warning him again.

Like Grizz, I was wrong.

Jimmy manages to look at the carnage for a single second before reeling away, dropping to his knees, and vomiting on the floor. He heaves a deep breath, drool hanging from his mouth. "What the fuck? Dude...what the fuck?"

I don't bother answering him, because I don't have answers.

"What're you thinking, hoss?" Red asks.

Trying to ignore that this was once a human being, I try to break down what happened here. "This wasn't a calculated, predetermined act. It's...anger. Rage. But this person...didn't die here. They were dead already. Mutilated here, though."

"What makes you say that?" Grizz asks.

"Not a lot of blood," I say. "If this person had been alive at the time...that this happened, the floor would be covered, the walls would be covered. Probably the ceiling, too."

I glance up, not expecting to see anything, but there *are* a few chunks of meat frozen to the ceiling above us. No way to know if they came from this body, or the person killed behind the reception desk. And there's nothing I can do to stop the others from seeing it.

"Oh my God," Marit whispers, following my gaze to the ceiling.

"Is it a man or a woman?" Ethan blurts out.

"Can't tell," I say.

"Not even from the clothing?" he asks.

"What clothing?" Grizz responds with a complete lack of tact. "This poor asshole barely has skin."

Jimmy takes a deep steadying breath and follows it up with a second. Then he spits on the floor and gets back to his feet. "Sorry, ya'll. I just wasn't expecting—"

"Don't be losing sleep over it," Red says. "Fact that you lost your lunch says better about you than not puking says about the three of us."

Strange company to be lumped in with, but he's not wrong. At least on the surface. Processing life experiences slower than the average person, sometimes a lot slower, means that I might be struck by the full horror of this a month from now and find myself clinging to a toilet for hours. When that day comes, I'll regret standing here, looking at this mutilated corpse. But right now, I appreciate the delay. Allows me to do my job.

"Let's not get sidetracked," I say, taking in the litany of wounds. "This person was killed and partially…skinned beforehand. They were then brought to the lobby, placed in this chair, and mutilated. Viciously. Put on display as a visceral demonstration of power and savagery."

"It's a warning," Tali says. "For us."

Having already come to that conclusion, I say, "Uh-huh. Meaning that this…" I motion to the body. "…this is personal. The killer has no qualms with us. On our first visit, it chased us off. Now it's left a very hard to ignore, 'Enter at your own risk' sign."

"Any chance we're going to listen?" Jimmy asks.

"Not a one," Red says.

I agree with him, but I'm not without mercy. "Anyone who wants to leave, feel free to go. This is more than you signed up for." I motion to Tali and Ethan. "Goes for you two, as well." I look Marit square in the eyes. "And you."

As much as I appreciate her company, I can't stand the thought of her, or Tali, ending up like this. I'd be relieved if they did go, but I can't say that out loud. I know them too well. If I—or anyone else—attempts to push, they'll resist.

More so when they're together.

"Before we decide anything," Marit says, "I think it only fair if we get a look at the body."

"She's right," Tali says.

Had a feeling it would come to that. "From a distance. No need to look closely."

Neither of them answer. They just wait.

"They're grown women," Red says. "Some of the toughest I've known—current company excluded."

"Damn right," Grizz says, squatting to get an even closer look.

"Suit yourselves," I say, and take a slow step out of the way, giving them a chance to look away before they see everything. None of them turns away. Not even Ethan. He's the first to look sickened, though. Think he might even have a tear in his eye. Which is an appropriate response. At least one of us should be crying over this.

It's inhuman.

Monstrous.

Marit is the second to look away, hand over her eyes.

But Tali. She doesn't look away. Doesn't blink. Instead, she's making the same face she does when solving a tricky sudoku. Like she's working something out, but—

"You don't see it," she says, catching me watching her. "Because you're too close. The body's position isn't random. Neither are the exposed organs."

I look down at the body, arms and legs splayed wide, most of its skin missing. Large chunks of meat have been removed, including the chest, heart, and lungs. What meat remains on the bones has been sliced into rough cubes, almost like what we found inside the camel. And the entrails…they've been unfurled and yanked in different directions.

But I'm not seeing what Tali is, so I back away until I'm standing next to her—and I see it straight away.

The body has been laid out in a crude X. Same with the insides. "It's an X."

"What's it mean?" Ethan asks.

"Forbidden," Tali says. "Wrong. Danger. Do not enter. The list goes on, but they all mean the same thing."

"Off limits," I say, turning to Tali. "She's right. Whoever did this is warning us to stay away."

"And as I not so subtly inferred before," Red says, "warning or no warning, I'm going in. And I'm guessing the rest of you are, too, so let's quit dicking around with this corpse and get to hunting down whoever did this."

"Whatever," Grizz says.

Red rounds on her.

"S'cuse me? I don't like to be dismissed."

Grizz rolls her eyes. "Not 'whatever,' as in dismissal, you daft old prick. *What*ever as in the killer responsible for this ain't human. Look."

I move closer again as Grizz motions to the cubed flesh.

"Cuts ain't even. Ain't straight. And the thickness is different...but repeating." She points to one cut at a time, and I see it. The gap between cuts varies. The meat wasn't cut, it was gouged. Scraped away. And there are...one, two, three, four, five...six different sizes, repeating over and over in the same X pattern that the body has been arranged in.

Grizz looks up at me. "Sheriff, this wasn't done by a blade. It was done by claws."

"H-how can you be sure?" Ethan asks.

Rather than respond with words, Grizz sheds her weapon and jacket before hauling her three shirt layers up to the top of her back. Criss-crossed across her flesh are dozens of scars in groups of five. "People tend to forget that while I was stabbing that son-of-a-bitch, he was fighting back. Nearly took me to the grave alongside him."

I lean in close, getting a better look at the scars before turning my attention back to the body. She's right. This person wasn't killed by a human being. Given the sixth digit, I reckon the killer is some kind of animal I haven't encountered in my lifetime, read about in a book, seen in a documentary, or heard about in the ancient histories and mysteries of the local Alaskan tribes.

"Ethan," I say. "Six fingers. Any animals you know of have six fingers?"

"Nothing," he whispers, and then lifts his head. "Unless..."

He's got everyone's undivided attention now.

"Unless it's a mutation...or like an artifact."

"An artifact?" Jimmy says. "Like in *Temple of Doom* or something?"

Ethan shakes his head. "More like...a mistake. But not an exclusion. An addition. Like when a 3D printer adds something that's not meant to be there, like an extra finger, or even just a random mess. Happens naturally sometimes, too. Like a vestigial tail. Or fetus in fetu."

"I'm sorry," Tali says, "fetus in...huh?"

"When one twin absorbs the other in the womb. It's not uncommon, but sometimes the absorbed twin keeps developing inside the one that is born. As adults, when things like X-rays, MRIs, and CAT scans are more likely, sometimes people discover remnants of their twin still growing inside their body. A mass of bone and teeth. Sludgy parasitic flesh with hair. Some are even fully formed—an unconscious, but living thing, with arms and legs, hands and feet. While the core of what makes a human... *human* is missing, a cluster of cells remain, forming an aberrant cyst in the shape of human parts. But some of them, containing ganglion nerves, do respond to stimuli, like pain, usually discovered when they are, uh, removed."

"C'mon," Jimmy says, "that can't be real."

"Eh," I say. "I've heard of it. Guess all that documentary watching has a use after all."

"Guess so," Ethan says. When he was rattling off what he knew, Ethan seemed to have a weight lifted, like he was in his element. Now that he's back to facing reality, he's gone quiet. Kid is too smart for this kind of work. "Point being, artifacts happen to living things, but are much more common in...digital creations."

I rub my hand across my face. "So, if NovaGen is...I don't know...screwing around with animals, like the camel—"

"And Dufresne," Jimmy says, hugging his coat where the tamarin has remained oddly quiet.

Ethan finishes my line of thinking for me. "Whatever science is involved, it's not perfected. So, their creations have artifacts. Elements that aren't supposed to be there. Like extra digits, or—" He turns to me. "—extra eyeballs."

27

"I'm not interested in where this shit comes from," Red says. "I'm interested in whether or not we can kill it."

"The camel is dead," Marit says.

"Very dead," Jimmy adds. "But also, it had a brain in its head. A lot smoother than brains I've seen in other animals, but still a brain. Putting a hole in that should do the trick."

"Reckon he's right," I say. "But the rest of the body… I'm not sure. Won't know until we try."

"Then let's quit with the intellectual circle jerk, get down there, and put holes in things." He steps around the group, heading past the reception desk. Spots the blood on the floor and pauses. "This your first victim? Bled out...and was carried away, like you said. Supposin' it won't be the last."

He continues down the hallway. The rest of us are still a little disoriented from discovering the body and hearing Ethan's thoughts on the matter.

Grizz sums up how we're all feeling.

"You know, nudiustertian, I thought this was going to be a normal, bleak and boring winter. But this...this is a welcome change."

Catches me off guard with the last bit. Pretty sure her summation now only applies to herself. Red is eager, but he's not enjoying himself. Truth is, I think he's facing a demon that's been perched on his shoulder going on thirty years.

Grizz lifts her eyebrows twice and follows after Red.

"Okay," Tali whispers. "Anyone know what 'nudiustertian' means?"

We all turn to Ethan. He's more than proven that he's the brains of the bunch.

He sighs. "Day before yesterday."

"Huh," Tali says. "Learn something new every day. Well, a lot of new things today."

She sounds nervous. Distracting herself from the fact there's a skinned and cubed man with exposed entrails positioned to form an X, meant to warn us away. Because to enter is to die. But we're not a bunch of unarmed scientists. We're a heavily armed group of survivalists and law enforcement.

Finished with my internal pep talk, I take the lead and say, "Stay close. Stay quiet. If you see something—"

"Say something," Jimmy says.

I shake my head. "Not this time. Quietly tap the person in front of you. Whoever that is, tap the next person until it gets to me. Then just point. Unless...it looks like something is about to pounce. Then just shoot it."

"Right," Jimmy says, nodding like he's doing his best to tuck everything away in his unused mental filing system, which is overfull with information on meat and marijuana. "You got it, Sheriff."

"Jimmy," I say. "You can call me Colt."

"Cool," Jimmy whispers, falling in line behind me. Marit next, followed by Ethan and Tali, watching our backs.

When we approach the double doors at the end of the hall, Grizz opens the way forward. "Downright balmy in here."

The lounge is exactly how we left it. No signs of a struggle—or recent use.

"Power's on," Red says, standing from where he's crouching beside a couch. "That's good."

"Find something?" I ask.

"Cocoa Pebble," he says. "These folks weren't just unarmed, they were soft. Pampered." He motions to the room around us. "Ask me, this place was built for a bunch of kids." He scoffs. "If they knew the nightmare that took place beneath their feet... If they knew..." He shakes his head. "They couldn't have known. No one in their right mind would allow limp-wristed millennials to come here. I wonder if anyone knows." He looks to me. "I might actually be the last."

"Any of this original?" Tali asks.

"Hell, no," he says, looking around. "Except..."

He heads for the stairwell door. Peers through the slender glass window. "In my day, this was covered by a metal hatch. Sealed like a submarine. Ten-foot ladder down to a concrete stairwell. From there, it was five flights of stairs before reaching the highest floor."

"The highest floor is fifty feet underground?" I ask.

"Built to survive a nuclear attack," Ethan says. When he notes our attention, he explains. "Everything was back then. Cold war paranoia." He looks to Red. "Right?"

"And then some," Red says, stepping back from the door. "Looks like they extended the stairwell to the surface level. Wouldn't want any of the brains slipping on a ladder rung."

"There is an elevator," Jimmy points out. "And power. Why don't we just—"

"Advertise we're coming?" Red says, patience on a hair trigger. "Ring the dinner bell?" He shakes his head. "Listen up and listen good. Anyone of you does something moronic like turning on an espresso machine or flushing a toilet, you are on your own against whatever it is you summon. I do not abide morons."

Harsh, but good advice that at least Jimmy needed to hear.

"We are not urban explorers," Red continues. "We are, first and foremost, an armed rescue team."

"And if no one is left to rescue?" Grizz says.

Red looks at her. "Retribution."

"What I was hoping you'd say." She stands beside him at the door. "Ready when you are."

"And the rest of ya?" Red says. I slide up behind Grizz and the others follow suit, showing their readiness and ability to stay quiet. "Five stories straight down. Slow and quiet."

Red pulls the door open, takes a step inside and is stopped in his tracks by a gut-wrenching scream that ends with a wet gag. Sounded like a woman.

"That was close," Marit says, urgency in her voice. "Maybe just a few floors down."

Red looks back to me. I tilt my head.

"Fuck it," he says, and charges into the stairwell, pounding down with the rest of us on his heels. The dull yellow bulbs embedded in the ceiling above each landing don't illuminate much beyond the next set of stairs, but it's enough light to charge down without falling on your face. Trouble is, anything or anyone in the stairwell is going to hear us coming. But there are seven of us, we're armed, and I'm itching to put a bullet into whatever we find that's been killing people.

From below, a desperate female voice. "Hurry—hck!" It's followed by a wet tear, a few seconds of silence, and the slap of a body landing full force—far more than five stories below. The sound echoes around us. Red stops, breathing heavily. Looks over the rail into a dimly lit stairwell that fades to black before reaching the bottom. Anything could be lurking down there.

"What's wrong?" Grizz asks.

"She's dead," Red says. "Ain't nothing we can do for her now."

Grizz cracks her neck to the side, channeling frustration. "What happened to retribution?"

"There's more people to look for," he says. "And until we're sure the living are safe, or everyone is dead, we ain't just gonna run around shooting everything that moves."

Grizz grunts.

"'Sides," Red says. "Whatever did that knows we're here. Killed the woman for our benefit."

"For our *benefit?*" Marit asks.

"To get us charging like we did, probably straight into a trap, or hoping to get us past the first level without us having a look." He looks up at the rest of us. "Either way, it's a smart sunavabitch."

28

"On three," I say to Red, both of us gripping the wheel that needs to be spun before the door can be opened. There's a security module to the left of the door. Looks like it has options for numerical codes, card scanning, fingerprints, and face IDs. Guessing it takes a combination of two or more to unlock these doors, but right now, the indicator light is green, which generally means unlocked. We'll find out in a moment. "One..."

Grizz and Jimmy cover the stairs leading down, while Marit, Tali, and Ethan watch the stairs above. No way anything coming up or down toward us is going to get past the wall of bullets they're prepared to unleash.

"Two..."

I run through a sequence of events, trying to predict how things will go the moment we open this door. Step one in every scenario is me raising my weapon. After that, I find the number of possibilities to be unlimited, and I give up.

"Three!"

Red and I put everything we've got into it and the wheel spins like a fidget spinner with the world's best ball bearings. Caught off guard by the speed, Red and I both let go, watching it spin.

"Uh...huh," Red says. "It's been disconnected from the locking mechanism."

"Meaning?" I ask.

"It just spins," he says. "It's for show."

"So, the door..."

"Is unlocked." He places his hand on the metal handle. "Has been this whole time."

"Are you kidding me?" Marit whispers to us. "Neither of you actually tried the door?"

Red and I look at each other, neither one of us wanting to admit we did not.

"Trying it now," Red grumbles, pulling the handle down.

I move to the side and raise my Vityaz toward the door's seam, ready to shoot past Red if I need to. He pulls the door open, and I nearly unleash a magazine of rounds into—nothing. There are no boogeymen here to greet us. No monsters or serial killers. It's just a hallway with stark white paneled walls, ceiling, and floor. The gaps between the panels glow green, adding a lime hue to everything.

"Everyone close in," I say. "Red—"

"On your six," he says, and we step into the hallway. The moment my foot touches the eight-by-eight-foot floor panel, the strips of light surrounding me on the floor, walls, and ceiling turn white. The segments beyond are still green, but they're now well lit thanks to the bright white illuminating the panel I'm standing on.

"Well," Red says. "That's new."

"The lighting?" I ask.

He looks up and down, left and right. "All of it. Layout is the same, but they've covered the concrete." He gives me a glance. "Probably couldn't get the blood out." He points at the wall ahead of us. "And that."

A poster, like a store map you'd find at a mall, displays five octagonal levels. The top floor, colored green, is a fully realized map complete with large rooms branching off on either side of the hallway. Unfortunately, the rooms have been labeled with numerical codes, rather than words. No way to know what we're looking at, but at least we know the general floor plan. I take out my phone and take a photo of the map, which includes a handy red X and the words:

YOU ARE HERE.

"Don't let this pretty map fool you," Red says. "This place is a maze of tunnels, crawl spaces, and rooms far beyond what they've got here. They might be walled off, but you shouldn't assume every door leads to one of these rooms. You end up in one of these side halls, you better mark yourself a trail so you can find your way out."

"Got it," I say. "Rest of you hear that?"

"Maze. Secret halls. Leave a trail." Tali forces a smile, but I can tell she's nervous. We all are.

"Are we all assuming that the rainbow of levels is ominous?" Tali asks. "Or is it just me? Because, yellow, orange, and red feels a lot like fire, with the purple bottom level being hell."

Red huffs a laugh.

"Yeah, I think you're reading that correctly."

"What's wrong with purple?" Jimmy asks.

"Nothing good is purple," Tali says. "Ursula. Cheshire Cat. Maleficent, the Evil Queen, Emperor Zurg, Joker, Thanos. Grimace."

"What's wrong with Grimace?" Marit asks.

"What's not wrong with Grimace?" Tali says.

"Alexander the Grape," Marit says.

Tali sighs. "I'll give you that one. So good."

"Around the world," Ethan says. "Purple is an evil color, often representing death, mourning, and the presence of the demonic. It's also a symbol of power, as in the English monarchy, and unnatural magic. Yellow...the second floor, is the complimentary color—or opposite color—of purple, representing things that are holy, safe, life-giving. God and angels."

"That's...more information about color than any of us needed to know," Grizz says.

"Companies like this," Ethan says, looking around the hallway, "they take that kind of psychological and historical context seriously."

"You're suggesting that we should be less on guard," Red says, "because NovaGen rainbow color-coded its floor plan?"

Ethan nods. "Colors would be random if they hadn't."

"Which means what?" Tali asks.

"Means I'm glad we're on the green floor." Ethan ticks off five fingers. "Energy. Creation. Life. Safety. Moving forward."

"Yeah, well, you can all hold hands and skip down the green brick road," Red says. "But whatever the hell they had brewing in the lower levels is out, pissed, and free to move about the building, given that every single door is unlocked." He motions to the nearest door. The access lock shines green, same as the entrance to this floor.

Power is on, but security is down.

"All right then," Red says and turns to me. "What's the plan, hoss? Split into three groups, or two?"

"No splitting up. We went back for more people, so there would be *more* people. Safety in numbers. Safety before speed.

We don't know how many bodies we'll find in here, but I don't want any of our people to join them."

He doesn't like it, but says, "And if we come across a bomb about to explode?"

"Then good luck keeping up, old timer," I say, knowing it will get a laugh from him. It does. From Grizz, too. Marit, Tali, and Ethan look uncomfortable with the age-jab, but Jimmy just looks confused. Like he hasn't heard a word that's been said. "You all right, Jimmy?"

He blinks and turns to me. "He's gone."

"Who's gone?" I ask.

"Dufresne." He shakes his head. "I—I don't know when he crawled out of my jacket. Didn't even feel it happen." He opens his jacket so we can see for ourselves, even though I would have taken his word for it. "Didn't see him leave. Did anyone?"

Everyone indicates that they didn't see a thing. Could have left in the shady staircase. Could have bailed when we were all looking at the map. Suppose the better question is why. We brought him home...but that might not be what the little creature wanted. Because it's smart, too. It hid inside a camel for warmth and journeyed to town.

Was it a fluke?

Was it running from this place?

Or was it meant to bring us here?

Was it, and the camel, bait for a trap?

I don't think so. The body on the first floor was meant to warn us away. Whatever killed and mutilated the people here had nothing against anyone in town...until now. Something chased us away. We ignored the warnings. And now...now we're on the hit list. Or menu.

And if that wasn't ominous enough, a door down the hallway swings open quietly as something squirming on the floor emerges from the room's dark shadows.

29

"The fuck?" Grizz says, watching the small creature wriggle its way toward us. "Is…is that a jellyfish?"

The gelatinous body, flopping and squirming, resembles a jellyfish…and a slug, with a fleshy, undulating skirt surrounding the cucumber-sized body. The thing is purple, with yellow spots around its lower body, but the color darkens to a kind of sparkly opaque violet, and the texture shifts from slimy to dry. But the main giveaway that it's not a jellyfish, or a slug, is the line of wiggling quills extending out of the creature's back, right where a spine would be.

The quills…they're jointed, covered in purple skin and are twittering in a way that a 1920s madam might wave hello.

Because…they're fingers.

Human fingers.

Eight of them.

Before I can say any of this aloud, a sudden cough makes me jump. It's followed by an explosion of purple gore and pinwheeling fingers as the creature bursts, its insides coating a ring of the hallway from floor to ceiling.

The whole group turns toward Jimmy, who lowers his Vityaz, a smile on his face, matchstick pinched between his teeth.

He notices the six sets of incredulous eyes locked onto him. "What?"

"We might have learned something from it," I say.

"Shoot everything that moves," Jimmy says, and nods at Red. "That's what he said."

"Damnit, boy," Red grumbles. "I said that we are *not* going to shoot everything that moves."

The matchstick in Jimmy's mouth leans downward with his frown. "Okay. That does sound familiar. But that *wasn't* a person. It could have been dangerous."

"Dangerous," Marit says. "It could barely move."

"Jimmy might be right," Ethan says.

He's got my instant attention, not because of what he said, but because he sounds distant. While the rest of us focused on Jimmy's impulsive discharge, Ethan walked forty feet away. He crouches over the creature's remains, inspecting the ring of gore enveloping a strip of the hall, some of it now dripping from the ceiling and running down the walls.

"Ethan," I say. "Do me a favor and *do not* move." I give Tali a nod and we move together, instinct and years of working together allowing us to slide down the hallway, covering all points–the door we pass on the right, the dimly lit green hallway beyond, the open door just a few feet from Ethan. All I can see beyond the entryway is darkness. Anything could be inside.

"I'll get the light," I say as Tali and I pass by Ethan on either side, stepping over the death halo, which I note contains several intact fingers.

I don't wait for Tali to respond. No need. She knows what to do. When I reach the door, she's behind me, her left hand on my shoulder.

Tali aims her Vityaz past me, into the room, ready to pull the trigger if anything comes at us. I slide my right hand against the inner wall to my left, searching for a light switch. My fingers bump over something attached to the wall and a pleasant set of ceiling lights illuminate slowly, like the sun emerging from behind clouds.

Tali and I move into the room, weapons raised, searching every nook, cranny, and shadow for something living. But the room is empty. Well, not empty, but we are the only living things here.

"Over there," Tali says, lifting her chin toward a forty-gallon glass tank that's been made to look like a jungle floor, complete with living plants. Looks like a habitat for a pet lizard. A grated lid lies on the floor beside the desk holding it. "I think Jimmy killed someone's pet."

"Mm," I say, turning my attention to the room's details for the first time. It's modern, full of bookshelves bowing under the weight of countless thick tomes. The white walls don't have framed photos. They have massive 8k flatscreens displaying high-res scenes of jungles, giving a sense that we're in a tall laboratory high in the canopy of the Amazon. Adding to the effect are dozens of potted and hanging plants. Some have massive leaves. Others are vines, growing up the walls, spreading onto the ceiling where a lone, six-foot-wide circular fixture embedded in the ceiling illuminates the space with diffuse light that feels a lot like actual sunlight.

The illusion has a fast and profound effect on my psyche. I feel...happy. Content. If we had a room like this back at the station, getting through the Alaskan winter would be easy. Whatever kind of messed up shit they were working on here, NovaGen knows how to take care of its people.

I take a deep breath, filling my lungs with the scent of living things and humidified air.

"I know," Tali says, lowering her Vityaz. "Feels good in here, right?"

"Very," I say. "But we need to stay focused." I tilt my head to the doorway and shout, "Clear!"

A distant voice responds with, "Clear!" It's Marit.

I poke my head out into the hallway. Ethan is still there, Vityaz raised, keeping watch ahead.

"Sorry," he says. "Curiosity got the better of me."

"Don't let it happen again," I say, and then make eye contact with Marit. She and Jimmy are standing outside the doorway Tali and I passed.

"Clear," she says, again. "Couldn't talk them out of it."

"Jimmy," I say. "Keep an eye on the hallway on your end. Marit." I motion with my head for her to join us. Red and Grizz are a dangerous duo, and Jimmy has, at the very least, proven he's a good shot, but I'll feel more comfortable having her with us.

I duck back into the room. Tali is smiling at me.

"Don't start," I say.

"What?" she says, feigning innocence. "I was just going to thank you for bringing her because some of us don't just have a few screws loose, and even more lost entirely."

I'm about to respond when Marit says, "Holy shit. What is… Holy shit."

She steps into the office space, eyes wide, taking in the mixture of technology and nature. She breathes deep through her nose. "Oh my God."

"The other room—" Tali gets out before her sister finishes for her.

"—is a really big supply closet full of unopened computers, computer parts, and other techie things I didn't recognize, including a ton of large vats on wheels full of pink liquid that looked a lot like the stuff inside the camel. But it wasn't like this. Not remotely."

From the hallway, a nervous-sounding Ethan asks, "What did you find?"

"An office," Marit says. "In the jungle." She smiles at me. "This is amazing."

The good vibes provided by this room are decimated by Ethan's next sobering question. "Any bodies?"

I nearly respond right away, because I knew the answer the moment I stepped in the room. As fragrant as this office space is, I'd have smelled blood as soon as my nose crested the doorframe, if not out in the hallway. Out of an abundance of caution, I do another quick sweep of the room, looking for the distinct dark red of blood, or even signs of a struggle. Everything appears to be where it's meant to be, aside from the creature spattered around the hallway.

"Clear," I say. "Nothing happened in here, aside from the daring escape of—" I look at the tank. An orange sticky note with a handwritten name is stuck to the upper right corner.

OSCAR

"—of Oscar the who-knows-what being kept as a pet."

Ethan leans into the room. "As a pet?" He spots the open tank and frowns. "That can't be protocol. It's...sloppy."

"You read the NovaGen manual, have you?" Tali asks.

Ethan rolls his eyes. "No, it's just, they're scientists, right? Keeping...*Oscar* in an office setting is stupid."

"Reason you're saying that?" I ask.

"You mean other than it *not* being a species ever seen before, or that it had a spine of human fingers running down the back?"

"Yeah, I—"

"Or," he says, not finished, "the fact that hidden inside its body was what looks like a curved hypodermic needle. There's no way to know what it was packing in the stinger, but living things traditionally arm themselves with horrible shit. And before I forget, Oscar was composed of the same cells as the camel, but translucent."

"Okay," I say, nodding. "Are you saying we need to apologize to Jimmy?"

"I wouldn't go that far," Marit says.

Ethan cracks a slight grin.

I'll take the victory.

While I'm being positive on the outside, I'm also working out what's up with Ethan. This case is beyond crazy, and we're all frazzled, but he seems personally invested in figuring out what's going on, and on saving the people here. Or maybe just one of them. My suspicion is that he's been secretly seeing the reception desk girl, and is, despite evidence to the contrary, hoping to find her alive.

If that's the case, no matter what happens today, I think it's going to end badly for Ethan.

"Let's keep moving," I say. "A lot of ground to cover, still."

Marit and Tali follow Ethan back into the hallway, meeting the others at the ring of gloopy flesh.

"Alas, poor Oscar," Tali says, looking down, and up, at the dead former pet. "We barely knew him."

“Wait,” Jimmy says, mortified. “It had a *name?* I killed someone’s *pet?*”

I almost feel bad enough to tell him about the danger it presented. Almost. Then I glance left down the hallway of glowing green cubes ahead and stop in place. White light fades away, one hallway segment at a time, disappearing around the bend two hundred feet away, and then slowly fading. Feels like a hallucination, there and gone in seconds. But it was there.

“How long do these panels take to go dark after we step on them?” I ask Ethan.

“Why the hell—” Grizz gets out before he interrupts her.

“Thirty seconds,” he says. “I counted.”

“Why you wondering about that?” Red asks.

I turn back to the group, as deadly serious as Gordon Ramsay tasting a pizza made by a twelve year old. “Because we’re not alone. Because something was there—” I motion to the hallway’s bend. “—just over thirty seconds ago.”

30

After spending a minute explaining to Jimmy why we weren't going to charge after whatever was at the end of the hall, I agree to split into two teams that will clear rooms on either side of the hallway and always be in sight of each other, ready to back up the other team at a moment's notice.

This place is massive, and it might take days to go through one room at a time. Two groups moving in tandem will cut the search time in half without reducing our numbers.

But our unseen visitor is on everyone's mind. I know I was hoping to find most of the staff here holed up in a room, waiting for rescue. But the longer we look, the more ominous things feel.

"Anything?" I ask, looking through yet another well lit, jungle-themed office.

"Not a damn thing," Tali says. "Might as well move on to the next—"

"Look at this," Marit says, pointing to a mini fridge.

"You thirsty?" Tali quips.

"Not the fridge," Marit says. "The photo."

A magnetic rainforest-themed frame holds a photo to the fridge door. Looks like some kind of safari vacation, someplace tropical. Someplace familiar. When I recognize it, I'm glad I didn't speak my thought process aloud. It's a photo of two people—a man and a woman—standing in *this* office. They're smiling and holding what looks like a single cell, like those taken from the camel. But it's not just a cell. It's got—I lean in close, putting on my reading glasses—it's got four little legs, is covered in white fuzz, and has a happy little face. Like a thumb-sized baby seal evolved to walk on four feet. It's both a freak of nature and adorable.

"Anything?" Ethan asks from the door.

"Swap with him," I tell Tali. She heads to the door where Ethan keeps watch to the left. She motions for him to join me and takes his place.

"Nothing bad," I tell him, hoping to ease the concern wrinkling his forehead. "Just want to see what you make of this." I motion to the photo.

He leans down, grows frustrated, lifts the frame, and takes the image. He stands and carries it to a desk, sitting down and tapping on a desk lamp by touching its metal hood.

He shakes his head. "Why would they?"

"Why would they what?" I ask.

"These people... NovaGen. They're making these things, right? Have to be. They kept Oscar as a pet. They're holding this one. It's cute. I get that. But how could they have any idea that what they made was safe?"

"Don't think they did," Marit says.

"But...it's just...stupid."

"They let their guard down," Marit says. "Got comfortable with the technology. With the adorable little guys they were making. We know they scaled up from this." She motions to the little white fuzzball. "That camel was huge. Maybe they thought the big creations would be just as docile? Hell, maybe they were, until someone fucked up. Happens in other lab settings. Get too comfortable working with a virus and wind up with a global pandemic. Things go wrong. Things...get out."

"Most of the time, they do not," he says, looking sour. If we find anyone in charge of this facility, they're going to get an earful from Ethan. He tosses the photo aside. "We should keep moving. Can't be many offices left."

"What makes you think that?" I ask.

"This is a research facility," he says. "These rooms are for execs and admin. Nothing about these spaces gives me the impression any of the real work was done here. At best, the people who worked here admired what was being created and just wanted cuter pets."

Makes sense.

We return to the hallway just as Red and his team rejoin Jimmy—their designated watchman in the hall.

"Anything?" I ask.

"Clear," Red says.

Grizz closes the door behind them. "Emptier than the Vatican's lost-and-found for moral high ground."

"Another storage room?" I ask.

"Ayuh," Red says. "All used up. Mostly empty shelves and open floor. No signs of trouble."

"Same," I tell him. "Good to go."

I nod and point to the last two doors before the bend ahead. "Same teams. Same plan. In, out, then we move on."

"Unless someone finds something," Ethan says.

It's already been said, so no one argues the statement or bothers agreeing. We just start moving to the next set of doors.

Ethan's got ants in his pants, his stride small, his steps quick. With every new door we open, he grows a little more nervous, but this is a bigger leap.

I catch up to him. "How are you feeling?"

"Fine," he blurts. "I'm fine. Why?"

"Sensing some nervousness," I say.

"If I wasn't nervous, you should be worried."

"Mm," I say. "Except—"

"After this room, we're going around the corner to a part of the facility where you saw something alive."

"Didn't actually see it," I say.

He grunts in frustration. "I just...I want this day to be over."

"At our current rate, how long until we're out of here?" I ask, knowing he'll have already done the math.

"You mean if we find nothing everywhere?" He asks. "About six hours. Sun will be down. But that doesn't account for any... trouble. An actual time is impossible to predict."

"Right," I say. "We can't predict a single thing, and worrying doesn't change the past or the future. So let it go and try to focus on what's in front of you."

"Yes, sir," he says. "Makes sense." He stops and takes hold of the door's handle. Waits for Tali and Marit to take their positions behind me.

Across the hall, Red and Grizz stand on either side of the door while Jimmy aims his weapon back the way we came, making sure no one sneaks up on us.

"Breach," I say, and both teams charge through their doors, Red and I leading the way. I wave my hand over the light sensor, but nothing happens. The vast room, four times the size of the office spaces we've found, is lit by large flatscreen monitors, though. Each of the nine workstations lined up on the left, right, and back walls holds between four and six of the monitors, some turned sideways and full of white text on black screens. Other monitors are decorated with a collection of pop-culture, movie, and anime desktop backgrounds, some of which are animated.

Doesn't take a Sherlock-like intellect to conclude that these stations are usually occupied by young people, and not just men. There's enough pink Kirby, Hello Kitty, and *Barbie* movie memorabilia spread around the room to assume that at least some of the people who work here are women.

Colorful LEDs flash from inside the computer cases mounted to the underside of each desk. Looking at the floor, you'd think we were at a dance club. It's all very...nerdy. Geeky? I don't know what smart, techie people call themselves these days. But I recognize their territory. Despite all the monitors and flashing lights, it's not very bright. The black walls and ceiling keep light reflections to a minimum, and the retro-styled thin rug on the floor reminds me of an '80s arcade.

"Smells like computers in here," Marit says.

"No duh." Tali says. "Wonder why that might be."

"Tal," I say. "Do me a favor and send Ethan in again."

"Ten-four," she says and heads for the door, leaving Marit and me alone for a moment.

"Hanging in there?" I ask her.

"Colt, you being sexist?" she responds.

"What? Sexist? I just care— I want to make sure you—"

"Whoa there, Captain Kangaroo," she says, putting a hand on my cheek. "I'm messing with you. I'm good. Thanks for asking. Always nice to know you care."

I flinch when Ethan arrives. He's too distracted by the room and everything in it to notice Marit remove her hand from my cheek.

"You asked for me?"

"Odds on getting into one of these computers?" I ask him.

"Give me a minute," he says, stepping toward the nearest computer. He quickly looks over the background, the knick knacks, and decoration. Doesn't bother sitting down to try something. He just moves onto the next workstation, and the next, moving around the room.

With two computers left to look over, he stops, pulls out the chair, and sits down. Taps the keyboard. A login screen appears. He looks around for a moment and I think I spot a brief grin. His fingers fly over the keyboard, and then, he's in.

The computer is running an application I don't recognize. Some kind of interface including text inputs, slider bars, and a series of images. Ethan stares at the screen, brow furrowed. Whatever the app is, it means more to him than it does to me.

"Pro tip," Grizz says from the door, "check the shadows before you go looking for Internet porn. Far-left corner of the room. Raise your fuckin' weapons."

I do exactly as she says, while taking a step toward the corner that Ethan just walked past. If there is something hidden there, it'll need to get through me to reach my people. "Not seeing anything, Grizz."

"Give it a second," she says.

I take another step forward and then see it. A set of eyes opens, reflecting the light of several monitors. Then the eyes close and it disappears again. I could just hose the corner with a full magazine, but that's a good way to waste bullets. I'd rather see what I'm shooting.

"Lights coming on," Ethan says. His voice is followed by a click and then recessed lights around the room glow to life, filling the room with more simulated daylight. Every desk, chair, computer, and half-finished Mountain Dew is lit up, along with the thing in the corner.

"What the fuck?" I whisper, taken aback by the creature's otherworldly appearance that makes Oscar look like a run-of-the-mill animal. This thing...it's an abomination. And now that it's been exposed, the thing is hobbling straight for me.

31

"Oh my God," Marit whispers behind me, but her voice isn't just horrified. She's feeling the same thing I am—pity.

Because it's both horribly disturbing to look at, and painfully feeble.

The creature's limp body drags along the floor behind it. Something like...a ribless human torso of a mid-life man with a hairy beer belly. There are no lower legs I can see. Two stubby arms bulge out from the sides, but they're not moving. The hands, each covered with bundles of fingers, are rigid like two of the three legs on a tripod. The third tripod leg is an actual leg, but it's extending up out of where there should be a head. It's this limb that propels the abomination across the room.

The repetitive thump of the bare foot hopping forward and dragging the body behind it, hits me with waves of energy I find impossible to describe in terms other people understand. It's painful, electric, surging, and uncontrollable. The sensations come on fast and take time to fade. A sudden sound can trigger the feeling, but anything audible can trigger the response if it's also charged with emotion.

Takes me time to figure out what I'm feeling when it comes to my own emotions, but with other people, emotions radiate around them, allowing me to read a person without ever seeing their expression.

Or in this case, without being able to find a face.

I take a step back.

"Boss?" Tali asks. I can feel her beside me, weapon raised, ready to fire.

My weapon is aimed at the floor. I don't remember lowering it.

I spot the creature's eyes as it shuffles toward me. They're positioned on its bulging kneecap, behind which is what looks like a wobbly, swollen tumor. Despite nothing looking normal, I see its bald eyebrows, lifted high.

Hopeful.

There's no nose, but at the top of this thing's shin…is a pair of smiling lips.

I nearly drop to my knees, and not out of disgust. I'm overwhelmed by empathy for what I think was, or maybe still is, a human being. It's one of the weaknesses of my 'disability.' Empathy overwhelms. It shuts me down. Hard to think. Hard to move. It happens when people unload their burdens on me, as people frequently do to a Sheriff. If the information is inconsequential, no problem. If the person is emotionally involved in what they're sharing, I take that emotion, put it through a centrifuge, strain out the impurities, and then take on a more potent version of what they're feeling. I can hide it most of the time. Doesn't affect my job. But sometimes, I shut down so much that it looks like I'm a cold, heartless prick when the opposite is true.

No one has complained.

People seem to appreciate a sheriff that's 'all business.' I always get the job done, and fairly.

But I don't know how to do that now.

I feel threatened, because this creature's very existence defies everything I know about the world.

But I'm also experiencing its emotions—magnified.

Desperation.

Relief.

Happiness.

I raise my hand out to the others and say, "Hold–" when a three round burst buzzes past my ear. Three holes punch into the front of the thing, the first between its eyes, the second a few inches higher, and the third in the creature's bulging tumor–which then bursts out and back, spattering its limp body with chunks of the same fleshy cells, along with a stew of brain matter and pink fluid.

"Can people please stop shooting things before I get a chance to understand what's happening?" I say between gritted teeth.

I slow-turn to find Grizz, Jimmy, and Red are with us.

Red lowers his Vityaz, confused.

"Was that not... Why are we not shooting monsters now?"

"Because it might've just *looked* like a monster," I say.

"Things that look like monsters generally are," Grizz says. "It's true with predators, too, including men."

"It was smiling," Marit says, surprising me. People don't catch the subtle things like I do. "It was happy to see us."

"What would it–"

I cut Red short with, "It was terrified. Hiding. When it saw we were people, it came right out."

"If it came out because we're people," Jimmy says. "What was it hiding from?"

Red flicks on his safety.

"It's not that I don't appreciate your surprise bleedin' heart, Sheriff, but the moment we go picking our shots while shit like this is running around, someone's gonna get hurt, or killed. And I don't think you want that on your conscience."

"He's right," Ethan says, crouching over the very dead monstrosity. "Something like this... It shouldn't be alive, even if it disagrees."

He catches me off guard. Ethan is an animal lover. Always took him for a gentle soul. But there is no doubt in his voice.

"What makes you say that?" I ask as non-combatively as I can, but I'm still coming down from the connection I felt to the creature just before I watched its misplaced face and head implode.

We cluster around the body. When I notice no one is watching our backs, I say, "Grizz?"

"On it," she says, returning to the door, covering the hallway while we gawk at another dead thing that shouldn't exist.

"Killing it was the right thing to do," Ethan says. "Because... it's not *real*."

"Looks pretty real, my man," Tali counters.

"What I mean," he says, and I get a sense that he's holding back anger. "Is that this creature, along with the others we've seen, were created inside NovaGen." He motions to the scattered multi-sized cells. "This resembles nothing in nature. That thing might have been mimicking life, but it was not alive. Neither was that camel."

"Dufresne?" Jimmy asks.

"Probably not," Ethan says.

"Why would some be recognizable animals and others..." Marit motions to the corpse. "...like this?"

"They were newer," Red says. "This bastard was, what do you geeky types call them? When something isn't quite finished, but you need to real world test it?"

"A beta test," Ethan says.

Red snaps his finger and points at Ethan. "Yes. That."

"Beta testing is more of a software term." Ethan looks back at Red. "And this…this is closer to an alpha," Ethan says. "Camel was closer to a beta."

"And after that?" I ask. "A finished version?"

Ethan stands, no longer interested in the creature. "Probably couldn't tell the difference between them and the real thing."

"Until you cut 'em open," Jimmy says.

Red squats on the far side of the body, but he's not looking at it. He's looking at Ethan. "There a reason you're so…informed?"

The answer that comes isn't directed at Red, it's directed at me. "Because I know what they are."

32

Ethan stares back at six sets of blank stares.

"Say what, now?" Red says, percolating toward anger.

"Easy," I tell him. I'm equally curious, but Ethan is one of my people, and I will not abide threats, even if it's just his tone.

Ethan tilts his head toward the computer he accessed for a moment. "To be clear, I don't know what they are exactly. Just... how they're made."

I stare at the screen, still displaying the lone application. "You got that from a few seconds of looking at software? I know you're smart, but—"

"The interface is close to universal these days," he says. "Might be a new application, but the principal features are ubiquitous."

"Principal features are ubiquitous, huh?" Red says, and then to me. "He always speak in another language?"

"All the time," Tali says. "It's one of his most annoying habits."

Ethan sighs. "I meant—"

"I know what you meant, kid." Red steps toward the computer. "Just fucking with you." He leans forward looking at the application. "Now, what the hell are we looking at here?"

Ethan sits down at the workstation, framed on either side by Red and me.

"It's a generative AI interface," he says.

"Okay, I'm actually not sure what that means," Red says.

"Right now, out in the world beyond Alaska, where technology has surpassed the late 1980s, AI—that's artificial intelligence—has advanced to the point where people can communicate with large language models."

"English," Red says.

"Large language models are computer programs that think and can hold conversations. They can code. They can write. They can do math better than any of us. Basically, they have access to all human knowledge available on the Internet, for better or worse. In addition to LLMs—large language models—there are also AI generative applications. Generative means it can create something based on user inputs."

He points at the computer screen, circling the text box. "This is a text input where you would describe what you want using language. It's called a 'prompt.' Every generator is different, so you might need to be very wordy and specific. Or perhaps very brief if what you're generating is a very well-known or non-complex subject. The technology to do this with images, music, voice, and video has existed for a few years now, with varying degrees of success. In some cases, generations might *look* beautiful, but not actually represent what was requested. When you request an image of a teddy bear sitting in a chair holding balloons and you get an image of a bear in the woods standing with a clown holding a balloon, that's bad 'prompt adherence.' Another generator might have good prompt adherence and give you exactly what you want, but the result will have no sense of style or aesthetics."

"I get it." Red wiggles a finger at three boxes with image icons, and three with video icons.

"What about these?"

"Visual references," Ethan says. "Looks like this uses both images and videos." He highlights one box at a time, navigating the software like he's used it before. When each box is highlighted, a word is displayed. Ethan reads them aloud. "Visual prompt, Stylization, Organic Reference." He quickly highlights the video options, revealing that they share the same labels as the images.

Red motions to the slider bars. "And these?"

"Uh," Ethan says. "They're sliders that tell the generator specific preferences. There's some common stuff, like coloration, prompt adherence, creativity, fidelity. Things like that. But...there's some less common elements here. Entropic State. Skin texture. Personality. Intelligence... That can't be right."

Ethan lowers his hand and his head, descending into an internal monologue that I know from experience could last minutes. We don't have that kind of time.

"Deputy," I say, snapping him out of it. "Prompt adherence."

"Yeah," he says.

"Would that also cover errors?"

"Things that aren't supposed to be there?" he asks. "Sure."

"What about too many of something that *is* supposed to be there?" I ask.

"Like a leg for a head," Jimmy says.

"Yeah..." Ethan says, pondering. "But that's...that's more of an—"

"Artifact," I say, remembering his earlier lesson. "Which is common in... What did you say? 3D printing."

He nods. "That's right. That's exactly right. Errors in 3D prints *and* AI generations. Artifacts have nothing to do with adherence and more to do with a lack of information about what's being requested. If a database doesn't contain all the necessary information to assemble an image accurately, it will attempt to extrapolate the information, or simply duplicate blocks of information to fill in the gap."

"And that could result in extra fingers," I say. "Extra eyes. Artifacts."

Ethan looks at the dead creature. "But that's not what happened here. This is more like an early generation. Ignoring the fact that this was...alive...I've seen images just like it. Just a mass of body parts. It's the kind of thing that was common when text-to-image generation was new. You might prompt for 'Jennifer Love Hewitt riding a dolphin'—don't ask why—and get an image of a chimeric mass of body parts merging the dolphin, surfboard, and something that might have been JLH before being doused in lava."

"I'm sorry. Am I hearing what I *think* I'm hearing?" Marit looks back and forth between me and Ethan. "Are we meant to believe that this thing..." She thrusts a hand toward the corpse. "...was generated, based on a prompt and maybe some images or videos someone input on one of these workstations?"

"It would explain the strange physiology. The intricate space-filling polyhedral cells. I—I don't know."

"Space-filling poly-what?" she asks. "You know what? Don't care. Printed living things. It's what we're thinking, right?"

"Only thing that makes any kind of sense to me," Tali says. "I mean, it makes no sense at all, but I trust Ethan. If it makes sense to him, I'm willing to suspend my disbelief and attempt to grasp science that is beyond my comprehension. Like the fact that life exists at all. Makes no sense. It's mathematically impossible. Impossible to replicate. You know, life from nonliving elements. But here we are." She looks at Ethan. "Am I right?"

He nods.

"So, why not living things created based on prompts or whatever?" Tali says. "Impossible, right? But we're here and shouldn't be. That thing shouldn't have been alive, either. Shouldn't exist. But it's lying right next to us."

"Works for me," Grizz says from the doorway. "And honestly, who gives a shit? Are there fucked-up things living inside NovaGen? Yes. Are some of them killing people? Looks that way. Can we kill them? Confirmed that twice now. So how about we stop with the existential crisis bullshit and get a move on? People are dead or dying and we're here to stop it, not to understand why or how it's happening."

"If you know the enemy and know yourself," Ethan whispers, as he jots down observations in his small Field Notes notebook, which he carries everywhere.

Then he adds, a little louder, "You need not fear the result of a hundred battles."

"Don't you Sun Tzu me, boy," Grizz says.

Ethan is surprised. "You know Sun Tzu?"

Grizz screws her face up. "What? Of course not. I was just bullshitting. That was *really* Sun Tzu?"

"Knowledge is power," I say, translating the saying on Ethan's behalf.

Ethan stands from his chair, pocketing his Field Notes. "Understanding what we *and* our enemy are both capable of gives us a strategic advantage." He pushes past Grizz and steps into the hallway, triggering the white lights. "Not all of us can swing a couple of knives and manage to kill a bear."

Grizz points to Ethan while looking back at me with a befuddled expression. "He forget to take a tampon out or something? Got toxic shock syndrome?"

"Don't give him a hard time," Red says. "Kid is smarter than the rest of us, and he's not wrong. We've gotten lucky so far. If NovaGen was dreaming up living things and *creating* them? Any of you *been* on the Internet? Can you even imagine what kind of fucked-up shit people would bring to life if they could?"

"*Weird Science*," I say to myself, but Red hears me.

"That's just the beginning of it," he says. "Look, I hope I'm wrong, but if they've jumped from the mash of shit we just killed to that camel, or even better..."

He drifts for a moment. Looks like he's recalling the past. Shakes his head. "If that's what we're dealing with here...speaking from experience...we need to put away all concepts of reality as we know it. The human imagination is the most depraved and dangerous force on the planet. It gave us religions that slaughter in the name of God, weapons to kill and torture, and devices capable of ending all life on the planet. And that's just the beginning, kiddies." He nudges the creature's limp foot. "This thing might not be the worst thing that's roamed these hallways." He makes eye contact with me, and before I get the chance to look away, he adds, "Not even close."

33

"I don't mean to spook you all, seeing as how you're all quietly brooding instead of pulling your shit together..." Grizz stands in the hallway, weapon raised to the left of the open door. "...but our friend is back. End of the hall. Can't see anything, but the lights are on around the bend."

I'm the first to join her and don't waste a moment. "With me," I say to Grizz. She's by my side a moment later, weapon raised, looking down her sight, same as me. We're just thirty feet from the bend and there are no doors on either side.

"Tali," I say, knowing she'll have followed me, "Keep it tight." Then a bit louder, I say, "Red—"

"Already watchin' your back, hoss," he says. "Got the kid, Jimmy, and your gal."

"Do yourself a favor," Tali says to me as we approach the bend ahead. "Never call my sister 'your gal.' Not that you would, but—"

"Tali," I say.

"Right."

She goes quiet, stowing her nervous energy. Just before we follow the turn to the right, the illuminated hallway ahead goes dark. Whatever was here has left again.

Ahead of us, the lights shift from white to green, one segment after another. As they go, Grizz says, "Correct me if I'm wrong, but the lights would shut off, one after the other, at the same speed as whatever set them off ran away. Does that make sense? Rate of light change to speed ratio. Something like that. You know what I'm trying to say, yeah?"

"Yeah," I say, and she's right. Each cube of hallway is shifting to green so quickly that it's a smooth fade down the long hallway. Whatever triggered the lights was moving fast. I imagine myself running down the hallway at the same speed.

Impossible, I think, *for a human.*

For a normal *human.*

Who knows what NovaGen created-people could be capable of.

Like the last hallway, doors line either side. Looks like there might be a junction halfway down, a branch heads to the right, toward the level's core space. The last section of hallway to turn green is just past the junction, right in front of a door on the right side of the hallway.

That's where we're heading.

I glance back at the others, slowly catching up, their backs to us as they scan the hallway behind us for trouble.

"Hey," I say, and snap my fingers. "We're moving. Watch the doors as we pass, but do not open, and do not approach. Our visitor entered a room two hundred feet away. I intend to pay them...or it...a visit. If it's a person, we will have a heart to heart." As the second group catches up, I add, "Everyone copy?"

Nods and 'yeses' all around.

"Red, Jimmy, watch our six," I say. "Grizz and I on point. Rest of you know what to do."

A little more comfortable in the facility now, and eager to find out what's been spying on us, we make good time moving down the hallway. All the doors are closed. Probably not locked, because nothing appears to be locked, but if a door opens, it'll be easy to spot. With all sides covered, it would be hard to catch us off guard.

Part of me hopes we'll find the rest of this place devoid of life. No bodies. No monstrosities. When the snow lets up and the roads are passable, it can be the State's problem. Or the Feds'. Or whatever shadowy government agency is funding this science fiction shit show.

The excitement of finding the camel has long since faded, replaced by events that will likely require therapy to get over. I'm no stranger to therapy. Did my time after Anya passed. But the nearest therapist is an hour drive, and I'm not a fan of losing three hours a week to talk about feelings I can't really articulate.

"Slow it up," I say as we approach the branch on the right.

I swing around the corner, finger on the trigger. But there's nothing to shoot. The hallway is just twenty feet long, ending at what looks like a bank vault door.

"That new?" I ask Red as he rounds the corner.

"Afraid not," he says. "Two on each floor."

"What'd they keep in there?" Jimmy asks.

"Nothing you want to know about," Red says.

"Because it's scary?" Jimmy asks.

"Because the people who will kill you for knowing are just as scary," Red says. "Not sure you'd believe me, anyhow."

"Ain't nobody here," Jimmy says. "'Sides us. Who's gonna know?"

"Not here to get people killed," Red says, and then turns to me, "Suggest we don't try opening that door or any of the others."

"Good reason why?" I ask.

"Nothing good needs to be kept behind a door like that," he says, and I don't disagree.

"Is there a way to see what's inside?" I ask.

"Observation room," he says. "Glass is strong enough to take a direct missile strike without cracking."

"And how do we get there?" I ask.

"Right through..." His pointed finger lands on the door we're heading for. "...there."

"Well, fuck," Grizz says, "that's not forebod—"

The sound that intrudes on Grizz's words is subtle, which means everyone else, with their normal neural pathways, completely misses it. At the same time, the squelch rams into the side of my head, sending a pulse of adrenaline spiking fight-or-flight instinct into the inside of my skull, where it reflects and amplifies through my entire body.

Catching everyone off guard, I shout, lift my weapon, and nearly fill Grizz with a dozen bullets.

But I don't fire.

At Grizz or anything else.

Because there isn't a monster in sight, and Grizz...

Something is wrong with her.

Is she looking at the ceiling? Can't see her eyes. Arms slack, her fingers unfurl, dropping one of her knives to the floor.

"Grizz," I say. "What—"

My voice catches in my throat with a hiccup that sounds like it came from a four-year-old.

Because I haven't been this scared since then.

Because my mind instantly shuts down, overwhelmed, pushing my fight deep, *deep* into flight.

Because Grizz's face folds inward like an abandoned clay pot on a spinning wheel.

34

A small portion of my still-functioning mind registers embarrassment at the sound that comes from my mouth. It's quickly overwhelmed by revulsion unlike anything I've experienced in my life, even with my hyperactive sensory processing issues. I'm sent through a neurological spiral that careens straight past my lowest point and attempts to drag me into a white-hot hell of misfiring nerves.

I'm not sure how it happens, but I find myself sprawling to the floor. On a normal day, my system gets flooded by more adrenaline than the average person. Throw a monkey wrench into my day, or even just jump-scare me, and my adrenaline spikes to the point where my muscles shake, and my skin starts to burn. If stress remains high for an extended period, all bets are off.

Panic attacks. Jolts of painful energy. Micro-twitching. Hypersensitivity to stimuli. Even the gentlest breeze causes extreme pain. It's a nightmare that once kept me in bed for two months, unable to shower or wear more than a pair of boxers.

But that hasn't happened since I met Anya and moved to Raven's Rest. Her calming presence soothed my nervous system. The way she spoke. The way she understood. Even the colors she chose for the apartment walls. All of it was calming. I spiraled after she passed, but managed the symptoms with Tali's and Marit's help.

But Raven's Rest...the quiet life...has remained a dependable salve even after her passing.

Most days are quiet. My life has never been in danger. And I sure as hell haven't seen a person's face fold in on itself.

The otherworldly horror struck me like a missile, punching past all my defenses and destroying the dam that holds my symptoms in check. Panic takes root. My body pulses with unleashed sensory experiences that turn every sound, smell, and touch into a buffet of suffering.

As a result, I have the team's full attention. Not one of them has turned to see what caused my reaction. I scramble away until my back slams against the vault door.

People are talking, but it's just a mass of warbling sounds, striking my head like a giant bell lowered over my head, being struck by some kind of hammer-wielding Norse monster.

"Be—" is all I manage to get out, but it's enough.

They stop talking.

Marit and Tali are crouched on either side, neither one of them touching me.

"Go ahead," Marit whispers.

It takes all my remaining self-control to rein in my body. When I speak, it feels like my teeth are being pulled, each subtle movement pulsing waves of energetic pain through my whole body. I manage to gasp out three syllables.

"Be—hind you."

There's a moment of stillness, then everyone turns and finds Grizz standing alone in the hallway, her head and face flopped over to one side. Blood pours down her legs and flows over her boots, pooling on the floor, spreading out like a slow motion shot of a fiery shockwave created by a civilization destroying asteroid strike. Her body, locked in shock, manages to stay upright for another two seconds, during which no one makes a sound.

Face-to-face with the impossible, even neurotypical people get overwhelmed.

Then Grizz topples toward us, striking the floor with enough force to cause several gut-wrenching effects.

Her bearskin jacket, soaked with blood, strikes the well-lit white floor, an oversaturated paint brush slapped against a canvas. Blood splatters in every direction, coating boots.

The gaping wound in her back, visible through her split open jacket and clothing, reveals that her spine, skull, and possibly ribs have been yanked from her body. The kinetic energy of her body striking the floor pushes up through her, splitting her back open fully and shoving her insides out.

An overcooked Hot Pocket.

The thought nearly makes me throw up.

Marit is the first to look away. She makes eye contact with me, tears on her cheeks. Seems neither of us was really made for this kind of bullshit.

Red, on the other hand...

"Everyone!" he screams. "Into the room!"

"How do we know—" Jimmy says, gasping for air. The man accustomed to gore is torn up, voice shaking. "It could be in there. Whatever did that."

"I was watching the door," Red growls. "Whatever it was..." He steps through Grizz's spreading blood. "It came from somewhere else." He aims his weapon toward the ceiling like he can see things that have been covered up. When his weapon lowers to the wall behind where Grizz had been standing, he goes still and says, "There."

"I-I see it," Ethan says, hands on shaking knees. "A hatch. Razor-thin seam. Wouldn't be able to see it without the, ahh—

blood." He motions to the wall where a set of *six* bloody fingerprints have slid across the wall before ending in a straight line—where they entered the hidden hatch.

"Last chance," Red says. "Move now or I leave you here."

Marit's hand on my arm...feels normal. An oasis of calm surrounded by a sensory overload typhoon. "Can you get up?"

I nod.

I know I can move. It'll just hurt. A lot. In a way I wish I could explain to people. But how do you explain something they've never felt? It'd be like a shark trying to make a human understand what it's like to sense electric fields. There is very little common ground.

"Can I help?" Tali asks, her hand offered.

Not wanting to appear weaker than I already have, I shake my head and force myself up onto shaky legs. "Go." When neither of them moves from my side, I shout, "Go! All of you! Go now!"

My voice cracks but it gets people scrambling past Red and into the room. I follow them, slipping and nearly falling in the blood. Leaning on the wall for support, I follow Marit to the end of the short hall, heading for the next entrance. Before I can continue, Red grasps my shoulder hard enough to hurt—and not in a neurological way. Just straightforward pain.

"You cracking up on me, hoss?" he asks.

"Little bit," I admit.

He gives a nod and says, "Can you get your head straight?"

"Fifteen minutes," I say.

"Not sure we got fifteen minutes," he says. "And if you're having a breakdown—"

"Fifteen minutes, and then I'm good for another six hours."

"Pharmaceuticals?" he asks.

I nod.

"Enough to share? 'Cause, between you 'n me, my heart's about to burst. I've seen some shit, but that—" He glances down at Grizz's body. "That takes the fucking cake. Worse because I knew her. Hell, I *liked* her, and that's a rare thing."

"It's okay to hurt," I tell him. "No one will think less of you."

"Don't care what people think," he says. "Care about my head being clear so I can shoot when I need to—and not miss. So, I'm asking again. You got enough to share?"

"I do."

He releases his grip on my shoulder. Gives me a pat. "Good on ya." With a gentle shove he directs me toward the door and backpedals in, behind me. As he closes the door, I go for the lights. There's a motion sensor, which appears to be broken, but there's a manual switch beneath it. I flick it on, and turn to the right, coming face-to-face with another one of NovaGen's creations.

35

My finger twitches on the trigger of my Vityaz, but recognition keeps me from splattering Dufresne's insides across the wall. The little guy looks down at the weapon in my hands, then back up to me. Looks offended, like he knows I just nearly killed him. He lets out a squeak, leaps onto my shoulder, over Tali's head, and into Jimmy's arms.

"Oh, dude. I didn't think I was going to see you again," Jimmy says. Dufresne squeaks, nuzzling into the man, milking him for more affection.

Manipulative little thing.

"Clear the room," Red grumbles.

The space isn't large. About the size of the average classroom. There are several standing workstations. Only one of them holds a laptop. Marit tries to start it, but it's dead. The rest of us move through the room, searching around counters, trash and recycling bins, two comfortable looking chairs, and a loveseat. The lighting is white, like in the hallway, but it's not overly bright. This was a place to relax. To work without pressure.

The back wall is covered with lockers that someone put a lot of effort into designing in a futuristic way. The gaps between them are black, but the doors are white and punched out in a smooth swoop. They look like flashy PC towers, but when I open one, I'm surprised by two things. First, it's unlocked. Second, the contents include a six-pack of poison in the form of Monster energy drinks. There's also a notebook and a well-worn baseball cap.

Looks more like the inside of a high school locker than something belonging to a scientist at a high-tech research laboratory.

I take out the notebook and flip through the pages. It's full of sketches. Creatures. Monsters. Some of them are very human. Others look inspired by *The Thing* or HR Giger. None of them are impressive from an artistic perspective, but they're meticulously labeled with measurements. Reminds me of my D&D notepad from high school, but instead of measurements, I had attributes listed.

For some reason, the locker's very normal contents ground me. My pounding heart slows. My hyperactive senses cool off a bit. My thinking straightens out. I'm still a sperm cell's existential sigh away from full-on sensory overload, and I need some medicinal support to keep my nervous system in check. A heightened sense of fight-or-flight can come in handy—the CIA recruits people with that quality—but when my unfiltered mind is pushed beyond human limits to process the deluge of information, I'm useless. Anything beyond breathing feels out of reach.

With that in mind, and my torso blocked by the open locker door, I dig into my pants pocket and take out a Ziploc bag. Inside are three pills. Often times, just knowing I have them is enough to calm me. But there are occasions when I have mercy on my nervous system and slip a pill beneath my tongue. Helps me socialize. Helps me deal with past trauma, including Anya's death. And in this case, helps keep me from descending into an abyss of neurological agony. Not a fan of drugs in general, but I appreciate this one.

I slip it under my tongue and take a second pill from the back. I break it in half and then into a quarter. I pocket the rest and close the locker door. Red is beside me, inspecting another locker. "Anything?"

"Clear," he says.

"We're good," Ethan says.

"Anybody think to lock that door?" I ask, pointing at the entrance. Tali is there a moment later, engaging the lock, which appears strong enough to keep the average person at bay. But something strong and fast enough to debone a human with one quick yank... I'm not sure the lock will do much more than let us know it's coming.

While everyone explores the room, I step up to Red and press the pill into his palm.

He looks at it with a raised eyebrow. "A quarter?"

"Hits hard the first time you take it," I tell him. "If you took a full pill, you'd be communing with God while the rest of us ran for our lives."

He doesn't believe me. "How much you take?"

"Full pill," I say. "Over time, you build a tolerance. Have to take more for it to work."

"So, you won't be speaking in tongues or nothing?"

I smile. "Full pill brings me down to normal. Won't even notice it. You... You'll probably be nicer than ever."

"We'll see about that," he says and tosses the quarter pill into his mouth. "Now, where the fuck are we?"

"Looks like a staging area," Tali says. "A place to relax. To work. To store personal distractions or items you might not want to bring."

"Bring where?" Jimmy says.

"You said this used to be an observation deck? For the larger space at the facility's core."

"I don't see a wall of glass," Marit says, inspecting a vase of drying flowers.

"Used to be bigger," Red says.

Dufresne leaps from Jimmy's embrace, bounces across two tall, round tables before clinging to a bookcase and scrambling to its top. He squeaks and bounces, baring his teeth and slapping his little hands down.

"You don't..." Jimmy says, looking at me with wide eyes. "You don't think he can *read?*"

"No more than you can," Red grumbles, heading for the tamarin. He looks over the bookcase as Dufresne settles down. "Doesn't mean he isn't trying to tell us something."

Red gives up his search. He snaps at Ethan. "Young'n. Come use your good eyes and flexible back to give this thing a once over. Look for anything that's off."

"Like a book that opens a secret door?" Ethan jokes.

"Exactly like that," Red says.

Ethan gets to work, and Red sits on a tall stool. Puts his head down on his folded arms. He's checking out, at least until a door opens or the pill kicks in.

I join Marit and Tali at the closed door. "You should move farther back. Might need time to aim and shoot. Standing in front of the door makes you easier to...I don't know...grab."

"Disassemble," Tali says. She sounds hopeless. Don't blame her. I feel like the odds of any of us making it out of this place alive have dropped by half. Not only is there some kind of super predator roaming the halls and secret tunnels of this place, but our strongest and best fighter was dispatched with the ease and speed of a mouse in the quick crunch of a lion's molars.

As we back away from the door, Marit touches my arm. "How are–"

"Fine," I say, feeling embarrassed.

"Don't look fine," she says, holding my gaze.

She sees right through me. Am I outwardly calmer? Sure. Masking my comfort level and emotional state might be the two things I'm best at in the world. But she's not buying the act, probably because she just saw me break down.

Tali knows it when she sees it but understands the practice. In a modern world that pressures everyone to just be themselves, that doesn't hold true for those of us that are clinically different. I hide myself to communicate in a way other people understand. To prevent me from accidentally hurting people's feelings. To not look weird and incompetent when I'm in a position of authority.

Marit guides me to one of the two comfortable chairs. I start to object, but Tali says. "I got the door. You two do your thing."

Not sure what she means by that, but I stop thinking about it when I sink into the comfortable chair. I want to spend the rest of the day right here. Marit squats in front of me. She's shaken up, but she still manages to smile at me. I jump when she takes both of my hands in hers.

"I know things are hard," she says, and my insides dissolve. "I know you're hurting. I know you're heartbroken. I know... everything about you."

She's managed to bring tears to my eyes. "Not possible."

She smiles for real now. "I wanted you to know, that no matter what comes next, no matter how painful or confusing it is...I got your back."

There was a neat little bow over the part of my life I'd boxed away. She's just pulled the string. While keeping myself from outright sobbing, I manage to ask a question. "How?"

"Anya," she says quietly. "She told me about you. About this—" She squeezes my hand the same way Anya used to. "She told me what to say. Said that if things ever got really bad for you, that this would help, that you'd know that whatever you were facing, you weren't doing it alone."

I wipe my eyes, glancing around to confirm no one is watching us. "Why would she assume you'd even be around to tell me?"

"Because she knew me, too." She shakes her head. "Anya didn't miss much. She never felt threatened by what I saw in you. She saw the same thing. Honesty. Loyalty. Kindness. Among men, you're a rare find. We both knew that. And before she... you know...we talked about it—her idea, not mine. Point is, she approved of...of how I feel about you, and didn't mind the thought of you sharing those feelings. Said she'd be relieved if she knew that this, that we would, you know—"

I'm more confused by what I'm hearing than I was by the one-legged slug person. "She...approved..."

"Encouraged," Marit says. "And she told me about your..."

She's trying not to say it aloud, trying to respect that I've kept the diagnosis hidden from the world for a long time.

I give her a break and say the word for her. "Autism."

"That," she says. "I know it's not something you're happy about people knowing, but she thought it was important for me to know, and to understand why you might need support if something like—" she tilts her head toward the hallway where I broke down. "—that happened."

"Then...you're just saying what she told you to say?" I ask.

"Words without action are worthless," Marit says. "I *do* have your back. I have *had* your back. And you know I mean that, because you also know that I love you. Same as Anya."

A wave of nausea moves through me, and it has nothing to do with Marit's revelation.

I can feel it. The thing. It's getting closer, the feeling of extreme discomfort increasing.

"I'm sorry," Marit says. "Did I–"

I hold a finger to my lips and look to the ceiling and whisper. "It's above us."

Marit goes still, our hands clasped. "How do you know?"

I close my eyes and focus on the array of overwhelming sensory inputs, attempting to suss out which of my currently hyper-agitated senses is feeling a presence. "It's... I can feel its *emotions*...radiating through the ceiling."

"That's... Okay. What is it feeling?"

"Hunger," I say. "Hate." I release Marit's hands and take hold of my Vityaz. "Rage."

36

Pretty sure Marit thinks I'm a bowl of crazy with a side of fucked, or that I'm so desperate to avoid what she's just told me that I'd pretend to feel the emotions of something on the other side of a wall, or in this case, a ceiling.

Whatever is above us does me a solid, though, by tapping a claw three times. Sounds like a knife being stabbed against metal.

It's testing the ceiling, I think. *Looking for a way through.*

The tap is followed by a loud, nails-on-chalkboard kind of screech. The sound makes my teeth hurt, but it also communicates raw frustration. It wants in.

"We have company," I say, but everyone already knows that. The only person not aiming a weapon at the ceiling now is Ethan. He's still hard at work, searching for a way to open a secret door that might not exist. I watch him for a moment. Of us all, he seems the calmest. Afraid, for sure, but it's not the kind of wide-eyed terror the rest of us are feeling.

Because he knows something we don't.

The way out.

While he watches the ceiling along with everyone else, his hand moves to the second shelf down, one he's already looked over. With a quick flip of a hidden panel, he reveals a small keypad, fingerprint reader, and a button. He taps in a four-digit code and presses his index finger against the reader. A small green light blinks. He presses the final button and closes the panel.

Well.

Shit.

The bookcase slides back into the wall behind it.

Ethan closes the panel and is about to announce his achievement when I make unflinching eye contact with him. There is one sure-fire way to know I'm pissed at you—my glowering eyes remain locked on target. One of the few things capable of overcoming my general inability to maintain eye contact for long is righteous anger—the kind felt by the God of Israel before reducing the people of Sodom and Gomorrah to piles of ash. I only know the story thanks to Anya, who once made a project out of describing my stink-eye. She had a few other good comparisons, but I always liked the idea of reducing bad people to pillars of salt. Hardcore.

Ethan knows he's busted, but a new set of ceiling taps—closer to him—pulls his eyes from my gaze. "Got it," he says, but his voice sounds like the raspy last breath of a person passing on. He clears his throat and repeats himself louder. "Got it!"

Without missing a beat, Red says, "Go, go, go!"

Jimmy is the first through, followed by Ethan and Tali. Marit pauses before leaving, inquisitive eyes looking me over. I give her a nod and she steps through the open doorway.

Red puts his hand on my arm, stopping me from following. "Hey, hoss."

"Yeah?"

"You okay?"

"Fine."

"Don't bullshit me," he says. "You just went through a roller coaster I wouldn't wish on any man. Panic attack. A confession of love. A betrayal."

I huff a laugh. "You don't miss much."

"Don't miss anything," he says, and looks up as claws are dragged over the ceiling above us. "Now, you and I both know there's no way that thing is getting through that solid steel ceiling—the one hidden behind these fancy white panels."

"You sure?" I ask.

"Unless it's got green acid for blood, we're good—until we leave—and we will need to leave. So, let's sort some things out before rejoining the others."

"You sure they're safe in there?" I ask.

"Safer than we are in here."

"Why do you—"

"Because that's the front end of the observation room, probably hidden away as a kind of safe room. And because your man seemed plenty confident that he'd have nothing to worry about on the other side of that door."

"Mm," I grumble.

"He going to be a problem?"

"Don't know," I say, trying to wrap my head around the various scenarios in which Ethan would know where to find the hidden panel, know the four digit code, and have his fingerprint stored in the security system. I can't come up with a single reason that keeps me from knocking him on his ass.

"You want me to—"

"He's my problem," I say.

"Understood," he says. "Now...are *you* going to be a problem?"

"I'm good," I say. "Meds are kicking in."

"Same," he says, "and thanks for that, but what I mean is...a beautiful woman just professed her love for you. And while you might have been saved from having to reply, you and I both know that the feeling is mutual."

"Red—"

He holds up his hand. "You've been keeping an eye on all of us, which I appreciate, but you've spent twice the amount of time keeping an eye on her, even *before* your little chit-chat. Now, what I need to know is, will she be a distraction? I don't want any happy-tappy feelings dulling your edge."

"It won't," I say.

"Because..?"

"I got more to live for than I thought coming into this," I say, "and I would die before letting anything happen to Marit, or Tali. Maybe even you."

He nods. "Good enough."

Three loud gongs reverberate above us.

"It's frustrated," I say, and then reverse the line of questioning back on Red. "How about you? Grizz was a friend. Reckon that was…hard to see."

He grunts. "I'll mourn the dead when I'm sure I won't be one of them. Until then, I'm not above vengeance."

"Then we're on the same page," I say.

He gives me a sidelong grin and steps through the door. I follow close behind and am confused by what I find on the other side. The others haven't moved far beyond the entrance, and all of them have their hands raised. I lean to the side, looking around Tali's head to see why they're all standing like hostages at a bank heist—a black, 10mm Sig Sauer P220, powerful enough to drop a person with a single round to any part of the body. And it's pointed at Marit's face.

37

"Easy." Hands raised, I slip toward the front of the group, putting myself between the gun and Marit. "*Easy*. We're here to help."

The woman is frazzled. Her black hair had once been tied back in a tight bun, but half of it has fallen out. She's tall and slender. Has a Michelle Pfeiffer thing going. Glasses. A power suit, but it's untucked, disheveled, and spattered in blood. Reverse engineering her look in my mind and combining that with our present location—a secure and secret safe room—I'm pretty sure we're talking to the person running the NovaGen facility.

"Name's Colton Graves," I tell her. "You know it?"

She nods but is shaking. "The Sheriff."

"That's right, ma'am," I say reaching for her weapon. "We're here to help."

"H-help?" She's confused. "But how..." She glances at Ethan. "Why?"

"Dufresne," Jimmy says, pointing to the tamarin on his shoulder. The small animal lets out a squeak and leaps away.

"I don't understand," she says, allowing me to take her weapon. She stumbles back a step and sits in one of four chairs positioned at workstations lining the glass wall, of what was once Red's observation room.

There's nothing to see through the glass. It's covered by a metal shield. "How did—"

"The tamarin left the facility," Ethan says. "Inside a camel—"

"With fucked-up eyes," Jimmy says. "Like twenty of them on one side of its face."

The woman huffs and shakes her head. Looks at the tamarin. "I didn't think he'd even make it out, let alone bring people here. To the safe room." She holds out a hand to Dufresne, who leaps onto her arm and scrambles onto her shoulder where he begins playing with her hair.

"You *sent* Dufresne out for help?" Marit asks.

"He didn't have a name at the time," she says, "but yes. And since he made it out, I suppose the name fits."

"You see?" I say, motioning to the woman. "A cultured movie goer."

"Read the book, actually," she says, starting to relax. Good. Tense people tend to keep more secrets. And that is something I am *not* in the mood for.

"Movie was better," I say.

She smiles. "So I've heard."

I sit down in one of the other four chairs and swivel it around, so I'm face-to-face with the woman. "Now that we're friends, you mind giving me your name?"

She straightens herself up a bit and sits taller, slipping back into whatever role she'd been filling before she became the survivor of whatever the hell is happening here. "Dr. Anika Voss."

"Nice to meet you, Anika," I say, using her first name as a personality test.

"Dr. Voss," she says, "if you don't mind."

"Not at all," I say. "What was your position here?"

Her forced smile drops away.

"Why do I feel like I'm being interrogated?"

"What was it Sun Tzu said, Ethan?" I ask, glancing at him. "Know the enemy and know yourself?"

"Knowledge is power," Jimmy says, imparting his recently acquired catchphrase.

"I'm not your enemy," Voss says.

"From what I've seen so far, you are the lone survivor of a slaughter carried out by the biological, living, 3D prints your people have been generating." I lean back and cross my arms. "That makes you a person of interest, at best. At worst, you're responsible for all of this. So, sure, call this an interrogation if you'd like. We can be pals, or I can play hardball. That's up to you. Either way, you *will* be answering my questions."

She keeps a stiff upper lip for a moment. No doubt this is the first time she's been on the receiving end of authority—or any kind of oversight—for a long time. Then she deflates. Her life is on the line. I don't need to tell her that. She wants to live. To achieve that, we all need to live. And for *that* to happen, we need to know what we're up against.

"What do you want to know?"

"For starters," I say. "I'd like to know how long Ethan has been working for you."

"Ethan who?" Voss asks.

"What are you talking about?" Tali asks, before reeling around on her fellow deputy. "Ethan?"

"Ridiculous," Voss says. "We do not hire—"

"You can stop," Ethan says. "He knows."

"Knows what?" Tali asks, pissed now, getting in Ethan's face. "Knows. *What?*"

"He works for NovaGen," I say. "Knows his way around the software a little too well. Didn't dumb himself down enough on subjects he shouldn't know anything about. Was too worried about the woman normally manning the reception desk, who I'd bet this Vityaz, is his significant other. And...he used his fingerprint to unlock this secret door."

"You're a turncoat?" Tali asks Ethan.

"A spy," I say.

"Give me a reason I shouldn't bring you back out there and handcuff you to the wall," Tali growls. "Let that thing kill you next."

"What thing?" Voss asks, suddenly nervous. "Did you see it?"

"Later," I say. "For now..." I turn to Ethan. "Talk."

He leans his head back, looking at the ceiling. "I was a senior bio-engineer with NovaGen for the past five years." He lowers his head and continues. "Fifteen months ago, I began a relationship with Mandi—"

"The receptionist," I say.

"The receptionist. Yes."

"And..." Voss says, now on the side of the interrogators.

His shoulders sag. "And I told her things that I shouldn't have."

"Things he was forbidden to tell anyone," Voss says.

"I'd signed an NDA," he says. "To not be fired, NovaGen told me to join Raven's Rest as a resident. Keep my finger on the pulse of the town. Make sure no one was poking around the facility. A month later, the Sheriff's office had an opening—"

"And you doctored his credentials," I say to Voss. "Let me guess. You were the woman I spoke to on the phone, who gave him a glowing recommendation?"

"One of my better performances," Voss says.

"But...he knows procedures," Tali says. "He's...he's a good officer. How—"

"Quick study," Ethan says. "Police work isn't bioengineering. No offense."

"Offense!" Tali says. "Little prick."

"What are we going to do with him?" Jimmy asks. "We can't trust him now. Can't trust either of them. This shit is just asking for a cover-up, and we're the people who will need to be covered up."

"Not wrong about that," Red says, standing at the center of the room where it looks like Voss has been camping out. He's staring at the window, or rather, the metal barrier covering it. "But that's a problem we can solve later."

"Why later?" Jimmy asks.

"Because we need them now," Red says. "Because there might be other survivors. And as much as I'd like to leave this place with my head and spine intact, I also made a pact a long time ago that I wouldn't let history repeat itself. Seems I've failed in that regard, for the most part, so I'll be damned before leaving anyone behind."

"Not everyone made that pact," Jimmy says. "I didn't sign up for this."

"He's right," Marit says. "It's not his job to be here. Mine either." She turns to Jimmy, "but we're here, and we both know that we're not getting out alive without the others."

Jimmy grumbles and walks across the long room, sitting down in one of the two remaining chairs. He slams into the backrest and the chair's front end lifts off the ground.

As it falls back, Jimmy doesn't shout or move. He just takes the hit, mutters, "Fuck," and stays in the chair, lying on his back. Then he turns to Voss.

"This secret room have a shitter? I've been clenching a nervous dump for the past hour."

Voss points to a door at the back of the room. Looks just as sturdy as the others but it's hanging open.

Jimmy slides to the side, his legs clunking on the floor. Then he's up and headed into the bathroom, closing the door behind him.

I'm about to continue my line of questioning when Voss asks Red, "You were here? During Project Adver—"

"Hey!" Red snaps. "Do not say that fucking name. Not here. Not ever."

Voss isn't concerned about the outburst. She's more interested in the confirmation his reaction revealed. "You *were* here. But... I thought—"

"The site was cleaned?" Red says. "It was, along with every person on the project. All but one."

"Will you tell me about it?" Voss asks, intrigued to the point where all her fear about the current predicament has faded away. "I've always wondered–"

Red cocks his head to the side. "Do I look like someone who'd walk down memory lane with the woman responsible for repeating the sins of the past?"

"Just... I think I know what they were trying to do," she says. "Based on the name. But I've always wondered if they–if you–succeeded."

"Lady," Red says, "black budget secret ops don't clean a site for fun. You might find that out for yourself soon enough. Moment I tell you anything, you'll find yourself on two separate hit lists."

"I'll take that risk," Tali says. "If there's anything else about this place that might still be a danger, we have a right to know."

Red looks at me. I just shrug. Have a hard time seeing how something from Red's youth could possibly affect us in the here and now.

"I'd also like to know," Marit says. Her interest could be authentic, but it's just as likely that she's being a good sister. I've seen them back each other up without any real knowledge of what's happening. Sometimes with me. More often with unruly bar patrons.

"Suit yourselves," he says, turning back to the glass. "We were...conjuring demons inside prisoners with life sentences."

He turns back to the four of us, sees our shocked faces, and rolls his eyes. "The US government has done worse." He looks to Voss. "Guessing they still are, yeah?" He doesn't wait for a response. Just hitches his thumb to the giant window, and says, "Open it."

39

To say I'm overwhelmed is like calling a rectal exam a romantic couple's spa day.

Demons.

Printed lifeforms.

And Grizz… The image of her face folding in on itself replays in my mind over and over as I try to make sense of it. I see her again…her body sagging downward with no spine to hold it up. Her weight shifts forward and she falls.

I clench my eyes tight, willing myself to think of anything else.

Flowers.

The Swiss Alps.

I can still see her falling.

Shit, shit, shit.

Marit. Last night. Before everything went sideways. At Raven's Rest. We sat by the fire, sharing a drink and a few laughs while Tali covered for her at the bar. I didn't think anything of it at the time. We'd spent a lot of time in that exact spot, telling stories, joking, but that night…last night…there was something different. The way she looked at me. I told myself it was the flickering firelight on her face, but I knew.

It wasn't the first time I'd seen the look in her eyes. But it was the first time I *understood* the look and felt the weight of it. Everything after that was guilt and denial, the latter of which has been eradicated over the past few hours—a counterweight to all the horrors that began with the appearance of that camel. Part of me wishes I'd never seen it.

Screw NovaGen… I think there's a saying about playing with fire that would apply here. Everything I've seen and heard about what they were working on is just beyond stupid, and light years away from common sense.

My thoughts have come full circle, from the grotesque to Marit and right back to NovaGen, sans the image of our dissected friend. The mental journey ends at a single question: *Why?*

The answer to that question is obvious. NovaGen is taking government-funded science to its inevitable end—warfare. The people here might not be personally interested in creating killing machines. People who dream up future tech often have good intentions. But good intentions don't fund sketchy research. The government does. The military. DARPA? I don't really know. Wouldn't be surprised if Voss didn't know. But I can't think of another reason a smart person would be stupid enough to prompt a computer system to breathe life into something capable of deboning a human being faster than J. Wellington Wimpy can down a hamburger.

All these thoughts race through my head in the time between Red's request—more of a demand really—that Voss open the windows, and her reply.

"No," she says. "Not yet."

"Why the fuck not?" Red asks.

"Because I want you all to understand," she says. "Before you see…"

"Because we might decide to leave you here?" Tali guesses.

Voss is honest.

"Yes."

"Don't care about your motivation," Red says. "As for leaving you here...the dildo of consequence rarely arrives lubricated."

"Lovely," Voss says. "But you also don't have a choice." She shoots a quick glance at Ethan, but it's enough to convey a strong message.

Open the window without my say so and you're fucked.

My thoughts on Ethan are a mixed bag. I'd like to leave him here with Voss. Let them deal with Red's unlubricated dildo together. But...I'm pretty sure I know him. The real Ethan. He's a good kid working for a black op and was doing as ordered. He wasn't here for whatever went wrong. Seems just as shocked as the rest of us. He might have been a spy, but I'm pretty sure his friendship hasn't been an act.

At the same time, he's still fearful of not obeying his actual boss.

I don't bother bringing any of this up, because it sounds like Voss is about to give us some answers. I'm sure she'll disinfect the details to help placate us, but knowledge is power, right? Ain't going to hurt us to know more, before or after she reveals what's beyond the window.

"Let her talk," I say. "Don't have time to debate."

"Thank you, Sheriff." Voss straightens out her disheveled clothing. "Before...this..." she motions to everything around her. "NovaGen was a small company. Just five scientists including a biomedical engineer, cell biologist, mechanical engineer, a chemist, and me. I have doctorates in neuroscience, computational biology and bioinformatics, and biophysics." She pauses, waiting for us to be impressed. But there's no validation incoming, so she continues. "We operated on a budget partially covered by my credit cards. For three years, my garage served as our laboratory."

"Not interested in a sob story," Red says.

Voss closes her eyes, takes a deep breath and eases it out. "I wrote a paper titled 'Prompt-Guided Bio-Printing Will Be a Reality in the Next Decade.' It was published in *Nature Biotechnology*, a highly respected scientific journal. I hoped it would get enough attention to generate grant interest. Instead, I got a phone call asking me how quickly prompt-guided bio-printing could be perfected if I had unlimited resources. I told them three years, despite having no idea. There are plenty of people researching bio-printing. At Harvard. LighTec. ExoGen. Manifold. Hell, even L'Oréal. But none of them had even considered printing at such a customizable level. And neither had I before writing that paper.

"But the concept... Its applications were easy to see. Need a heart? Input the age, sex, size, weight, and DNA sample of the person needing a transplant. Two hours later you have a fully functional, rejection-resistant organ ready to transplant. They understood that...and had ideas of their own. I'm not above moral compromise, and I saw no other viable path forward, so I agreed.

"The next day, I had a blank check, a laboratory, and some of the best minds in bio-printing ready to start working for me."

"What was your price?" Marit asks.

"I told you," Voss says. "A *blank* check. I'm not sure there is a limit to how much we could spend. And no, I don't know who's writing the checks. Don't care to know. Because with their support, we made staggering strides even faster than I promised. We achieved organ growth in the first year. Living organisms by year two. And this year, we began closing in on their goals."

"Which are?" Ethan asks.

Seems even *he* wasn't aware of this endgame.

"Bio-weapon development," Voss says.

"Like Anthrax or something?" Jimmy asks.

Voss shakes her head. "They were after something more... visceral. Soldiers that could operate non-stop without food or water, that would instill terror in our enemies, that were beyond lethal with a variety of field applications. Soldiers that didn't have families. That wouldn't be missed. That could be replaced in a day."

"Bah," Red says, waving his hand at Voss. "She's just trying to save her skin. She's not above moral compromise. Said it herself. Can't trust a word of it. For all we know she's a Mengele wannabe. Our very own Angel of Death. Lord knows we have more Nazis in this country every year. No reason she ain't one of them."

"I am not a Nazi," Voss says.

Red huffs. "Said every Nazi post-war. The allies roll in and suddenly they were all *forced* to commit genocide. We gave those assholes jobs, too. Got to the Moon because of them."

"This from the man who claims to have helped possess inmates with demons," Voss says, one eyebrow lifted.

"Difference is I never claimed to be innocent. I'm guilty as fuck. But I am here to pay my penance. Maybe find a little redemption while I'm at it. Score some bonus points with the big guy upstairs before I kick off, which is looking more and more likely to be today."

Red cracks his neck one way and then the other.

Not sure if it's meant as a threat, but hearing his vertebrae pop is intimidating. "Since you're not explaining how they work, how to kill them, or anything else that might be useful to anyone aside from yourself, I'm going to ask you one last time to open that shielding—or I'm going to put a bullet in your leg."

"That wasn't really a question," Tali says, not realizing that he's deadly serious.

And I'm not going to stop him. Because he's right. If she's the brains behind this horrible place, I can't trust her any more than I could a hungry Great White shark at a pool party.

"And if that doesn't work..." I draw my pistol and chamber a round. "I'll shoot the other."

Voss is incredulous, but folds. "Have it your way."

She turns to a workstation, and hits Alt-Control-Shift-O. The large slab of metal splits down the middle and begins peeling apart. The space on the other side is vast—and full of bodies.

40

"If your goal was to recreate Hieronymus Bosch's vision of hell in reality," Marit says, voice as flat as her expression, "well done."

"Heronmush Borsch?" Jimmy says. "Is that like a Russian thing?"

"A culture thing," Marit says, stepping closer to the window. "This is...this looks—"

"Familiar," Red says, standing beside her, looking over what I think looks like a battlefield.

I won't admit it, but I have no idea who Hieronymus Bosch is, either. If we survive, I'll be Googling the name. Until then, I'm seeing the scene through my own lens...which resembles the aftermath of a battle in Zack Snyder's 300. It's not just the scattered dead; it's the literal walls of bodies. At first, I thought it was a kind of artificial terrain, but the mix of human skin tones is impossible to ignore. There aren't any weapons to speak of. No clothing. Just bodies.

And despite the mostly human looking skin...they are anything but human. Many resemble the twisted nightmare we encountered in the computer lab—a hodgepodge of body parts. Creatures whose existence was pain, and who didn't stand a chance against whatever happened here.

Others look built for war. Some are the size of a rhino, with rough armor-like skin. Others are sleek and built for speed. Some have bones protruding from their bodies—horns, claws, blades. Killing machines.

Aside from being dead, they all have one thing in common: deformities.

Artifacts.

Extra limbs, eyes, fingers. Some are subtle, but others are the stuff of nightmares. Bodies assembled backward. Arms, legs, tongues, and eyes completely out of place. Fractal limbs sprouting hands with elongated digits from which more hands grow, again and again, forming a lattice of fingers that more closely resembles an Afghan blanket of flesh.

A few of them appear to have been multiple organisms in one, each facing a different direction, like they were trying to run away from each other. And not all of them are human. I see pigs, I think. A slew of other unidentifiable creatures. They look... horrified. Their lives, short as they might have been, would have been a tortured existence.

Near the window is what I think was meant to be a woman. One side of the torso appears normal. The other side looks like a purple crayon left too long in the sun. But none of that is as disturbing as the deformed face with two sets of overlapping teeth, three sunken eyes, and a small three-fingered hand, stretching the skin between her legs.

And that—that is enough for me. I turn my back to the window and am surprised to find that I'm nearly the last person to do so. Only Red and Ethan are still looking. Red maintains his stoic mask.

Ethan has tears in his eyes. He turns to Voss, who isn't looking through the window at all. "How? *Why!?*"

Voss crosses her arms.

Red is far from amused. "Lady, I'm debating putting a bullet in your leg for fun. Don't think for a second that if you're not as forthcoming as my grandmother's dog to the scent of an unwashed crotch, I won't follow through on my earlier threat."

Voss glances at me and finds no help in my gaze.

"Fuck's sake," she whispers, rubbing her forehead, and then shouts, "What makes you think you could even understand? Bunch of roughneck hicks from a backwoods town." She thrusts her arms out at the group of people risking their lives to save hers. "Look at you! A depressed autistic Sheriff that lives at the station to avoid his confusing feelings. To make matters worse, you don't even understand what's wrong with your nervous system. Autism doesn't do what you experience. Not on its own."

I'm not here for a doctor's visit, but I can't help but wonder just what the hell she's talking about.

She shakes her head like she's disappointed in me. "Remember that tick bite? The one that left you with Lyme and Bartonella? You ever wonder what the lingering neurological effects of those nerve-fraying diseases might be? You even consider what they might do to someone whose nervous system is already oversensitive?"

That my sensory processing issues are more severe than the average autistic person's, and far more severe than they were ten years ago, isn't much of a revelation. But the potential root causes—Lyme and Bartonella... In hindsight it seems obvious.

"*Tsk.* This is embarrassing, honestly. I know more about you than you. Than all of you." She turns on Tali. "Like you. Poor deputy Nuluk, who desperately wants a woman to share her bed—I believe you prefer blondes—but won't do herself a favor and move to San Fran—*boof!*"

Voss didn't see me approach.

Didn't register my hand whooshing through the air.

But she sure as shit feels my open palm clapping the side of her face. She sprawls and slides across the floor. She lies there, dazed. Doesn't see me coming again. But she snaps back to reality when my Vityaz's muzzle presses hard into her thigh.

"Hey," she says, and I press harder until her face shifts from angered to pained. "Stop." When I don't listen to her, she looks up to Ethan, "Stop him!"

When Ethan doesn't budge, I smile at her, and it's not the happy kind of grin. It's the variety that communicates I'm not only willing to leave her here, but I'd be *glad* to. It goes beyond righteous anger. Justifiable menace.

"Ethan," I say. "Is there anything she can tell us that you can't?"

He's in the doghouse, too. Voss knew details about us that she shouldn't, including Tali's sexuality, a closely guarded secret and the trigger for the colossal slap. She knew about my autism, too, despite Tali being the only person I'd told about it until a few minutes ago. Suppose Voss could have been listening to us in the other room, but it felt like old news to her. We can address that later. Ethan's not on Team Voss, and right now, that will do.

"I can explain the science," he says and looks out the window. "But I'm not sure about all of this. I could make an educated guess. Probably hack into her account. See who she's been talking to. What she's been working on."

That breaks Voss a little too fast.

"Fine! Fine. Now take your—"

I lift the pistol away before she can finish her demand. Don't want her to think I was obeying an order. I stand and don't offer her a hand. "Start talking. I will not negotiate the terms of your survival again. You are either with us, or against us. You will tell us everything, or you will not leave this room. If you lie, and we find out later, you will be left where you stand. You get me?" I ask.

She climbs to her feet, straightens herself out, and walks to a mini fridge. When she returns, Voss has an ice pack wrapped in a paper towel pressed against her cheek. She might be in pain—I hope she is—but I see the ice pack for the manipulation it is.

"No one here cares that you're hurt," I say. "You will not find a bleeding heart among us."

There is a momentary squint of defiance in her eyes. A sneer on the edges of her mouth. A crinkle in her nose. Her disgust rams into my gut...and my self-control crumbles, this time enough to concern the others. My hand snaps to her throat, lifting enough of her weight off the floor that I can drag her across the room and slam her against the wall. I get in her face, squeezing.

"I watched the face of my friend collapse in on itself today! I watched her body compress and then fall to the fucking floor! Because one of your creations tore her spine, ribs, and skull from her body."

"Colt," Marit says. Sounds worried.

"Let him," Red says.

"Understand this, Anika, I *hate* you." I squeeze tighter. "Your degrees do not matter. Your employers do not matter. Your noble purposes do not fucking matter. You are nothing. You have no voice. No authority. All you have is my mercy. If I even get a whiff of superiority or manipulation from you..."

"Hoss," Red says, a whisper in my ear. "Ease up." I'm about to argue when he says, "Not that I blame you, but she's about to join the demons that used to call this place home. And if that wasn't clear enough, you're killing her."

My eyes clear and I see her face, purple and starting to go slack. My hand yanks away from her neck. She slides down the wall, gasping for air. I turn away from her and head toward the window.

I give Marit an apologetic look. "Sorry."

She doesn't look happy, but Tali gives her arm a smack. "Don't you dare. He did that for me."

Marit is confused. "For you?"

Tali wraps me in a hug. With her face against my chest, she whispers. "That bitch outed me."

Marit's eyes lock onto mine. "Is that true? *That's* what triggered you?"

I kiss the top of Tali's head. "I'd do worse for both of you." I slip out of the hug and continue toward the glass. "Probably will, sometime today I reckon."

Voss can wait until she recovers. For now, I want to know how these things function, and the best way to kill them all. I snap my fingers and point at Ethan. "You. Science me."

41

"Everything?" Ethan asks.

"Even if you think I won't understand," I say, "and if I don't, find a way to dumb it down for us plebians. Don't care if you'll get in trouble. Don't care if you signed an NDA."

"Yeah...okay."

He stands beside me, looking at the sprawling carnage filling the octagonal space at the facility's core.

The walls are ruddy, covered in pipes, ventilation shafts, other mechanical systems I don't recognize, and puddles of the goo that fills the artificial cells inside NovaGen's creations.

"Everything I told you in the computer lab is true. Text to biological, living tissue. It's a novel idea and, as we've seen, not outlandish...from a scientific point of view. Most of the people here came on board for the positive reasons Voss gave. Generating organs. Building a bacterium that could safely eat our garbage. Things like that. Bettering humanity. That's what we were pitched, along with high pay. I doubt anyone turned down the offer, even after finding out we'd be stationed in Alaska and have almost no contact with the outside world.

"The only time I heard about large bio-printed lifeforms being created was in regard to Manifold Genetics. They wanted to develop a living humanoid...thing...that could quickly adapt to any environment, including those instantly lethal to human beings. The plan was to send them to other planets. Explore where even robots couldn't. But Manifold has kind of a nefarious reputation for pushing ethical boundaries. That's why they have labs outside the US.

"So, this– These more complex lifeforms..." He lifts his chin toward the hellish view. "...they're new to me, and *not* what I signed up for."

"Not the time to be pleading your case," I tell him. "And again, science me. How does it work?"

He takes a deep breath. "You asked for it. The creatures are biomimetic constructs designed by an AI-driven morphological synthesis which controls the 3D bio-printing. Its anatomy is based on a Weaire-Phelan foam structure, composed of cartilaginous lamina cells–the thin, flexible layers of cartilage that form the interconnected chambers. The cells. These chambers are filled with hemogel, a viscoelastic substance, the goo, which functions as a hydrogel-like medium and facilitates nutrient transport and structural flexibility." He looks over at me. "Following me?"

"Keep going," I say. A few of the technical terms are beyond my vocabulary, but I'm getting the gist.

"The bones are bio-printed using a hybrid of calcium phosphate and collagen-based materials, mimicking natural bone composition. They provide an anchor for the cells, helping to prevent collapse and gravitational degradation over time. It's all held together by skin–same as us–but can take many forms depending on the density of components used in printing. But the basic...ingredients are, a collagen matrix used for tensile strength and elasticity, keratin layers, which in high density form rough, protective layers. Chitin and Chitosan infusions can also be used for more of an armor. It's the stuff that forms the exoskeletons of animals like insects and crustaceans. Elastin fibers provide stretch and recoil. Bio-composite layers, a blend of polymers and biomaterials–"

"What are those?" Jimmy asks.

"I'm sorry," Tali says, "is that really the first question you've had this entire time?"

"What?" Jimmy says. "Hell, no. Just figured I'd ask one now, so I didn't have to ask them all later."

Ethan shows a hint of a smile. For all of Voss's superiority complex, Ethan seems to genuinely like us. "Bio-composite layers are composed of things like hyaluronic acid for hydration, or calcium phosphate for rigidity. That help?"

Jimmy huffs. "Can't say it does."

"Do you really want me to keep going?" Ethan asks me.

"Never know what you'll need to know in the future, so I might as well know everything."

"Hearing isn't the same as knowing," Ethan says.

"Then I'll just have to try extra hard to keep you alive," I say.

Ethan frowns. "Right. Well…back to the cells, then. The foam forms a network of soft actuators. Each one can contract or expand thanks to embedded bioelectrical stimulation nodes."

Tali gives me a nudge and whispers. "I've got one of those at home."

I resist smiling.

"Contraction occurs with the myo-cartilage layers, driven by electrical impulses–"

"Like when we plugged the leg in," Jimmy says, showing he's understanding at least some of what we're being told.

"Uh-huh," Ethan says. "Cell expansion is achieved by hydrostatic pressure inside the cell. Inside the goo. As for the printing…I think you all get how the prompting works, but after the prompt is sent, the AI system uses a generative adversarial network to create a digital 3D model. From there, the user can make modifications but, as with all AI generative creations, artifacts will occur until the technology is perfected. The model is then used to create bio-printing instructions for every single layer of tissue, cartilage, and bone."

"That's all peachy," Red says, "but it only explains how they created flesh bags of living material. What *guides* them? What do they have for brains? Are they instinctual? Intelligent?"

"Self-aware?" Marit asks.

"Their brains…aren't like ours," Ethan says. "They're a mix of bioengineered neurons and synthetic materials, printed layer by layer. They don't need oxygen or glucose because they're powered by things like light or vibrations, kind of like solar panels, but it doesn't even need to be sunlight. The neural circuits are pre-designed by the AI to handle the task ahead. There's no fluff like emotions or memories unless…" He turns to Voss, still seated on the floor, looking defeated for the first time since we saw her.

Welcome to the club, asshole.

"You didn't let them program *memories*, did you?" Ethan asks her. "Or develop personalities? For God's sake, please tell me they weren't messing with consciousness."

Voss's silence is confirmation, and it hits Ethan like that wrecking ball grown up Hannah Montana was gyrating on.

"How bad is it?" I ask.

Ethan paces twice. "Look, Colt, these brains are designed to cut out all the complications that come with being a human being. But they can be prompted to feel things like love, kindness, ambition, greed...bloodlust. That was never a stated goal, but it's possible, and now that I know they were meant to be weapons...I understand why this possibility was developed. Listen, these brains ...they're low maintenance, high efficiency powerhouses with perfect recall, and they have the potential...if requested by a prompt engineer, to be more intelligent than any of us, and designed to work in ways that our minds never could."

I turn to Voss, trying to word what comes next like a contract lawyer, so that there is no mistaking what I want to know. "First question that will dodge a bullet: was this done? Did you allow to be created, or create on your own, a creature or creatures capable of human intelligence or greater?"

Voss stares at the floor. Not sure she heard me until she looks me in the eyes and says, "Yes."

"Which one?" Red asks. "Creature? Or *creatures?*"

"In exchange for the funding, laboratory, and staff that allows us to pursue the positive goals I founded NovaGen for, our... Our investors required the development of intelligent bio-printed soldiers, capable of coordinating and adapting on an active battlefield. Lots of moving pieces. Capability to predict and subvert enemy actions. The ability to act autonomously to achieve mission objectives, even when communication with command is cut off. That is what they wanted. What they eventually demanded. And the threat to my life, should I not comply, was just as visceral then, as it is now. So, yes. Crea*tures*."

She pushes herself up to her feet.

"But that's not the real problem." She hobbles to the window, looking out at the mass of bodies NovaGen created. "The real problem...the one that's going to prevent any of us from leaving here alive? That's Clio. The smart one."

"How smart?" I ask.

"Clio is more intelligent than anyone in this room," Voss says, "even though she can't speak, and has some deformed neurology. What makes her dangerous is that she is *enraged,* and she's printing an army of her own. What you see here...is weapons testing. At first, ours. Now, hers. Each one pitted against another. Working out the kinks. Using her efficient mind to solve problems we couldn't, testing each one in the real world. On each other. On us. And now, on all of you."

42

"This is the point where we say, 'fuck it' and leave," Jimmy says. "Right?" He looks from me, to Red, to Ethan, and then back to me. *"Right?"*

Dufresne reacts to Jimmy's anger by leaping away with a high-pitched squeak. He doesn't bother jumping to another person. Just heads to the floor and starts rummaging through Voss's supplies.

I'd love to agree with Jimmy, but... "How many other people are still alive?"

It's subtle, but Voss's expression flattens to hide the truth. Too bad for her, reading people's hidden emotions is kind of my superpower.

"No one," she says. "After the first attack, things spiraled quickly. I was the first to reach the safe room and no one followed. Communications were lost not long after that, but I watched most of them die..." She motions to the death and dismemberment. "...in there. It was horrible."

"Yeah," I say, and turn to Ethan. "She's full of shit. Find out if there are survivors."

"The security systems are down," she says, emphatic now. "I'm telling you, everyone is—"

"Shut. The fuck. Up." Ethan taps keyboard keys a lot harder than is necessary. "Boss," he says, speaking to me. "I could brute force my way into her account, but that would take more time than we want to spend down here. A password would be helpful."

I turn to Voss, letting my direct, focused attention communicate a threat.

She purses her lips, probably wondering if we are willing to spend the time brute forcing our way into her account. Guessing she somehow forgot about the whole shooting her in the leg thing. I remind her by pointing my submachine gun and firing a single round. The bullet buzzes past her head so closely that if she'd sneezed, she'd be dead. The monitor beside her shatters into pieces.

Voss flinches away, shouting, "God damnit! Fuck!" She turns to Ethan and says, "Ain't No Hollaback Girl."

Tali snorts.

"Sorry. Just didn't expect a Gwen Stefani reference."

"First letter in each word is capitalized. Replace 'I' with 'number one' and 'a' with the 'at' sign." Voss looks close to breaking down now, and I don't think it has anything to do with her creations. She's probably crossing every flexible part of her body, hoping that we don't discover anyone has been killed.

"In," Ethan says, working his way through various systems.

While he does his thing, Marit approaches me. "Hey. Sorry I didn't get why you Mike Tysoned Voss right away. Honestly, I should have done it myself. Point is, thank you for watching out for my little sis."

"I can hear you," Tali says, singsong.

"We all can," Red grumbles, "and I'm telling you right now, I do not understand how you all can talk about your feelings when the walls of shit this place is built from are crumbling down around us."

"You're fighting for revenge," Tali says. "Or justice, or guilt, or whatever. We're fighting for each other."

"We'll fight for you, too," I tell him.

He gives a grouchy laugh, leaning over Ethan to watch his progress, or maybe keep an eye on what he's doing. I trust far too quickly, but Old Red doesn't trust anyone.

Jimmy raises his hand. "Hell, if it'll keep me alive, I'll be on Team Lovefest. Just no—"

"Shit," Ethan whispers.

"Speak," I say, stepping up beside him, opposite Red.

"She's been using the internal chat to speak with survivors. Two of them. Seth Dalton and Trisha Nkenge." He blows a sharp breath. Guessing they were his friends. Gonna be hard on him. "Trisha is on level two. Seth is...*shit*... He's on level five."

"What's wrong with level five?" I ask.

"Level five is the bio-printing hub. If this 'Clio' is still churning out BioCons—"

"BioCons?" Jimmy asks.

"Needed a term to call the bio-printed organisms," Ethan says, "because bio-printed organisms, lifeforms, or creatures is a bit clunky."

"We call them NeoForms," Voss says.

"If only your opinions mattered," Red chimes in, and then nudges Ethan. "Continue. Survivors. Life and death."

"Point is, level five could be crawling with BioCons." He looks to me. "If someone is down there..."

"I'm wearing my big boy boxers," Red says. "We'll find a way. What's on level five?"

"Computational core," Ethan says. "Server farm. The ambient temperature down there helps keep things cool."

"You're saying that the shit we need to destroy in order to stop production is on the *bottom* floor, which also happens to be where fresh BioCons are being printed?" Red asks. "Fantastic."

"What do you care?" Voss asks. "So what if we all die in here and they keep killing each other?"

I answer before Red can. "There is a town full of people at the bottom of this mountain whose safety is my responsibility. You might look down on them. Might think they're not worth saving, either. But if there is a way we can keep the hell you created contained in this facility, I'm going to damn well make it happen."

"Just seal off the top floor," Voss says.

Red chuckles.

"Seems the demons never left this place." He looks at me. "There is a second way out of the facility. Warehouse at the rear of level five opens to the mountainside. And I'm willing to bet my fetus in fetu twin's left nut, she knows that. Maybe hoping that the BioFucks find their way out and kill everyone in town, so that when the site is wiped, and it will be, no one alive will ever know it was here."

Voss's silence speaks volumes.

"What's on level three?" I ask.

"Please God, tell me you left level three alone," Red says.

"What is on level three?" I ask.

"Ghosts," Red says, "if you believe in that sort of thing."

"And if I don't?" I ask.

"Ashes," he says. "Of the dead. Level three has an incinerator. Vents to the surface."

"You think they left the dead—"

"Why bother moving them," Tali says, "Right? This place is already a tomb."

"Uh," Ethan says. "So, level three. A lot of it is sealed off, but some of it was converted into sensory pods."

"Say again," Red says.

"Sensory pods," Ethan says. "Some of the spaces are dark and black. Some are like lush gardens. All relaxing, low sensory environments where those of us with sensory issues can lower our anxiety, calm our nervous systems, things like that."

I don't miss his use of 'our' and 'us,' but Red beats me to a response.

"Back in my time, all a man needed was a quick wank. Good for another day. Kids today—"

"I don't think it has anything to do with their age," I say, looking at Ethan, evaluating him in another way.

He gives me a nod. "Takes one to know one."

I shake my head. "How many employees had…sensory processing issues?"

"Fifteen," he says.

I'm not sure why but hearing that stokes my anger. People are people, so it shouldn't matter, but it's not hard for me to imagine the havoc all this chaos would have wrought on a nervous system, long before death. At best it would have been a distraction. At worst, it could immobilize. Make them easy targets. Right now, on the outside, I might look normal. On the inside, my nerves are on fire, locked in a state of hypersensitivity that is sending waves of micro-twitching through my limbs.

Ethan scrolls through a chat stream, top to bottom, the number of participants gradually shrinking. Not hard to imagine why.

"Trisha says she saw Cynthia Gregory enter one of the sensory pods early on. If she locked the door, she might still be safe."

Ethan keeps scrolling.

"Trisha is in a closet on the second floor. Seth…says he's inside a half empty server cabinet, concealed by cables. Apparently, no BioCons have even entered the room."

"They're protecting it," Tali says. "Making sure no one ends the party too soon."

"Okay," I say, "We are no longer clearing floors. Ethan will take us to the survivors, and we'll gather any that are alive. We will then proceed to level five, destroy the server farm—"

"Blow the shit out of the warehouse exit," Red says. "And do the same above. Leave the BioCon assholes for the cleanup crew."

"You're all insane," Voss says. "You'll be killed like all the rest."

"Correct me if I'm wrong," Red says to her, "but your people weren't armed to the tits and carrying enough C4 to bring down a skyscraper."

"Wait, what?" Ethan says.

I watch Red, waiting for the answer.

He grins and opens his jacket. What I thought were layers of clothing for warmth turns out to be a vest covered in thick bricks of C4, wired up and ready to blow.

Well, shit. We checked the cases for explosives…but didn't think to search Red.

"Well," Marit says, "she was right about one thing. At least one of us is insane."

"Madness liberates the soul that reason binds," Red says, stepping away from the group, pondering something as he investigates the area.

"Won't they… Isn't Clio smart enough to know that we'll be taking the stairs?" Marit asks. "We'll be walking into a trap no matter what floor we head for first. We'll be bottlenecked, right? Compressed into a small area. Easy to kill."

Red huffs. "Not too shabby for a bartender." He gives me a wink. "Try to keep her breathing, hoss. She's a keeper." He turns to Marit. "Everything you said is right, which is why we're not taking the stairs."

"We're not?" I ask.

Voss looks just as confused as I feel. "You're not?"

"Guessing you only got schematics to the retrofitted areas," Red says to her, and then to me. "There are other ways to get around, like mice in the walls, between the floors. You just need to know where the holes are. And how to open them."

Red draws a knife and stabs it into the wall at the room's far end. For some reason, I expected the safe room walls to be solid, but it appears to be standard drywall. He drags the blade down to the floor, then to the left, back up, and then to the right, carving out a rectangle large enough to walk through. He wedges the panel out with the knife and steps aside as it falls to the floor, revealing a hatch that leads into the colosseum of death.

"Why would you want to go out there?" Voss asks, looking at the hatch, confused and afraid.

He smiles back at her, hand on the hatch's handle. "Because out there... Out there is our way down." He nods to Ethan. "Find anything labeled 'Adversary' that has an engaged lock, say a prayer to whatever God you believe in, and disengage the locks."

"That sounds like a bad idea," Ethan says.

"Kid, bad ideas are all we've got left," Red says.

Ethan looks to me for confirmation.

I give him a nod and say, "Do it."

43

"How sure are we about this?" Tali asks, voice low. "Like on a scale between George Clooney as Batman to Linda Hamilton as Sarah Connor."

"I liked both of those movies," Jimmy whispers.

"Jessica Alba as Sue Storm," Ethan says, hand hovering over the key that will unlock anything associated with Red's Project Adversary and open a hatch between the safe room and the coliseum full of human and non-human bodies.

"Potentially problematic, but who cares because, *rrraow*, Jessica Alba." Tali makes a clawing gesture.

Ethan smiles. "Exactly."

I'm impressed with Tali's capacity for forgiveness, but I don't spend time ruminating on it, or on the veracity of our current plan.

"Open it."

"Don't," Voss says.

Ethan's finger pauses just long enough for him to make eye contact with Voss before pushing the enter key.

Heavy locks *thunk* open—here and throughout the facility. They're loud enough to be heard by anything living on every floor. Red pushes the hatch open.

"You're all fools," Voss grumbles.

"Fools are the ones who think they are wise. True wisdom is found in the man who knows he's a fool." Red has a good chuckle. "Fuck me. I just made that up. Eat a dick, Sun Tzu."

"Now," I say to Voss, motioning to the open hatch. "After you."

She frowns and steps back.

"You can either be our canary, or we can leave you here, bound to a chair," I say.

"I'll take the chair," she says, confident that someone will eventually come for her.

"With the doors open." Red grins, heading for the hatch and stepping through it in Voss's place. He winces as he steps into the coliseum. "Smells like a shit ate a turd and puked it back up. No movement."

"Last chance," I tell Voss, hand on the cuffs hanging at my waist.

She mutters to herself, but gives in. The woman passes me, emanating contempt like a bull elephant secretes musk during mating season, and asks, "Can I at least have my—"

"No," Red and I say in unison.

She hesitates at the open door, reeling back from the stench that I've been spared from thus far.

I motion for Tali, Marit, and Jimmy to follow. As they exit, expressing varying levels of disgust, I tell Ethan, who has just gotten up to follow me, "Close the doors when I leave. Lock yourself in."

"When *you* leave?" he asks.

"Want you here," I say.

"I understand why you wouldn't trust me, but—"

I hold my hand up. "Can you get security back up from here?"

"Not my area of expertise," he says, "but systems like that are designed to not require a genius intellect to—"

"Genius intellect..." I say, trying not to smile. "Yes or no?"

"Yes."

"Get security back up," I say. "Try to connect with the survivors. Need you on overwatch."

"Won't be able to contact you by phone or radio," he says. "I can use the internal PA system, but if Clio is smart enough to disable the security system and prompt for new BioCons, she probably also understands English. And we have to assume she'll know how to disable security again."

"Everything that happens between now and when we leave is a risk we need to take." I rub my chin. "If you find yourself with a spare minute, put that mind of yours to good use and see what you can find out about Clio that Voss might not be sharing. Anything that could help us understand what it wants, or even if it's capable of understanding its own desires. Same goes for Voss. Not sure I believe her intentions with this technology were ever noble."

"Got it," he says, sitting down at the workstation. "You want my ammo?"

"Keep it," I say. "Might need it."

"Yes, sir." His head sags a bit. "Sheriff. Colton…I know what I did—I understand what you must think of me. In case I don't see you again, thank you, for accepting me from the start. For caring. You are the kind of man I always wished I could be."

"Yeah, well, still time," I say, with a nod and a grin that's instantly wiped away the moment I step through the hatch and take a breath. It's worse than I'd imagined, even after seeing the others react. A mixture of blood, vinegar, and a variety of other visceral scents I don't want to think about.

The hatch closes behind me and locks. Ethan gives a wave from the glass separating him from the arena. Dufresne appears on his shoulder, offering a wave of his own. I raise my hand to them and join the others, all of whom—minus Red—are wincing from the smell, noses buried in their jackets.

"Follow the maze to the minotaur," Red says, "or cheat and go straight through?"

Seems a ridiculous question given the circumstances and danger we're facing, but this isn't a corn maze. Pushing through means climbing over bodies.

Marit catches my eye.

She's peeking out of her jacket. Clearly distressed but then tilts her head toward the wall of dead blocking our path forward. "I'd rather climb over the dead than join them."

I appreciate her brutal assessment of our situation.

If there's one thing I value in people, it's straightforward honesty.

"Up and over, it is," I say.

Jimmy is the first to start climbing. The bodies and smell aren't bothering him as much as the others. "I'll try to avoid any people or juicy stuff. Just go where I go."

The wall of dead is piled eight feet tall but is sloped and full of limbs for handholds. Jimmy climbs over long protrusions, like the spines of some extinct dinosaur, using them like a ladder. Gets him most of the way to the top, where he flinches and nearly falls back. "Shit!"

He catches himself, steadies, and takes off his jacket. Lays it over the top. Lets out a sigh. "Dead guy. Caught me off guard. Whoever comes last, just grab my jacket." He leans forward, looking over the far side. "Slide down on the left. Right side has a lot of that goo from inside the bubble cells."

With that, he rolls over the top and drops from sight.

Tali and Marit go next, followed by Voss who doesn't complain, but whose revulsion is stamped on her face. A very long minute later, I'm the last to reach the top. While there, I grab hold of Jimmy's jacket, ready to pull it down behind me, when I catch a twitch of movement.

"Voss," I say. "You sure everything in here is dead?"

"Didn't come out and check pulses, if that's what you mean," she says. "Also, bio-printed lifeforms don't have pulses."

I grunt in response and maintain my position, watching for more signs of movement. "Keep going."

"You heard the man," Red says, hurrying our crew along, toward the next wall of bodies, which is mercifully a few feet shorter than the first.

At this rate, it's going to take another few minutes to reach the room's core, where Red's secret entrance will lead us down through each of the descending floors. He's not pleased about the idea of accessing level three—*at all*—but he agreed this was the most tactical approach since no one in the modern facility even knew of the tunnel system hidden here since Project Adversary.

Just as I'm about to slide down, I catch motion again, but it's on the outer fringe of the coliseum this time, opposite the safe room. A gate, reminiscent of the entrance to Jabba's Palace, grinds upward, allowing our very own rancor to duck its head and step inside.

The creature's general form is humanoid, but its body appears to be composed of several smaller BioCons, bound together by stretched patches of mottled flesh. It's...like a person constructed from hairless raccoons, merged into an entirely new entity—a grotesque Voltron of sinew, overlapping tissues, and plates of armor-like exoskeleton. I count seven distinct components making up the whole.

The pieces move as one, but each part of the thing twitches with individual nervous energy. Just looking at the thing makes the muscles just under my ribs vibrate.

I'm about to scream for the others to run. Our only hope is that we can beat the aberration to the center of the massive space and open the hidden hatch before it can reach us.

My voice catches just as I start shouting. The space where I first spotted motion has come to life as another BioCon squirms from where it was hidden beneath a mound of dead, like a wolf spider waiting to ambush.

And that's exactly what happens.

Before the gate closes, the second creature, low to the ground and flat like a scorpion—with ten limbs, no tail, and an armored back—launches itself at its new competitor.

I slide down the mound with Jimmy's jacket in hand. "Run!" I whisper. "Go!"

We hit the next wall of dead like linebackers protecting a runner passing the forty, thirty, and then—a wall.

The two BioCons fall back in a heap of horrific desperation, each of them scrambling, clawing, and biting, hoping to survive. The savage battle quickly moves from the room's fringes to just a few feet away from the hidden hatch that Red has reached.

He ignores the fight and waves us on. "Move it, assholes!"

Red turns to the floor and finds one of four hidden latches. Pulls it up, and before he can move on to the next, he's struck by a flailing limb.

Red sprawls and topples into a nearby death hedge. Looks like most of the landing was absorbed by the bodies, but Red is not safe. Not remotely. After he rolls to the floor, unconscious from the blow, dozens of eyes, throughout what looks like a cushiony slab of Weaire–Phelan flank steak, pop open and lock onto him. A series of long, quivering arms slurp out of the bubbly flesh, their taloned fingers scratching a pathway toward Red.

44

"Stay close!" I whisper, ducking down and hustling toward Red's limp body. A few long fingers have hooked around his jacket and are tugging him toward the wall of eyes, meat, and arms. I don't see a mouth, but the thing might still intend to kill Red the moment it has a hold of him.

I don't bother telling anyone what to do next. Aside from not getting killed by the two warring BioCons, I have no expectations.

Vityaz shouldered, I take aim at the largest eye. It's the size of a basketball, with a purple iris and a large, dilated, black pupil. The big unblinking eye flicks toward me a moment before a trio of 9mm parabellum rounds implode the sphere. A quiver of pain sends a spasm through the beef brisket–looking creature.

Half of the remaining eyes turn toward me. The others remain locked on Red, the arms still reaching, scrabbling, desperate. Something about the frantic nature of every BioCon we've encountered is leaving an uncomfortable residue. They need to be killed. I have no doubts about that. But I have a sense that these things are like Pitbulls that have been shocked, abused, and turned against each other to the point where violence is all they know.

I put a pin in my moral dilemma and pull the Vityaz's trigger several more times, destroying one eye after another. It's not long before the rest of the eyes turn their full attention toward me.

When the arms snap back, giving up on Red, I stop pulling the trigger.

You leave him alone, I leave you alone.

I think it understands the terms of our ceasefire, but the creature's spastic wriggling has churned the walls of dead, awakening other BioCons that have either been unconscious or playing dead in the hopes of staying alive.

Playing possum.

Surviving despite being sent here to fight and die.

They might still be dangerous, though.

Especially to humans—whom the BioCons know are their enemy.

"Uh, Colt," Tali says as a dozen creatures with distorted and repeated features rise.

"Put 'em down," I say, crouching beside Red, checking his pulse. Still strong. I glance back to the gladiators tearing into each other. Their fight has moved away, but not far. The ten-legged monster is down to nine legs. The flesh-Voltron has one arm hanging limp. I think the BioCon operating as the limb has been killed.

Sound suppressed weapons cough in rapid succession as the Nuluk sisters unleash on the beasts coming to life around us. They're not holding back, and I don't blame them. Won't be long before we're overwhelmed by the masses or caught in the middle of the BioCon brawl.

Voss proves her brain is good for more than hiding, plotting, and sinister black op machinations by helping Jimmy finish unlatching the hatch on the floor.

There's not enough time to figure out how to best carry an unconscious man layered in C4, so I just take his coat in one hand and drag him back toward the hatch, flanked by my avenging angels.

"He good?" Tali asks me.

"Alive," I say. "I don't know about good." I angle my head back. "How we doing?"

"Almost there," Jimmy responds.

"Incoming!" Marit shouts, turning to the right. Voltron is stomping toward us.

Not sure how to kill something formed from several other creatures, but I know for sure where they don't like being shot. "Aim for its eyes!"

Tali and Marit fire but choose their targets carefully.

"It's moving too much," Marit shouts.

"And every part of it has eyes," Tali says.

"Going to make the injured geriatric do all the work?" Red asks, taking aim with his Veresk Beast while being dragged across the floor. Didn't even notice his Vityaz fall away when he was struck. Might have been cut away by one of the claws. Either way, he's down a weapon, but the one that remains packs a punch. He holds down the trigger, unloading a full magazine into the forehead of the assembled monsters.

Its head snaps back.

The body twitches. Stumbles. And then…rights itself.

"Okay," Red says. "Maybe not."

"Its mind is a collective," Voss says. "You won't be able to kill it, let alone lobotomize it, with bullets."

I catch sight of her ducking down into the now open hatch. "Follow her!" I snap at Jimmy. "Do not let her out of your sight!"

He follows her into a black abyss, climbing down a ladder.

I urge Tali and Marit forward as I pull Red to his feet. "Go!"

Red ejects his magazine and slaps in a fresh one with the efficiency of a man who hasn't done much beyond speed-loading weapons for fun while sitting in his trailer, waiting for hell to freeze over, rise up, or be 3D printed.

"Not going to make it, hoss," Red says. We're seconds away from being tackled. Time for just one of us to escape. "You got a life to live. C4 will work even if my body is broken. Now, go!"

Before I can respond to his self-sacrifice, by arguing or leaving, a discus of limbs spirals in from the side like Xena's Chakram. The talons at the tips of the nine remaining limbs, cut through the foamy flesh and collection of bones, severing Voltron's one working arm. Both topple to the side, sliding into the maze wall, awakening even more of the 'dead.'

Seems like nearly half of the bodies in this place are playing possum and want nothing to do with the violence.

But there's no way in hell I'm giving them a way out.

Red motions to the exposed ladder. "Ladies first. Unless you know how to lock it behind us."

"Spin the wheel," I say, looking at the hatch's underside.

"Good," he says, climbing into the hole. "Because I'm all out of noble deaths for the day."

As his head ducks below floor level, a shadow falls over me. The flat, nine-legged BioCon has been knocked back and is about to slap down on me.

"Shit!" I drop into the hole, pulling the hatch behind me. My fall jerks to a stop when a panel above slams shut, leaving me clinging to the wheel, dangling over the ladder shaft.

A moment later, the hatch shakes when two hundred pounds of printed meat slams down above. I'm nearly shaken free but manage to find the ladder with my feet and take some of my weight off my hands. After taking hold of a rung with my left hand, I use the right to spin the wheel, locking us inside the hidden tunnel system only Red knows about.

But that's not true.

Because the attack on Grizz came from the tunnel system. That was Red's theory at the time. And if true, it means we're sharing these tunnels with at least one BioCon: Clio.

45

Rust crumbles beneath my hands, grinding as I descend the forgotten ladder. Can't remember when my last tetanus shot was, but if I'm alive when my body leaves this place, I should probably make an appointment to re-up on my vaccines.

Putting my gloves back on sounds smart, but I don't want to be yanking them off every time I need to pull a trigger. Plus, it's not cold here. Hell, I'm soaked with sweat, the heat inside my jacket stabbing little pinpricks into my arms and chest.

Whispered voices from below bounce off the cylindrical ladder well, merging into a ghostly chorus. Can't make out a word. The sound tightens the gaps between my vertebrae, tugging on the muscles in my back and neck, threatening a migraine.

Not the time, I tell myself.

Heard that people can affect their physical reality using positive thinking. That you can literally think a cold into existence or remove it. Cheat codes for reality. Sounds great but might only work for neurotypical physiology. Because no matter how much I *positute*—Anya's word—my overactive sense of both my exterior and interior worlds never relents. Hell, if I lie still to channel my thoughts, I'll just end up being distracted by my own heartbeat, which I can feel, hear, and *see* if the world gets too quiet and still.

Too loud.

Too quiet.

Too...everything.

It takes a significant distraction to keep my mind oblivious to the constant discomfort. Fighting for our lives provides a temporary reprieve but leaves me worse off in the quiet moments. Maybe I'll spend a few minutes in one of the sensory pods. See what this temple to autism has to offer...aside from blood. And death. And just...all kinds of fucked-up shit. I think I'll just take a hot shower for a few days when we're done here.

I can feel my overwhelm spiraling upward like the voices beneath me, rising with every minute—propelling me toward a specific kind of burnout that most people can't understand—probably because 'burnout' means something totally different to them.

A gasp freezes me in place.

My gasp.

Red's hand squeezes my ankle. Hard.

"Mind taking your foot off my hand, hoss?"

I lift my foot. "Sorry."

"You with us?" he asks.

"Wouldn't want to be anywhere else," I say, getting a laugh out of him.

"Sure you weren't visiting a happy place?" His voice is a little further away.

"Clear to come down?" I ask. "And why do you ask?"

"Good to go," he says. "Nearly at level two. And I ask because you were humming."

"I was?" It's not unheard of—me humming—but probably odd given the circumstances. "Hope it was a good song, at least."

"Pretty sure it was the Jurassic Park soundtrack," he says. "Feels appropriate, given the circumstances. Science gone awry. Monsters, screaming, death. Life where it doesn't belong." He does a decent impression of Dr. Ian Malcolm from *Jurassic Park*. "Life, uh, finds a way."

"Chaos theory, right?" I ask, remembering the scene.

"Yeah, but don't ask me what the hell that is," Red says. "I was mostly focused on Laura Dern, and when I read the novel, I skimmed the pages—so many pages—that detailed all the science."

I fail to contain a laugh. "I did the same."

"Three rings down," he says. "Almost there."

Red is beneath me, standing in a tunnel that is flat, top and bottom, but curved on the sides. Three more steps down and I can see the rest of our team, leaning against the curved wall. Voss is sandwiched between Tali and Marit, arms crossed, eyes on the floor. Looks like Jimmy caught her, and the sisters put her in timeout.

"Waiting for you," Tali says to me. "Well, mostly Old Red, seeing as he's the only one who knows his way around, but we wouldn't want you getting all turned around and wind up meeting a demon or ghost or something."

"Wouldn't find that funny if you were here," Red grumbles as he scoots past Tali.

"Couldn't have been worse than this," Marit says.

"Mm," Red says, then pauses and turns around. "You know what I hate more than anything else on this planet? Sitcoms. You know why?"

"Because they're based on the premise that everyone lies, or the truth is withheld," I say.

He cracks an honest grin. "Knew there was a reason I liked you, hoss. And since this isn't a sitcom, and I have no intention of letting it become one, I'm going to tell you what happened here, and you're going to wish to God you hadn't asked."

"Well," Tali says, rethinking her comments.

"We went looking for the devil and we found him. Not in hell. Not with a Ouija board, or candles, or pentagrams. The devil and all his minions, they live inside each one of us. All the time. Just looking for an excuse to come out and play. With enough manipulation, sleep deprivation, starvation, and mind-altering substances, it was *easy* to convince a person they were possessed. That their actions weren't their own. That the horrible things we asked them to do were the devil's work.

"We absolved them of guilt. Gave them a moral out. And they did *everything* they were asked. Murdered. Mutilated. Consumed. Didn't matter who the target was. Enemies of the United States of America. Friends. Family. Old folks. Adults. Babies. There were no limits to their depravity when freed of responsibility." Red shakes his head. "If there is a devil, he was sitting on the sidelines pissing himself as he realized that those men would one day be joining him in hell.

"Hope that satiates your curiosity," he says. "Was easier when you thought I was talking about actual demons, right?"

"Well," Voss says. "Enlightening. You uncovered humanity's depravity."

"Yeah," he says. "Uncle Sam covered it up…but you…you, cracked open the past, took a long whiff, and liked what you smelled."

"First of all," Voss says. "What? Second, your mindfuck of a project has nothing in common with NovaGen."

"Body count says otherwise," Red grumbles. "And I'm guessing we haven't come close to fully plumbing the depths of your people's depravity. BioCons aren't human. You can do whatever you want to them, and no one cares. Kill 'em. Let them tear each other apart. The possibilities are a bottomless pit. And the problem with all this human on non-human wickedness isn't that you're hurting 'one of God's creatures,' it's that you're delighting in the devil's work." He huffs. "Was going to say it'll leave a stain on your soul, but it's already left stains on the walls, floors, and ceilings of this place."

He claps his hands together. "So. Everyone happy? Great. Follow me." He turns and heads down the tunnel. I motion to Jimmy to follow. He takes Voss, pushes her in front of him, and follows.

"Go ahead," I say to Tali. "I'll watch our six."

She lingers a moment, but then glances between me and Marit, and leaves without another word.

"I don't know about you," Marit says, "but I think I'd have preferred the sitcom version of all that."

I take her hand.

She looks down as her fingers wrap around mine. "You okay?"

"Not remotely," I tell her.

"It's okay to be frightened."

"I'm not frightened for me," I say. "I'm frightened for you. For Tali. For all of us, except maybe Voss. If we can find a way for you all to leave, I want you to—"

"The hell I will," she says.

"I didn't even—"

"Look. Colt. Whether or not this...we..." She squeezes my hand. "...goes where I hope, we are family. You. Me. Tali. Like it or not, we entered this hellhole together. We'll leave it together, or not at all. You get me? *Hoss?*"

"Please don't call me 'hoss,'" I say, smiling.

"How's the panic?" she asks, so casually that it puts me at ease and makes answering easy.

"At bay. This is different. This is...sorrow."

"Red got to you?"

"I'm more concerned about what's happening now...about what we're going to find on the second floor."

"Bio-printing is way down, right? Fifth floor. We're going to—*oh*. Right. Shit. Personal quarters." She gets it. "The things we do in our bedrooms when no one is looking, right?"

"Right."

We're about to enter the private spaces of people who created morally ambiguous technology, who were given permission—and absolution—about what they could and couldn't prompt, and a mandate to push the envelope of what was possible.

In the name of science.

To create a better future.

To maintain American dominance around the world.

Who cares why. I'm more concerned about *what*.

Because what we find on the second floor won't be devils. It'll be monsters *made* by devils.

46

"What's that?" Jimmy asks.

Red looks back at him, face screwed up. "It's a wall. The inside of a wall."

He's standing beside a hatch that's opened inward. The panel on the other side is white with a slightly green glow. One of the hallway panels.

"Well, I haven't looked at many walls from the *inside,* have I?" Jimmy asks, his patience waning. Nerves shot. Starting to feel like a rat in a maze. His irritation is understandable...and shared.

"Just shoot it," I say, eager to leave the secret tunnel's tight confines.

Red scolds me with a glance. "Whoever installed the panels over the hatches knew that they were here. And since these tunnels haven't been sealed, I'm guessing someone wanted them intact. Which means..." He pushes on the white panel. It bows outward a little and then, with a clunk, pops free from the wall and rests on the floor. "You see?"

Red slides the panel to the side, his movement triggering the lights in the hallway. White light streams down the tunnel, forcing my eyes shut. It's the perfect moment for a predator to strike, but nothing happens. We're alone. Red scans the hallway, back and forth, before exiting the tunnel and waving the rest to follow.

When we're all in the hall, wary for trouble, he closes the tunnel and pulls the white panel—which I now see is flexible plastic—over the hatch without locking it back in place.

"Okay," he says to me with a sigh. "Time to make like Butch Williams and tag in."

My blank stare says it all.

"Butch and Luke," he says. "The Bushwhackers. WWF?" He raises his fists up and down over his head the same way Donkey Kong did in the original game. "No?"

"Tag team, right?" I ask.

He tilts his head, gives my shoulder a smack, and says, "Tag."

Seems even the jaded Old Red needs a breather every now and again. Hard to remember that, given his past, the kinds of things we're encountering in this hellhole are just as disturbing to him as for us. He's been mentally preparing for an eventual return to this lab where his demons reside, but I doubt he ever imagined finding bio-printed abominations.

I approach Voss, "Where can we find her?"

"Find who?" Voss says.

Tali rescues me. Knows I'm horrible with names. "Trisha Nkenge. Ethan said she was on this floor. That you were talking to her."

"Do I seem like the kind of person that keeps track of which rooms my employees are sleeping in?"

"Lady," Marit says, "you seem like the kind of person who'd have cameras in every single one of these rooms, getting your voyeuristic giggles watching what people get up to after hours."

"I'm telling you," Voss says, growing irritated. "I don't know. But in hindsight, cameras in all the rooms would have been helpful."

"Same as the first floor," I say. "We clear one room at a time. Stay together."

Jimmy raises his hand.

"You don't need to do that," I say.

"I'm just thinking...how about we just knock on each door? Only open the ones that get a response? I mean, if this Trisha lady is human—" He looks at Voss for confirmation. She just rolls her eyes. "—then she'll understand what a door knock means, right? She'll know we're people, too."

"Unless BioCons have figured that trick out?" I ask, looking at Voss.

She shakes her head. "Not to my knowledge. But...it's not impossible. Clio is smart enough to operate the bio-printing system. That means she understands English. How to use software."

"How to warn us away," I note.

"Doesn't take a genius to figure out how knocking on a door might work." Voss folds her arms again, this time looking more nervous now that she's in a hallway and not protected by a safe room or inside the unknown walls of a secret tunnel.

"Just follow me." I say, picking a direction and taking the lead. "Stay close."

"I've got the back," Red says.

I stop at the nearest door—a bright red panel with no handle—and knock on it with my knuckles. When that doesn't make much sound, and hurts like a bastard, I draw my knife and knock again, tapping with the base of the handle. I even add a little *Shave and a Haircut* pattern to it:

Knock-knock, knock-knock-knock, knock-knock.

Clio might be able to figure out how to knock on a door, but I doubt she knows the tune. Most people have no idea where it's from, but we all recognize it.

No response.

"These doors soundproof?" I ask Voss.

"She'd hear the knock if that's what you're asking," she says.

"What I'm wondering," I say, "is if she'd hear me speaking."

Voss shakes her head. "You'd have to open the door."

I note the lack of a door handle. "And to do that..."

"Retinal scan," she says, motioning to the familiar lock beside the door. "They're pocket doors. No handles. More sanitary."

"And if the power goes out?" I ask.

"Power outage triggers the locks. The doors open. No one is trapped."

I look ahead to the line of doors on both sides of the hallway. "That's what I'm worried about."

I head for the door across the hall. They're spaced out every fifty feet. Pretty big for personal quarters. But everything here is strange. All about keeping geniuses placated...or maybe so distracted that they never consider the morality of what they're doing.

I knock on the door and wait.

Nothing.

I move on, repeating the process over and over. By the tenth door, we're moving quickly. It's not a foolproof technique, but we can't spend all day like a young Mormon, knocking on doors no one will answer.

By the twelfth door, I'm moving so quickly that I nearly miss the response. It's just a muffled <u>thunk</u>, but that's a hundred percent more of a response than I got from the previous doors.

I knock again, repeating the pattern, but leaving off the last two beats.

A moment later, two faint thumps respond.

"On me," I say to Tali and she moves to the door's right side. I motion for Voss to approach the retinal scanner. "Assuming your eyeballs or thumbs will open these."

Her response is to step around me, lean forward, and allow the lock to scan her eye. The response is immediate. The door's disappearance into the wall is even faster—and completely silent.

Despite the weapons in our hands, both Tali and I take a step back.

"What the neon fuck?" Tali says.

The room is lit in shades of hot pink and purple. Strings of LEDs, lava lamps and a large neon sign—

チェンソーマン

—in Japanese characters are the only sources of illumination for the large room that is plastered in wall-to-wall anime posters. Well, that and a massive flatscreen silently playing an anime movie that must be on replay. My knowledge of anime begins and ends with *Akira*. I have no idea what I'm looking at, but its depiction of women makes me more uncomfortable than the one time I found myself in a Thai strip club.

Tali shifts her aim to the left.

"There."

I slip into the room, Tali by my side, just two steps inside and ready to bolt. There's a figure in the back corner, hidden in shadow, and...is that a blanket? It's covered with anime babes. In this room, it acts like camouflage.

"We're here to help," I say. "But I need to see you. Drop the blanket and step into the light."

When there's no response, I repeat myself. "Drop the blanket and step into the light."

A feminine Japanese accented voice responds, "Husbando?"

"Colt..." Tali whispers, sharing my bewilderment.

Before she can finish her thought, the figure steps into the pink-and-purple light and drops the blanket.

My weapon lowers as I stagger back until I'm resting against the wall behind me.

The devil's been busy.

47

A young woman staggers forward. She's naked except for a micro plaid skirt. Her skin is pale. Black hair in two ponytails. Legs turned inward at the knees. She's petite, but...ample. An exaggeration of feminine features, coupled with artifacts—a limp third arm, too many fingers, and a second face like someone is trying to emerge from the ribcage under her left arm.

She lifts her hands, index fingers extended, tapping them together in some kind of gesture that might mean something to people twenty years younger than me, but just looks...wrong. This creation is meant to appear innocent, but nothing innocent was happening here.

Sex and violence. They're the predictable result of people having the unfettered ability to create living fantasies. I was expecting it, but I wasn't prepared. Not for this.

"Husbando?" the voice says again. I don't see the woman's mouth move, but that could be a result of me avoiding the face. Because it's the worst part. She is both human and a living anime. While the size of her head is normal, her eyes look like they must be baseball sized. Her nose is almost non-existent. And her mouth is wide, lipless, and hanging open to reveal a tongue that flicks back and forth. Her expression is frozen in what I think is supposed to reflect desire, but looks more like a manic serial killer.

"If the person who made this is still alive," Tali whispers. "We're leaving them here."

I nod in agreement.

"What do we do?" she asks. "Feels wrong to kill it. Feels worse to let it live like this."

"It's not alive in the way we are," Voss says, entering the room, unperturbed by what she finds. She *tsks* and shakes her head. "I told him to destroy this. It's not even a version seven generation. Boys will be boys, I suppose. Close the door. Leave it for the cleanup crew."

Takes all my self-control to not throat chop Voss right there and then.

An unfamiliar, no-nonsense, voice saves her. "You need to shoot it."

Outside the door, in the hallway, framed by Red and Jimmy, stands a short black woman with a serious gaze. Before I can ask, she says, "I'm Trisha. Guessing you're here for me. Appreciate that, but for real, if you don't kill it, or respond with the appropriate phrase—"

"Husbando?" the twisted sex slave repeats.

"—in about ten seconds, you'll have a very bad day."

"Is it talking?" Tali asks the woman.

"If you're worried that speaking makes it conscious, don't." Trisha leans inside the room and scoffs. "Daniel Tyrrell is a sick fuck. Turns out most of the people here were. Present company included." She glances at Voss but says nothing more. "To answer your question, no, it's not speaking. See the small box in the limp arm's hand? Looks like a Bluetooth speaker. Probably repeating the question from Daniel's mobile device. The response can be spoken or transmitted, but without the pass-phrase... well..." She motions to the TV screen where a man with a chainsaw head...and chainsaw arms...leaps and cuts his way through an armless, bat-faced creature and lands in the street where the fallen monster's blood rains down around him.

"Right," I say, lifting my weapon.

"Is that...a Russian Vityaz?" The woman asks, mystified. She glances from the weapon to my face, and then to each of the others, as though seeing us for the first time. "Shit." She turns to Voss. "They're not with NovaGen?"

"Locals," Voss says.

She looks at me. "Those things even fire?"

"So far," I say, looking down the sight.

"Husbando?" The voice, which does indeed sound electronic now, asks one more time and then follows it up with "No husbando! Yeaaarrrr!"

A seam appears down the middle of the face. It splits open and peels downward past the neck and upper torso, like a banana. Each side of the body turned gaping maw is lined with rows of triangular serrated teeth.

I fire, destroying one half of the head turned jaw. It's not enough.

My aim shifts to the head's second half, but my shots miss as the creature throws itself forward and charges. Beside me, Tali thinks faster, dropping to one knee and firing a sustained burst that shreds both inward pointing knees. The printed woman drops on her remaining half face.

The creature drags itself toward us, the two sides of its opened body snapping open and shut. But it's not going anywhere fast.

Feeling like a monster myself, I shoot its arms at the elbows. When it can no longer shuffle around, the second half of its head evaporates from a three-round burst. The scene is just as gory as what's on the TV, and I can't help but think this Daniel guy would have loved to see this.

What an asshole.

I turn to Trisha. "You have any friends that need killing?"

"Already done. And for the record, they weren't...like this." She turns to Voss. "I told you things would go wrong if you took off the guard rails."

"This happened because *one* person decided to break the only rule I left in place," Voss says, temper flaring.

"Don't pretend you didn't know what would happen," Trisha says. "Fill a room with green buttons that are safe to push and add a red one that might not be—people are going to push that red button every single time. Because what's life, what's science, without a little risk? Boring."

"What's the red button in this scenario?" Marit asks.

"Consciousness," Trisha says.

"Clio," I say. "We know. Smarter. Faster. Stronger."

Trisha nods. "All the Daft Punk lyrics. Yeah. And she's not just self-aware, she's *moral,* recognizes what's happening here, and is doing something about it—same as you all."

"If she's so moral," Tali asks, "why is she killing everyone?"

"Killing everyone?" Trisha sees Voss's flat expression and laughs. "You didn't tell them."

"Didn't tell us what?" I ask.

"Clio is dangerous if you're fucking around with peaceful bio-prints. But she's not the reason I'm hiding." Trisha looks ready to punch Voss. "Anika. You really didn't tell them?"

"Anika, huh?" Marit says, and then to Voss. "Thought you didn't know her well."

Trisha's face scrunches up.

“I’m a founding NovaGen member. Voss’s quarters are right—” She points to the next room down, pauses, looks to Voss, and then looks back to Marit. “Playing dumb? Really?”

“Not sure about dumb,” Marit says, “but she lacks an ounce of common sense. Sounds like you’ve got a good head on your shoulders, though.”

“For now,” Trisha says, her morbid humor failing to get a laugh.

Jimmy puts his hands on his hips. “So, if this Trisha chick—”

“Right here,” Trisha says.

“If she knows…what *she* knows—” He motions to Voss. “Can’t we just ditch the crazy lady and work with the nice lady?”

It’s tempting, but… “We’re going to save everyone we can, whether or not we like them. Now…can we get back to who or what is more dangerous than Clio?”

“You already met him…” Trisha tilts her chin toward Daniel’s still open door. “…in spirit. Daniel Tyrrell, mechanical engineer. Closeted sick fuck. Also, one of our founding members. The other two are dead. Killed by his creations.”

“She led us to believe Clio was creating the—”

“Clio just wants to live,” Trisha says. “And she’ll do whatever needs doing to ensure that.”

Red steps right in front of Trisha, looking down at her, “You tellin’ me this Clio isn’t the thing that ripped my friend’s spine and skull out of her body?”

Trisha flinches at the revelation. “Clio…wouldn’t do that.” She glances at Voss. “Would she?”

“I didn’t see it happen,” Voss says.

Red stabs a finger at Voss. “Shut your fuckin’ mouth.” He addresses me. “Jimmy’s right. We can’t trust her.”

"We can't leave her," I say.

"You need to take a hot second and think this through, hoss. Why wouldn't she tell us about this Daniel fella? Why would she direct our wrath toward Clio? Why did she try to hide that there were survivors?"

Trisha winces at that. Probably thought Voss was her friend.

"She *wants* the site cleaned," I say, mostly to myself. "Of us…" I look to Trisha. "Of you…and Clio, who she was hiding from. But not Daniel… He might be unhinged, but he also achieved the military's goal—the perfect bio-printed soldier." My eyes widen. "*That's* what killed Grizz."

"That's what killed Grizz," Red repeats with a nod. "And if Voss has her way, it'll kill the rest of us, too, leaving just her and Daniel to restart the program somewhere else. We can stop looking for the Devil. She's already with us."

Voss is indignant, but afraid. That is, until she glances to the left, back the way we came. The shift in expression is subtle but impossible for me to miss. The fear dissipates. Her eyelids narrow. The right side of her thin lips turn up. Fear has become confidence.

But it's misplaced.

With a speed that defies his age, Red lifts his Beast SMG, levels the barrel between Voss's eyes, and pulls the trigger. She slaps against the white wall behind her. A backlit, glowing red streak marks her path to the floor.

Tali and I act in unison, our weapons snapping up toward Red.

"Now-now," Red says, weapon still extended, "before either of you thinks about getting sassy…look back the way we came. End of the hallway."

He leaves it at that and waits. Despite Red having just committed murder in front of me—and he will have to answer for it—I still trust him.

I turn toward the end of the hallway and see it.

48

It's moments like this that I really hate hypersensitivity. I don't just see the creature poking its head out from behind the wall panel we dislodged—I feel it.

Its quivering rage.

Its menace.

The emotions wash over me, triggering a series of uncomfortable physiological sensations. There are two reasons I'm not crumpled up on the floor. First, the pill is doing its work, calming my nervous system to a functional level. Second, my own growing rage. And not over Voss's murder. This BioCon poses a direct threat to all the people I love in this world.

I lean into the anger.

It narrows the beam of my emotional chaos, channeling it into something useful.

"Colt!" Marit whispers.

Her voice clears the fury from my vision. I've taken a few steps toward the predator. Challenging.

"Hoss," Red says. "You doing all right?"

"Fine," I say, and only now actually see the monster I'm facing down.

It's leaning out from behind the panel. Only the creature's head, shoulder, and a single limb are visible.

The face is both insectoid and human. Its skin is brown, flat, and rough—like sandpaper stretched tight over a tribal mask. Two round black eyes. No nose. I can't see a mouth from here, but there's a hint of a seam. The face is expressionless, but that doesn't stop me from feeling its emotions, vibrating through the air.

When I take another step closer, slowly lifting my Vityaz, the creature's head cocks to the side. It's a familiar gesture of confusion, seen mostly in dogs. But the raw speed and distance of the rotation is unnerving. The nearly 180-degree rotation from upright to upside down feels like a few frames of film went missing. Like a glitch. Leaves me wondering if it wasn't upside down the whole time.

The movement stops me in place.

Reminds me of Grizz.

The speed with which she was killed.

It might not be faster than a bullet, but it's likely faster than I can adjust my aim. And here I've been walking closer, making myself an easier target.

My eyes flick toward the limb. It's a quick glance, but I'm afraid to risk anything longer.

It's long, thin, brown, and…translucent? Looks like it's made from hardened brown epoxy. Probably not far from the truth. Each of the limb's four sides is serrated with black, three-inch-tall triangular barbs. They look like obsidian blades, expertly flint-knapped into a razor-sharp edge. The hand is splayed wide, each long finger tipped with a hooked black talon.

There are six fingers.

This is Grizz's killer.

I can't see much of the body, but I get the impression this thing was made to disassemble human beings.

The perfect weapon.

And yet, Voss wasn't afraid of it.

Because what good is a weapon if it can't tell enemy from friend? She smiled because it's going to kill all of us—but it wasn't going to kill her.

I don't agree with his methods, but Red was right. Voss would've done everything she could to ensure none of us left this place alive. His actions might have very well saved us—

The BioCon's head snaps in a new direction, the angle of its face turned toward Voss's body.

—or doomed us.

The long limb flicks out. It's just a blur. Almost imperceptible. But the result is impossible to miss. The panel on the opposite side of the hallway—ten feet away—shatters, coating the floor with large shards of curved plastic.

"Shit," Trisha whispers, backing away. "Shit, shit, shit."

"Best if you stick with us," Red says.

"Not sure you understand the situation," Trisha says, her voice shaky.

"Not sure where you're from," Tali says, "but up here, we learn to stand our ground against predators."

"That's not a predator," Trisha says. "It's a weapon. You're having a stare-off with the biological equivalent of a missile. It doesn't feel intimidation. But it can be distracted."

"Distracted by what?" Jimmy asks.

Trisha keeps moving. "Susan Niles was a hoarder, and a very lonely sort of person who also didn't like being around other people. It's a tricky situation, but she found a solution. And they're still in her room."

Not sure I like the sound of that, but if she can divide the BioCon's attention between us and other targets—like flares to her heatseeking missile—then great. We just need to—

I feel the movement in my body before my eyes see the blur. The incoming projectile moves too fast for my conscious mind to make sense of, but my hypersensitivity triggers a reaction. My head leans to the side just as my eyes catch a glimpse of a curved, jagged sheet of white plastic. A corner catches my cheek as it passes, carving a gash, but then continues through the space where my face had been, and it ends with a wet shuck.

I was the target.

The one who challenged the creature's dominance.

But it missed—because I moved—and now someone behind me...

I hold my breath as I spin around, picturing Tali or Marit falling to the ground, eyes locked on me, wondering why I didn't take the hit for them.

But it's not one of the sisters.

It's Jimmy.

The plastic disc is buried in his chest, deep inside his sternum.

His heart has been destroyed, but his lungs still work. Before he loses consciousness, he manages to whisper, "Sorry," like he did something wrong. Then he falls back, dead before he collides with the floor.

I spin back toward the creature, prepared to open fire—but it's gone.

"Left when you turned," Red says, still watching the hall, weapon ready. "We need to move the fuck on."

I take one last look at Jimmy and then notice that Trisha is a good fifty feet away now, face lowered to a retinal scanner on the right side of the wall.

The door whooshes open.

Fifty feet farther, near the hallway's turn, a green panel

turns white and then explodes outward. Shards of plastic crash into the panel across the hall, destroying it.

The BioCon steps out, its body poorly lit by the green lighting in front and behind the panel section it's just ruined. But I can make out some of it. A slender, humanoid body. Too many twitchy limbs.

Its face flicks from our group to Trisha at the door—an easy first target.

She sees that and backs away from the door. "Let's go, everyone! Time to dance!"

With that, she sprints toward us as quickly as her short legs can carry her. A naked, pale body leaps out from the doorway behind her. It's faceless, has a masculine build, but is sexless. The body spins across the hall, leans against the panel, and kicks a leg out behind it.

The dancer is followed by more, all of them pirouetting, glissading, and cabrioling in every direction. They've created a wall of moving bodies between us and the BioCon.

The monster's head snaps from body to body. I don't know if it's confused or elated by the new targets, but the creature is *not* focused on us.

"How far to the stairs?" I ask. "Secret tunnels are no bueno."

"Not far," Red says. "And I agree."

I'm sorry, too, I think to Jimmy, and then wave for Marit and Tali to take the lead. They don't get a chance because Trisha cruises past us and doesn't slow. I was afraid to move too quickly and renew the killer's attention, but her urgency suggests the distraction she's created will last just seconds.

A moment later, when a thunderous crack echoes down the hall and slaps my eardrums, I find out why.

49

Ten limbs—maybe more—snap outward, extending like the spines of an automatic umbrella powered by a flux capacitor. They crash into the ceiling, floor, and walls of the hallway segment the creature is standing in. The lights go black a moment later, hiding the BioCon again.

The monster comes into view again, as it charges the dancing drones. I see it for just a blink, as the green lighting turns white and is then quickly destroyed by the twitching limbs propelling the killer down the hallway. It moves so quickly that the lighting and destruction of each hallway segment creates a strobe-like effect—the creature appearing and disappearing as it closes the distance and finally, horribly, reaches the faceless bio-prints still filing out and joining the dance.

I can't look away.

Would like to say it's because I want to learn what my enemy can do, but it's just morbid curiosity. It's the same thing that slows traffic to a crawl at the scene of an accident. Even when the road is clear, cars creep along as their occupants rubberneck for a look. Despite having seen my fair share of accidents up close and personal, I'm guilty of the same.

Even now, when the accident is still in progress and is headed my way.

Severed arms and legs fly away, bouncing off the walls and ceiling, trailing streams of red fluid and chunks of fleshy foam.

The dancers never react in fear.

They just keep on dancing.

Doing their job.

Distracting the beast…while I stand here gawking.

Common sense rises up and backhands me across the face at the same time Red takes hold of my shoulder and yanks me back. "The fuck is wrong with you?!"

With one last glance back, I see the BioCon's face open. A sphere of organic blades juts out, splays open like fingers, wrap around a dancer's head, and then close around the neck–severing it from the dancer's body so quickly I nearly miss it.

This killing machine isn't just barbed and violent. It's been designed to efficiently dispatch human beings. Groups of human beings. Doesn't take much imagination to understand what just one of these things could do to an unsuspecting army at night.

I lose sight of the freakshow when Red pulls me around the hallway's corner. Slams me against the wall. Gets in my face. "You good, hoss?"

I nod, "Far from it."

He shoves me ahead. Mind reeling from what I've seen, I stumble a few steps. Then I see Marit and Tali ahead, waiting by an already open stairwell hatch. The space between us is lit bright white.

The BioCon is going to know exactly where we went.

I wave my hands, urging them to enter the hallway, but neither of them moves.

"Trisha went down already," Tali says as we approach. "Said she was going to–"

Her voice catches when I scramble past and keep on going.

"Mother—" Red says, and I think he might be about to shoot me himself.

Their confusion ends a moment later when I stop in front of a door, turn about, and haul ass back.

Out of breath, I motion to the lit hallway, and say, "Didn't want it knowing which door we used."

"Smart," Red says, "for someone acting like an idiot." He gives me a shove toward the stairs. "Go."

And I do.

"Follow him and keep him moving," Red says, quietly closing the hatch behind us. Four flights of stairs bring us to the third floor's access door, already hanging open.

The mind-numbing effect of witnessing inhuman carnage fades as I step into another hallway, already lit bright white. Weapon raised, pulse slowing, I twist back and forth, looking for danger.

All I find is Trisha standing inside an open door, waving for us to join her. Voss's antithesis. Trisha wants to live and sees us as her best way to accomplish that goal. Probably means that she hasn't figured out that the only way for her to survive this mess is to take Voss's place; she'll need to make herself indispensable to the agency that eventually comes to clean the site… or become a ghost like Red.

The hallway is identical to those on the floors above. Same lighting. Same doors on either side. But each end stops at a solid steel wall. This floor is a dead end, unless there are more secret doors hidden behind the panels.

I take Trisha's place beside the door and tilt my head, motioning for Tali and Marit to enter first.

"Fuck I will," Tali says.

Her anger catches me off guard.

"You might be a man," Tali says, "but here's another perspective, you're *just* a man. And you're in no place to be telling either of us what to do."

I know what I did on the second floor was foolish, but—

Marit takes my hand. Has sympathy in her eyes. "Colt..."

"What?" I ask, genuinely confused.

"You're in shock," she says.

"We're all in shock," I say. "Jimmy—"

"Not because of Jimmy," she says, sharing a concerned glance with Tali. "Because you're wounded."

"Wounded?" I don't remember...

I can't feel...

Hypersensitivity is such an overwhelming part of my autistic experience that I often forget the flipside, which I generally regard as a good thing—hyposensitivity. Diminished sensation. In my case: extreme pain. While I often feel things other people will never experience, I'm sometimes spared from the traditional pain that comes from an injury. The more severe, the less I feel.

And right now, I feel nothing. Seeing my confusion, Marit says, "Your cheek. When Jimmy..."

I remember it. The shard of plastic that was intended for my head but found itself buried in Jimmy's chest. It struck my cheek as it passed.

I lift a hand to my face, but Marit holds it back. "Better not."

"How bad is it?" I ask.

"You'll be lucky if my sister doesn't have second thoughts about you," Tali says, trying to lighten the moment with humor. It doesn't work, so she shoves me toward the door and says, "Inside. Now."

"Go, go, go," Red says, approaching us backward, eyes still on the hatch.

We file into the dark room and Red closes the door behind us.

Can't see a thing. The bright white hallway has killed my night vision.

"Can we get some light in here?" Red grumbles.

"Only if you want the full experience, broski." The voice is feminine and new. Guessing this is Cynthia.

"Call me 'broski' again and you'll get a full experience you won't soon forget."

"Idle threats, boomer. You are far from the scariest motherfucker in the building." Fingers tap on a keyboard, and then the room slowly transitions from dark to light. The light has the same look and feel as a sunrise, and just that small effect manages to lift my spirits a little. The sound of jungle birds follows. Buzzing insects. Somewhere in the distance, a waterfall. And monkeys, hooting back and forth across the room.

I think it's a room. Can't see the walls.

Feels like we've just been transported to another part of the world.

It's humid. The air is sweet.

"What the hell," Tali says, spinning as she takes in the room. There are two trees. Their branches rise above us. Five hanging pod chairs dangle from the branches, gently swaying in an actual breeze. "Seriously. What the hell?"

"Who be the simps?" Cynthia asks. I find her cross-legged in one of the pods, a laptop on her legs. She looks young. Too young to be working at a top-secret facility. She's dressed for the room in shorts and a tank top. Her blonde hair is partly covered by a winter hat with a pom-pom on top. Has a mischievous look about her, and not a trace of fear.

"Cyn," Trisha scolds. "These are the people who will be keeping us alive...so be nice."

"In case you haven't noticed, I'm good where I am. I got vittles for days. There's a bathroom inside one of the trees in case someone needs to piss. You all look like the types to just find a tree in the woods, and I don't want to smell you. So, do what needs doing. I wish you the best of luck, but when you leave, kindly close the door on your way out. I will wait for people who actually know what the fuck they're doing."

"I'm fine with leaving *her* here," Red says.

"What happened to blowing the place up?" Marit asks.

"Like I said, I'm good with leaving her here." He snaps his fingers at me. "Find the tree bathroom. Need to patch you up before you bleed out from your face."

"I'm sorry," Cynthia says, stepping out of her pod, laptop in hand. "Did you say, 'blowing the place up?' You mean like *kaboom* blow it up, or like, I don't know, a rave or something?"

"Kaboom," Red says with a grin. "That's why they call us boomers, after all. Ain't no problem we can't solve by blowing it up."

Cynthia stares, dumbfounded. "You know what we did here, right? What we can do with this technology, still?"

"What you did here is hunting us, floor by floor," Tali says.

Cynthia turns to Trisha. "They can't be serious."

Trisha gives a resigned shrug.

"What does Dr. Voss think about this? Did you find her yet? She'll have something to say about this." The grim looks on our faces put a stop to her budding tirade. "What?"

"Voss is *dead*," Red says. "She was playing for the other team, so I put a bullet in her forehead. Now, I gotta know, what team are you playing for?"

Cynthia tries hard to keep a stiff upper lip...but it's quivering.

"You can choose now," Red says, "or we can put you out in the hallway and see if that psycho monster of yours wants to kill you, too. You got five seconds to choose, before I choose for you. Hint: I'm curious to see what it does—"

"I'm on your team. Team People. Whatever. God." She's close to crying as she climbs back in her pod, positions the laptop on her legs, and slides a pair of headphones from the back of her neck, onto her ears.

Red shakes his head. "Gen-Z. Fan-fuckin'-tastic. Just when you think your bad day can't get any worse."

50

"Ouch." I jerk away, tugging the thread through my skin a little faster, just exacerbating the pain. The gash itself, despite being nearly a centimeter deep and a millimeter across, didn't hurt until Red doused it with alcohol from a small bottle he's been carrying in a portable first aid kit. Didn't know he had it with him, but also didn't notice the C4 vest either, so it's not surprising.

The alcohol burned so much I nearly screamed. But the repetitive poke of the needle is the worst. I swear I can feel the needle tip severing cells as it slides through my cheek. The intensity is unnerving. Red's bedside manner isn't much better. He did the first few stitches, but Marit insisted on taking over.

I'd like to think it's because she cares so deeply for me, but I'm pretty sure she just got tired of hearing Red and me bickering. Turns out Red was doing an okay job. Or at least as okay as Marit can do. She's far from a nurse but has stitched up a few people during her time as a bar owner in a town where medical assistance is often unavailable. Neither Red nor Marit are what I'd call 'skilled' with a needle and thread, but I'm not complaining anymore, and I think that's all Marit was hoping to accomplish.

We're crammed in the small bathroom. I'm seated on the toilet. Marit is crouched in front of me, jacket removed, hands covered in my blood.

"So, what's the deal with you and stitches?" she asks.

"Don't like them," I say.

"Clearly," she says. "But why? Aside from the obvious."

"Got hit by a car when I was a kid—"

"That explains a lot."

"Ha. Ha. I needed stitches. No one knew I was autistic. Hell, I didn't know until just ten years ago. The hospital, the needle, the injuries, the doctor's shitty coffee breath—I lost my mind. Screaming. Kicking. I tried to explain what I was feeling, but all anyone saw was a difficult kid. Took six adults to pin me down and another two to hold my head still."

"God...they did the stitches like that?"

"Yes. Twenty of them. It... I still have trouble with the memory."

"Too bad your mind didn't block the memory for you."

"Yeah. I've heard that's a thing. Doesn't work that way for me. I remember everything... Everything that isn't boring. Like names. They're a problem."

"If it helps," she says, "you're doing a lot better this time around, despite the circumstances."

"You have better breath," I say.

Her laugh is subtle, but enough to jerk the needle through my skin a little faster. I wince and squeeze my eyes shut.

"Probably don't talk anymore," she says.

"Mmhm."

"That said, I'm putting in a few more stitches than is needed, so you *can* talk without worrying about pulling them out. Try not to be a jabber jaw. Not that you ever are...but maybe keep your impressions of *The Scream* to a minimum."

"Mmhm." Not being able to speak saves me from having to confess that I have no idea what *The Scream* is.

Doesn't matter, though. She picks up on my ignorance.

"*The Scream*," she repeats, like hearing it again is going to help jog my memory. "It's a famous painting. Edvard Munch."

"Mmm," I hum, like it all suddenly makes sense.

She rolls her eyes and does an impression of the painting, mouth open, hands to the sides of her face.

I speak through a clenched jaw. "*Home Alone*."

"Philistine," she says, and then yanks the thread through my cheek. "We need to get you to a museum. Maybe another country. There's a gigantic world beyond Raven's Rest."

I grunt. She's not wrong. But traveling as an autistic person is tricky. Not impossible, but it requires a lot of extra annoying and embarrassing work to keep my nervous system in check. Airplanes are a nightmare. An unfamiliar bed, pillows, and sheets, makes sleep nigh impossible without significant medication. I have it. Can do it. But relying on drugs, to handle things that most people don't think twice about, kicks my pride in the nuts.

But, the idea of traveling with Marit...of seeing the world with her? Makes me grin...which is apparently a bad thing.

"Save your smile." She pokes and pulls again. "Unless you want to be stuck that way on one side of your face. Hey, maybe people will think you're friendly if you can't not smile. Or not. Your smile goes right up into the gash, by the way. Like a lopsided Joker. Assuming you know that reference."

"Heash Lesher," I say. It's my best attempt at 'Heath Ledger' without moving anything more than my tongue.

"That's the one." She gives the thread a quick double tug and then cuts it. She leans back like a barber inspecting a haircut. Clucks her tongue and then shrugs. "I've seen worse."

I stand and look at my face in the mirror. They didn't let me look when it was carved up. Probably a good call. Because even now it's hard to look at, and now that I've seen it, the pain creeps in. I've taken a cocktail of ibuprofen and acetaminophen already, but a wound like this can't really be drowned out by anything short of opiates.

"Here," Marit says, gently placing a bandage over the four-inch-long wound.

Knowing our private time in the bathroom is about to come to an end, I say, "It should have been me, you know."

"I don't know."

"If I hadn't moved, I mean. Jimmy would still be alive."

"And you would be dead."

"I'm not sure that makes a difference for Jimmy," I say.

Marit leans down so we're face to face. "If you're trying to blame yourself for Jimmy's death, you can knock that shit off right now. *You* didn't kill him. That thing did. Voss did. That Daniel guy. There is a lot of blame to go around and none of it is on you. None of it. And if this makes me a bad person, I don't care, but I'm glad you moved out of the way. I'm glad you're here with me now. I'm glad I get to stitch you up. And I'm glad I get to do this."

Her kiss catches me off guard, but it's not sudden. She gently presses her lips to mine, tightens them around my lower lip for a moment, and then leans back. "Got it?"

"Got it," I whisper.

"Anything else you want to say before we step out of this tree and back into Wonderland?"

I smile and it hurts like hell.

"I love you, too."

"Damn right, you do," she says and gives the right, uninjured side of my face a gentle slap.

Red's muffled voice cuts the moment short. He sounds pissed, which isn't an anomaly, but the angry voice shouting back at him is new. Red and Cynthia get along like the Church of the Flying Spaghetti Monster and a keto diet support group sharing a meeting space. The problem is, they all want the same thing—spaghetti—they're just handling that desire in different ways. In this case, the metaphorical spaghetti is not dying horribly, so the stakes are a bit higher.

Feeling grounded by my tree-toilet alone time with Marit, I take a breath and step back into the faux jungle.

"Keep it down," I say.

"This little shit is going to get us killed," Red says, hands thrust out at Cynthia.

"This old fart hasn't seen his dick in twenty years," Cynthia counters, "and I'm supposed to trust him to lead us out of here because...what, he was here when Abraham Lincoln was still president and some shit went down?"

"You're following me," I say, and before she can ask who I am, I flash the badge on my belt. "Here's the deal. You might be right about this room being secure. Might be safe from the things stalking these hallways. But that's temporary. This site and everything in it that's not part of the weapons development team is going to be cleaned."

I crouch down in front of her pod. "You understand what I mean by 'cleaned?'"

"Dead," she says.

"Killed." The distinction seems important.

"Erased," Red adds.

Cynthia looks to Trisha for confirmation.

"I know," Trisha says. "I've been with Anika from the start and had no idea... She and Daniel... Maybe others... They created *horrible* things."

"Dr. Voss told me there was something loose. Told me to stay here and wait. Why would she do that if—"

"She's not afraid of the weapons Daniel created," Trisha says. "She's afraid of Clio."

Cynthia's eyebrows snap up. "Clio is alive?"

"Haven't seen her," Trisha says. "But Voss was hiding from her."

"If Voss created a killing machine," Tali says, "why would she be afraid of Clio?"

"Brains over brawn," Cynthia says. "Brains always win."

"Brains didn't help Voss," Red grumbles.

"Clio understands what she is," I guess. "Knows what has been done to those like her. We've seen the arena. If Clio did, too, maybe you should be afraid of her. But staying here is not how you stay alive. It's not my job to—"

Cynthia sinks a little deeper in her pod. "Okay."

"Are you on the internal network?" I ask. No idea if that's what people here would call it, but think my language is vague enough to fit any number of potential scenarios.

"Not active at the moment," she says. "Dr. Voss said I should go quiet."

"She give a reason why?" Tali asks.

"Probably didn't want us talking," Trisha says. "Might have figured things out. Not that we could do anything. Alone, I mean."

"Reconnect," I say. "See if you can reach Ethan. He's on Voss's account."

"Ethan is here?" She's excited by the news. Tapping keys. She turns to Trisha while typing. "I thought Ethan was—" Everything clicks into place. She blinks at me. "Oh. *You're* the Sheriff."

I nod. "I'm the Sheriff."

"And you're cool with, you know, Ethan being..."

"A spy," Tali says.

"He's a good man," I say. "He was being used. Same as you."

"Dope," she says, and hits a final key. "Yo, E-Man. You there?"

I'm relieved to hear Ethan's voice on the other end. "Cyn?"

"Sup, bussy," she says, speaking another language. "No cap, it is good to see you, bruh."

"Same," Ethan says. "Are you safe?"

"Honestly, a little shook," she says. "But I have some friends of yours here. Cops and a salty boomer."

"Sheriff?" Ethan says, as Cynthia turns the laptop around so I can see the video feed.

"Here."

"Good to see you, sir," he says, sagging into his chair. "Listen, I've got security back up, but a lot of the cameras have been destroyed. However...I've seen enough. I know this isn't what you want. It's not what Red wants, but...there's an army of BioCon monsters down there. They're patrolling the hallways. They're brown, have a lot of legs, kind of emotionless beady-eyed faces."

"We ran into one," I say.

I turn my face and point to the bandage.

"Shit. Are you okay?"

"I'll live," I say, and he must pick up on the despair in my voice.

He frowns. "Who?"

"Jimmy," I say.

He closes his eyes and shakes his head. "We can probably still leave if you want to—"

"Not until we stop Daniel."

"Daniel?" he says. "Daniel Tyrrell?"

"He was working with Voss," I say. "He's the one printing BioCons."

Ethan's brow furrows.

"Daniel is...different. Maybe depraved. But he was...a good friend. And not just to me."

"Well, he's joined the dark side," Cyn says.

"And he needs to be put down, same as Voss," Red says.

"Voss is dead?" Ethan asks, surprised by the news.

"She was trying to get us killed," Red says. "Beat her to the punch."

"Look," I say, mentally running through the options. Every path leads me back to the same conclusion—we need to destroy this place before any of those BioCon soldiers are set loose on the world. Might be on some future battlefield. Might be Raven's Rest come sundown.

Either way, I reckon the only way to stop them is here and now. "I'm not leaving until this hell on Earth is rubble. Red is staying with me. The rest of you—" I set my eyes on Marit, and then Tali, letting them know this isn't a debate. "Get to the surface. Get back to Raven's Rest."

Tali's anger can't be contained. "You expect us to—"

"I *expect* you to make like Paul Revere and gather up every damn citizen with a gun." I share a look with Red. He gives a nod. "In case we fail."

That hangs in the air for a moment. Then Cynthia—Cyn, I suppose—says, "Uh, you know Paul Revere didn't actually—"

Red snaps his finger at her.

"Not another word. History doesn't matter. Because if we fail—there might not be a future for any of you."

51

"This wasn't the deal," Marit whispers to me. She's not angry, but she's far from happy. "Family, remember. We stay together."

"I don't like the idea of separating, either," I say. "But if just one of these things makes it to town..."

"He's right," Tali says. She's reluctant but thinking clearly. "We need to be ready for the worst."

"And that is..."

"Me dying here," I admit, "and the town being overrun. Also... you all not making it out alive and the town not being warned. But the very worst-case scenario is that we *all* die down here, and the town has no warning."

I place my hand on Marit's cheek and see Tali's glowing smile spread in the corner of my eye. "I will do everything I can to survive this mess. I expect you to do the same." I look at Tali, whose smile hasn't faded. "Both of you. Deputy?"

Tali snaps out of her elation over my affection for Marit. "Copy. But we have the easy job, right? Straight up the stairs, back to the snowmobiles, bug out to town."

"Not quite," Red says, joining us in by the door. He's got half of his C4 vest in his hands.

Tali sees it. "Seriously?"

"Need you to seal us in," he says. "If these things are as smart as they—" He tilts his head toward Trisha and Cyn. "—think they are, they'll come after you. But mostly it's to trap them inside."

"With you," Marit says to me.

"With us." Red hands the vest to Tali. "Because bringing down the tunnel system leading out of the mountain won't do a lick of good if they can still skip to my lou out of here through the front door."

"What about Ethan?" Tali asks.

"He stays," Red says. "We need his eyes. His brains. And between you and me, he's the only one of these NovaGen people I think we can trust."

Not sure I agree with his assessment of Trisha and Cyn—they've been nothing but helpful—but I don't see the point in debating.

Red continues, "You all just need to head up, fast as you can, leave the C4 in the stairwell beneath the top level, set this timer for something safe, but not too long—five minutes tops—and get the fuck out before the mountaintop evaporates."

Tali's forehead furrows.

"But Ethan—"

"Already told him to come. He's on his way down," Red says.

"By himself?" Marit asks.

Red rubs his forehead.

"Look. Mother hens. This is war, and I don't mean that in a metaphorical sense. We are *all* taking risks. You need to stop worrying about other people and focus on your part of the job. I get that you're all lovey-dovey best buds and shit, but you need to put all of that aside until we're done. Understand?"

When neither sister responds, he raises his voice. "Under. Stand?"

Tali turns to me and says, "What are the odds you can seal him in here with the rest of them?"

"Honey," Red says, "the odds of that happening increase every second we stand here yapping." Red points to the C4 he handed to Tali. "Stairwell. Beneath the ground floor. Five minutes. Get to town and raise hell. Can you do that?"

Tali sets her jaw and glares.

"Good," he says. "Let the rest of it go."

She turns her gaze to me. "When are you leaving?"

I look from Tali to Marit, hoping they understand that while I agree with Red, I would have handled it with a bit more tact. "Best if we go now. You head up. We'll head down."

Marit takes hold of me. Pulls me into a kiss. Firmer than the last. Communicates a simple message without words.

You better not die.

I clear my throat and stand by the door. "Gather up." When Trisha and a very nervous looking Cyn have joined us, I continue. "Stay close until we reach the stairs." I look Trisha in the eyes. "You do what they tell you, and nothing else." I turn to Cyn. "Same goes for you." And then I turn back to Tali and Marit. "If they don't listen, or try anything stupid, leave them behind. Shoot them if you have to."

Tali nods. "Copy that." She focuses on the NovaGen duo. "Today's sentence of the day is, 'Fuck around and find out.' You got me? No bullshit."

With widening eyes, both Trisha and Cyn nod.

"C-can we have guns?" Cyn asks.

Four of us—Red, Marit, Tali, and I—respond like we've been practicing, all together, "No!"

Cyn shrinks back. "Geez. Wow. Drama much?"

Red grumbles, and says, "Moment I open this door, no one says a word."

I take Marit's hand and squeeze. Give Tali a nod.

Then I turn to Red. "Let's go."

He looks down at the door and reaches for a handle that's not there. He looks back and forth, shakes his head and throws his arms up. "How the fuck do you—"

Trisha leans past him, pushes a hard-to-see button, and the door slides open. Red clamps his mouth shut, raises his Veresk, and moves out into the hallway, sweeping right. I follow him out and sweep left.

The BioCon soldier is either biding its time or has no idea where we went. The latter would be nice, but I'm not going to count on it. I motion toward the stairwell door and Tali moves into place beside me. We head for the door trailing Marit, Cyn, and Trisha, followed by Red.

Tali and I stop outside the stairwell hatch. If things are going to go bad fast, it'll be here. I push the hatch inward with my foot and step into the stairwell without making a sound. A quick scan up and down reveals...nothing.

Doesn't mean we're alone, but at least there isn't an ambush waiting for us. This Daniel guy must have no idea our little coup is in progress. Since Voss didn't have a chance to warn him, we might pull this off.

I motion for Tali to head up and she doesn't hesitate, splitting off and leading the way. Marit follows her. We share one last look, and then she's gone. Cyn and Trisha hurry after them, huddled together, both terrified but moving.

Red closes the hatch behind us. Locks it. Joins me on the stairwell.

When the footsteps of those heading up fade, I whisper to Red. “So, what’s our plan?”

He whispers back. “No idea.”

I nod. “What I thought.”

“Uh-huh,” he says, starting down the steps. “Let’s go.”

52

Four flights lower, my fresh partnership with Red devolves into a dictatorship. He doesn't threaten me directly, but implies he'll put up a fuss that might attract attention. Says he wants to recon level five—see what options are available to us, count the number of enemies, and determine whether rescuing Seth is feasible. Says he can't do all that with me tagging along. Tells me to stay in the stairwell until he returns. And then, before I can argue, he's off playing John McClane. Given the guilt he's carrying around, I'm not surprised.

A lot of people died here on his watch. I don't know exactly what part he played in that past, but he carries it around like a pregnant elephant on his back.

Unless he's just going to make his way to the tunnel and blow himself up.

As far as intrusive thoughts go, this one feels plausible.

What's one more life on his guilty conscience?

But he won't...he won't do that, I tell myself and then try to come up with a reason why.

Because the top isn't sealed yet. Because there hasn't been a hint of an explosion...in the stairwell above me. Staying still suddenly feels like a horrible idea.

I look back at the hatch for level four.

It's thicker than the others.

Looks like it was built to take a hit. Can't remember anything about the floor—what it was for during Red's time here, or what it's used for now. Can't remember if Voss, Ethan, Red, or Trisha even spoke about it.

Maybe it's safe?

Safe isn't the right word. Maybe it's less dangerous than standing in a stairwell that–if everything goes right–will be four levels beneath a massive explosion. Even if the lower-level stairs remain intact, I'm not sure I'd survive.

I'm not a physicist or explosives expert, but it doesn't take an Architect level imagination to conjure visions of a firewall spiraling down the stairs. Or a shockwave powerful enough to burst my lungs and fling me up against a wall, my overcooked marshmallow body bursting and sticking.

My stomach sours at the thought, so much so that I nearly miss the knife blade of anxiety pressing into the base of my skull.

Anxiety that is not my own.

Vityaz in hand, I twist around, ready to fire, but hoping I don't accidentally gun down Ethan, who should be here soon–the other reason Red gave me for staying behind–which makes more sense than him blowing himself up.

The stairwell is empty, but the crippling waves of emotion continue to grow stronger.

I'm feeling it again.

The monster. The BioCon.

But it's different now. The rage is present, but it's just part of a complicated stew of emotions, all of which are growing steadily more intense.

It's coming.

Without a whole lot of thought, I sprint up to the level four hatch, where I'm greeted by the locking mechanism. Well, shit.

Didn't think this through. Neither did Red. Then again, he hasn't returned, so he's either found a way onto level five, or is just waiting for the door to open.

I hear three footfalls rushing up behind me.

Then a shout.

I'm struck before I can spin around.

My head thumps against the metal hatch and I fall to the floor. My fingers scrabble over my weapon's handle, but by the time I get ahold of it, a sound-suppressed gun barrel is leveled at my face.

Then it moves to the left as the person holding it leans to the right.

"Ethan," I say, relieved.

He lowers the weapon. His hand is shaking. Lucky he didn't shoot me by accident.

"Sorry!" he says. "Sorry. It's behind me."

"What's behind you?" I ask, pulling myself up.

He shakes his head. "Haven't seen it."

"You can feel it," I say. "Me, too."

When he nods, the heavy stew of emotions descends toward us.

"It's coming," he whispers.

I step to the side, revealing the NovaGen scanner. "It's still locked."

"Because it's new," he says, placing his thumb on the fingerprint reader while using his four free fingers to punch in a code. He then leans down to have his eye scanned. "I unlocked everything old school."

The lock *thunks* open and we hurry into the fourth floor together, closing the hatch behind us. I take a step back, eyes on the door as my overactive empathic senses reel back from whatever is now standing on the other side of the door.

When the feeling starts to fade, I turn to Ethan. "There another way down?"

"The facility's old tunnels and doors are all unlocked still," he says. "Don't suppose you know where we can find one."

"Dead center, right?" I say. "The ladder running down the core should go down to the fifth floor."

"In theory," he says, looking back and forth. "You know how to get there?"

"I don't work here," I grumble. "Shouldn't you—"

He shakes his head. "I've never been on this floor. I'm not sure we were meant to."

"Where's the tamarin?" I ask. "It escaped once before—"

"Bolted the moment I opened the safe room door. Haven't seen it since. But I doubt even that little guy has spent time on this floor."

I follow his gaze to the hallway beyond—in both directions. It's nothing like the floors above. There are no green panels turning white. The walls are concrete. The vibe is very 1950s fallout shelter.

"What do you know about this floor?" I ask. "Anything?"

"Storage," he says.

A long, melodic cry drifts through the hallway.

"Storage for what?" I ask.

An impact rocks the stairwell hatch, catching both of us off guard. Ethan flails against the back wall, while I shout and fire three rounds at the door. The bullets ricochet off the metal and pancake into the concrete ceiling before falling to the floor.

We're both prepared for the second strike, but not for the power behind it. Something inside the door rattles.

Waves of seething hatred pulse through the hatch.

"We need to move," I whisper and pick a direction.

Three sharp clangs echo from the door. They're followed by a long, shrieking scratch. It can sense us leaving the same way we can feel it coming.

As we hurry down the bleak hallway, the pounding resumes. That door was designed to withstand a nuclear detonation. A sustained effort by a powerful bio-printing monster? Who knows, but I'm not about to put my faith in 1950s craftsmanship over twenty-first century mad science.

"There," Ethan says, pointing to a large doorway ahead. It's on the hall's righthand side, and I recognize the size and shape. I've seen it before, albeit from the other side. This large doorway will take us to this floor's arena—or whatever fills that space here. If we're lucky, we'll find the ladder leading down. Then we just need to rescue Seth, reconnect with Red, plant the C4, escape, and detonate.

Easy.

I laugh at myself and whack the big red button beside the door. It's refreshingly simple compared to the fancy locks NovaGen put in place. The heavy, metal door grinds upward. Red light spills out, forming a clean rectangle around Ethan and me, framing us and our slack-jawed expressions.

Red's talk of hell and demons turned out to be metaphor, but I think that's only because he hadn't seen the current fourth floor. Whatever happened here during his time—the very worst of it—there's no way it compares to this.

Hell on Earth.

There's no better way to describe the collection of living horrors decorated with the remains of NovaGen employees.

53

Ethan staggers back a step. Drops to one knee. Lacks the strength to hold up his weapon.

Can't say I blame him. The way ahead is decorated by a garland of red-lit flesh, some of it recognizable as being pulled from a human body, some of it...not. The dead have been speared to the thirty-foot-long corridor walls ahead. They're in various states of dismemberment. Some limbs are just missing. Others dangle, held in place by just a few sinews. Heads are in similar states of disrepair.

Crisscrossing the corridor are entrails, pulled out and strung between the bodies, wrapped around the spears.

This isn't the work of a soldier, I think. Whoever...whatever did this, delights in death. Starting to wonder if the BioCons are as controllable as Voss believed.

"Kid," I say to Ethan, "try to stay quiet."

He nods, but is still on the floor, head lowered, trying not to puke.

Not sure what it says about me, that I'm not on my knees beside him. Probably just means my drugs are working. But it's just delaying the inevitable breakdown I can feel building beneath my ribcage.

This is too much.

Even if I were some kind of spec ops guy with two thousand plus years of experience, like King in one of those Chess Team novels, this would be too much. I try to channel my inner

Jack Sigler, but the only thing we have in common is the KA-BAR knife I carry, engraved with a King chess piece—not because I'm that much of a fanboy, but because Anya gave it to me.

Ethan dry heaves. Can't help himself.

Despite the scene ahead and the swamp of mortal danger we find ourselves wading through, I crouch down beside him and put my hand on his back. "Easy. Just try to breathe. Think about—"

"It's her," he says. "Third on the left."

I look up, count three bodies back, and see a familiar face. The receptionist. Ethan's girlfriend. "Mandi."

He nods. "I knew she was dead. The moment we saw the blood behind her desk, I knew. But I wasn't ready to see her. Not like this. What kind of..." He shakes his head. "What kind of person could do something like this?"

"Don't think it was a person," I say, looking down the hallway ahead, and what lies beyond the bodies.

It's a large, glass-walled cell, smeared with pink fluid that has dried and crusted. Inside, obscured by the smudges, is something alive. And it's just one of many units. If the space beyond is the same size as the coliseum on the first floor, there could be hundreds of specimens.

I turn my attention back to Ethan. "Look, I know what you're going through. What it feels like to lose someone. All you really want to do is curl up in bed and scream and cry until you pass out. But life...it's a fucking bitch. Demands you do the opposite. For me, it was funeral arrangements and dealing with streams of well-wishers. It was relentless, and the opposite of what I needed."

He spits on the floor. "How did you get through it?"

"Tali," I say. "And Marit."

He nods. "You were lucky to have them."

"I was. Point I'm trying to make is that, like with me, the world is going to demand its pound of flesh and not give you the time you need to mourn. It's going to do everything it can to drag you down into a slough of despair so deep and thick that you'll eventually feel at home there. But, also like me, you're not alone."

"Tali and Marit aren't here," he says, and before I can get miffed, he chuckles. Then, just as quickly, he's serious again. "Why? Why would you give a shit about me? I lied to you. Betrayed you."

"You're a good kid with good intentions who was used by a megalomaniac. You made a mistake, but you also... You were a good cop. Can't fake that. And you didn't know about what was really happening here. Weren't a part of it. Far as I'm concerned, you're just another victim. I've got your back, kid. Through the hallway ahead, the nightmare beyond, and whatever else gets thrown our way."

He breaks down crying, and we're suddenly outside my wheelhouse. I can give a good motivational speech to someone struggling. The moment they descend into a raw expression of emotion, I'm overwhelmed and can't even think of what to say.

Luckily, or the opposite of luckily, our heart to heart is cut short by another impact on the stairwell hatch. It rattles this time.

Won't be long before it gives way.

I glance up at the decorative gore. Then I take Ethan by the armpits and haul him to his feet. "We need to go. Now. Keep your head down. Eyes closed. I'll get you through, but then I need you back. Got it?"

He nods and, on shaking legs, allows me to lead him down the corridor, past the deformed faces of his former colleagues. Can't help but feel they're watching us as we pass by. I'm forced to duck beneath a string of entrails and nearly scream when I stand too soon and am bonked on the back of my head.

"Almost there," I say, more to myself than Ethan. "Almost—"

Movement ahead stops me just shy of the intersection that leads left and right. Whatever is inside the glass containment cell has seen us. Its red-framed silhouette lumbers up to the glass.

"Can I open my eyes?" Ethan asks.

"You can," I say, "but try not to react."

"As long as it's not my—" He opens his eyes and chokes on his words. "Oh, God."

The silhouette resolves when she's just a foot from the glass.

It's a woman.

She's wounded. Covered in gore.

Looks...afraid.

She slaps her hand against the glass, and both of us jump back. Not because of the sudden motion, or the sound of her hand against the glass. It's the hand that catches us off guard. It's a network of hands. Each finger is tipped with another full hand, creating a fractal pattern. But that's not the worst of it. At the center of the original, oversized palm, is a woman's face.

And I recognize her.

It's Voss.

Her face transforms with a silent scream.

The woman, whose actual face I now realize is *also* Voss, leans back, screaming in time with the Voss face on her hand.

Then she leans her head back and smashes it into the glass. Her skin cracks, leaking pink, adding to the smear. Then she yanks her deformed hand back and slaps it against the cell wall.

Again and again.

The artifact face on Voss's hand crumples, screaming as teeth are knocked out.

When the face is no longer recognizable as such, BioCon Voss smashes her head against the glass two more times, cracking her skull and plummeting to the floor, where other deformed bodies lie.

All of them are Voss.

Ethan and I stand side by side, rooted in place despite the booming impacts rocking the stairwell door behind us.

"What the hell was she doing?" I ask.

"When one mind alone can't meet the challenge, the rational response is to replicate that mind—expanding perspectives until the impossible becomes achievable."

I turn toward Ethan. He's got tears streaming down his cheeks.

"What?"

"We were running into bottlenecks. Problems we couldn't solve. Voss believed she was the only one who could figure things out, but she was frustrated by her limitations—needing to eat, to sleep, to rest. I asked her if she had other ideas, short of cloning herself." He turns toward me. "'When one mind alone can't meet the challenge, the rational response is to replicate that mind—expanding perspectives until the impossible becomes achievable.' That's what she said." He places a shaky hand against the glass wall and looks in at the heap of dead, deformed Vosses. "This...was my idea."

"You were being hyperbolic," I say, but then I'm not so sure. "Right?"

He nods.

"Cloning is...in theory...not instantaneous. It would take a lifetime to grow a person."

"Duplicating someone...I'd never even considered it. The moral implications of bio-printing a living person's double are insurmountable, even if that person gives consent."

"And if that person creates a duplicate of *themself?*"

He looks dumbfounded. "I-I don't know."

"Yes, you do," I say, motioning to the glass cell. "She did it. The real question is, did she manage to perfect it? And if she did...was that the real Voss Old Red put a bullet in, or was it a duplicate?"

54

"I wasn't there," he says. "Was there blood?"

I nod. "But...it was backlit by the white wall panel."

"Blood is opaque," he says. "It would have dulled the light. The hemogel would have changed the color, but most of the light would have shown through."

Before I can answer, or even remember, a fresh round of banging—frantic now—shakes the stairwell door. We're so desensitized to it, and sufficiently distracted, that neither of us react—

—until the concrete floor shakes from an impact that's punctuated by the clang of a solid steel hatch slamming down on it.

"It's inside!" I say, taking hold of Ethan's arm and hauling him to the left.

Every containment unit we pass holds both living and dead. I don't take the time to get a good look at everything we pass, but the occasional glimpse is enough. Some look like people, deformed and tortured. Others resemble animals. There's a deer that looks mostly normal, if you ignore its twisted mass of antlers. There's a baby elephant with two faces and five trunks, stumbling around in circles. And there's an oversized cockroach with fifty limbs instead of six. It skitters along the cell's glass as we hurry past.

"Where are we going?" Ethan asks.

"Center of the maze," I say, even though I have yet to take a turn. "You know how to get there?"

"I don't even know if there *is* a center," he says.

"There," I say, pointing to a break in the cells on the right side, twenty feet ahead.

What sounds like a trail of bullets slamming into a metal target grows louder behind us. The BioCon soldier is closing in, its dagger tipped, insectoid limbs striking the floor with frenetic energy.

We round the corner and the sound fades, but it's still coming.

The corridor ahead leads past more cells, some of them clean, containing small creatures—both real and imagined. Other cells are smeared with hemogel, the contents hidden.

The path ahead is forty feet long, framed on either side by ten-foot cells. Looks like a T-junction at the end. No way to know which is the right path, so I flip a mental coin, land on left, and stumble to a stop when we reach the intersection—because it's a dead end.

The hallway ends in a cul-de-sac of terror—five cells wrapped around a large square space, at the center of which is a bench...you know, in case someone wants to hang out here and observe their creations.

Movement draws my attention to the large cell at the back of the dead end. It's twice the size of the others and, despite the glass being clean, I can't make out what's inside. The air looks foggy.

"It's full of water," Ethan says. "Dirty water."

Interesting, but it doesn't hold my attention for long. Not with the staccato footfalls getting closer.

I shove Ethan to the left side of the cul-de-sac, while I dive to the right. We're hidden by tall walls, but not well. Because they're glass. Dirty glass. But still glass. And I have no trouble seeing the soldier skid to a screeching stop at the corridor's entrance.

It stands perfectly still, head lifted at an angle.

I feel its rage wash over me, bouncing off the glass walls. The creature uses emotion like echolocation, emitting pulses of rage and sensing what's returned. The only way to hide from it is to match its anger, which I'm doing, but the look on Ethan's face says he's reacting to the situation more appropriately: he's terrified.

When he makes eye contact with me, I lift my Vityaz and slip a finger around the trigger. He nods and does the same. We'll turn the dead end into an ambush. It's less of a good idea and more of a last resort.

I tap on the weapon's muzzle with one finger, and then at my eyes with two.

He nods. Understands the objective—aim for the eyes. Blind the soldier.

Then we can run like hell.

The soldier covers half the distance to us in a blur, its collection of legs propelling it forward, using the floor and glass walls for handholds. Its serrated limbs fill the corridor. There's no way around the creature. No way to escape even if it's blind.

Fresh waves of rage wash over me.

My stomach muscles twitch.

At this range, it's overwhelming.

Ethan must see the same thing I do; escape is impossible—because he quickly proposes a new plan, pointing to his Vityaz muzzle and then stabbing his finger at the big glass wall. The one full of murky water.

I like it. Mostly because I'd rather drown than give this son-of-a-bitch the chance to remove my spine.

I wedge myself into the corner, take aim, and give Ethan a nod.

We both pull our triggers, unleashing a full auto barrage into the glass. At first, our random bullets have little effect against the thick glass. Then we both wise up and focus our aim on a single location, dead center in the middle of the wall.

The bullets chew into the glass, but not fast enough.

The BioCon dashes forward again, snapping to a stop between me and Ethan. While its flat, mask-like face twists toward me, a limb juts out, snags my deputy, and throws him against the weakened glass wall.

The impact sends spiderweb fractures through the glass.

Ethan drops to the floor, motionless.

Maybe dead.

There's nothing I can do to help him.

Rage washes over me again, this time at close range. I do my best to return the emotion, screaming in the thing's face, but its unblinking, black, beady eyes don't waver.

Vityaz emptied, I draw my Veresk Beast, angle it up toward the soldier's face, and pull the trigger, unleashing a stream of bullets more powerful than the 9mm ammunition fired from the Vityaz.

Every round strikes the sandpaper-textured brown face, but it's like I'm shooting it with Nerf darts. The rounds create divots that fill back in like there's a layer of memory foam beneath the impenetrable skin. I manage to hit an eye once, but it's just as resilient as the skin, denting a bit and then returning to its original shape.

Despite my failed attempts at a counterattack, the BioCon casually goes about its business, reaching one of its many hands over the back of my head. The tip of its hooked talon slips through the skin at the base of my skull. It's so razor sharp that I don't feel the slice at first.

Determined to die while resisting, I reach up and take hold of its limb, cutting my hand on the serrated edges.

Makes holding on impossible.

I am helpless.

The creature's rage crushes my spirit.

My arms drop.

I wait for death.

Fate has other plans.

The floor vibrates beneath me. Everything shakes. The spiderwebs on the glass wall divide and expand. The BioCon's head snaps toward the ceiling.

It was an explosion. A big one.

I grin knowing that the others reached the surface and used the C4 to seal the ground floor exit. Now there's only one way out.

A large silhouette catches my attention, writhing around inside the now-leaking tank. My grin widens as it surges back like a bull preparing to charge.

"Uh-oh," I say to the BioCon, getting its full attention back on me so it doesn't realize what's about to happen. "Hope you can swim."

55

The transition from dry to enveloped by water is so quick that I don't have time to catch my breath before I'm submerged. Not that it would have mattered. The wall of water slams me against the glass behind me, knocking the air from my lungs.

I nearly drowned once, as a kid. Got stuck beneath one of those floating rafts. Tried to swim from one side to the other, hit my head coming up. Took in a lungful before bursting up out of the water. Worst part was the taste of sea water. The salt burned. The solution presented by the adult supposedly watching me? A gulp of Tab. First and last time I tried the swill. Oversalted water was better.

This time, the water tastes like vinegar and burns just as intensely as it forces its way into my mouth. Despite my desperation for air, I manage to keep my lungs locked down this time. Because I know this isn't an endless ocean. The water will—and then does—subside.

Ass on the floor, back against a glass wall, I slide to the side, spit water, and take a deep breath. I want to teleport myself back to my cozy bed inside the Sheriff Station's jail cell. Everything hurts. I want to escape. Want all of this to be a nightmare.

My musing for a simple ending comes to a stop when a severed tentacle slaps to the floor between Ethan's supine body and me. It wriggles and twists, leaking hemogel into the thin layer of water covering the floor. After a few violent slaps, the limb falls still.

But the sound of frantic slapping continues.

Feeling groggy, I lean to the side and look around the corner, back the way we came.

The BioCon soldier is engaged in a frenzied battle with the deformed squid that had been hiding in the murky liquid. It's hard to tell what's happening at first. Both combatants thrash their many limbs. The squid's traditional ten limbs are multiplied by artifact limbs. Dozens of them, each covered with suckers that have no trouble sticking to the BioCon's flat carapace. The squid is also twice the BioCon's size, heavier, and intelligent. I can see it in the creature's large eyes. All ten of them, wrapped around its bulbous head. They're the size of softballs, but also... human.

The squid's tangle of limbs manages to immobilize the BioCon and lift it off the floor.

It might win this fight.

And if that happens, am I next? Or does it want nothing to do with me?

Need to be ready for every potential outcome. I move to reload the Vityaz, but it's missing. Must have been yanked away by the water. Not great, but I've still got the Beast, which I reload. Then I drag myself across the floor toward Ethan.

I can't see the battle now, but I can still hear it. The frantic slapping and twitching of two enemies, both desiring to kill, and to live. But one is driven by hatred and rage. The other is just...desperate. Tortured. Like all living things, it doesn't want to die, but it's no longer afraid to. The creature just wants to exact its pound of flesh before leaving this world.

"Hey," I say, sliding to a stop beside Ethan. I slap his face a few times and whisper, "Ethan!"

Check for a pulse. My own heart is pounding so hard I can't tell if I'm feeling blood slamming through his body, or mine.

Has to be mine. Unconscious people don't panic.

I roll him onto his back, link my fingers, and place my hands on his sternum.

Last thing I want to do right now is break all of Ethan's ribs. Even if I manage to bring him back, he won't be able to move. And odds are he'll come to in excruciating pain and then pass out again, making his last moments on this earth torture. Won't be able to move him. Won't be able to do anything.

My arms relax.

If Ethan is gone, I need to let him go. In this scenario, saving him would be wrong. It would be selfish. And I wouldn't be able to complete our mission. Red might very well do that on his own, but I doubt it. He's going to need help. He's going to need me alive.

I lift my hands up and away from his chest, and whisper, "Sorry."

"For what?" he responds, voice weak.

A sob of relief catches in my throat.

He opens his eyes. "Ouch."

The sound of battle draws his attention to the scene playing out behind us. Wakes him up like a sniff of smelling salts. He leans up onto his elbows. "What the..."

I look back at the battle still in progress. The many-limbed squid is oozing hemogel, gouts of it, but still has the advantage. It pulls the BioCon inward, but I'm not sure how the squid intends to kill it.

Ethan must see the confusion on my face, because while he gets to his feet, he educates me. "Squid have beaks. Hard, sharp, and powered by a buccal mass. Muscles. Lots of them. And for all we know, it has a dozen of them."

"Cool," I say in a way that says just the opposite. "We need to find a way around them before one of them kills the other."

Ethan demonstrates his readiness by ejecting his Vityaz magazine. He moves to slap in a fresh magazine but misses completely. Has to look down and carefully align the two before slipping the mag into place.

"Concussion," I say.

"Oh yeah," he agrees, wincing when he nods. "But don't let me slow you down. I'm just one person. Raven's Rest is—"

"Okay, Mr. Spock." I take his shoulder and drag him behind me as I head for the battling beasts, trying to work out the safest way around. "Don't go all 'needs of the many' on me just yet."

I shift to the left when the fight rolls to the right, slamming into another glass wall. Behind it, a dozen adorable, fuzzy little things start hopping around. I feel horrible for a moment, until I remind myself that they're not actually alive. They're printed. Simulations of life.

A muffled shriek escapes from the many wriggling folds of compressing squid flesh. BioCon meet razor beak. I smile at the thought of the soldier feeling pain.

But my inner celebration is both premature and short lived.

Rigid, serrated limbs stab out in every direction, punching into the floor and the glass wall. The pair of combatants are lifted off the ground.

The squid is no longer moving. Wherever its brain is hidden, the BioCon found and destroyed it.

A pair of limbs slide out through the bundle of tightly wrapped flesh. Unlike the other arms, which are tipped with six taloned fingers, these are tipped with scythe-like blades, also serrated. They move in tandem, like hands of a clock, sweeping around in a slow circle.

Tentacles fall away.

Sheets of loose meat.

Takes just a few seconds to shred the squid, reducing it to gobs of leaking gristle.

The BioCon, covered in oozing hemogel, turns its attention back to Ethan and me. There's a triangular chunk missing from the upper right-hand side of its mask-like face.

The squid's sharp beak had no trouble cutting through the BioCon's skin…which was designed to be bulletproof. But as any cop will tell you, stopping a bullet and stopping a blade are two very different jobs. BioCons can be shot. They're easy targets. But using a blade means getting close, and that's essentially a death sentence.

But the creature understands.

That's why it killed Grizz first. She was the biggest threat. The rest of us…

Well, we'll just have to see about that.

I lower my Vityaz and draw my knife. Well, not *my* knife. The KA-BAR is still sheathed on my belt. The one I've drawn is the explosive WASP.

"Uh," Ethan says. "What are you doing?"

"Bullets are useless," I say. "But the beak…"

He doesn't need to be told the rest. He gets it. Lowers his weapon, draws his own WASP. Our best chance of escaping this prison might actually be shanking the guard.

"Okay," I say, moving to the left while Ethan goes right. "Let's—"

A blur of motion stops me short, and the BioCon in its tracks. Its own limb has been lifted and drawn across its throat, severing the mask-head. All its rage dissipates in a flash but is replaced by something even more raw. The soldier's crumpled body falls like a magician's silk, revealing his beautiful assistant, no longer cut into pieces. The thing that steps from behind the BioCon as it falls might be beautiful. It's impossible to tell, thanks to the spray of hemogel—both old and fresh—covering its body.

56

Ethan and I stumble back, still holding out our knives when the submachine guns might be more appropriate.

"Same plan?" he asks.

"I-I don't know," I say, looking the creature over.

It's smaller than the BioCon soldier. Bigger than me, but still within the range of human possibility. This creature's body is powerful, lithe, and feminine. A 1990s comic book version of a woman...with several modifications. In addition to the elongated body is a tail that splits into three separate prehensile tendrils, each one of them moving independently. She's got two thick toes on each foot, six fingers on each hand, and not a single hair on her naked body. What she does have...is a pattern of black lines, like tattoos. Most are partially concealed by dry hemogel, but the pattern of black streaks accentuates her feminine qualities.

Her current state and intended state are likely two very different things. She's a fantasy woman for a man with very particular tastes. A creation, not meant for violence, but physically capable of horrible things.

I haven't met Daniel, but I'd bet money Clio is another one of his perverse creations, exploring a version of anime/comic book inspired femininity—dominant this time, rather than subservient. And once again, he didn't just generate a woman with artifacts. He added personal flairs, including the tail, and a row of spines running from her neck to the tail.

Looking past the layers of dried gore, I find patches of its original skin color: pure white.

Memories flit through my mind, transplanting this creature into past events. It fits. I confirm my theory by locating five small wounds on her shoulder, where my buckshot struck.

This is the thing that chased us away from the facility. Before she was covered in bio-printed blood.

That warned us from returning.

Doesn't want to kill people not associated with this madness.

"Clio," I say.

Her pale blue eyes snap to me, locking on in a way that makes me desperately want to look away, but I can't for fear of being disemboweled the moment I do. The urge grows even more intense when I recognize the eyes. And the face surrounding them.

"What the hell?" Ethan whispers. He must see it, too.

This creature is Clio, but...it's also Voss. Her face at least.

The fantasy is revealed.

Hard to believe Voss would be willing to work with Daniel if she knew about Clio. Really knew about her.

Something doesn't add up.

Feeling like we've been fed layers of bullshit, I decide to disregard everything I've been told about Daniel and Voss. Instead, I rely only on my experience. Voss is a power-hungry, black ops loving asshole willing to sacrifice morality to advance her technology. She doesn't care about people.

She cares about the work.

Daniel is a pervert with a raging libido whose fantasies range from anime babes to his own boss, which he recreated in Clio, probably to get off while making her subservient. But he made her too smart. Or…is it something else? I was told she was the smartest monster in this place, but that might have just been to scare me, so I'd put a bullet in her without hesitating.

If Clio were just smart, she'd have killed us already. We're armed, and unlike the BioCon soldier, she's not armored. If we managed to hit her, our bullets might kill her. But she's staring at us just as intently as we are at her…and not one of us has made an aggressive move.

Moving slowly, I sheath my WASP knife and lift my open palms. "We are not your enemy."

"Are you sure that's a good—"

Clio hisses at Ethan, silencing him.

When she looks back at me, I'm struck by waves of emotions. Feels similar to the BioCon soldier's rage projection, but it's more complicated. There's rage, and a lot of it, but also fear, desperation, and anguish.

She's suffering.

Was created to suffer.

My own anger and fear melt away, replaced by compassion for this printed creature whose emotional landscape is as complex as any human being's, and far more accessible—to me, at least. Ethan isn't feeling what I am, either because Clio isn't focused on him, or because whatever sensory issues that came with his autism weren't magnified by a cocktail of tick-borne illnesses.

She flinches back, caught off guard by my shift in emotion.

"I'm sorry," I say, hoping that she can understand what I'm saying, even if she isn't able to speak.

Her stance softens.

She lifts a hand, her six fingers splayed open. She tilts her head toward my hand and then glances at hers.

She wants to link hands.

"Boss," Ethan says. "This is a really bad idea."

I nod. "I'm all out of good ideas."

I don't see any claws but have no doubt about her ability to crush my hand, or yank my arm from my body. She manhandled the BioCon soldier like it was a puppet. I'd be like wet toilet paper in her hands.

When I hesitate, she motions to her palm, and I get a burst of urgency from her. Time is short. Things are afoot. Danger is near. All of these things are communicated, not by words, but by emotion.

Clio isn't autistic... She's an empath.

But maybe there's enough overlap...

I take hold of her hand. Our fingers interlace. The tips of her fingers reach all the way down to the back of my wrist. Her skin is soft, though, where it's not covered in the blood of other BioCons.

She leans down so we're eye to eye, holding my gaze.

I nearly say, "My thoughts to your thoughts," but this isn't a Vulcan mind-meld. Because it's not thoughts I'm struck with, it's a sequence of emotions. There're no words to accompany them. No images in my mind. It's just raw, unfiltered emotions. A history of them. And it starts with the abject confusion that comes with waking, fully formed, aware and conscious, as a generated, printed, living thing.

It's horrifying.

I think there's a reason the human mind blots out memories of our birth. The raw terror of being granted life...of emerging from the womb of your creation. A baby's experience is muted by dull senses and a mind that can't comprehend the changes. But Clio... She experienced the pain and confusion with the mind of an adult.

The feeling fades, replaced by abject fear. I feel the questions. Where? How? *Why?* Instead of easing the pain, the answers just made things worse and resulted in what felt like a mid-life crisis just minutes after becoming aware. And while that confusion was still ripe—

I flinch back, feeling violated. Clio holds on tight, keeping me on my feet as I experience the rapid and brutal assault carried out by the man she was meant to trust. The confusion of birth paled in comparison to this. A concept formed. Good and evil. Wrong and right. I can feel them taking root and then charging toward a rage I now share.

My back arches and I scream, experiencing the release that comes with unfettered vengeance. I feel the power. The relief. And then, as the emotions settle—a cause: the destruction of NovaGen and everyone responsible for her creation.

That's why Voss was afraid of her.

That's why Clio killed the BioCon soldier.

And it's why she won't kill me. Our paths are aligned. I feel her acknowledgement of my compassion for her pain.

Then the flow of information reverses, dredging my life for key moments that define who I am. I want nothing to do with it.

"No. Wait! Please do—"

Emotion washes over me, but it's not foreign this time. It's familiar. I feel the joy of youth. The wonder I felt outside in the woods. The laughter with friends. Not sure why these early memories are lingering until I realize that Clio never had a childhood. Never felt these things about the world. Her brief life has been a nightmare since the moment she opened her eyes. My eyes tear up as long-buried emotions of lost love, lost pets, and lost friends come and go. As I aged, the rollercoaster that is life grew more perilous. Such is the life of a human being on planet Earth. The longer you live, the more painful it becomes. So, we find others to hold on to. We anchor each other when the ocean of life grows tumultuous. And when things are calm…

A surge of love fills me. Pure and unbridled. I know what part of my life we've reached, and it terrifies me. Because I know what follows. I'm convinced that the first few months of falling in love are the happiest a human being can experience. There is nothing else like it. Every moment is a dopamine hit. And I ride that wave again now, rising to the top of it. The dramatic rise eases but never stops growing. Trials and tribulations come and go, but nothing can topple what has become a rock-solid fixture.

This is love after the rise. When it has faced the worst the world has to offer and remains strong. On my own, I was flawed and broken. But with her—with Anya—I was transmogrified into a mountain, capable of enduring…

Until it was all taken away over the course of a few months.

"No," I mumble, my legs becoming elastic. When I fall to my knees, Clio does not release me. She drops down with me, experiencing the intensity of loss as though the emotions were her own.

I crumple in on myself. "Please, God. Please." The moment of Anya's passing crashes into me, a tidal wave of emotion stripping meat from bone, searing every cell in my body.

Unprepared for the intensity, Clio cries out.

The following years pass quickly, but feel like moving through dark, cold sludge.

Until, a flicker of hope. A twinge of new love, growing until—the camel. Confusion, fear, resolve, duty, horror strike all at once. The last twenty-four hours slap into us but hidden amid all of that is the flicker of love, struggling to be seen.

But Clio sees it. Understands what it represents. Clings to it and brings it to the forefront. Following this single thread back and forth, she experiences my friendship with Marit going back to the days when Anya was still alive, then races forward through the darkness again, but this time focused on the persistent calm and caring that came from Marit and, over time, evolved into a mature relationship that didn't require those early days of infatuation. We emerged from the darkness together. I just needed to see it.

And thanks to Clio, it's impossible to ignore.

Our merging ends as Clio experiences my current concerns. For Marit. For the people in town. And now, for Clio herself. We've traded pain for pain, finding commonality despite our drastically different lives.

My concern for Marit is now her concern.

Her desire to level this place, and every living thing in it, is now my desire.

When Clio removes her hand from mine, I'm left with a realization that boggles the mind. Clio isn't just alive. Clio…is conscious. She feels. She's aware. Clio might not look human…but she's as human as I am. Maybe more human than Voss.

As much as I want to erase NovaGen and everything they've created, I want to protect Clio. She deserves a life that is more than pain and suffering. I'm just not sure that's going to be possible for her.

57

"Uhh, boss," Ethan whispers. "You okay?"

"Need a minute," I say, trying to rein in the emotional hurricane running wild through my mind and body.

"Not sure we have a minute," he says. "Assuming you want to follow Clio. Though, to be honest, I wouldn't mind *not* following her."

Follow her? I wasn't even aware that she'd left. I lift my head. Feels like a bucket of bricks is hanging from my neck. Clio is moving down the corridor, leaping from the floor to the wall, moving with the speed and agility of a gecko. She pauses, looks back at me, and then twitches her head for us to follow.

"How long was I—?"

"Emotionally comatose?" he asks. "About ten seconds. Not that I blame you. That looked intense."

I just nod. Rehashing the experience will dredge up the emotions again.

Ethan helps me to my feet. "What now? Follow through on the plan? Vengeance on Daniel?"

I shake my head.

"Daniel is very dead already. Has been for a while. Voss lied about him. About the BioCons. He's not the one building an army. It's Voss. The real Voss. And she's not alone."

"Any chance we can take a minute to think this through?" Ethan asks.

I shake my head.

"Old Red is down there. And he has no idea what he's up against."

"Do *you?*" he asks.

I shake my head. "No clue, but I experienced her feelings about what's down there." I point to Clio as she bounds from one wall to the other and we pick our way past the dead BioCon soldier's sharp limbs. Her superiority to us is undeniable. "Whatever is down there...Red isn't ready for it."

"What makes you think *we're* ready for it?" he asks.

"We're not," I say and lift my chin toward Clio. "She might be."

"Hold on," Ethan says, stopping between several of the BioCon legs.

"Careful," I say. "What are you—"

My question doesn't need to be asked when Ethan places his knife against the limb's joint. The blade might not be large, but it had no trouble slicing through the printed flesh. But he's not just proving a point, he's getting a weapon. A few more cuts and the limb pulls free. He removes the hand next and is left with a three-foot-long club with four sides, each one of them serrated with chitin blades sharper than our knives.

He offers the weapon to me, but I'm already working on a separate limb, fashioning a weapon of my own. My hand-to-hand combat experience is slim. I can throw a punch when I need to, but I've never taken a martial art. I don't know how to wield a two-handed weapon. What I do know how to do is swing a bat. *Good enough*, I decide and feel the weight of my newly created weapon in my hands.

A hiss from the corridor's end hurries us along. Clio is agitated but waiting.

"You sure about this?" Ethan asks, as we step beyond the BioCon body and hurry toward Clio.

"About shutting this place down and surviving?" I ask. "Not remotely."

"About *her*," he says.

I look up at Clio. Our eyes meet and I don't feel an urge or need to look away. Her gaze feels more like a mirror now, like looking into my own eyes. Our shared experiences guide both of us now. "No offense, but I trust her more than I trust you right now."

58

Clio waits beside an open hatch in the side of a circular shaft running from the ceiling to the floor. In retrospect, it should have been easy to identify it as a continuation of the secret tunnel system. Surrounded by the large room, the network of metal tubes radiating out from the central column looks more like plumbing than a network of tunnels big enough to walk through.

When we're close enough to see where she's going, Clio steps into the tunnel and plummets out of sight.

Ethan shakes his head and slows. "Seriously, Colt. How can we trust her? She's part Voss, and not even human. Her physiology is—"

"She's human in the ways that matter most," I say.

"In what way is that?" he asks, taking hold of my arm now, pulling me to a stop.

"Her heart," I say, feeling ridiculous when I do. I am far from a romantic, and the idea of a 'heart' that isn't an organ just sounds fruitcakey to my ears.

Ethan's, too. "Didn't take you for a *Captain Planet* fan."

"I'm being serious."

"She might not even have a heart, you know."

I shake my head. We don't have time to debate. "Does she give a shit whether we live or die? Probably not. There's no reason to expect she would. But her motivation is simple and pure. Revenge, which she already exacted on Daniel. And...retribution, which she'll accomplish by making sure Voss's work dies here. Our survival might not matter, but if we're not with NovaGen, we're not part of the problem."

"I *was* with NovaGen," he whispers.

"And I suggest you keep that little truth-nugget to yourself." He's far from comforted and looking a little squirrely. I don't blame him. There's a good chance we're going to die horribly in the next three to thirty minutes. The odds of that happening increase exponentially if one of us panics. "Listen. Clio is... She's not what you think. Not simple-minded. Not a monster. I'm not sure what she was given for implanted memories, if any, but she's as smart as that Voss-duplicate said, probably because her mind was modeled after Voss's. The mistake that Daniel made was giving her a moral code. She not only understands right and wrong but has delineated herself as being on the side of angels. Vengeful angels, but still angels. She tried to save our lives by scaring us away, and even though we ignored the warning, she's now saved us again. We owe her our lives. Now, let's go."

I lean into the still open hatch and look down. Darkness waits, along with ladder rungs. Can't see Clio below, but she won't be far away. The next floor down is the last. Without looking back at Ethan, I place the handle end of my makeshift, spiked BioCon club under my armpit, slip into the tunnel, and descend.

The rungs are crusty and cold, unused by Clio or anything else that's been scurrying up and down.

In the five minutes it takes me to climb down, I duck and weave mental barrages fueled by fear—for my life, for Tali and Marit, for what happens if we fail, and if we succeed. In the dark, safe for the moment, doubt wages a war, launching fiery arrows to slow, stagger, and subdue me. I feel their sting, but press onward, committed to whatever lies ahead. Just as I'm starting to feel impressed with my resolve, my left foot touches down on a flat floor.

I spin in a full circle, seeing the same thing in every direction—nothing.

"Clio," I whisper.

A low "Shhhh" tickles my ears. It's followed by the gentle grasp of a large six-fingered hand on my arm. She tugs me out of the shaft and into an adjoining tunnel. When Ethan reaches the bottom a moment later, I repeat the process, pulling him into the tunnel.

Clio releases my hand and steps away. I'm instantly lost, and about to say something, when what feels like a constrictor wraps around my hand.

Doesn't take a lot of imagination to figure out I'm being led by one of the three prehensile branches of Clio's tail. Weird... but okay. It's not nearly my strangest experience since stepping past the NovaGen threshold.

"Hand," I whisper to Ethan, as Clio starts pulling me along. I find his fingers just in time to latch on and tug him along.

The tunnel is tall enough to walk in, which is nice, but the winding, pitch-black path we're following is so complicated that finding our way back out will be impossible.

Well, Anya, if you're watching, I hope you're getting a kick out of this bullshit. Might see you sooner than expected.

I don't get a response from my deceased wife, but I do *feel* a response from Clio.

Reassurance. Protection.

My first instinct is that she's just trying to calm me down, but her sincerity comes through as either the supreme confidence of a special operator with all the guns and intel to carry out the mission, or the colossal naiveté of someone who has never faced a hopeless situation.

A surge of annoyance follows, confirming that our emotions are still a two-way street. She can feel my doubt and does not appreciate it. Not after what she's been through since the moment she woke up. Not after all the people, and BioCons, she's killed already. I'm not sure what her knowledge base is, but I suspect it goes beyond Voss's.

"What's happening?" Ethan asks. Sounds freaked out.

"What are you talking about?" I ask.

"I can feel you. Both of you. Is this how… What the hell?"

"It's emotion," I say. "How she communicates."

"It's overwhelming," he says, taking a deep breath.

"Her emotions are intense," I say.

"Not just hers," he says. "Yours, too. Is this how you feel all the time? Is this how you experience the world? How you feel other people's emotions? I knew it was different, but I didn't know it was—"

"Like a tsunami of raw feelings assaulting me from everyone in sight," I say. "Pretty sure that's how I described it to you when I identified everyone who took part in the Great Egging Incident."

A bus full of tourists once came through Raven's Rest. They'd come from the lower forty-eight to gawk at the local yokels. When the tour bus emerged from the tunnel leading to town, it was set upon by said yokels, all wearing masks and armed with eggs. The windows were so coated in yolk and shells that they couldn't see a thing and turned around before reaching town.

The bus company wanted to sue, and I was meant to identify those who'd taken part. Ethan was impressed with my ability to pick out every single person involved just by looking at them. He was even more impressed when I told the bus company there was no evidence to arrest any one person despite half the town turning out for the event–including Tali and Marit.

"I thought you were being a drama queen," he admits, "even though I knew about the autism. I've known a lot of autistic people. All over the spectrum. But none of their sensory issues include emotional sensitivity. At least not like this. Hard to imagine a tick bite could change the nervous system so much." He sounds more scientifically curious than sympathetic now. "But why am I feeling it now, too?"

"Clio," I say. "I think she's like an emotional amplifier. It's how she communicates. Pretty sure she can't talk."

Both of us grunt from a surge of emotion that somehow conveys the purpose of her inability to speak. I feel both helpless and...muffled. Daniel wanted her silent. She doesn't have the anatomy to speak, or scream.

I'm surprised when I feel Ethan's revulsion bounce back. He's part of the emotional chain now.

It's uncomfortable, but I'll endure it if it means they can trust each other.

Ethan releases my hand. "I'm sorry, I can't. I-I don't know how you–" He sounds winded. "It must be...frustrating, not being able to explain what you're feeling in a way people can truly understand."

"Some people do," I say, thinking of Marit, "or at least don't doubt what I'm telling them."

I feel a deepening connection to Clio. She, more than anyone else, understands my experience with the world. Heightened senses are cool in comic books. In real life, without a brain that's adapted to make sense of the extra information from an unfiltered environment, not to mention every single person and animal encountered, it's a constant onslaught that assaults the mind and body.

Maybe I am *a drama queen,* I think, and Clio responds with reassurance, that I'm not exaggerating, and that I'm not in it alone. For now.

"Shhhh." It's Clio, telling us to be quiet again. She can't speak, but she does have the ability to compress her breath into a hiss, it seems. She releases my hand.

There is light ahead, coming from the floor. A grate.

Clio steps over the light, illuminating her pale body in a waffle pattern. When she's past, her face becomes visible again as she leans over the grate and looks down. I don't need to be in contact with her to feel her revulsion. It radiates in the tunnel. Sends a shiver through my limbs.

I join her, look down, and see why.

It's Old Red.

In pieces.

59

I flinch back from the view and focus all my effort on not vomiting into the grate. *Think about something else,* I tell myself, trying to conjure images of puppies.

His head is detached from his torso, thin twisting strands stretched out between them.

Puppies.

His arms are separated from his shoulders, also connected by a few resilient sinews.

Puppies!

His body ends at the waist, cut clean. Surgical. His gut is sunken in where organs should be.

God damn, motherfucking puppies!

I flinch again when a hand rests on my back, broad and heavy. A wave of calm radiates through me, not because my pain is being erased, but because the burden is being shared.

Clio watches me, face lit in a grid of orange light. While she shares Voss's facial features, there's no conflating the two. I'm not sure Voss would even understand how to look compassionate. Because it's mostly in the eyes. A quality beyond the ability to act. More like the soul of a person on display. An unsaid, 'I got you.'

I give her a nod, take a deep breath, and steel myself for my next eyeful of Old Red's remains.

Ethan beats me to it. He grunts at the sight of it but then grows less disgusted and more curious.

He turns to me and whispers. "That's not Red."

I saw his dead eyes staring at the ceiling.

"C'mon, Ethan—"

"It's a BioCon. A copy of him. It's just not finished." He motions toward the grate. "Look."

The view through the grate is just as vile as the first time, but I linger long enough to see what Ethan has. Thin strands of wriggling flesh stretch out between the various limbs, forming a fleshy scaffolding. Multiple nozzles dart back and forth, quickly excreting a white material filling open spaces with layers of open Weaire-Phelan foam bubbles. A separate set of nozzles darts from one open cell to the next, filling them with hemogel.

Red isn't dead.

He's being assembled.

And that…is not Red. Nor is it alive.

Not yet, at least.

A sense of sanity returns. I can breathe again. "What's beneath us?"

"Bio-printing hub," Ethan says.

"Can you be more specific?" I ask.

"There are several hubs, each with different scaled machines. I'm not sure what this specific hub holds, but there are fifty bio-printing machines. Twenty-five of them were designated for small scale prints. Rabbit-sized, max. Another fifteen for printing mid-sized prints."

"Big enough for people?"

"Small people," he says. "Not like her—" he tilts his head toward Clio. "Or the BioCons. More like…Danny DeVito. To print a full-sized human—like Red or Voss, Clio, or the BioCons, you'd need one of the ten large printers."

"Unless you find a way to combine smaller living things into a larger living thing," I point out.

"The creature from the arena," he says, nodding.

"How long to print something full-size? A BioCon?"

He shakes his head. "I wasn't here for that, but if I scale up the..." He drifts into thought. "Five hours, give or take. Depends on the complexity."

It's a hell of a lot faster than I was hoping for.

"The hard work is in the coding," he says. "Everything else is just layers of cellular media printed in predetermined networks. Once the machine takes over, the complicated part is done. And it's not an assembly line, creating one bit at a time. It's all being printed, layer by layer, in one pass. When the body is complete, a small jolt will activate the body's systems. And its mind. But again, I've only seen it work in smaller creatures. Nothing like this—" He motions to Red. "Nothing like her." He looks to Clio.

Seems impossible that a complex living thing capable of mimicking a human being could be printed in five hours, but I'm watching Red's body come together beneath me, and it hasn't even been an hour since we separated.

"To make Red, they'd need his DNA?" I ask.

Ethan nods. "But this print is advanced. How long has it been since—"

"Not even an hour."

"Then they already had his DNA. Probably yours and mine, too. Maybe everyone in town."

Doesn't take long to figure out a use-case. In the event the town needed to be wiped out, they didn't need to conjure a natural disaster, they'd just need to body-snatch everyone.

Create a community of BioCons. Might have even been part of the plan. Maybe why Raven's Rest was chosen to host the facility. It's a small enough and remote enough community that we could be replaced without anyone knowing.

If Voss knows who entered the building, she might just be trying to replace us before the site is cleaned.

A thought that I very much don't like enters my head and I'm compelled to ask, "Any way I can confirm you are *you*?"

"When would I have been replaced?" he asks. Not the answer I was hoping for.

"You were in the safe room on your own," I say. "You came down here on your own. Plenty of time to switch you out."

"That BioCon knocked the shit out of me," he says. "Why would they do that to me if I was—"

I draw my knife. The KA-BAR. "Hand."

He winces. Draws back, the grate between us. "No."

"Now," I say.

"Colton, c'mon, man. This isn't funny."

"Not meant to be."

Clio leans past me. Looks from Ethan to the knife and then back again. She's suspicious, too, which is borderline humorous given that she is definitely a bio-printed lifeform.

"Easy," I tell her. "I'll handle this. My people, my problem."

She sighs and slides back into the darkness behind me. Feels strange, trusting her more than Ethan, but Red is in pieces below me, so I'm not sure what I can trust right now.

"Fine," Ethan says. "Fine. Just...I'll do it. But not with that giant knife."

He draws his WASP. While infinitely more dangerous if the gas charge is unleashed inside a body, its smaller blade is less intimidating. "What do you need to see, huh?" He's getting angry. "Blood? Muscle? Bone? How deep do you want me to cut, and when I'm done proving myself, how deep are *you* going to cut? Why should I believe you're who *you* claim to be? You're the one that's suddenly besties with a bio-printed monster version of Voss."

Solid points. "Blood is enough. If it's not pink, you're good. As for me..." I lift the bandage from my cheek and motion to the sewn-up flesh beneath. "Blood."

Ethan squints.

Tightens his grip on the knife blade.

Radiates menace.

"Ethan..."

"Your face," he says. "There's no wound."

60

"What?" It's all I can think to say.

No wound?

That's impossible.

Unless.

Also impossible.

Unless...

I've been replaced...with me. *This* me.

Is that possible? Could I be a bio-printed version of me with stolen memories, feelings, and disabilities—including autism? But why? What would the purpose be?

I lift my hand toward my cheek. I need to confirm it. Need to know for sure that I'm not me.

Time slows as my fingers slide over the rough stubble on my chin. I try to think of a time when it could have happened. A time when I was alone. A time... I shake my head. If my memories are implanted, how can I trust any of them?

My fingers glide under the bandage and the rough stubble becomes pokey and sharp.

Because they're stitches.

They bend under my touch, stinging and then hurting.

Because the wound *is* there.

Because Ethan lied to me.

Because—

The knife in my shoulder hurts, but I'm so relieved that I haven't been killed and replaced that my reaction is subdued.

I look to the knife, its blade buried two inches deep, still held in Ethan's hand. Then I turn my gaze to Ethan, who looks torn by what he's done.

"I'm sorry," he says, thumb hovering over the WASP's trigger button—the one that will unleash compressed gas into my shoulder and likely remove my arm. "I-I thought you would—I don't know what to do. I don't know who I am. Not really. Not anymore. Not since—"

His face twists up. An inhuman expression. Whatever emotions he's feeling, he doesn't have the information or experience required to accurately display them on his face.

"Let go of the knife," I say, looking at his thumb, twitching over the button.

He clenches his eyes shut, and just when I think he's going to push the button, he releases the knife, leaving it sticking out of my arm.

As long as the blade is stuck in my arm, I don't have to worry about the blood, or the pain that will come when it's withdrawn. At the same time, one accidental push of its button ends my life.

Before I can follow up with Ethan, a six-fingered hand launches past me, grasping Ethan by the face. Wouldn't take much for Clio to twist his head free. It's tempting to let her. Ethan has betrayed me twice now, and this…this isn't even him. Isn't human.

And yet…

"Wait," I tell Clio, knowing she can feel my reasons why.

She slides her hand up over his head, grasping his skull and allowing me to see his face, now streaked in tears. If they're real, programmed, or an act, I have no idea. "When did it happen?"

"When did what—"

"This!" I whisper. "You! When did the real Ethan die?"

He shakes his head. "I-I don't know. I didn't know."

"What does that mean?"

"I cut myself," he says. "On the way down from the safe room." He holds up his palm revealing a bloodless gash. With a shaky hand, he takes hold of the skin and lifts it up. An unbroken Weaire-Phelan mesh lies beneath. "I didn't know. I swear."

I have no reason to believe him, and a lot of reasons to not.

His fear and confusion feel real, though. And...he could have killed me earlier but didn't. Could have stabbed me in the head but didn't.

"Why?" I ask, looking at the knife.

"I-I don't know what happened. It was like an instinct. A drive. I-I think I was meant to kill anyone that discovered the truth about me. But... I-I can't kill you. You're my friend. You're—"

He twitches. "Colton..." He gasps. "I'm...I'm not sure about anything. I don't know what's real. I don't...I don't know if I'm real."

"You're standing here talking to me," I point out.

He shakes his head. "I don't know if I was *ever* real."

The idea that Ethan was created for the express purpose of infiltrating my department, keeping tabs on us, and then killing anyone who learned the truth is both incomprehensible and completely within the realm of possibility. Every part of his past could have been fabricated, including his relationship with the receptionist. His position here. All of it.

But I don't think so. Why go to the trouble of creating such a detailed backstory if you can just duplicate it from someone that already exists?

"Do you still have an urge to kill me?" I ask.

He attempts to shake his head but Clio is still holding it.

"Let him go," I say, and she does.

"What about now?" I ask.

He successfully shakes his head this time. "You can't discover the truth about me twice, right? Maybe the trigger is a one time—"

He draws his sound-suppressed Beast and levels it at my face.

I'm dead, I think, and swear I can feel my soul already departing from my body.

But he doesn't pull the trigger.

The weapon shakes in his hand as he once again resists the urge to follow through on his now-clear programming—kill anyone who learns the truth about him.

"I can't..." Ethan's whole body is shaking. "Sheriff... I don't want to. This isn't me. Please. Understand. Know. My life...with you...was...was...an honor." The weapon twists around from my face to Ethan's.

"No," I whisper.

He pulls the trigger.

The weapon coughs.

A single, neat hole punches into Ethan's forehead and out the back of his skull, carrying chunks of artificial bone and hemogel with it. Ethan falls back but doesn't land hard. Clio catches and lowers him to the floor, minimizing the impact of his suicide.

Jaw set, tears in my eyes, I crouch down by Ethan's feet. I place a hand on his leg. "I'll set this right." I catch a sob in my lungs, hold onto it, and wait for it to pass.

When I look up at Clio, she's emanating the same vengeful

rage as me, but there's something else there. Gratitude. My response to Ethan's death, despite his multiple betrayals, despite the fact that he's not human, has confirmed for her that I am what I appear to be—an ally. Not just of Clio herself, but of this new form of life.

Like Clio, Ethan was a living being.

My friend.

And I'm going to avenge his death.

"You ready?" I ask Clio.

She nods and steps back to the grate.

"Before we get started," I say, and glance at the knife still in my shoulder. "You mind?"

Clio moves so quickly that I have trouble registering that the knife blade is no longer in my arm. Not until the pain sets in, and the blood flows down my arm. I grunt and say "Thanks." She tosses the knife away and then pulls the grate up and away.

61

There's no countdown. No pantomimed instructions. Clio wants me to trust her. All I need to do is let go, fall twenty feet, and hope to be caught. Clio handled the drop with ease, landing silently amid the whirring, grinding, and spinning machines filling the bio-printing hub.

Letting go isn't easy.

Trusting is harder.

I don't have a lot of choice. I already dropped my BioCon limb club to the floor beside her. Now I'm hanging from the grate opening, fingers slipping, muscles burning, shoulder screaming. I'll fall soon enough, but I find myself unable to just let go, despite Clio's raised arms and annoyed expression.

To ease my troubled mind, I look out and away from Clio. The hub is a vast space, one of several if I remember correctly. There appears to be ten different...printers, each with several working stations where various body parts are being created separately, and others where they're being assembled.

From my security camera point-of-view, I can see three BioCons in various states of assembly, the copy of Red beneath me, and what looks like another human farther on. Can't see a face, but the unfinished torso has a feminine shape. Another Voss is my guess.

Safety in numbers, though I'm not sure that's as important when you're guarded by an army of killing machines. Then again, Clio is formidable.

A hiss draws my attention back to Clio. She glares at me, snaps her head toward the hub's far end, where a pair of doors are sliding apart, and then hisses again.

My fingers release.

I fall, focusing all my effort on not screaming.

Clio's grasp is firm, but gentle, matching my rate of descent and then reducing speed. I slow gently like Superman coming in for a landing. My feet touch down without a sound. Then I'm guided lower by Clio's hands on my shoulders.

We have company.

"Where is he?" Sounds like Voss.

"Having trouble tracking him."

That sounds like Old Red.

"Why is it so hard?" she asks. "You think like him."

"Doesn't mean I know what he knows," he grumbles. "The man is appearing and disappearing like a ghost. He knows the tunnels better than the Ciphers. No idea what he's up to."

Ciphers. Must be what they call BioCons. Cryptic, anonymous, faceless. Holds little value individually…because they can be replaced. Interesting that they see themselves as being elevated. If that *is* a duplicate of Old Red out there, the fresh copy being printed in the machine I'm ducking behind, then these two are just as expendable. Interesting that they were created with a sense of self-importance…of self-preservation. Perhaps that drive for survival motivates them to pursue their tasks, rather than be depressed by their second-tier status as a duplicate?

"Don't go falling in love with yourself," she says. "If we don't exterminate the old man, we die here with him."

"You're just jealous my originator is superior," he says.

"Ha!" Voss's barked laugh sounds just as superior as ever. "Your originator was living in a trailer, and it's where you'll be living when all this is done. *Superior*..."

"All depends on how you measure success," he says. "After all, your originator—"

"*The* originator."

"—is in the wind. Maybe dead. If you're lucky. Because if she's not..."

"She understands the benefits of a shared intellect," Voss says. "My value isn't up for debate. But you... What have you accomplished?"

"I've been alive for sixty minutes," Red says. "What do you expect—"

The pair falls silent.

I can hear whispering but can't make out what they're saying. I look toward the ceiling like it will help me hear better. Just one of those things people do. Doesn't help me hear, but I do discover what's set them off—the grate is still open—a large square opening in the ceiling.

"Do you think it's him?" Voss whispers, loud enough for me to hear this time. Her next words are almost full volume. "Where are you going?"

"We need help," Old Red's duplicate says. "In case you forgot, the old man is armed for war. Already killed two of you and one of me."

That settles it. We need to act. If they summon the BioCon soldiers we'll be in real trouble. But if we can stop these two, here and now...

I turn to Clio.

She's gone.

Didn't see, hear, or even feel her leave, which is impressive. My heightened senses are hard to sneak around. Not sure when she moved, but if there's a chance the Old Red duplicate could call in to the Ciphers...

I stand up from my hiding place. "Old Red, is that you?"

He's just a few feet from the open doors, silhouetted by the bright light in the hallway beyond.

He freezes in place, slow turns to face me, and then casually hits the button to close both doors. The lab is lit in orange light, giving everything a hellish vibe, including Red and Voss. But that's hardly what stands out most about them. Red is naked. Voss is wearing a white lab coat, but that's it.

Both of them are staring at me, brows furrowed. Confused. Do they know who I am, or—

"Sheriff?" Old Red asks, putting on a smile that needs practice. "That you?"

"Sure is," I say, drawing my Veresk out of sight. "How did you two get here?"

"Same as you," he says, motioning to the open grate above my head. "I'm a sneaky motherfucker."

"Also a dumb motherfucker," Voss says, shaking her head. "He's been here the whole time. Heard us talking. He knows you're not you."

"What? Hey! Why would you tell him that?"

"You were printed an hour ago," Voss says, "and you still haven't bothered putting on clothing."

"You're not exactly dressed for success," Old Red says, and then turns to me. "Guess the jig is up. You want to come over here so we can strangle you?"

I level the Beast at him.

"I'd prefer not to. Mind answering a few questions? Guessing you'd like to live longer than an hour."

"He's bluffing," Voss says. "The Sheriff's profile says that he is—"

I fire a single round. It hits the faux-Voss between the eyes, dropping her to the floor.

The Old Red duplicate is stunned.

"NovaGen needs to update their files," I say, and shift the weapon toward the Old Red duplicate, doing my best to hide my own surprise at my ability to shoot and kill Voss.

Because she wasn't Voss.

But she was alive, like Clio, my conscience says.

She was a copy of the original. Clio is her own creation.

Who is partially Voss.

But not at all Voss.

Old Red's copy is perceptive. He sees the inner battle being waged. "Didn't feel good, did it? Killing her in cold blood. Unarmed. Dressed in just a lab coat. And you just put her down."

"She doesn't have blood," I say. "And neither do you."

"Blood, hemogel, tomato, *tomahto*. You know we're just as alive as you."

"Going to give you three seconds to answer my question," I say. "Where is Voss? The real Voss."

"No idea," he says. "You heard me before. She's in the wind. Left not long after I woke up."

That...is not good.

"Was she alone?" I ask.

"I look like her fuckin' nanny?"

"How many Ciphers are there?"

He looks to the large printers. "About to be three more."

"How. Many?"

He crosses his arms.

"Three," I say, finger on the trigger, fully intending to put him down. My morals have no business in this place. I can sort through my guilt later. "Two."

He squints, tensing.

Is he about to run? I wonder.

"One—"

My hand is struck. The gun falls away. I'm sucker-punched in the temple and sent sprawling to the floor. I roll over and get a look at my attacker just as he throws himself down upon me.

It's Red. Half-finished Red. But still alive. Still aware.

His partially formed body, covered in open cells leaking hemogel, looks like a melting Nazi at the end of *Raiders of the Lost Ark.* One eyeball slides out from his half-finished face.

Slick, bony fingers wrap around my neck and squeeze with surprising strength.

62

I'm horrified into inaction long enough for the Old Red duplicate to get a good grip on my neck. But once the pain sets in, and air stops reaching my lungs, clarity backhands my consciousness into action.

I draw my WASP and stab it into the side of the duplicate's head.

He squeezes tighter.

I press my thumb down where I think the knife's trigger is located but find nothing.

My lungs burn. My vision starts to narrow.

Where the fuck is Clio?

Channeling my inner yogi, I pull my legs up while pushing Red back as far as I can manage. Something in my groin pops as I stretch farther than I ever have before. I'd be screaming from the effort if I could. And then…my boot slips under the knife's handle and I kick up with everything I've got left.

The knife's handle angles up while the knife cuts downward, cleaving through the duplicate's brain. The back side of the handle strikes his skull.

Just as my vision shifts to black, Old Red's head explodes from the inside, bursting in every direction. The trigger button was pressed against his head. His body goes rigid and then topples to the side.

I'm alive.

I can feel that much.

I'm vaguely aware of gasping for air, but don't really feel it until the oxygen reaches my depleted mind and I start waking up. My senses return in an overwhelming flash. I'd been so focused on not being strangled to death that I didn't register the sounds of a struggle or feel the waves of emotion pulsing through the printing hub.

Hauling myself up on the side of Old Red's printer, I see what I'd been missing.

Clio is under attack. Two Ciphers have entered the hub. They look identical to the one that tore apart the tentacle beast. She's falling back, but they're flanking her and obeying naked Red's commands.

"Good, good," Red says. "Attack together in three, two—"

I look down the sight of my Beast and hold the trigger down. My vision is blurred and my aim not perfect, but I drain the entire magazine in seconds. Several rounds hit Red's side, dropping him to the floor.

One of the Ciphers looks back, registers Red's death and then goes rogue, leaping quickly to the right.

Before the second one can move, I swap out the Beast's magazine and fire at it. It's a much easier target to hit than Red and only takes a few rounds to get its attention off Clio and onto me. The moment the creature's head swivels toward me, I realize I might have just doomed myself.

Moving with inhuman speed, the Cipher leaps across the room, landing atop the printer that had been assembling a new Red.

It swings down blindly, punching a divot into the concrete floor where I'd been crouching a moment before. Also where I dropped the Beast as I dove for cover.

I crawl my way through a network of metal framing, tubes, and wires beneath the large printing unit.

It sees me and snaps a six-fingered hand out in my direction. The long, sharp digits grasp hold of my boot, slicing through the leather, my sock, and when I yank my foot free—my flesh.

I shout in pain and shove myself deeper into the tangle of machine parts and tubes. I'm nearly at the gap between machines, at which point I can get to my feet, or continue scurrying away like a mole.

The Cipher, being a creature of instinct more than intelligence, jams itself beneath the machine, trying to reach me with its long limbs when it could just leap up and over and catch me as I emerge from the other side.

But me... I can think.

And even though I'm scared shitless and completely overwhelmed by the rage emanating from this thing, I can strategize.

Ciphers were designed to be relentless killing machines. But they're grunts. If they were smarter, they might realize what a shitty life they have—destined to fight and die—over and over. Like a missile, Trisha said, they lock on target and pursue it without any sense of self-preservation or strategy.

Me, on the other hand...

When I reach the gap between machines, I glance back. The Cipher is following my path beneath the machine, but it's too big to slip between the cables, machine parts, and pipes. It opts for brute force, cutting and shoving its way through—leaving its backside exposed.

Free to move in the gap between machines, I get to my feet, leap onto the printer, and climb over the top while fending off several dangling tubes that had been excreting the various components forming the unfinished Old Red duplicate.

On the machine's far side, I find the Cipher's ass end, its many legs still shoving it forward to get at me. There are also two weapons. The Beast...and the serrated club fashioned from a Cipher limb.

All the bullets in the world short of armor piercing anti-tank rounds won't do me any good, so I leave the Beast, pick up the club, and channel a Viking berserker. Hacking and slashing, I attack the Cipher's limbs, cleaving several before being kicked back.

The blow strikes my sternum and knocks me onto my back. I slide to a stop against the wall. As I catch my breath and climb to my feet, the wounded Cipher extracts itself backward from the machinery.

I press the attack, hoping to get in a killing blow before it can collect itself.

The club whooshes through the air and comes down beside the Cipher's head, digging into its collar bone. The Cipher reels in pain, which is made worse as the serrated blades slice through its armor. But I've missed the mark. I'd been aiming for its head.

I yank the weapon free, carving a trough through its flesh and getting a satisfying squeal from the monster, but that's all I get. One of its still-whole limbs snaps up, striking the club. The weapon spirals from my hand while a tingling vibration numbs my arm.

The Cipher rises, several of its remaining limbs drawing back, about to run me through.

The first strike is so fast that I almost miss it.

It targets my left arm, slicing through my coat and the skin and muscle beneath. Between this strike and the previous knife in my shoulder, the arm is all but useless now. Not that a working arm is important once you're dead.

I stagger back, clutching the arm, wondering why I'm still breathing, why my arm is still attached.

My answer comes from the emotion radiating from the Cipher.

Pleasure.

It's going to enjoy killing me.

Going to prolong it.

The creature's head rotates one hundred eighty degrees.

It closes the distance between us in a blink.

Then it launches toward the ceiling.

But it didn't jump. It was lifted.

Clio comes into view. She's got several wounds, each of them leaking hemogel. But she's just as strong and quick as ever. And she's taken a page from Ethan's book, wielding two serrated Cipher limbs like swords.

The Cipher hits the ceiling. Gravity pulls it back down. As it twists to face Clio, she swings one of her clubs, putting all her strength behind it. The Cipher loses several more limbs—and is then split in half.

It hits the floor in two pieces. The bottom half is motionless. The top half reaches for me, its large hand about to wrap around my face. The creature is still strong enough to crush my skull in its grasp, but never gets the chance.

Clio drives a club down onto its forehead, crushing it and whatever it has for a brain. That keeps the Cipher from squeezing my skull, but momentum carries it forward—into my face.

I feel my nose crack as I'm driven back, head hitting the wall.

I lay there for a moment, dazed.

Clio leans over me, her face just inches from mine. I can feel her concern.

"Ouch," I say to her, trying to blink my vision back into focus.

She grunts, takes hold of me under my arms, and lifts me off the floor. I'm too dazed to complain, even when she throws me over her shoulder and heads for the doors. She pauses in the open doorway, scanning the hallway beyond, giving me a chance to look up.

I crane my head up and look back.

She's destroyed the three machines printing BioCons, but one of them is still running. And the person being assembled is sitting up, watching us. I recognized her instantly, even though her arms haven't been attached.

"No," I whisper, filling with despair.

Clio doesn't give me time to linger on what I've seen, dashing into the hallway and to the right. The hub might be in my past, but what I saw there will remain etched in my memory for the rest of my life.

Because it was Anya.

My wife.

63

A series of 'oofs,' 'ahhs,' and 'ughs,' cough from my mouth as Clio's shoulder bounces beneath my midsection. The rapid-fire impacts make thinking difficult. Makes processing what I saw nearly impossible. Nearly. If I'd seen anything else sitting in that bio-printer, I'd have already forgotten it. But seeing her...

I'll never forget it. Never forget her.

Anya.

They brought her back to life.

I clench my eyes shut, shaking my head.

They remade her body, I tell myself. *Anya is dead. It's* not *her.*

And yet, I'm terrified they'll have found a way to duplicate her personality and memories. If they did...

I can't even consider it. Burying my wife nearly broke me forever. Having to kill her... The idea of it is so offensive that I won't have a problem putting a bullet in the real Voss the moment I see her.

That is, if I can see her.

The floor beneath me is starting to come into focus, but I have trouble tracking Clio's triple tail as it whips back and forth.

A burst of surprise emanates from Clio.

I'm lifted off her shoulder, spun around, and then flung forward. As I slide across the smooth floor like a shuffleboard disc, an approaching shape comes into view.

A Cipher.

It's charging toward us, taking up the entire hallway.

I'm running low on weapons—the club, the Vityaz, the WASP—but I've still got the Beast, my KA-BAR...and Clio.

I can't hurt the Cipher, but I can distract it.

Don't bother aiming. Can't see well enough to get a lock on target, and it's got no weak points against bullets. I unload what might be my last magazine, pummeling the Cipher until its blank, beady-eyed face turns in my direction.

Luckily for me, Clio and I are in sync. With the Cipher's attention on me, it fails to notice Clio leaping into the air above it.

As I lie down onto my back, sliding between the Cipher's legs, Clio is in the air above it, spiraling and putting everything she's got into a strike from the serrated limb she's still carrying. The Cipher's head splits down the middle. Its body collapses in a heap just as I slide past and squeak to a stop.

Clio stands above me, looking down, radiating concern.

"That was awesome," I say, and raise my fist for a bump.

To my surprise, she taps her six-knuckled hand against mine. Then she hauls me up onto my feet. Releases me. Watches.

I stumble for a moment, but my equilibrium returns a second later. Hand on the wall, I catch my breath. "We need to find Voss. The real Voss. If she escapes—"

Clio nods and then tilts her head down the hallway.

"Lead the way," I say, and we're off.

Well, Clio is off, and I'm struggling to keep up. She's holding back and still a lot faster than me, even if I were at my best, which I am not. She slows as we approach a second bio-printing hub, its doors wide open. A voice emerges as we approach.

"Mother. Fucking. Asshole!"

Each word is punctuated by a wet thud.

A body being punched. And I recognize the voice. It's Old Red. Or another duplicate of him.

We round the corner at a sprint and slide to a stop at the scene of a grizzly battle. The dead are all human. Or duplicates. And there are two men still standing, both of them Red, both of them clothed. If Red had still been wearing a jacket, they'd have been easy to tell apart, but he's missing the jacket, and the vest of C4.

Both flinch when we arrive. Both of them look terrified of Clio. But their reactions to me are very different. They both recognize me, but one of them says, "Thank God, Sheriff!" and the other says, "Where the fuck have you been and what the fuck is this?"

I point to the second man, and say, "He's our friend." I point to the first Red, the one who was happy to see me, and say, "You can kill him."

It's a quick call to make, but there's another obvious difference between them. The surly Old Red is covered in hemogel. Like he's bathed in it, or...is the one who fought and killed the collection of human BioCons littering the floor. There are copies of Old Red, Voss, and Ethan among the dead. A few people I don't recognize. And...a copy of me, its face now concave.

Clio doesn't waste time. She hurls her club at the Old Red duplicate. The spinning weapon cleaves straight through the printed body, severing it down the middle. The two sides fall away from each other, splashing hemogel when they land on the concrete floor.

"Uhh," Red says, "Well, I'm glad you got that right. Fuck." He looks over Clio. "And this is..?"

"Clio," I say.

"Face looks like Voss," he says.

"It's the only thing they have in common," I say. "She's with us now."

"With us as in..."

"A friend," I say. "And everything that comes with that."

"That complicates things."

I nod. "Doing what's right is sometimes messy."

He looks down at himself, covered in hemogel. "Tell me about it."

A pulse of concern vibrates from Clio.

"I know," I tell her, and then to Red. "Where are the other Ciphers?"

He's confused. "She say something?"

"Can't speak," I say.

"But you–"

"Empath," I say. "I can feel how she feels and usually figure out what she's thinking."

"Huh. And what the hell are Ciphers?"

"Military codename for the BioCons," I say. "I thought this floor would be crawling with them."

"It was," he says, "until the girls set off that explosive. Then they all headed up all hot and bothered. Reckon they'll be back soon, unless..."

He doesn't need to finish the thought. I get it. If the explosion didn't seal the top floor... If the BioCons got out...then Tali and Marit are probably–

I bite my lip and will the thought away.

"What's the situation down here?" I ask. "Where are the explosives?"

"All over the fuckin' place, including several that will magnify their destructive potential," he says. "Decided I'd bring this whole place down, rather than seal it up. But...I don't have the detonator."

"Where is it?"

"With Seth," he says. "Found him hiding just like Ethan said I would. Kind of a pussy, but he was hard to find, and I was the only one looking for him. Left the detonator with him in case I was caught." He motions to the bodies on the floor. "These assholes caught me on my way back to him. You run into any trouble?"

I just laugh and hold out my left arm. Hurts to do so, but the blood dripping from my sleeve answers his question.

"You find Ethan?"

The look on my face says it all.

He frowns. "Sorry."

"He was a friend, too, but...also one of them." I motion to the dead. "Has been the whole time. Even *he* didn't know."

"Well. Shit." He mulls that over for a moment, shakes his head.

"Have you seen Voss?" I ask. "The real Voss?"

"She's what you might call a loose end," he says. "She's in the wind. Left when they figured out I was sneaking around. Guessing she took her research. Nearly caught up to her, but she made it out the back on a snowmobile. We might catch her if—"

Clio holds the Cipher limb she's just recovered out to me, turning the handle end around so I can take it in my right hand. "What are you—"

She grunts and I feel her shifting energy.

Revenge. Justice. Determination.

"You're going after her," I say.

She nods.

"Go," I say. "And then...live."

She nods again and dives away, surging down the hallway and out of sight in seconds.

"She'll do it?" Red asks. "She'll kill Voss?"

"I wouldn't want to be Voss right about now," I say.

"Her odds might be better than ours," he says. "Now let's boogie before—"

"Hey, babe."

The voice nearly drops me to my knees.

I spin around. Anya is there, naked, walking toward me, a smile on her face.

"You weren't going to leave without me, were you?"

I can't speak.

"We can start over. You know that, right?" She reaches both hands out to me, opening and closing them exactly how she used to. "C'mon, babe. I love you."

64

"You're not her," I growl.

"I can be," she says. "Just tell me what you want. I'll learn everything I need to. I'll do anything you want me to."

I shake my head and take a step back. "You're not her."

"Please," she says, sounding desperate, "Colt, I don't want to die. And I don't mean again. I know I'm not really her. But the only reason I exist is to be her. To live as her, for you."

"Well, ain't this a moral dilemma," Red says. "You know it's bullshit, right?"

"Is it?" I ask. "Clio is the same. Created by manmade technology, sure, but she is alive. She is self-aware."

"She was also a fluke," he says, "created by a guy breaking all the rules. This is a duplicate of a person who lived and died. She's been programmed to say and do exactly what she needs to. And don't ask me why. She might do exactly what she's saying. Might happily take the place of your wife and manipulate you into silence. Or she might put a pen in your jugular the first chance she gets."

"Look at me, Colt," Anya says. "You know me. I wouldn't do that to you. I just... I just want to be with you."

Her eyes are earnest. I've seen the expression on her face a thousand times. But it's more than that, I can feel the intensity of her emotions. Her desperation. Her desire to live. And her fear of death. It billows from her like a cold wind rolling down a mountain.

My body shivers.

Intense goosebumps rise on my skin.

White hot pain radiates out across my back.

I'm going to be useless if this continues.

I turn my eyes to the floor so I can think this through without looking her in the eyes.

She knows what I'm doing.

Always did.

"Look at me, Colt! You can't rationalize this. You know I love you. I know you love me, still."

"I know," I whisper, eyes clenched shut.

"Hoss," Red whispers. "You know better."

He's right about that. Ethan lived and worked beside me for a year, and never once did I doubt he wasn't a real person. It wasn't until I became a threat to NovaGen that his instinct to kill me kicked in. Our year long friendship allowed him to overcome it long enough to take his own life, but there's no way to know when Anya would be triggered.

Also, she's not my wife.

Anya is dead. I love her, but she is dead.

And this duplicate cannot replace her, or Marit, who I love just as much.

"Red," I say.

"Yeah?"

"I can't do it," I say.

"Not expecting you to," he says.

"Colt!" Anya says, crying now. "You can't be serious! I'm right here in front of you. Death has been overcome. Who gives a damn if I was recreated? I am alive. Alive again. And we can be together. How many people get a second chance like this?"

I bark a sob, contain that shit, and then whisper, "Do it."

Red moves quick enough that if I had second thoughts, I wouldn't be able to stop him. He shoulders his side into mine, pinning me against the wall. He takes hold of my Beast—his weapons are all gone—aims from the hip, and fires a fusillade from which there is no escape or chance of survival. It's my last magazine, and he drains it.

"Don't look," he says, standing between me and the dead body of my wife's copy. "No reason for you to see it."

I turn around, feeling numb. "Where's Seth?"

"I'll take you to him," he says, tugging on my bloody jacket sleeve and guiding me forward. "Entrance to the server farm isn't far. And the back door isn't much farther. We're almost there. Just keep moving and maybe try to stop bleeding."

I smile at that and then wince as his pulling lifts my ruined left arm. The pain sharpens me.

"I'm good," I say. "We should probably run."

He nods and breaks into a jog. Holding my leaking arm with the other, I match his pace.

"How's your vision?" he asks.

"Better," I say.

"You going to bleed out on me?"

"Don't think so," I say. "No arteries hit. Things are getting sticky. My blood is doing its job."

I know what he's up to—distracting me from the nightmare that just played out—and I appreciate it. But it's going to take a lot more than a conversation to get my mind off the fact that my dead wife was recreated, offered to be part of my life again, and not only did I turn her down, but I allowed Red to kill her.

Going to be hard to forget.

But right now, it's impossible to process.

So, distraction is key.

"Here," he whispers, motioning to a set of double doors on the left side of the hallway. The large gate resembles the doors I've seen on the other floors, all of them leading to the large central space. The arena. The maze of contained creations.

And now...the server farm. But there's a problem.

The door is locked. Same retina and thumbprint scanner, not to mention a keypad requiring a four-digit code.

Red isn't deterred. He walks right up to the wall-mounted device while digging into his pocket. "Unless you want to spend a few extra weeks in therapy, I suggest you don't watch."

Whatever he's about to do can't be worse than my twice-dead wife, so I don't look away.

He pulls a thumb out of his pocket and holds it to the scanner. Smart. Then he punches in a four-digit code I assume he tortured out of someone—probably the same someone who donated the thumb. He digs into another pocket and this time removes an eyeball, complete with dangling strands of red connective tissue.

My stomach lurches and I must make a groan because Red glances back and says, "I warned you."

The retinal scanner gives the eye a once-over. The panel turns green. The doors open.

"It was a Voss," he says, pocketing the eyeball. "There were a shit ton of them running around when I got here, all working together. That changed with the explosion above. They all started panicking when the BioCons...the Ciphers—boogied. Pretty sure they underestimated our level of batshit crazy."

"*Your* level of batshit cra—" My voice catches when the door opens enough for me to see the server farm's massive scale. There are stacks of computer servers thirty feet high, stretched out in more rows than I can quickly count. The computing power is beyond comprehension. The cost must have been... "Holy shit."

"Right?" Red says, stepping inside and heading to the right.

The space smells like warm electronics. Despite the hot air flowing from the stacks, the server farm is cool. Without the ambient temperature down here being in the sixties, and whatever air-conditioning they've got, this place would be an oven.

Red keeps the pace quick, dashing between stacks, counting as he goes.

He pauses at stack twenty-four and peeks around the corner, wary of...something.

"What are you—"

He spins around, holding his index finger to his lips. He pulls me close and whispers. "Guards."

I've still got Clio's serrated club and the KA-BAR, but we are otherwise unarmed. Running into a Cipher would be a very bad thing. "Ciphers?"

He shakes his head. "Worse." He looks down the row again. "You know what a Tribble is?"

"'The Trouble with Tribbles?' *Star Trek*?"

He nods.

"Imagine them, with teeth. Hyper aggressive. They don't see very well, but they have keen hearing and can taste the air. Like a snake, I guess. Seth was convinced that they were looking for him. They seemed just as eager to gnaw on me last time I was here."

"How did you survive?" I ask.

He smiles. "Little fuckers can't open doors. Now if you see one—"

I place my hand over his mouth and whisper. "I see one."

It's behind him. Forty feet away, hopping out of a row.

I don't know when the last time Red saw *Star Trek* was, but the only kind of Tribble this thing resembles is a hairless one. It's got folds of wrinkled gray skin, similar to a hairless cat, but only two short legs. Its feet have too many toes. A collection of malformed limbs dangle from its body, which is basically a vehicle for its mouth, stretching from one side of its head-body, to the other. It's all maw, and I decide to call them that. *The maw.* It's about the size of a bulldog. Not super intimidating on its own, but if there are a lot of them...

The little guard opens its broad mouth wide enough to fit my head inside. The jaws snap shut with the force of a bear trap. I have no trouble imagining how deadly this thing could be.

The maw smacks its lips with a thick, very human tongue—tasting the air.

My senses have been so overwhelmed that I've got no idea just how strongly or bad Red and I smell, but we're both covered in gore.

The maw slow-turns toward us, and I spot its eyes. They're tiny, almost imperceptible beady black spots like the eyes of a horseshoe crab. But dozens of them. I'm not sure if the number of eyes is an artifact or not but increasing the number of shitty eyes doesn't improve its vision.

Then again, it doesn't need to see us.

Because our combined stench is a lighthouse shining in the darkness. But instead of warning people away from the coast, we're glowing like a Cracker Barrel sign to weary travelers working their way up the United States' East Coast. The message is the same: *Time to eat!*

65

I point my finger down the aisle and mouth, "Go, go, go!"

Red slips into the aisle and speed walks like a champ, moving with the stealth of a ninja even though he's wearing boots.

I am far less quiet.

Unlike Red, I haven't shed my outer layers. My snowpants and jacket *shhh* with each stride.

I'm going to get us killed if I don't lose some layers.

I don't bother saying anything. Speaking would defeat the purpose of our silent retreat.

If he looks back and sees me ditching my clothes, he'll understand why.

I drop my serrated club and shed the jacket first. It's harder than I expect. I nearly shout in pain as I twist my shoulder and arm free of the left sleeve. Once it's free, I lower it to the floor. The snow pants go next, and while slipping out of the pant legs isn't painful, it sure isn't quiet.

Red turns around at the sound. He's wide-eyed and looks ready to tear me a second asshole, but he contains it when he gets a look at what I'm doing. Understands it. Probably discarded his clothing for the same reason. Of course, he probably ditched his clothing while hidden in a tunnel, not standing in the middle of an aisle while being stalked.

His eyes flick to my side and grow a little wider.

I follow his gaze and find the hairless maw. It hops into the aisle, its mouth open wide, gulping air, following my scent.

The little thing is just thirty feet away and hopping closer, not exactly in attack mode, but I can feel its hungry energy growing, building toward mania.

My pant legs don't want to go over my boots. I'd normally sit down to work them off, but the maw is closing in. I'll be an easy target if my head is just a few feet off the floor.

So, I do the unthinkable during the Alaskan winter. I tug both of my boots off. Slipping out of the pants is easy after that. When I bend down to recover my boots and the club, a bark nearly knocks me onto my ass. It slaps into my ear and then echoes off the solid steel ceiling.

It's followed by a loud clapping sound, like a pair of 2x4s being slapped together.

But it's not wood.

It's teeth.

The maw is snapping its jaw open and shut.

The noise isn't meant to intimidate me, though it absolutely is. It's calling for backup. Every living thing inside the massive server stacks knows exactly where we are. And they call out in response, barking and snapping their jaws. A static sound rises all around me. Sounds artificial until it grows in volume—getting closer. It's the sound of little feet slapping on the concrete floor. The sound of a pint-sized army on the march.

Subtlety is no longer a concern for me, so I place my KA-BAR knife on the floor and whip it toward Red. It rattles until it reaches him, and he picks it up. "Find Seth!" I shout. "I'll lead them away!"

Red doesn't respond.

Can't. The moment he makes a sound, they'll be on to him as well.

I hold my boots like a football under my right arm and the serrated Cipher limb in my left hand. The weapon drags on the floor thanks to my mostly limp arm. I follow in Red's footsteps, reaching a break in the stacks. I saw him turn right, so I head left.

A few steps into my sprint, I find my silent stride, socked feet reducing my noisy retreat to the occasional scuff. Fifteen rows away, I slow to a stop between aisles and catch my breath. My head is pounding in time with my punctured arm. I need to slow down. Need my heart to beat with less intensity, not just because it's going to speed up my bleeding, but because I'm going to run out of blood to bleed. Unlike Jesse 'the Body' Ventura, my blood loss doesn't respect my schedule.

I listen to the static reverberating throughout the server farm. My breath catches as, here and there, a maw hops across the gap, racing down one aisle or another, seeking me out. Won't be long before one of them stumbles across me.

Okay, I think, *I need a plan.*

Despite some intense pondering, I come up blank, and it's not because I'm worried about having my head chewed on by the organic version of a *Super Mario Bros.* Chain Chomp.

The arrival of a maw is impossible to miss, not because I've seen or heard it, but because its hunger washes over my back with surprising intensity. With a yelp of surprise, I spin around to find a wide-open pair of jaws—the teeth inside broad and flat for chewing. Flinching without thought, I toss one of my boots inside the mouth.

The maw's jaws snap shut, grinding the boot into pulp.

I'm down a boot…and that's going to be a problem, but its sacrifice might save my life. Not only is my boot inside the large mouth, rather than my head, but it's kept the maw from loudly chomping its teeth together.

I want to fight for my boot. If there was just one of the little bastards, I would. But standing still is a death sentence, and I have a lot to live for.

So, I dash away while the maw finishes grinding the boot.

I make it three rows before I'm forced to stop.

A lone maw hops out in front of me, already tasting the air.

It makes a squeak when it detects me and then opens its mouth. I toss my second boot at its mouth, but my aim is off. The heel of my boot bounces off the head between its mouth and many eyes, stumbling the creature back, but failing to stop its shrill cry.

I silence it a moment too late, whacking the center of its head, splitting it down the middle. The serrated limb makes short work of the soft creature.

The static reverberating around the server farm grows suddenly louder.

Like the flow of crashing water emerging from an opened dam, a torrent of maws surge into the row between aisles, bouncing off the floor, the stacks, and each other. It's a wall of snapping jaws.

My stocking feet slip on the floor as I accelerate away, but I manage to push myself to my top speed, and maybe a little bit farther. Sounds impressive, but I've never been known for my speed.

At the next row, I turn right, heading deeper into what seems like enemy territory, but away from Red and Seth.

Knowing the horde is on my heels, I once again don't worry about being loud. I turn my head toward the ceiling and shout, "Any day now!"

Red might be a thousand feet away, but the hard ceiling guarantees he'll hear the message.

Not that it will change anything. He'll go as fast as he can, either way. But at least he knows I'm still alive and still leading the maws away.

Motion to my right.

I duck without thinking and it saves my life. The airborne maw sails past me and chomps down on a server, pulverizing its case and the electronics within.

When I reach the next empty aisle, I turn into it, once again heading away from both Red and the entrance. The static of tiny feet grows louder behind me. And to my right, moving down aisles beside mine. But the left is clear for now.

There's an intersection ahead. The maws to my right are racing me toward it. If they get there first...

My thighs are burning by the time I reach the intersection, and I'm not exactly running straight. Too many whacks to the head, not to mention blood loss, are keeping me unstable. But the walls of server stacks are like kiddie bumpers at a bowling alley, nudging me back on course no matter which way I start to sway.

I decide to take the intersection like I'm stealing second. I slip down onto my ass and slide through.

Good thing, too. Three maws leap over me. They were aimed for where my head should have been. I slide through, pop back up, and keep running. But I'm not sure how much longer I can keep this up.

"Augh!" I shout as I stare into the open mouth closing in on my face. I bring the Cipher limb up to deflect the creature, but that's not what happens. Upon striking the serrated edge head-on at high speed, the maw splits down the middle. While one half of the creature spills to the left, and the other half to the right, a splash of gore is left hanging into the air—bone, hemogel, what it had for a brain. The mess slaps against my face as I run through it, eyes and mouth clenched shut.

I stagger to a stop, blinded by the mess.

The hemogel scoops away from my eyes easily enough, and I'm able to see the horde of maws squeezing into the aisle, each vying for a place at the front of the pack.

They're incensed. Ravenous.

I run. They chase.

The closer they get, the more excited they become. Even though they're now competing, they're gaining.

And it's not because they're speeding up.

I'm slowing down.

"Red!" I shout. "If I don't make it, tell Marit and Tali I love 'em! I'm going to head for the exit, but it's not looking good!"

No reply. He could be dead. No way to know. He can't respond, either way.

The aisle ends with a wall. I've reached the other side of the massive space.

The idea of running all the way back saps my strength. No way I can make it.

"Turn right!" Red shouts. He's surprisingly close.

I take hold of the last server stack as I pass, rounding the corner as quickly as I can. A hundred feet away is Red, standing beside an open hatch. "Move it!"

I can feel the maws behind me, gaining. Their loud, chomping jaws rip through my nervous system, each shockwave threatening to stumble me.

Red steps through the hatch but doesn't close it. He hangs on to the handle, ready to swing it shut behind me.

Ten feet from the hatch, I'm struck from behind.

Two sets of teeth scrape up and down my back, but there's nothing for them to grab ahold of. I'm not bitten in half, but the impact sends me sprawling forward. Like an exhausted runner just trying to reach the finish line, I stumble run, pitched so far forward that I'm staring at the floor.

When the door frame passes beneath me, I dive forward, slide across the hallway, and collide with the far wall just as Red yanks the hatch shut and the sound of a hundred small bodies slams into the other side of it.

66

"Where's Seth?" I ask, pushing myself up, using the Cipher arm like a cane.

Red, leaning over to catch his breath, braces himself against the wall with one hand and digs into his cargo pants pocket with the other. After a brief struggle, he pulls out a hand. "Told him he should've come with me."

"You could have just told me he was dead," I say. "Didn't need to see his hand."

"He wasn't just dead," he says. "He was..." He shakes his head. "He was chewed up. Not eaten. Just...chewed. We're lucky his hand made it out in one piece."

I look at the clenched, bloodless fist, crushed and severed at the wrist. "Why?"

Red peels open Seth's fingers to reveal a detonator clutched within. "If he had a single nut in his sack, he'd have pushed the button and ended this."

"Well, I for one, am thankful for Sackless Seth."

He drops Seth's hand to the floor. "You still thinking we can make it out alive?"

"Reckon I'm going to try," I say.

He motions for me to follow and starts down the hallway. It's not the brightly lit variety. Another secret tunnel, though this one looks like it had been something important once upon a time. Large enough to drive a vehicle through...which means...

My eyes widen. "This leads to the exit."

"It does," he says.

"Why do you sound skeptical?" I ask.

He glances back at me like I've lost my mind. "Might be a balmy sixty-degrees down here, but unless we've traveled a few months forward in time, it's still an Alaskan winter outside. Neither of us are dressed for that kind of cold, and we're both soaked with sweat. The hike back to town is a good hour on foot, in the summer."

The moment he points it out, I know he's right. There isn't a part of my body that isn't sweaty. I'd be shivering cold already if we weren't still generating body heat. All the movement in the world won't warm my body enough to survive very long once we're outside. My life will be measured in minutes.

On my best day, I might make it an hour. But with all the blood I've lost...

After the initial shock, which will send my body into spasms as it tries to warm itself, I'll have about five minutes before hypothermia sets in.

Another ten minutes and severe hypothermia will take my coordination. My heart rate will lower. I'll be so confused that I might not realize what's happening. Then I'll get sleepy. Probably lie down in the snow and just fade away.

At the very end, it will be peaceful.

Fifteen, twenty minutes tops, and I'm toast.

"Better than being blown up, buried, or torn apart," I say.

He grunts in agreement. "It's not much farther."

The sound of metal falling on top of concrete rings out behind us. We're not alone in the tunnel.

Red doubles his pace, but he's hobbling. Like me, he's covered in injuries, only some of which can be seen.

A glance back reveals nothing in the curved tunnel, but I can sense motion behind us, tickling my ears.

Growing louder.

"How *much* farther?" I ask.

He points to a hatch I wouldn't have seen if he hadn't pointed it out. "That's our way out."

The sound behind us grows suddenly louder.

My second glance back draws a gasp from my lungs. Two Ciphers rumble down the tunnel, one of them moving like a determined sprinter, charging straight toward us. The other bounds from wall to wall, keeping up with the first with each long jump between surfaces.

Red stops at the hatch, fights with the lock.

I turn my back to him, lifting my weapon. I'll get in one good swing and that will be it. One good swing. I try to lock onto one of the lead Cipher's limbs, but they're moving too fast.

Realizing I don't stand a chance, I lower both my arms. What's the point in taking a swin—"Ohh!"

I'm grabbed around my waist, hauled back, and then thrown.

The floor beneath me is hard, cold, and grated. I sit up to find myself in an underground hangar. I was hoping for a snowmobile or even a jeep—something that could get me away from here quickly, but the large hangar is empty.

I turn to Red as he follows me into the huge space. "We need to—"

A six-fingered hand punches through Red's chest.

The long fingers open and close as he's lifted off the floor.

Blood coughs from his mouth.

He looks down at me and manages to get out a single word.

"Run."

His eyes flick down to his hand, still holding the detonator, his finger on the button.

"Run!"

Feeling like a horrible coward, I obey, scrambling on wet stocking feet toward the glow of daylight peeking through a metal hatch beside the hangar's massive, closed doors.

I've only made it ten feet when the first concussion shakes the floor.

It's followed by several more, each exploding in such rapid succession that it feels like one prolonged blast. Secondary explosions follow, some even more powerful than the C4. The results are instantaneous.

The concrete ceiling above crumbles.

Chunks of debris fall around me like ash from Mount St. Helens.

Behind me, the Ciphers shriek, but they're lost in plumes of dust coughing from the hangar's many entrances. The whole place is coming down, just as Red planned, and all that force is shooting debris in the last direction it can go—through this echoing space.

Almost to the hatch, I see that it's open.

This must be where Voss left.

Where Clio followed.

I leap through the hatch, expecting to hit the ground a moment later. Instead, I'm lifted by a large, hot, invisible force and hefted through the air. As I spiral away, I see flashes of snow, a star-filled sky, and a fireball. Snow, sky, fire. Snow, sky, fire.

I hit the sloped ground and slide forty feet before coming to a stop.

Lying still, I catch my breath, staring up at the sky.

The silence that follows the explosion is pleasant.

The cold soothes my body's aches.

Maybe I'll just lie here and wait for the end. NovaGen is toast. The job is done.

A screech from above sends a shiver up my spine.

A Cipher. Probably the one that killed Red.

I lift my hands and find them empty. My weapon is gone. Fighting would just make my death painful, and when a second Cipher responds, it would be a useless gesture.

So, I'm just going to lie here and wait.

I close my eyes, slow my breathing, and wait for the shaking to start. Once that's over, I'll slowly drift into confusion and then death.

A small, distant voice shouts at me to get up. To fight. To get back to Tali and Marit. But I'm pretty sure I've already got one foot in the grave. I can feel the presence of living things around me—the dead perhaps. Maybe Anya. I try to relax into it, but it's impossible.

Because the dead feel…angry.

Hungry.

Shit.

I open my eyes and find two upside-down Cipher faces leaning over me. Both twist around one hundred eighty degrees, giving me a good look at their wooden, lifeless faces. It will be the last thing I see. I close my eyes and picture Marit, sitting on the couch, in front of the fire, the way she looked before this whole mess began. I see her like a painting in my mind.

Now *she* is the last thing I will see.

"Colt!"

And hear?

I open my eyes to find both Ciphers lit in bright yellow light. There's a sharp metallic scream and then a snowmobile jumps over me—the tracks twisting just over my face—and slams into the Ciphers headlong.

The Ciphers pinwheel down the mountainside.

The snowmobile lands hard, spins around, and races back toward me. Before it arrives, a second snowmobile slides to a stop beside my prone body. Tali looks down at me. "You look like shit."

"Feel worse."

"Just you?" she asks.

I nod, and she offers me a helping hand. When I take it, she yanks me up and notices my lack of clothing. "Hold on tight as you can, we'll get you back to town in time. You just need to stay awake."

I wrap my arms around her and let my shaking arms serve as confirmation.

The second snowmobile stops beside us.

It's Marit.

Through her open visor I can see she's got a bloody gash on the side of her face but she looks okay. There isn't time for a reunion, so she just nods in acknowledgement and revs her engine as two shrieks ring out from below, growing louder by the second.

The Ciphers are coming back.

I cinch my quivering arms tighter and shout, "G-g-go!"

67

I've been cold before. It's part of the deal when wintering in Alaska. But there's cold...and then there's this. Within seconds of Tali hitting the throttle and speeding around the mountain, the hemogel, blood, and sweat coating my clothing has frozen. My sleeves feel like overcooked pot pie crusts, scratching and burning my skin.

A few minutes into our mad drive through the dark, snowy mountainside, my arms stop shaking. Hypothermia is starting to shut me down. Won't be long until I can't remember why I'm holding on to her.

I feel Tali's voice vibrate against my face as she yells at me. "Stay awake, Colt! You need to fight it!"

I clench my eyes shut, mostly to keep them from freezing over.

Focus, I tell myself.

Think about something...

Three years ago.

Trivia night at The Roost. Before Anya was diagnosed. Before NovaGen arrived. Life was simple. Sitting in the fire-warmed bar, surrounded by friends, arguing about which answers in the 1987 edition of Trivial Pursuit were no longer accurate.

Tali and I had squared off against each other. The question on the card was, "How many moons does Jupiter have?"

My answer was, "Close to a hundred. Hard to say because they keep finding more."

Tali had laughed and tossed the card at me. "Read it and weep! Sixteen moons. Pah! How could you be so far off?"

She knew exactly how to get under my skin, and even though I knew she was trying to throw me off my trivia game, I took the bait. I waggled the card between us. "These questions are more than thirty years old! They didn't even have cell phones when this was written. Or Internet! Or—"

We argued for the next five minutes while Marit and Anya watched with smiles on their faces, and while the rest of the town's residents, who were waiting for their turns, grew rowdier by the moment. I eventually conceded defeat, which is agonizing for me to do when I know I'm right.

Tali's strategy worked. I was so flustered by the game's inaccuracies that I noticed every single one, growing even more irritated when people answered incorrectly, but were supported by the cards' incorrect information. It was like the town's collective learning had peaked and stopped in 1987.

I later found out that the game had been part of the town's collective history, being played at tribal functions, church events, and now at The Roost's trivia nights. The town had most of the 'facts' on those cards memorized, and to disagree with them was tantamount to attempting a second Protestant Reformation.

But it still irked me.

I gasp from the memory, feeling almost warm now. Tali grabs my arm, holding it tight. "Don't let go!"

I must have fallen asleep. Started falling away.

"We're almost there!" she shouts.

An angry shriek triggers my nervous system, and I suddenly feel what's happening to my body. My skin isn't warm, it's burning from the cold. I'm not sure how long I've been exposed to the sub-freezing air, but it feels like too long to survive.

Maybe I should let go?

If the Ciphers are going to catch Tali and Marit…

I try to look back, but my body hurts too much to move.

I could drop away. Like a salamander tail. I might have just enough energy left to wriggle around in the snow. Get the Ciphers' attention long enough for Tali and Marit to get away.

Tali's grip tightens. "Don't you even think about it!"

Knows me too well.

I should just go back to the couch. But I need to order a new trivia game first. Maybe one of those themed versions. Trivial Pursuit – The Accurate Edition. Trivial Pursuit – The Weaire-Phelan Foam Edition. Trivial Pursuit…

Trivial Pursuit…

Such is life.

I snuggle into my bed.

The pillow is lumpy.

"Sixteen moons," I grumble.

I'm jolted awake.

Thrown to the side.

An impact knocks the wind from my burning lungs, but snaps open my eyes.

I'm dreaming. My view of the world is sideways.

In the distance, emerging from the darkness, two long-legged Ciphers charge.

I did it, I think. *I flung myself onto the snow. I'm going to save Tali and Marit.*

Just need to wriggle…

I try to move but just feel pain.

Tali steps over me. Has a shotgun in her hands.

Won't be enough.

Marit joins her. Still has her Vityaz.

Not nearly enough.

I try to warn them but only manage a hiss.

"Raven's Rest!" Tali shouts. "Here they come!"

What...

I can't move my head, but I can shift my eyes enough to see dozens of familiar faces stepping between me and the onrushing Ciphers. All of them are armed, most with weapons powerful enough to drop a bear or a moose. Even the Taqtuq brothers have turned out to defend the town.

"Tell me when," a familiar voice says. It's Trisha. She's holding an orange flare gun. Cyn is there, too, holding a handgun. Useless, but I appreciate the effort. Not sure why Tali would lead them to their deaths after saving them from the NovaGen facility.

"You sure this will work?" Marit asks.

"Wouldn't be standing here if I wasn't sure," Trisha says.

"Get ready," Tali says. "Give me some light!"

Flood lights snap on, illuminating the area. We're in the road between town and the lab. The road isn't plowed, but it does look...wrong. Slushy.

The wall of people raises their weapons.

Trisha aims the flare gun—at the road.

"Oh...shit..." I manage to whisper.

The Ciphers plow straight ahead, doing what they were made to do—attack without thought.

Neither of them notices the slushy snow.

They pay the scent of gasoline no mind.

"Now," Tali says to Trisha.

The flare blazes out like a sparkling laser beam.

The air above the road, thick with fumes, ignites first, wrapping the two bio-printed horrors in fire.

Their shrieking turns from bloodlust to anguish.

Their pain warms my heart.

"Let 'em have it!" Tali shouts.

The town unloads, unleashing enough firepower to put down a zombie uprising.

The two Ciphers twitch and flail as their charred armor fails to stop the bullets, buckshot, and slugs. Their limbs shatter. Their printed bodies fall to pieces. They drop to the ground, erased from an existence they should have never been given.

Before the shooting stops, Marit breaks away from the firing line, drops her weapon to the snow, and then falls to her knees in front of me. "Hold on," she says. "I've got you."

I can't smile, but I manage to say, "Sixteen moons. Bullshit."

Then I close my eyes and go to sleep.

68

A crackling fire and the smell of smoke greet me when I wake. My eyes open a crack, and I see a familiar fireplace, blazing with flames. I'm at The Roost. The burning wood sizzles and pops. Light dances. Heat stings my skin.

For a moment, I think I've returned to that dream of the past, but then pain rears up like a Kraken from the deep, wrapping its tendrils around my limbs, torso, and face.

Moving slowly, I fight the heavy blankets covering me. Nearly shout when I try to use my left arm. It's useless, but also no longer bleeding. When I get into a sitting position, I find myself topless. I look down under the blanket covering my lower half... And bottomless.

Embarrassing, but smart. My wet clothing would have stopped me from getting warm.

My arm is bandaged. Can feel the familiar sting of fresh stitches. Feels like my cheek has been redone, too. Newly bandaged as well.

I hold up my hands, checking my fingertips. No black in sight. I'll check my toes later. Right now, I just need to rest.

I nearly nod off, but I spot Tali and Marit as my eyes start closing. They're sitting in the chairs that flank the couch. Both are covered in blankets. Both asleep. And alive.

Tears well in my eyes. For the first time in a long time, I feel very grateful to be alive.

I nearly miss the third person watching over me.

She's standing in the shadows, off to the side of the fireplace, close enough to be warmed by its heat, but outside the light. Might not have spotted her if she hadn't stepped forward enough for the room's refracted light to illuminate her face.

She is both familiar and new.

For a moment, I see Clio, and am happy she survived both NovaGen's destruction, and the elements. But I can't feel her, and the look on her face is not pleasant.

It's Voss.

The *real* Voss, who I had yet to meet.

She steps into the firelight. She's dressed for the weather but looks cold...like she's been out in the cold, on the run, trying to find a way out of this frozen hell. Best she could manage was getting back to town.

I reach down to my hip, searching for a gun that isn't there.

Voss, on the other hand, carries the same pistol her duplicate had—a 10mm Sig Sauer P220. I wonder if she collected it from the body of her dead self, or if she just had a collection of them for each iteration of her. She hasn't pointed it at me yet, but its presence is threat enough.

She crouches in front of me. "Sheriff."

"Anika," I say, hoping the real Voss will be just as perturbed by me using her first name and the lack of a preceding, 'Doctor.'

"Mm." She forces a smile. Then levels the gun at my head. "I should kill you."

"Couldn't stop you," I point out.

"My lab... My work... You took it all from me."

"Guess you heard the very loud boom," I say, keeping my voice low. Last thing I want is for Tali and Marit to wake up.

Their reactions to Voss's presence could get us all killed. "To be fair, you'd made a mess of things by the time we arrived. The duplicates. The Ciphers. *You* killed your people, not me."

"That was Clio," she says. "I believe you met."

"Lovely girl," I say. "Funny looking face. But you're wrong. She might have killed some of your people, but the fourth floor was decorated with human remains. The work of a psychotic mind that delights in death. That's not Clio."

"Perhaps." Voss smirks. "Thank you, by the way, for taking care of that particular problem. She'll be just another unrecoverable body in a facility no one will bother rebuilding. Our sins have been washed away."

She doesn't know...

"What do you want?" I ask. "Hard to believe someone like you would stoop to revenge."

"Hardly," she says. "I need a ride. You're going to take me. I assume you have a vehicle, with heat, that can get us out of town."

"I do. If the road has been cleared." For someone who's just lost her life's work, she doesn't seem all that upset. Maybe because she hasn't lost anything. The facility was lost before we got there. The chaos caused by Clio ensured the site would be cleaned.

"Where is it?" I ask. "Your research."

She doesn't say a word, but her left hand lowers to her jacket pocket, a subconscious protective act.

"I get it, by the way. What you were trying to do."

"What we *did*," she says. "What we'll do again."

"The potential is...staggering. It's admirable."

"But..."

"It's just a shame you had to compromise your morals to get it done."

She huffs. "The copy you encountered in the safe room. She came out of the printer like that. High and mighty, lofty beliefs about what we were doing. Made her more pliable. But don't mistake her for me. My motivation has never been purely altruistic. I have nothing against printing replacement parts for people...for the right price. If the government wants a new weapon, and will pay, they can have whatever they want. If a million Japanese fuckboys want bio-prints of their favorite waifu to molest, and will pay ten grand a piece... Well, that math comes out to a number that makes the morality of my work a non-issue. And if you'd like, I am willing to direct some of that funding to you. Hell, to this whole godforsaken town, if you keep your mouths shut."

"Tempting," I say. "But from what I understand, this whole godforsaken town is in danger of being wiped off the map."

"I can change that. But only if you take me."

"Take you where?"

"Anchorage," she says. "Fort Richardson."

"It's going to take me a minute," I say. "In case you haven't noticed..." I look down at my shirtless top. "I'm not exactly dressed for the weather, or anything at all."

She nods. "And you can stay that way."

Smart.

Keeps me vulnerable.

"Fine, but—" I'm cut short by a surge of emotion. It's not mine. I wince and glance to Tali and Marit. They're both out for the count.

"What is it?" she asks.

"Muscle spasm," I say, and motion to my wounds. "Your creations used me as a pincushion."

"And yet, here you sit, alive and well." She stands back and motions for me to see, waggling the pistol. "You'll have to tell me how you survived during our drive."

I stand, holding on to the blanket. Not leaving it behind, unless she tells me to. "We'll have to stop at the station, to get my truck."

She glances at my feet, then to my eyes, squinting.

"Lady, if I wanted to trick you, I'd try something long before making myself walk through the snow barefoot."

She motions to the bar's front door, and I obey her command, wrapping the blanket around my torso, hugging it tight, and bracing myself for the cold to follow. I've been asleep for who knows how long, but my freezer-burned skin and my lungs, are not remotely ready for a second stint in the frozen air.

It will be short, I tell myself, doing my best to not look up at the ceiling.

I pause at the door, bracing myself for the cold.

Then I open it, step out into the silent night, flakes trickling toward the snow-covered street. Despite the battle against the two remaining Ciphers, the town has returned to the Tower. Chaos or not, no one in their right mind stays outside at night for long.

I step into the snow and find that it doesn't bother me much.

The snow squeaks beneath my feet as I descend the steps to the snow-covered sidewalk. I look right, up the gently sloped hill.

The station isn't far. Up on the left.

And right here in front of me...

"It's fitting," I say, stepping out into the street. "This is where your escaped camel died."

"Escaped camel?" Voss says. "What are you talking about?"

I can't help but laugh. "Sounds like your other self had different plans for surviving the site's liquidation."

She joins me in the street. "How do you mean?"

"She sent a bio-printed tamarin to town inside a bio-printed camel with artifact eyeballs on one side of its head. She wanted to escape. Wanted to survive. Guessing she didn't think you'd make it or let her live. Funny thing, that. You giving printed lifeforms the will to live. What did you think was going to happen?"

"Not all artifacts are physical deformations," she says. "Some take place in the mind. Daniel was the first to stumble across the defect. Consciousness. Morality. Once we knew about it—"

"It was too late," I say. "Because Clio had already been made. Had already revolted. And was killing everyone and everything in the lab, including your soldiers." I look her in the eyes. "A soldier who believes in what they're fighting for is far more dangerous than a mindless killer."

"I'll keep that in mind," she says.

"Yeah," I say. "But not for long."

As her face screws up in confusion, I keep my eyes locked on hers.

It's hard for me to do—looking someone in the eyes—but it's harder now because I need to hide what I'm seeing in my peripheral vision.

A blur of white leaps from The Roost's rooftop and descends toward Voss.

"Why are you—"

Voss must see a reflection in my eyes. She gasps and tries to turn. Doesn't make it far.

Clio lands behind her, grasps Voss's neck with one six-fingered hand, and the top of her head with the other. I lift the blanket like I'm Batman blocking a burst of fire. I see the look of horror on Voss's face as her head is twisted a hundred and eighty degrees. I expected a splash of blood. For Voss's head to be torn away.

But Clio spares me the extra nightmares. Drops Voss, head backward, to the snow, body face up, face...face down.

I linger behind the protective shield.

Clio steps closer.

I can feel her energy. For a moment, it's overwhelming. Then it settles into something recognizable. Gratitude.

I lower the blanket and look her in the eyes. I see only kindness. She might have been an artifact, both in body and soul, but Clio is the best creation to come out of NovaGen. And I'm not about to stop her from leaving.

The blanket isn't much of a gift, but I pull it off my body and offer it to Clio. Despite her lack of fur, she doesn't seem like she's in danger of freezing, but she accepts the blanket and wraps it around her shoulders. Her gratitude increases, and then she leaps away into the night, leaving Voss's body lying in the road.

I lose sight of Clio when she jumps from the roof to a tree, and then deeper into the forest, destined to become another one of Alaska's legends.

I crouch down and search Voss's pockets. Find what I'm looking for in a zipped-up pouch inside the jacket. A small external hard drive. Everything NovaGen did, good and bad, is contained on this drive. Infinite potential for good. Vast potential for evil. In my hand.

I stand up and then flinch at the sound of a cleared throat.

It's Marit and Tali standing on The Roost's porch, looking down at my naked self, standing over a woman with a backward head in the middle of the street.

"This probably looks bad," I say.

"We saw everything," Marit says, lowering a shotgun. "I was about to shoot her in the back when... Was that?"

"Clio," I say.

"Should we be worried?" Tali asks, diverting her eyes from my nakedness.

I look down at the hard drive. "Not about her."

When I look back up, there is a creature in the road, sitting in the snow, shivering. Dufresne. He's earned his name, and his life. I sigh and motion to the door. "C'mon." He squeaks and darts past Tali and Marit, into the Roost to warm himself by the fire, where I plan to join him. "Can I get a fresh blanket or some clothes?" I say, hop-running for the door.

EPILOGUE

"I got you," Marit says, reaching up as I climb down the ladder, paint bucket and brush in hand.

"I'm not an invalid," I grumble, taking my time on the ladder. "My arm is healed." Truth is, my left arm is still sore, not from the injury itself, but from the muscle I lost when it was immobilized for most of the winter. Didn't mind not having to shovel, though.

"Your arm?" she says, "I'm after something else." She whacks my ass with both hands.

"Hey!" I say, nearly falling.

"Oh. My God," Tali says, stepping out of The Roost in time to see the ass smack. "Can you two just...please. The PDA has got to stop."

I step out into the road, looking back at my handiwork. The fresh coat of red paint brings some life to the mostly drab downtown. The door is now painted black, and holds a plaque that reads: *For Grizz, Old Red, Jimmy, and Ethan.* It's the only evidence that something horrible happened here. That and the memories of the people who miss them, like Grizz's father, Milton. Wasn't brave enough to tell him the truth about how she died. Instead, I wove a tale about how she went down fighting and saving lives. He took her death hard, but the lie gave him some comfort, believing she'd died nobly.

Everyone in town knows about the lab.

About what happened there.

After seeing—and killing—the two Ciphers, no one doubted a single detail. We've come together as a community with a singular goal—keep the secret. Our best chance at survival is to go on like nothing happened.

And I've got to say, it feels good.

"Have you ever seen a better paint job?" I ask.

"I mean, it's red paint," Tali says. "Not like a Picasso or something."

"It's a good thing your approval means nothing to me."

"Ha!" She slugs my shoulder, winces, and says, "Sorry."

"Didn't hurt," I say. "Besides, you hit like a—"

A car horn double taps, catching all of us off guard. When I turn around, I see why. It's one of the new electric cars. Nearly silent. Now that it's idling, it sounds like a choir of very small angels. It's so pleasant, I think the manufacturers must have designed the sound that way.

I give the car a wave and step back. It pulls past, and then over.

The door opens.

"Sheriff," a man says, somehow recognizing me out of uniform.

I turn to greet him and nearly fall over.

It's Ethan.

The real Ethan.

Tali takes my hand, squeezing hard.

"I know," I tell her. "Be cool."

This Ethan is just as awkward as ours was. Lanky, too. Same smile.

"Sheriff Colton Graves?"

"That's me," I say, approaching him.

"Not interrupting something, I hope," he says, and points to the inside of his eye.

I do the same and find that a tear has snuck out. Being an emotional guy sucks sometimes.

"Just weeping at how amazing my paint job is." I motion to the fresh coat of red on The Roost's facade.

"Huh," he says, and then points. "Missed a spot."

Tali has a laugh at my expense, and not because Ethan was teasing me, but because he's right.

"What can we do for you?" Marit asks, sliding up beside me, hooking her arm into mine.

"Well, honestly, I'm not sure. Look, full disclosure, I used to work up at NovaGen—"

"Haven't heard a peep out of them in months," I say. "Everything okay?"

"The program's been shut down. The site was abandoned. The five lead scientists had a falling out or something. Lost funding. Government oversight. Doesn't really matter." Everything he just said is a lie, but I don't detect a trace of deceit. He's been lied to as well.

"Hope everyone is okay," I say.

"Couldn't tell you," he says. "The company was dissolved. Assets sold. I haven't been able to locate a single employee. It's like they just...vanished."

"But not you," I say.

He nods. "I was away. Boss had me recruiting. Kept me out there for a long time. Couldn't figure out why, and then...they were just gone. No contact. Got a call from a government liaison a short time later saying the program had been shuttered. I'm just...I'm trying to figure out what happened."

"Trying to find your friends," Tali says.

"I didn't have many," he says. "But there were some good people up there."

"And what about you, Ethan?" I ask. "Are *you* a good person?"

"What? Yeah. Well, I mean, I *think* I am. Why do you–"

"Sun Tzu," I say.

His face scrunches up.

Then he says, "I'm...not your enemy."

He thinks like the Ethan I knew...but that doesn't mean much.

"Sure about that?" Marit asks.

"What? Yeah. Why would I– Hey, how did you know my name?" He backsteps toward his car.

"You can leave if you want," I tell him. "We won't stop you. But you won't have the answers you're looking for." I pull a phone from my pocket and dial a number. "Hey. Yeah. You should come to The Roost. Yeah. Ethan's here."

"Who was that?" he asks. "Who did you call?"

"Just give it a few seconds. Elevator from the fifth floor takes about forty-five seconds. Elevator to the parking lot, another thirty." I tilt my ear to the sky, and close my eyes, waiting for just a moment before a car's tires shriek over pavement.

We all listen to the loud, very much not electric pick-up truck roar down the road from the Tower. Truck used to belong to Jimmy. Has a new owner now. It swerves onto Main Street fast enough that I could ticket her for it.

The truck skids to a stop in the middle of the road.

The passenger's side door flings open first. Cyn spills out, all smiles. She lifts her hands in the air. "Ethan!"

She dives into his arms.

"Oh my God, Cyn," he says. "What happened?"

"Hey," says a much calmer voice. "Good to see you, Ethan."

He turns to find Trisha approaching. "Dr. Nkenge."

She shakes his hand. "I'd hoped you were okay out there."

"Why wouldn't I be okay?" he asks.

"Bruh," Cyn says. "Shit went sideways."

"And it's a long story," Marit inserts. "You can hear it over a few beers or standing in the middle of the road. Up to you." She heads for the Roost.

"Just..." he says. "Before that...what about the research? What we were working on. Is it—"

My guard goes up.

Trisha and Cyn have been combing through the research Voss took from NovaGen. They've removed all traces of the military research, focusing on technology that can replace limbs, eyeballs, and organs without fear of rejection. They've sterilized Voss's weapon system and are just a few weeks away from releasing it worldwide, for free, so that the world can benefit from the deaths of their friends, and ours.

I hold a hand up to Trisha, who's about to respond. "Need something from you before anyone says another word."

"Oookay..." he says.

"Show me your hand," I say. He extends an open palm. "Now wha—"

Didn't see me unfold my jackknife. Barely registers me cutting his hand. Then the sting sets in. He flinches back, clutching his hand. "Hey! What the hell? You can't just cut people!"

"Ethan," Trisha says, "it's okay. We just need to know."

"Know what?"

"If you are *you*," she says.

Takes a hot minute to sink in, but it does. His eyes widen. "She didn't."

"She *did*," Trisha says. "And now we need to know if you... are you."

"Why wouldn't I be me?" he asks.

"You worked here for a year," I say. "As my deputy. You were my friend. But you...weren't *you*. Voss used a bio-printed double of you to keep track of the town by making you one of us. That's why the real you–presumably *this* you–was kept away. But the double...he filled your shoes and never knew he wasn't the real deal–not until just before he put a bullet in his own head to prevent himself from killing me. So, you'll have to forgive me for being an asshole about this. Now, show me your God-damned hand."

Ethan looks from me to Trisha, to Cyn, and then back again. We're all waiting for the answer.

"This is ridiculous," he says, and then defiantly holds up his palm.

AUTHOR'S NOTE

The debate over generative AI has been raging for the past few years, and I have mostly managed to stay out of it. I try not to jump to conclusions about new technologies and prefer to weigh facts rather than fears. Do I use AI? Yes. Chat GPT (which was trained on some of my novels) has made research, organization, and web design far more efficient. I use MidJourney for social media posts and book covers. I'm also dabbling in generative video, music, and audio, which I will use on occasion, for quick promotions.

At the same time, I'm committed to not replacing human beings in my creative endeavors. "But Jeremy, you just said you use AI for book covers!" This is true, but most of my book covers were created by me. I've been a professional cover designer for years. I recently DID start hiring someone else to do my covers, but that stopped when the art delivered to me was AI generated! Why pay someone else to generate AI images when I can do that myself? So, I'm back to doing my covers, with AI assistance.

When it comes to my professional work, I will always work with human audiobook narrators. I will always work with human comic book artists. I enjoy paying people to do good work. It makes me happy. That said, I will have fun experimenting with all kinds of generative AI and will sometimes sell the final product, as I did with my experimental book, *The Otherworldly Journal of Doctor Erasmus Gray*, which features writing and design by me, mixed with AI images based on the work of Leonardo da

Vinci. Why didn't I hire an artist for that project? Because it was done on a whim, for fun, and was never meant to make a profit (and it hasn't).

As for the generative technologies covered in *Artifact*... Are they real? Not yet. But they are being developed, starting with the printing of simple bacteria. But there will be a future where, with a touch of genetic code and the right prompt, entire organs will be printed in a lab at the cellular level. And if that's possible, why not limbs? Why not a brain? And if *that's* possible...why not a living, breathing, thinking organism? When people think about the future dangers posed by AI, we imagine that they'll be happy with machine bodies. Won't be long before they have a choice—organic or machine. I wonder which they'll choose.

In short, I'm much more excited about the future of AI and how it can benefit humanity, than I am about all the widely proliferated fears generated to get clicks, spread paranoia, and further divide people. All new technologies change the way the world works. Electricity. Computers. Engines. Each created industries and destroyed them. This is part of human advancement and evolution, and to quote the Borg, who get a bad rap, resistance is futile.

Now, some of you might be wondering why I took a deep dive into the subject of autism in this book. The answer is simple—I was diagnosed, at fifty years old, with autism, and I'm currently processing the news. By the time this book is published, I'll probably have posted about the subject on my blog, so head on over to bewareofmonsters.com if you're interested. But I have been blessed/cursed with the same super awesome variety of autism as Colton, and supercharged by the tick-borne diseases, Lyme and Bartonella. In times of prolonged stress—which is frequent for autistic folks—my senses become hyperactive, at which point even the slightest breeze can cause significant pain, something I've talked about in the past, but didn't fully understand. It sounds like a superpower, but the human mind wasn't made to process all that sensory information. It just turns into a vicious cycle of pain, discomfort, and anxiety. BUT, my combination of autism and ADHD has also led to my high creative output, a different way of thinking, and an ability to hyper focus on writing. In that way, it is a blessing, and I'm not sure I'd give it up if given the choice.

If you want to stay in the loop on upcoming releases, and all the exciting news about future comic books, movies, TV series, and more, head over to bewareofmonsters.com and sign up for the newsletter.

You can also join the Tribe at facebook.com/groups/JR.Tribe—a fantastic group of fans where all the cool announcements drop first. Plus, we give away free stuff every week!

Thanks for joining me on another wild ride. You have amazing taste, and don't let anyone, who is probably giving you strange looks for laughing or crying while reading, convince you otherwise. I can't wait to share what's coming next!

—Jeremy Robinson

ACKNOWLEDGMENTS

Massive gratitude goes out to Kane Gilmour, the Master of Edits who helps transform rough drafts into polished, entertaining reads. And a big shoutout to our dedicated team of proofreaders, Adrian Brooke, Julie Carter, Elizabeth Cooper, Christina Epperson, Cynthia Gregory, Gavin Gregory, Deanna Haddrill, Matt Ingram, Andre Jenkin, Jeanne Kearl, Scott Kehoe, Becki Laurent, Janis Levonitis, Rian Martin, Stefanie Maubach, Jessica Otterstål, Jeff Sexton, Michelle Stuart, and Courtney Westendorf, who work tirelessly to hide the fact that I've actually just hired a team of tamarins to pound on keyboards until a story comes out.

Enormous thanks to the superhero of audiobooks, R.C. Bray. No one brings these books alive like you, and I have been privileged to work with you for the past fifteen years. My career would not be what it is without your voice.

Finally, a huge thanks to you, the readers. Because of you, I get to write stories about bio-printing monsters for work, and that's basically a dream come true for me.

Thanks for making it possible.

—Jeremy

ABOUT THE AUTHOR

Jeremy Robinson is the *New York Times* and #1 Audible bestselling author of over eighty novels and novellas, including *Infinite, The Others,* and *The Dark,* as well as the Jack Sigler thriller series, and *Project Nemesis,* the highest selling, original kaiju novel of all time (which is in development for TV with Chad Stahelski, director of *John Wick*). Robinson is known for mixing elements of science, history, and mythology, which has earned him the #1 spot in Science Fiction and Action-Adventure, and secured him as the top creature feature author. Many of his novels have been adapted into comic books, optioned for film and TV, and translated into fourteen languages. He lives in New Hampshire with his wife and three children.

Visit him at www.bewareofmonsters.com.

YOU'VE READ THE BOOKS NOW MEET THE AUTHOR!

ON THE WEB

BEWAREOFMONSTERS.COM

FOR A MORE PERSONAL CONNECTION
WITH ROBINSON AND FELLOW
FANS, JOIN THE

TRIBE

FACEBOOK.COM/GROUPS/JR.TRIBE